First Wives Club Vol.1
Melanin Magic

By: Keisha Ervin

FIRST WIVES CLUB VOL.1: MELANIN MAGIC

Chyna Black thought she'd finally gotten her happily ever after. Her melanin is popping, her career has taken off like magic, and her love life is like something from a fairytale. After rekindling her love affair with Dame, he came back in her life, showed her how to move in a room full of bitches and swept her off her feet. When they met 20 years ago, she never knew the impact she'd made on his life. Because of her, Dame didn't even know bitches. With him, she found her forever. His love was like no other. The stars in the sky were aligning perfectly. Then, within a blink of an eye, her dream became a nightmare. When the smoke clears, and the dust settles, will Chyna be able to hold on to everything she holds dear, or will she end up alone - all over again?

Gray Rose and Gunz have two kids and a home together. You would think, after 10 years together, she'd have a ring too… but Gunz still isn't ready for marriage. Maybe it's because he's always fly, stays in the cockpit and can't stay out the streets. Gray is over trying to keep a man that doesn't want to be kept and Gunz ain't beat, she can jump off his dick. All it takes is one nigga to remind her that she's bad as fuck, and that they're a real nigga.

After 11 years, four kids, a house and a dog, Mo and Boss finally got married. From the outside looking in, everything seems perfect, but Mo is secretly drowning. When she looks in the mirror, she doesn't even recognize herself anymore. She used to have that up North glow, body looking like cinnamon, but between breast-feeding, soccer practice, ballet class, keeping house, a bitchy, loud-mouth mother-in-law and a husband who won't keep his mama in check but constantly wants to fuck, Mo is five seconds away from putting everybody on the front porch. Can she keep it together without losing her sanity?

Chyna, Gray and Mo are going through it, but with their girls, Meesa, Mina and Dylan by their side, they'll go through their trials and tribulations with love, laughter, a few tears and style every time they touch the city - STOP IT!!

Other Titles by Keisha Ervin

The Untold Stories by Chyna Black

Cashmere Mafia (Material Girl Spin-off)

Material Girl 3: Secrets & Betrayals

Paper Heart

Pure Heroine (Sequel to Me and My Boyfriend)

Emotionally Unavailable (Chyna Black 2)

Heartless (Chyna Black 3)

Radio Silence (Chyna Black 4)

Smells Like Teen Spirit Vol 1: Heiress

Mina's Joint 2: The Perfect Illusion

Cranes in the Sky (Messiah & Shyhiem Book 1)

Postcards from the Edge (Messiah & Shyhiem Book 2)

Such A Fuckin' Lady (Chyna Black 5)

Dedication

Cherita, aka the real Selicia, thank you for putting up with my nonstop calls. I know you hate that you went from being one of my loyal readers to now one of my friends because I make you listen to every chapter after they are written. Without our late-night calls, this book wouldn't be what it is. Thanks for being the Philly bully you are and for evoking the spirit of Cam. You are truly the best friend and junior editor a girl could ask for!!!

"She ain't know no better but I did." –
6lack, "MTFU"

Chapter 1

Chyna

Chyna lay in a hospital bed with an IV, heart monitor and oxygen tank attached to her body. Her breathing had been irregular since she arrived. She didn't want to stay another second in the dreary confines. The room she was in was devoid of beauty. It was a typical hospital room, sparse and practical. There were no decorations, except a limp curtain that separated her from the other patients in the emergency room. The beeping sound coming from the machines were driving her mad. She needed to get out of there before she lost her mind.

Hospitals reminded her of nothing but death. She wasn't ready to meet her maker. The reality that she could've died rattled her faith in God. What had she done to be put through such a harrowing, life-altering experience? None of that mattered when Dame pulled back the curtain and stepped inside. A fresh set of tears slid down her cheeks, as she gazed into his concerned brown eyes.

Even in a crisis, he was immaculately dressed. He was missing his suit jacket but the crisp, white, button-up, black tie, gray, pinstriped vest, matching pants and Christian Louboutin dress shoes made Chyna's heart rate spike. His handsome face reminded her of the stupid decision she made by getting in the car with L.A. She should've taken an Uber, or a cab as planned. Now, here she was with a fucked-up face and a fiancé who was probably about to leave her.

She couldn't tell by the expression on his face what he was thinkin', as he neared. She didn't know if he wanted to slap her or kiss her. His face was stone - as usual. No one, not even Chyna, could see past the mask on his face. Dame only let you see what he wanted you to see, which was a gift and curse. She never knew where she stood with him.

At that moment, she needed to know her position in his life more than ever. When she told him she was in the hospital because she'd been robbed at gunpoint while in the car with L.A., she expected him to hang up and never speak to her again. She honestly couldn't be mad if he had. If she was him that would have been her response. She had no business being in the car with her ex-boyfriend, especially at that time in the morning. It didn't look good no matter how she spun it.

To her surprise, Dame gently took her feeble hand in his and sat beside her bed. He was never the type of nigga to cry but seeing Chyna in such a vulnerable state weakened him. The despair he felt would come in waves, stealing his appetite and sleep for days. The man was genuinely fucked up. It was hard for him to look at her. The right side of her face was severely bruised to the point that it had swelled and her eye was swollen shut. He didn't know what to expect when he walked into her hospital room, but he didn't expect this. An anger like no other surged through his veins.

"Tell me what happened again?" His raspy voice croaked.

"I just wanted to surprise you." Chyna talked slowly, as tears slipped from her eyes.

Every time she talked a sharp pain spiked, causing her to wince.

"I saw L.A. at the award show. He asked me to come to his hotel to talk to him. At first, I was gonna go. I even went to the hotel, but when I got there, I couldn't get out. There was nothing for me to say and I didn't want to disrespect you, so I told the driver to turn around. The only thing I wanted to do was get home to you, so I caught a red-eye home." Chyna licked her dry lips.

Her face was on fire. The pain meds hadn't kicked in yet.

"Take your time, Belle." Dame rubbed the outside of her hand with his thumb.

"I know this might sound crazy, but when I got on the plane, L.A. was on the same flight. I tried to avoid him, but he ended up being seated next to me. He told me he missed me but I told him I love you. It took him a while, but he got the hint and let it go. When the plane landed, I was gonna catch a cab to the hotel, but L.A. had a car and offered to give me a ride. I didn't feel like waiting on a cab and it was dark out, so I said ok. Baby, it was completely innocent. Nothin' happened. I swear," Chyna sobbed.

"All I wanted to do was get back to you." Her bottom lip quivered, as her chest heaved up and down. "Then, these men..." She broke down and cried hysterically.

"Shhhhhhh... it's ok, Belle. I got you, baby girl." Dame rose from his seat and took her in his arms.

The flashback of L.A. being shot in the chest and Chyna being smacked in the face with a gun was stuck in her brain on repeat. She couldn't get the frightening images out of her head. Dame's vision clouded with tears, as Chyna cried even harder. Nothing else needed to be said. Chyna had no need to fear his wrath. He believed every word that came out of her mouth.

If Dame didn't know shit else, he knew when Chyna was lying. She was telling him the complete truth, which made him feel like shit. No woman deserved the kind of beating she'd been given. He could barely recognize her. Chyna's face was fucked up, but he loved her all the same.

A black eye, swelling and bruises wasn't gonna change the fact that she was the most beautiful girl in the world. She was his sunshine, his lover, his best friend. He'd gladly lay down and die before anything bad happened to her. If he could, he'd shield her from all pain. Unfortunately for Chyna, he'd be the one to cause her the worst pain of all. Like Chyna, he too had thoughts that haunted him. Dame had fucked up. He'd fucked up badly. If it was possible, he'd rewind time and erase everything that happened before he got her frantic phone call.

Dame was posted up at the Four Seasons Hotel with Mohamed and a few of his men. He'd had a long day of scouting land for his next casino. All he wanted was a good meal, a glass of whiskey, a nice, soft bed and the sound of Chyna's sweet voice to lull him to sleep. He hadn't talked to her since earlier that day. He couldn't wait to hear all about her experience on the red carpet. Witnessing his baby excel in her field turned him on to the fullest. When she got back to St. Louis, he was gonna pipe her down until her legs shook.

Lying back on the couch, he stretched his long legs and sipped on a tumbler of whiskey to unwind. Room service would be up at any moment with his food. Dame's stomach growled, when he heard a light knock on the door. When Mohamed approached him without a tray of food behind him, he furrowed his brows.

"What is it?"

"You have an unexpected guest." Mohamed said, with his hands clasped in front of him.

"Who?" Dame screwed up his face.

Nobody but Chyna knew he was in town.

"A young lady by the name of Brooke."

Dame drew his head back, perplexed.

"What the fuck she want?" He said, out loud to himself.

Something bad must've happened to Chyna. That was the only reason she would be there.

"Let her in." He sat up straight.

Seconds later, Brooke sauntered inside the living area like a runway model. Dame couldn't front, shorty was pretty as fuck, but Brooke didn't have shit on Chyna.

"Is Belle alright?" He asked, right off the bat.

"Who?" Brooke asked, confused.

"Chyna." Dame grunted.

"Well damn, I don't get no hi, how you doing or nothin'?" Brooke arched her brow.

"Cut the bullshit. Is Chyna a'ight?" He questioned, worried.

"Calm down. She's fine." Brooke huffed, rolling her eyes.

"Then why are you here?"

"May I have a seat?"

"Go ahead." Dame took another sip of his drink.

He didn't know what the hell she wanted but she'd already overstayed her welcome.

"I missed you."

Dame screwed up his face. This bitch is crazy, he thought.

"You look good." Brooke eyed him hungrily, while crossing her shapely legs.

She hoped him seeing her bare, thick thighs would entice him, but Dame felt nothing. Homegirl was a little too thirsty for his taste.

"Chyna know you here?" He cut right to the chase.

"No."

"Then what the fuck do you want?"

"I see that temper of yours hasn't changed." Brooke made herself comfortable in her seat.

"Does my fiancée know you're here?" Dame repeated, hating to repeat himself.

"Well, after I tell you what I know, you might wanna get that ring back." Brooke chuckled.

"You got ten seconds and I'ma have Mohamed toss yo' ass up outta here," Dame said, over the cat and mouse game she was tryin' to play.

"I just gotta know. What is it about her that you love so much? What does she have over me?"

"What's with all the questions? You was just a fuck and fucks don't get to ask questions." Dame looked at her like she was crazy.

Brooke swallowed back the tears in her throat. Hearing him say she meant nothing to him was all the ammunition she needed to rip his heart into shreds like he'd done her.

"You know what's funny?"

"This whole, entire conversation," Dame quipped.

"No. What's funny is, even though you did me dirty by fuckin' my friend, I still have your best interest at heart. That's why... when I learned that your fiancée..." Brooke mocked by making air quotes. "...was going to see the man she really loves tonight, I felt it was only right that I tell you."

"What the fuck are you talkin' about?" Dame ice-grilled her.

"Chyna; she's with L.A. right now."

"Bullshit. How you know that?"

"I'm her best friend. She told me, duh. She ran into him at the MTV Awards. He asked her to come by his hotel room after the show, so they could talk, and they did. Sorry to tell you, homeboy, but she leaving you for him."

"You a goddamn lie." Dame's heart rate increased, as he snatched up his phone.

"Call her. I bet she don't answer 'cause that dick in her mouth." Brooke said, confidently, with a smirk on her face.

Dying to prove her wrong, Dame dialed Chyna's number and let the phone ring until his call was forwarded to voicemail. At that moment, his heart dropped. Chyna always answered his calls. The only time she didn't was the night she was with L.A. at her crib and when he caught her kickin' it with that lame-ass white boy. Some foul shit was definitely up.

"Yep, he's balls deep. You believe me now?" Brooke arched her brow.

Unwilling to believe that Chyna would dare step out on him, Dame tracked her location on his phone. Sure enough, she was at the James Hotel. Brooke was telling the truth. Dame was so mad, he saw red. If Chyna was in front of him, he would've choked her until she took her last breath. He'd asked her to marry him and this was how she would repay him by being on some ho shit. Dame felt like a complete and utter idiot. It was like he'd been duped.

From that moment on, Chyna was dead to him. He would never look at her the same. She'd disrespected him in the worst way. He'd let go of all his other bitches 'cause he loved her and here she was fuckin' around with her ex behind his back. Nah, it wasn't going down like that. Furious, Dame threw the glass of whiskey in his hand across the room. The glass shattered into pieces, as it hit the wall.

He could barely function, he was so mad. He couldn't stomach what Brooke had just told him. Didn't Chyna know that she was his weakness? Nothing or no one could unravel him like she did. Because of her, he now knew what it felt like to live life to the fullest. Before her, every day was mundane. He was a walking corpse. Then, she reentered his world and turned everything upside down. In the beginning, Dame thought he'd be the one to break her heart, but here he was bleeding internally.

Brooke watched as Dame paced the room. She should've felt bad for what she'd done but she didn't. Chyna fucked her over when they were 16 and she was simply returning the favor. Revenge was a dish best served cold. This had been 20 years in the making. Chyna had fucked over so many people, it was high time she got her just due.

Brooke was the one that should've been on Dame's arm, not her. Chyna didn't know what to do with a nigga like Dame. He needed a bitch like her on his team. And yeah, she'd promised herself to Gabe; but if she had a shot with Dame, she'd dead that shit with the quickness. He could pretend like there was no chemistry there, but Brooke knew better. All he needed was the space and opportunity to act on his desires.

"Dame, calm down." She stood up and grabbed his hand.

"Fuck that. I'ma kill her," he fumed, barely able to breathe.

"This is what she does to everybody. Chyna only cares about herself. She don't give a fuck about you."

Dame's chest heaved up and down, as he tried to contain his anger. Chyna's disrespectful, disloyal-ass had to pay. Dame hadn't felt a pain like this since he used to get beat by his father. This was why he closed himself off to people. People couldn't be trusted. They'd let you down every time.

This couldn't be how their love story would end. He had to be sure she'd really dipped out on him. Dame tried calling her again. Five rings later, the voicemail clicked in. Irate, he ended the call. All Dame could do was nod his head repeatedly, he was so upset.

"Forget about her. Let me make you feel better." Brooke slowly glided in front of him and slid down to her knees.

Dame looked down at her like she was crazy but there was no hiding the bulge inside his slacks. Eagerly, Brooke placed her hand on his crotch and stroked him through the seam of his pants. Dame's cock got harder by the second. It was begging to be unleashed. Never breaking eye contact, Brooke lustfully unbuckled his belt and unzipped his pants. Dame watched intently, unable to move. His mind was telling him what Brooke was doing was wrong, but his stiff dick couldn't comprehend the concept. Chyna had done the unthinkable, so all bets were off. He didn't owe her shit but the same courtesy she'd given him, which was none.

If she could so easily disregard everything they'd built over the summer, then so could he. Dame had no business giving his heart to a woman anyway. He knew it was a stupid idea from the jump, but his love for Chyna outweighed any common sense he had.

"She still got your heart now?" Brooke teased, as she took his hard flesh into her hand.

Twenty years later and he still had the prettiest dick she'd ever seen. Tenderly, she placed her lips around the swollen tip of his dick. Dame was too big to take all at once. He had the kind of dick you had to work into your mouth slowly. Brooke could only get half of his cock into her mouth before she had to come up for air. As his dick grew bigger in size, she knew that he enjoyed every second of fucking her warm mouth. Brooke alternated between unhurried, languorous licks to fast, rhythmic strokes of her tongue while glancing up at him.

The harder she sucked, the louder Dame groaned. Visions of Chyna giving L.A. head tormented his brain, causing him to grip the back of Brooke's neck extra hard. He fucked her mouth roughly, as if it was Chyna sucking his dick. Gagging noises filled the room. The next day,

Brooke's throat would be sore, but she didn't mind that he was being aggressive. Dame could fuck her mouth any way he liked. She'd dreamt of this day for far too long to complain. She knew if she bided her time, she'd be back with him again.

Chyna may have won the battle, but she'd won the war. In a matter of seconds, her belly was full of Dame's cum. Hot semen squirted from his dick, as he pumped feverishly into her mouth. He intended to deposit every drop of cum onto her tongue. None of it would spill onto the floor. As soon as his orgasm subsided, Dame's dick went limp. He was surprised it got hard in the first place. He wasn't even attracted to Brooke. She was nothing but a warm hole for him to nut in. Her presence meant nothing to him, as he zipped up his pants and poured himself another drink. She was nothin' but a slut whore like her friend. He hated Chyna for doing this to him… to them. Brooke wiped her mouth and rose to her feet.

"That was nice." She purred, wrapping her arms around his back.

"Fuck off me." He jerked his arms away.

Brooke stumbled back, surprised.

"C'mon, Dame, I wanna fuck like we used to." She tried reaching for him once more.

"If you don't get yo' ass on." He curled his upper lip in disgust.

The sight of Brooke repulsed him.

"You really ain't gon' give me no dick?"

"Mohamed!"

"Yes, Nephew." He appeared, stoically.

"Escort this ho out."

"Ho?" Brooke said, appalled. "Yo' bitch the one fuckin' somebody else! She the fuckin' ho!"

"Make this bitch disappear." Dame retook his spot back on the couch, so he could stew in his misery.

In his world, Brooke no longer existed. What they'd done was a minor lapse in judgement. He wasn't in his right mind. Now that he was, he remembered that Brooke couldn't offer him shit except a fuckin' headache. Heated, she snatched up her purse.

"On everything I love, you gon' regret this, muthafucka!" She pointed her finger at him before storming out of the room.

When she'd said it, Dame took her threat idly; but now, as he held Chyna securely in his arms, he regretted every decision he'd made that night. She hadn't done him wrong. He should've known better than to let a conniving bitch like Brooke get in his head. She'd been preying on their downfall from the start and he'd fallen right into her trap. He should've waited till he got ahold of Chyna before he jumped to conclusions, but he didn't, and now things were all fucked up.

He'd fucked over his dream girl because he let his temper and insecurities get the best of him. All the courting, wooing and getting her to trust in his love would completely go down the drain if she knew what he'd done. The guilt was already killing him. Every time he gazed into her pretty, brown eyes, he felt like shit. The right thing to do would be to tell Chyna the truth. They'd made a pact to never lie to one another; but if he did, they'd be through.

Dame couldn't risk that. He couldn't fathom a world where she wasn't in his life. She was his belle, his future wife. Besides, she'd been through enough in one night to last a lifetime. Adding to her misery wouldn't help anyone. Chyna could never find out about what happened between him and Brooke. He couldn't risk her leaving him over a bullshit-ass mistake he made in the heat of the moment. She was his. He'd worked too hard to capture her heart. There was no way he was letting her go. Dame could stomach killing a muthafucka in cold blood, but he couldn't stomach losing Chyna. His deceit would have to go with him to the grave. Dame was gonna make sure of it.

"Take that shit off. Move I'll break you off properly. I get mine the fast way. Ski mask way." – 50 Cent, "Ski Mask Way"

Chapter 2

Gerald

Gerald stood over the bathroom sink, huffing and puffing, as sweat poured from his forehead. He could barely catch his breath; his heart was beating so fast. The black hoodie he wore was suffocating him. Quickly, he pulled it over his head, so he could get some air. The white tank top he wore underneath clung to his chest. The stick-up he'd done with his man, Berg, was a success, even though they had to shoot an NBA superstar and slap up his bitch.

A few hours before he'd received the call about the job, Gerald was in bed with Asha laid up for the night. She didn't even know he'd stepped out. He'd slipped out while she was asleep. He'd been told that the job was some last-minute shit. Berg offered him half the cut he'd been offered, which was a hundred grand. Gerald desperately needed the money, so he was down for whatever.

The plan was to get in and out. They went in with no intentions on hurting anyone, but when L.A. refused to come off his jewels and money, an executive decision had to be made on the spot. Gerald had jacked plenty of niggas in his day, so he didn't give a damn about L.A.'s celebrity status. If the nigga had to be put down, then so be it. He didn't give a fuck.

He had Asha and a baby on the way that he had to feed. He had to get it how he lived. If L.A. hadn't been a hardheaded nigga, then his fate would've been different. It was his fault he'd been shot. At least that's what Gerald tried to tell himself. Honestly, if L.A. died, the guilt would consume him. Gerald had done a lot of grimy shit, but he'd never witnessed a murder. The visual of blood seeping from the bullet hole in L.A.'s chest kept flashing before his eyes. Gerald needed a bump of coke to calm his nerves.

Reaching into his pants pocket, he pulled out a small vile of coke and the pink diamond engagement ring he'd taken off the finger of the pretty girl in the passenger seat. Gerald wasn't supposed to keep anything that was stolen. He'd given Berg the Rolex watch and pink diamond earrings but kept the ring for himself. It was too exquisite and rare to give up. He'd been thinking about proposing to Asha since he found out she was pregnant with his child. With the stolen ring, he'd now be able to. The good part about it was he wouldn't have to come out of his own pocket to buy a ring.

The only thing that plagued him was the girl. He couldn't get her out of his mind. The panicked sound of her voice haunted him. He'd seen her face somewhere, but he couldn't pin point where. Maybe it was because he was high while doing the robbery that he couldn't remember where he knew her from. It really didn't matter. The dirty deed had been done and now he needed to erase the harrowing memory.

With a shaky hand, he poured the addictive white powder onto the bathroom sink. Holding down his left nostril with his index finger, he leaned down and snorted the line of coke until there was none left. The rush of the of the powdery white substance went straight to his brain. A calming euphoria washed over him. Suddenly, all his worries disappeared, and he felt more confident than ever. Gerald was invincible. Nothing or no one could stop him.

"Baby." Asha tapped lightly on the bathroom door, scaring him.

Gerald, swiftly, placed the vile of coke and ring back inside his pocket and then wiped his nose.

"Yeah!" He turned on the faucet.

"Where did you go? I woke up and you were gone."

"I just stepped out for a second and had a drink with my boy. You were sleeping so I didn't wanna wake you," he lied. "Go back to bed. I'll be out in a second."

"Ok." She quietly went back to their bedroom.

Asha had a bad feeling in her stomach but dismissed the notion. Things in her life were finally picking back up after Dame fired her. She and Gerald were madly in love and preparing for the birth of their first child. The only thing in their way was Dame. He had no idea that Gerald was living with her. If he knew, he would surely demand that she put him out or make her pay her rent herself. Asha planned on telling him but had to figure out the best way to go about it. Her brother could be a loose cannon when pushed to the edge. She'd witnessed firsthand when he killed Yayo. She was already stressed out enough. Preparing to be a new mom was a scary thing. She didn't need her over protective, ticking time bomb of a brother to add to her worries.

“How can you get tired of a dude who was so fly?” – Bow Wow & Omarion, “Can’t Get Tired Of Me”

Chapter 3

Mo

"Really, Boss?" Mo huffed, throwing a dirty cup in the sink.

"What?" He screwed up his face, as he walked inside the kitchen.

"How many times do I have to ask you to wash the fuckin' dishes before you go to bed at night? You ain't even wipe the countertop down." She snapped, pissed. "I swear, you wanna see a roach up in here; and if you do, you gon' be the main one crying."

"Watch yo' mouth in front of my son." He ignored her complaining and kissed her on the cheek then did the same to his nine-month-old son, Zaire.

"And you ain't take out the trash. Really, dude? This what we do now?"

"I'ma do it in a minute. Calm yo' cute-ass down. I got this." Boss assured, slapping her on the butt.

"It's always, I'ma do it in a minute but don't shit get done."

"No, yo' controlling-ass just want me jump when you say so. I ain't Ryan, Makiah or King. I'm your husband. Remember that shit. You either gon' wash the dishes yourself or wait till I do it. Either way, it's fine with me 'cause it's gone get done."

Mo could feel it in her bones. It was only a matter of time before she ended up on an episode of Snapped.

Closing her eyes, she inhaled deeply and counted to ten. She was seconds away from slapping the shit out of her husband. She didn't ask Boss for much. All she asked was his assistance around the house, and with the kids, but the smallest shit he could never find the time to do. Meanwhile, she cooked and cleaned like a Hebrew slave. Boss had her and life all the way fucked up.

Even though she'd cooked dinner the night before, helped their twin daughters and their son, King, with their homework, monitored bath time, read them a bedtime story, put them to bed, pumped, washed and ironed clothes, she was not Karen White. She was not his Superwoman. She was only human, and a human being could only take so much.

Mo never wanted to be one of those wives that nagged and complained all the time. She wanted to be the fun, go with the flow kind of girl. Once upon a time, she was; but after having four kids, all that shit went out the window. Being a mother of four, she had to be disciplined and structured or else she'd be swallowed whole. That's why she needed her husband's help. Mo had asked him to do one thing before going to bed and that was clean the kitchen and he couldn't even do that.

He could however find the time to turn over in the middle of the night and press his hard dick in the crack of ass, so he could fuck. Mo looked at that nigga like he was crazy. A) She was too damn tired for sex. B) She'd barely had enough time to wash her ass let alone shave her lady bits and C) She was fuckin' tired! Pissed that he even had the balls to initiate sex after the long day she had, Mo politely elbowed that nigga in the chest and told him to get the fuck back.

Being a stay-at-home mom was hard as fuck, especially when she had no help. Mo was a hands-on mom.

She didn't have a nanny or a maid, although she desperately needed one. After years of being the head of A&R for Bigg Entertainment and managing a slew of artists, Mo quit to be at home with her kids. Managing a full-time career and three kids was already stressful enough, so when she became pregnant with her fourth child, something had to give. She couldn't be successful at both. As a matter-of-fact, she was failing big time at being a mom.

When she was working, she often missed her girls' cheerleading competitions, recitals and King's football and baseball games. Half the time, she couldn't make it to parent/teacher conferences, school plays, doctor's appointments or help with any of their class projects. Mo felt like the worst mom on the planet. Once a week, she found herself crying over her shortcomings at her desk.

The kids hated that she was gone all the time, which made her feel worse. Most times, she didn't make it home until after they'd gone to bed. Mo's kids were growing up right before her eyes and she was missing every second of it. Other mothers turned up their noses at her for being a working mom. On top of that, she and Boss rarely got to spend any time together. They were like two ships in the night, passing each other by. And their sex life had gone down the toilet. They went from fucking at least five times a week to maybe twice a month.

It was a no-brainer for Mo to put her career on hold and focus on her family; but after almost two years of being a stay-at-home mom, she was starting to drown. Homegirl was fuckin' miserable. She missed her old life and constantly felt guilty about it. She thought her days of being torn were over. On one hand, she wanted to be an independent career woman; and on the other, she loved devoting all her time to her children and husband. Being a wife, mom, maid, nurse, mediator, therapist and a freak in the sheets was stressful as fuck, especially when her husband acted like he was her fifth child. *That's what you get for marrying a young nigga,* Mo thought, looking at him.

The longer she did, the angrier she got. It was 10:30 in the morning and there she was with her hair up in a messy ponytail, with a ratty t-shirt on, worn-out jogging pants and old house shoes, while he was dressed like a trap star. Mo was pissed off and turned on all at the same time. She could barely find the time to brush her teeth let alone get dressed up. It wasn't fair that her husband still had it all together.

Boss was fine as fuck. Even after 11 years of being together, he was still the flyest nigga she'd ever seen. Most people took him for a thug based on his appearance, but he was anything but. He owned several luxury carwashes, gas stations, real estate and a brand-new hookah spot he and Mo had just opened up called Babylon. He was a 31-year-old, 6'1 nigga with a big dick and a cocky attitude. Bitches stayed on his dick, but he only had eyes for her. She was his bitch and he was her nigga. Boss worked her nerves but nothing or no one could tear them apart. He'd loved her even when she thought she wasn't loveable. There was no way in hell she was giving his sexy-ass up.

Mo looked him up and down. The black Chicago Bulls snapback, white, red and black Chicago Bulls sweatshirt, small, gold chains, gold Rolex, several gold rings, Gucci belt, black, fitted jeans and J's made her pussy cream on sight. Her nigga stayed fly, but his thin brows, almond-shaped eyes, nose, dimples, kissable lips and full beard were what really drew her to him.

Every time she looked at him, she melted. His athletic build, which was covered in tattoos, only added to his sex appeal. From his neck down to his dick was a mural of ink. The tattoo she loved the most was the one of her name – Monsieur - covering his heart.

"Since you too good to wash a dish in this muthafucka, come hold your son while I clean up the kitchen, AGAIN." She held Zaire out at arm's length.

"Come here, li'l man." Boss happily took his son. "Mommy trippin'." He kissed his mini-me all over his face.

"No, you trippin'. Get on my damn nerves. You can't do shit I ask you to do."

"And neither can you, nigga. How many times I ask you to suck my dick, but you can't never do that? It's always *my neck hurt, my jaw hurt, I'm tired,*" Boss mocked her.

Mo shot daggers at him with her eyes.

"How about, I do the dishes and you suck your own dick? How about that?"

"You got jokes today, huh?"

"Shut up." She rolled her eyes at him.

"You shut up."

"No, you shut up!" Mo argued back, like a li'l kid.

"Grow up, Mo."

"You grow up!"

"I'm not about to argue wit' you." He went to walk away.

"Then shut up talkin' to me. Go in the room and play the game until you leave to go to work, wit' yo' nonuseful-ass, while I clean up everything by myself - as usual." She turned on the faucet.

"I don't know what yo' problem is but you need to chill," Boss warned.

"You, you're my problem. You take my kindness for weakness. One day you gon' wake up and I'ma be gone."

"Here you go with that shit." He groaned.

"I'm serious." Mo scrubbed a pan.

"Uh huh. Yeah, sure, you gon' leave me." Boss scoffed. "Who you think gon' put up wit' yo' crazy-ass?"

"Don't get it twisted. I will leave you and bounce to the next dick, boy."

"Beyoncé gon' get you fucked up. Yo' mama tryin' to get punched in the mouth today, Z." Boss made funny faces at his son.

"Think it's a game." Mo kept on.

"Don't get yo' ass beat." Boss glared at her.

"Boss, ain't nobody scared of you."

"You scared of this dick. *Boss, it hurt. Scoot back. Ouch-ouch! Wit yo' ouching-ass.*" He screwed up his face.

Mo eyed his package, lustfully. She couldn't even deny it. They'd been together 11 years and she still ran away from the dick when he piped her.

"Whatever. Have several seats, sir," Mo chuckled.

She hated that she could never stay mad at Boss. One look at his magnetic smile and she turned to mush.

"I ain't no young bitch. I take that D like a champ. That's why I got four kids now and that's why you act the way you do."

"Li'l Mama." Boss took her by the hand and made her face him. "Talk to ya man. What's the problem?"

Mo let out a long sigh.

"I'm overwhelmed. I need help. I really think we should think about hiring a maid or a nanny."

"Nah." Boss shook his head. "I don't want nobody in my house."

"I can't take care of the kids, a baby, keep the house clean, cook and do everything else by myself."

"That's why you got me."

"Nigga, you can't even wash the dishes when I ask you to."

"If you need help so bad, we can have my old bird come help. She ain't doing shit. As a matter-of-fact, we can talk to her about it right now 'cause I gotta call her back." He pulled out his iPhone.

"No!" Mo snatched his phone out his hand.

"What you doing?"

"You can't call your mother." She hid his phone behind her back.

Mo's day was already starting off badly. She didn't have time to deal with Boss and his miserable-ass mama. Phyliss Carter was a certified bitch! At first, she and Mo got along great. They talked on the phone, went shopping and out to eat together all the time; but when Mo had words with Boss' little sister, Shawn, their relationship immediately soured. Since then, Phyliss made it her business to fuck with Mo every time she was in her presence. The only reason Mo hadn't got in her ass was because she was Boss' mother and her kids' grandmother. Their family dynamic was already strained enough. More fuel didn't need to be added to the flame by cussing his mama out.

"Why not?"

"You know she don't like me."

"You trippin'. Yes, she do." Boss took his phone from her.

"No, she don't and you know it."

"I'm not having this conversation wit' you today."

"Boss, please don't call her. I don't wanna have to fight yo' mama today," Mo begged.

"Why? She wanna come over to see the kids." He placed the phone up to his ear.

"Aww… hell to the no!"

"You really gon' keep yo' kids away from their grandmother?"

"If that means me staying out of jail, then yes. I got too much shit on my plate and going to prison ain't one of 'em."

"You over-exaggerating. My mama ain't that bad."

"Shiiiiiiiiit, I will literally get down on my knees and suck your dick right now if you hang up."

"For real?" He squinted his eyes. "Don't fuck around."

“On my mama,” Mo assured, unzipping his pants.

Boss quickly ended the call.

“Shit, if I would’ve known this was all I had to do to get some head, I would’ve had my mama move into this bitch.” He put the phone down, as she wrapped her lips around his dick.

"Never trust no nigga, bitch. All these niggas counterfeit. Baby girl, when you gon' learn? That is not yo' nigga." – Kash Doll, "For Everybody"

Chapter 4

Gray

The fact that Gunz hadn't come home the night before should've bothered Gray but after ten years of dealing with his shit, she honestly could give two fucks. She was done running behind that nigga. Knowing him, he was laid up with some bitch. Lord knows, she wasn't fuckin' him. It had been eight months since he had a sample of her black and Korean pussy. She'd be damned if that muthafucka ran up in her when she knew good and well he was fuckin' other bitches.

She'd put up with Gunz and his cheating ways for far too long. The only reason she'd stayed with him was because he was the father of her six-year-old daughter, Press. He was also the only father figure her ten-year-old daughter, Aoki, knew. He'd raised her as his own, and although he was a shitty boyfriend, he was an excellent father. Yeah, after ten years of being together, she was still his 'girlfriend'. He'd given her an engagement ring a few years into their relationship; but after constantly asking him to set a wedding date and him continuously putting it off, Gray realized she'd been given a shut-up ring. The ring was meant to placate her while he ripped and ran the streets.

At one point, she thought Gunz was the love of her life, but that nigga was for everybody. Gray stopped fooling herself into believing he'd change, and that they'd get married. Gunz wasn't shit to her but her baby daddy. Hell, she barely wanted to call his ass that. As far as she was concerned, that nigga was just a roommate. Gray had bigger things to worry about… like the fact that in ten minutes she would have to tell her staff of 100, hardworking people, that her self-titled magazine was shutting down. No one was buying magazines anymore. It was the digital age and blogs like the Shade Room and Fameolous got more traction than Vogue and Time magazine.

Laying off 100 employees wasn't an easy fete. They were more than her employees, they were her family. On top of that, Gray had no idea what she was gonna do with her life. Being a magazine editor-in-chief had always been her dream. She worked from the bottom to get where she was, and now it was all being taken away from her. She had no idea who she was without her magazine.

She'd never be the type to sit at home and bake cookies all day. She was a working girl. How she would rebuild her life, she didn't know. Before she could even figure out her next step, she had 100 people waiting on her in the auditorium. Just as Gray gathered what little strength she had, her iPhone rang. It was Aoki's school calling.

Gray hung her head low. The last thing she needed was for Aoki to be in trouble. Lately, she'd been acting up at school. Gray assumed it was because Gunz was never home and they could no longer shield her from their relationship problems. Aoki was ten years old now. She could feel the tension in the room when they were together. Gray was pretty sure she heard them arguing at night. This wasn't the life she wanted for her or her children. Something had to change - and fast.

"Hello?" She put on her best, professional voice.

"May I speak to Miss Rose, please?" The school principal, Mrs. Glanville, asked.

"This is she."

"Hello Miss Rose. This is Mrs. Glanville from Forsyth school calling regarding your daughter, Aoki."

"Yes, is there a problem?" Gray prayed it wasn't.

"There is."

Gray slumped down in her seat and rolled her eyes.

"I'm afraid Aoki has been in a fight with two of her classmates, Ryan and Makiah. You know our school has a strict no fighting policy, so all three girls have been suspended for two days."

"Well, obviously she was jumped, so why is Aoki being suspended?"

"I'm afraid Aoki initiated the fight. She slapped Makiah in the face during recess because she jumped in front of her when it was time to go down the slide. The girls began fighting and when Makiah's twin sister, Ryan, saw her on the ground, she jumped in and pulled Aoki off her sister. Then, Aoki pushed her, and they began fighting. Makiah was still very upset, so she got up and started hitting Aoki too, before one of the teachers could break up the fight."

"Oh my god," Gray groaned. "I'ma kill her li'l ass."

"We're gonna need you or her father to come pick her up from school early."

"Ok, I'll call her father." Gray ended the call, on the verge of tears.

Her day was already shitty and hearing the news that her daughter had been suspended for fighting only made it worse. *Not today, Satan*, she thought, FaceTiming Gunz. With her hand covering her eyes, she listened as the phone rang. After three rings, he finally picked up.

"What you want? Gunz sleep," some girl answered the phone.

Gray quickly uncovered her eyes and looked at the screen. Her eyes had to be playing tricks on her. She knew Gunz was a disrespectful bastard but no way in hell was he letting his side bitches answer his phone. This wasn't even a grown woman on the other end. This girl couldn't be any older than 21. Gunz was officially robbing the cradle. Gray didn't even know why she was surprised but she was.

The girl was the total opposite of her. She was petite, with long weave flowing down her back and thick, false lashes on her doe-shaped eyes. A small earring was in her nose and several tattoos covered her arms and chest. A million thoughts ran through Gray's mind. She couldn't believe that things had gotten so bad between her and Gunz. The little respect she thought he had for her had completely gone out the window.

"Who are you?" She finally asked.

"Tia. Gunz girlfriend, why?"

"Umm… li'l girl, put Gunz on the phone."

"Didn't I tell you he was sleep?" Tia panned the camera over to him.

Sure enough, there he was shirtless, knocked out asleep on his stomach. If Gray could, she would've reached through the phone and stabbed him in the back like he'd done her. Tia put the camera back on her.

"Anything else?"

"Girl, where is your mother?"

"Ma'am, I am 20 years old. I am grown."

"Ma'am?" Gray drew her head back. "No you did not just call me ma'am."

"Look, we over here sleep." Tia yawned. "Don't call his phone this early no more."

"This li'l bitch is so disrespectful. Who the fuck arc you talkin' to?" Gray said, in disbelief.

"You, old lady. Gunz is not yo' nigga. He wit' me now. That's why he don't never come home no more. He too busy suckin' and fuckin' me. I don't even know why you thought he would stay with a square bitch like you. You a lame and you fat. Don't nobody wanna be wit' no big bone bitch. But I'ma do you a favor, sweetheart. When I'm done with 'em, you can have him back."

Gray cracked a smile and laughed. *This heffa really think she doing something,* she thought. If Tia thought calling Gray fat was gonna get her riled up, she had another thing coming. Calling her fat was an amateur read. It didn't matter what size Gray was. At the end of the day, she would still be prettier and more successful than the prosti-tot on the other end of the phone. Little Miss Tia thought she was pulling rank on Gray 'cause she had Gunz in her bed. Little did she know, but Gray had been here before. Tia wouldn't be the first or last bitch to think they held court in Gunz's life, only to wind up broken hearted in the end.

"Let me tell you something, sour puss. That dick you over there suckin' is for everybody. Ain't a bitch in St. Louis that ain't had that. So, while you gassed up 'cause he got yo' nails and feet done, bought you some bundles and a Gucci bag, remember, everything he has got my name on it. So, fuck him good so that old-ass heart of his can give out and I can cash in this life insurance."

"Girl, bye." Tia laughed. "Just 'cause y'all share a light bill don't mean shit. You been wit' that nigga for ten years and all you got is a mortgage and a baby. If it wasn't for your kids that nigga wouldn't even acknowledge you."

"Oh, baby girl, you have no idea who you over there fuckin' wit'. But see, I know exactly who that nigga is. Yo' dumb-ass the one that's gon' have to learn the hard way. You a damn fool if you think Gunz gon' fall in love with you. That nigga will never love you; but since you have no parental guidance, let me inform you. You ain't shit but a cum rag, li'l girl. You a whore, and when he get done nuttin' up in you, he gon' come right home to me. So, enjoy it while it last. Oh, and by the way, before you try to play a chick like me by answering my nigga phone, wipe the drool from your mouth. You slut bucket bitch." Gray spat, ending the call.

Holding her head back, she tried her best not to scream. Seeing Gunz in the bed with a girl that was young enough to be his daughter was the last straw. That li'l bitch could have him. Gray was officially done. This was the final nail in the coffin. She'd been through enough. She wouldn't be disrespected by his side chicks. She deserved to be happy. Holding on to a man that didn't mean her no good for the sake of her children wasn't helping her. It was hindering her. Remembering the meeting, Gray rose from her chair and held her head high.

She wouldn't let her circumstances or Gunz break her. The meeting with her staff was short and sweet. There was no point in prolonging the agony. It was best to rip the Band-aid off. No one was shocked by the news, but the revelation they'd all be laid off still hurt. Gray promised all her employees a nice severance package to ease the sting. She was surprised she was even able to hold it together.

Tears stung her eyes, as she talked, but not one fell from her ocean blue eyes.

Gray couldn't afford to cry. If she did, she'd never stop. Maybe she was able to keep her composure because she had to head to Aoki's school. Asking Gunz to go was out of the question after her confrontation with his baby whore. She'd deal with Gunz later. Right now, her focus was on her daughter.

The sound of Gray's red, Le Silla, pointed-toe, suede pumps echoed as she switched down the hall. All the children were in class. Gray made her way to the main office. After announcing herself to the secretary, she was led inside the principal's office. Gray took off her Dolce & Gabbana shades that was cascaded with flowers and jewels. To her surprise, she was the last to arrive. Aoki, the twins, their father and the principal all awaited her arrival. Gray glared at Aoki, as she walked inside. There were a few scratches on her face, but other than that, she was alright. Aoki sank down in her seat with tears in her eyes. She knew when they got home her ass was grass.

"Sorry I'm late." Gray said, as she sat down.

"No problem, Miss Rose." Principal Glanville smiled.

The twins' father, however, said nothing. He barely acknowledged her presence. He sat slouched down in the seat like he didn't want to be there. There was a noticeable scowl on his face that sent a shiver down Gray's spine. She'd been around Gunz's mean-lookin'-ass for ten years but this man actually kind of scared her. Gray tried not to trip off how fine the twins' daddy was but it was impossible. The man was fine with a capital F. For some dumb reason, she had butterflies in the pit of her stomach.

The sight of him alone made her nervous. She hadn't seen a man this handsome since she met Gunz.

The nigga had heartbreak and ho written all over him. He was too damn cute for his own good. Judging by the length of his long legs, he looked to be about 6'4 in height. A blue jean dad hat rested low over his diamond-shaped eyes. He had sweet, caramel-colored skin, a sprinkle of freckles on his cheeks and pointy nose, pink, full lips and a well-groomed beard. There was so much ice on him, she could barely see. A gold, diamond, Cuban link chain, two, gold, tennis diamond necklaces - one with a Jesus piece and the other a cross - rested on his broad chest.

On his left wrist was a $46,000, yellow gold, Cartier Juste Un Clou bracelet. A gold ring was on his ring finger, but it wasn't a wedding band. An Audemars Piguet watch was on his right wrist. The rest of his look was laidback. He wore a white, fitted tee that showed off his tattoos, ripped jeans and Timbs. Gray wished she could clear out the room, lock the door and have her way with him but quickly reminded herself that he was someone's father. Plus, by the looks of him, he wasn't shit. She already had one ain't shit nigga on her nerves. She didn't need to add another to the roster.

"Miss Rose, we called Ryan and Makiah's parents but weren't able to reach them, so the next person on their call list was their uncle, Mr. Parthens." Principal Glanville pointed.

Gray placed her red, leather-trimmed, suede Gucci bag down and extended her hand to him.

"Hi, I'm Gray. Aoki's mother."

"Yep." Mr. Parthens nodded his head and kept his eyes focused ahead of him.

Gray screwed up her face to match his.

"Rude… but ok." She caught herself looking at his crotch.

She wondered if his dick matched the size of his cocky attitude.

"As you both know, you've been asked here today because the girls had a physical altercation. Fighting is prohibited here so the girls will be suspended—"

"That's some bullshit." Mr. Parthens interjected.

"Excuse me?" Principal Glanville cocked her head to the side.

"You excused." He sat up straight and looked over at Aoki. "Her li'l bad-ass fucked wit' my nieces so she deserve to get her ass whooped."

"Bad-ass?" Gray repeated, appalled.

"Mr. Parthens, please refrain from cursing." Principal Glanville urged.

"Stop wit' all the Mr. Parthens bullshit. I told you my fuckin' name is Cam." He mean-mugged her.

"I know you didn't just call my daughter bad." Gray continued. "Have you lost yo' damn mind?" She furrowed her brows.

"Nah, but obviously you have." Cam turned and looked at her for the first time.

Instantly, his breath was taken away. The angry expression on Gray's face did nothing to hide her stunning beauty. Miss Rose was bad. He'd never seen a woman that looked like her. She had an exotic appeal about her. Cam wondered what she was mixed with. He guessed

Polynesian. Whatever she was, she was gorgeous. Her skin matched his and she even had a sprinkle of freckles on her nose and cheeks too. Her tranquil blue eyes were what captivated him the most. They were mesmerizing, but the angrier she got, the more they turned gray.

Her long, brown and honey blonde wavy hair was pulled up in a top knot. Cam didn't like her hair up like that. He wanted to see her hair down. The top knot was too constrained. Everything about her look was too prim and proper. There was only a hint of sex appeal to her attire. The Rodarte, black, fitted blazer, spaghetti strap, black and white stripped Dolce & Gabbana bodysuit and red, wide-leg pants fit her curves perfectly but hardly showed any skin. Baby girl was thick and needed to show that shit off.

Cam liked a woman with meat on her bones. Gray was a nice size 18, but she wasn't sloppy with it. Her breast sat up and her stomach might've been pudgy, but you couldn't tell through her clothes. Her thighs were full and firm. Cam couldn't wait till she stood up, so he could see how fat her ass was. Shorty was dangerous and didn't even know it. She needed a real nigga like him to loosen her up and bring her inner bad girl out.

"I need for both of you to calm down." Principal Glanville tried to gain control of the room.

"No, the hell with that. He needs to apologize." Gray crossed her arms and stared at Cam.

"Fuck outta here. What I look like apologizing to you? It was yo' daughter that got her ass whooped. I ain't apologizing for shit."

"I ain't get beat up and she need to watch herself on the slide or the next time I'ma slide her ass." Aoki rolled her neck.

“Aoki, hush.” Gray warned, and then focused back on Cam. “You got to be out yo’ damn mind to talk to me like that. You must not know who I am.”

“Yo’ sexy-ass could be Michelle Obama and I still wouldn’t give a fuck. Check yo’ attitude, ma, ‘cause yo’ daughter obviously got it from you.”

“Hold up. You think I’m sexy?” Gray placed her hand on her chest.

Cam grinned.

“You a’ight.”

“A’ight? Boy, bye. Whatever. That’s neither here nor there.” Gray waved him off.

“You the one that came in her with all them titties. Fuck I’m supposed to say?” Cam said, with a straight face, knowing he had her flustered.

“First you say my daughter deserve to get her ass beat, then you gon’ talk to me like I’m a piece of meat?”

“Name one thing I lied about and if you find that out, I’ll show you my dick. I see you been lookin’. How you like that print?” Cam sat back in his chair and grabbed a handful of his penis.

“You know what?” Gray shot up from her seat. “I can’t deal wit’ you niggas today.”

“Nigga?”

“Did I stutter? Yeah, you a nigga. You’s a disrespectful-ass nigga at that.”

“Miss Rose! Your language, please!”

"I'm sorry, Mrs. Glanville, but I have had one hell of a day. I had to lay-off all my employees, my daughter's father side bitch tried my life, I haven't eaten lunch and then this muthafucka here talkin' to me like he crazy. I can't win for losing."

"Miss Rose, I understand that, but we still need to discuss this."

"No, we don't need to discuss shit." She grabbed her purse. "I'm about to take my black-ass the fuck home."

"You about a rice box away from being black anyway." Cam said, nonchalantly.

Gray gasped so hard she thought she was gonna pass out.

"No, this nigga didn't. You racist bastard. You know what? Aoki, c'mon before I slap the shit out of him."

"Only thing that's gon' get slapped is that fat ass I'm lookin' at right now."

Gray looked him up and down with fury in her eyes.

"Nigga, I will fuck you up."

"*Nigga, I'll fuck you up*," he mocked her, in a high pitch tone. "And I will fuck you." He glared at her, without a hint of a smile on his face. "Sit yo' ass down."

"Excuse you?" Gray rolled her neck, indignantly.

"You heard what the fuck I said. Sit yo' ass down so this old-ass lady can finish talkin'."

"Excuse me?" Principal Glanville gasped.

"I don't know what the fuck is up wit' y'all and all these excuse me's but y'all need to hurry this shit up so I can go." Cam cocked his head to the side and sat with his legs wide apart.

"Mr. Parthens—" Principal Glanville tried to speak before he cut her off.

"Bitch, I know you old. Didn't you hear me say my name is Cam?"

"Mr. Parthens, I—"

"I see Cicely Tyson don't listen. C'mon, Ryan and Makiah." Cam shot up, pissed. "The next time they fight, if the li'l bitch ain't dead, don't call me with this bullshit." He pointed at Principal Glanville.

"And you, ol' thick-ass, rice patty with the cute eyes." He pointed at Gray, while holding open the door. "You need to get a handle on yo' daughter, or the next time, I'ma have my nieces run up in her shit." Cam warned, before strolling off with an attitude.

“She smiling in yo’ face, but you don’t even know, so I can’t even say.” – 6lack, “MTFU”

Chapter 5

Chyna

Leaving her hospital bed was the last thing Chyna should've been doing but she wouldn't be able to rest until she checked in on L.A. From what she'd been told, the two bullets to his chest miraculously missed his heart by a half an inch. However, the doctors had to surgically remove the bullets. After hours in surgery, L.A. was now in the ICU in critical but stable condition. Dressed in her hospital gown with the pole from the IV drip in hand rolling beside her, Chyna made her way off the elevator. Against her better judgement, she begged one of the nurses to take her to his room, even though she was still woozy from the wound to her head and the pain meds she'd been given.

Chyna knew she had no business being up on her feet in the condition she was in. She could only see out of one eye, but the need to see L.A. consumed her. Now was the only time she'd be able to do it. In the 24 hours she'd been in the hospital, Dame hadn't left her side once. She practically had to threaten him into going back to the hotel to shower and change. Little did he know, but her making him leave was her way of going to see L.A.

Dame would black her other eye if he knew what she was doing. L.A. was officially on his shit list. He blamed the whole jacking on him. He felt if L.A. would've given up his jewels and cash, then Chyna wouldn't have been in the hospital with a fucked-up face. It took everything in her to stop him from finding L.A.'s room and finishing the job the robbers started his self. If L.A. made it through this, it was only a matter of time before he was back in the hospital but on his death bed.

"You got five minutes." The nurse gave Chyna a warning glare.

She wasn't trying to get her head chopped off by Dame. He'd been a tyrant her whole hospital stay. He stayed on everybody's asses to make sure his belle got the best care the hospital had to offer.

"Ok," Chyna nodded, walking into L.A.'s room slowly.

As soon as she stepped inside, she frowned. For some odd reason, the first thought that came to her mind was that he didn't look comfortable. Chyna's eyes zeroed in on the bed. It was lumpy with padding and sheets that tried to mask the thick plastic that covered the hard mattress. Chyna didn't like it one bit. A man in his condition needed to be as comfortable as possible. What if he woke up and his back hurt? He would never get better laying on a bed like that. Chyna wanted to fix the problem but didn't know how. She was fucked up herself. Concerned for his well-being, she examined his room.

It was cramped, to say the least. The large hospital bed dominated most of the space. The machines, Get Well balloons and bouquets of flowers took up a lot of space too. There were so many flowers it looked like she was in a floral shop. Next to his bed was a bedside table and comfortable chair that looked like someone had been in all night. Like her room, his was painted in a color that some might've considered soothing, but to her, it only conjured up thoughts of a funeral home. A heavy door attached to his hospital room and private bath was engineered to open quietly so it wouldn't slam. The private bath had a handicap railing on the toilet, a shower and a tub.

Chyna thought she was hooked up to a ton of machines, but it was nothing compared to what L.A. had going on. A transducer beeped every few seconds, echoing throughout the room. A heart monitor and oxygen tank were attached to him. Reluctantly, Chyna focused on his face. L.A. lay like a corpse with his eyes closed. The only way she knew he was alive was because his chest moved up and down. All the color had been drained from his beautiful face. It was now an ash gray. He looked sickly. Nothing like the strong, virile man she'd come to know, and at one point loved. Chyna had never seen him look more fragile in his life.

Angry and sorrowful tears threatened to fall from her big, brown eyes as she gently placed her hand on top of his. His tattooed hand was slightly cold because of the frosty temperature in the room. Chyna clutched his hand tightly, as she broke down and cried. Tears burst forth like water from a dam, spilling down her cheeks. She could feel the muscles in her chin tremble like a small child, as she hung her head low.

"Why didn't you just give them the jewels and the cash like they asked?" She wept. "Why?"

Chyna cried so hard, her chest hurt. She cried for their breakup, the hurt they'd caused one another, him being so damn hardheaded, the bullets shot into his chest by unknown assailants and the right side of her swollen and bruised face. She wept for the love they once shared but had been destroyed by their egos, rash decisions and bad timing. None of it had to go down the way it did but it had and now here they were. Nothing between them would ever be the same after this. The jacking had changed everything for the worse.

"Why do you have to be so fuckin' stubborn?" She cried even more.

Chyna wanted to hate him for what happened, but she couldn't. They were both victims. The robbery was neither of their faults. She just hated that he'd almost lost his life because of it.

"What the fuck are you doing in here?" Bellamy spat, with venom in her eyes.

She couldn't believe Chyna had the audacity to be inside her husband's room, weeping like he was her man. Chyna released her hand from L.A.'s and wiped her eyes before turning around. She would be damned if she let her arch nemesis see her cry. Bellamy looked like she was going to go into labor any day now. Her belly was big as fuck. Four months before, Chyna would've been incredibly jealous to see her in such a state, but the love she had for L.A. was no longer there. In the past, she would've been ready to fight and argue with Bellamy but that was the last thing she wanted to do. It wouldn't help anyone. They'd all been hurt enough.

"I just came to see how he was doing. That's it." She explained, calmly.

"I don't give a fuck what you came to do! Get the fuck out, bitch!" Bellamy's bottom lip trembled, she was so upset.

L.A. was her husband. It was bad enough that he was laid up in the hospital, fighting for his life. It was even worse when she found out he'd been robbed and shot with his ex in the car. Bellamy wasn't a dummy. She knew that L.A. still had feelings for Chyna. She just hoped and prayed that he'd never act on them. Learning they were in the car together at 3:00 in the morning verified her fears. There she was seven months pregnant with his little girl, waiting for him to return home so they could spend time with his mother, and his ass was out fucking around with his trifling ex-girlfriend.

Bellamy was crushed. When she'd married L.A., she prayed that he'd get over his feelings for Chyna. Apparently, he hadn't. The unconditional love she had for him, their marriage and baby obviously didn't mean a thing to him. Almost a year and a half later, he was still hung up on a bitch that didn't love him half as much as she did.

Chyna grabbed the IV pole and prepared to leave. She was determined not to lose her cool, even though Bellamy was pushing her.

"Yeah, that's right. Get the fuck out." Bellamy rolled her neck, as Felicia walked into the room.

"Chyna!" She exclaimed, taking her into her arms. "How are you feeling? I came by to see you earlier, but you were asleep." Felicia examined her face and body.

"I'm ok." Chyna took in her heavenly scent and smiled.

She missed Felicia terribly. She hadn't seen her in months. Felicia's breast cancer was in remission. She looked better than she had in ages. It was so good to see her back to her old self.

"Ma, are you serious right now?" Bellamy shouted. "This bitch was creeping around with my husband and your hugging her? What kind of disloyal shit is that?"

Before Felicia could even respond, Chyna stopped her.

"First of all, watch your fuckin' mouth. Secondly, ain't nobody fuckin' your husband. L.A. was doing me a favor by giving me a ride to the hotel my *fiancé...* was staying in. I don't want your man, sweetheart. I been let that dick go; so for the sake of you and that baby, it's time you let this sick infatuation with me go too."

"You can try to convince yourself and everyone else that you're over L.A., but I know the truth. You ain't foolin' me, bitch. I can see right through your li'l innocent act. You asked him for a ride 'cause you wanted to be near him. Aren't you tired of trying to weasel your way into our lives? The man don't want you. He's married to me! We have a baby on the way! Leave us alone!" Bellamy pushed Chyna in her chest, causing her to stumble back.

Fortunately for her, she didn't fall.

"Bellamy, stop!" Felicia stepped in-between the two women.

"No! I will not! This bitch has ruined my life not once but twice! It's because of her that I lost Carlos! Now, because of her, L.A. is laying in the hospital fighting for his life! He almost died because of this cum-sucking ho! It should've been her that almost died! Not him!" Bellamy tried to swing and hit Chyna in the face but was stopped by Felicia.

"You are not gonna lay a hand on her." Felicia gripped her wrist.

"So, this is how it's gonna be?" Bellamy said, as tears rolled down her puffy cheeks. "You gon' stand here and take her side like she ain't just try and fuck my husband? I'm the one married to your son! I'm the one carrying your granddaughter! She ain't your family! I am! She ain't shit but a delusional, home-wrecking ho!"

"I'm not gon' be too many more bitches and hoes," Chyna fumed, ready to lay hands on her.

“Bitch, fuck you!” Bellamy tried to get at her, but Felicia continued to hold her back. “Get the fuck out my man’s room! Security! Security!” She screamed at the top of her lungs.

Instantly, an armed guard rushed into the room. It was like when Chyna ran up on L.A. and Bellamy in California all over again. Except, this time, the guard had a gun. Chyna rolled her one good eye hard. Even when she was trying to do the right thing, shit always went left. She wasn’t even trying to turn up. She was genuinely on some peaceful shit, but Bellamy’s insecure-ass wouldn’t let her live.

“What’s the problem?” The armed guard asked, with his hand on his gun.

“This bitch is trespassing! Get her out of here and make sure there is a guard outside of my husband’s door from now on! We don’t need any more of his delusional fans getting inside his room!”

“You heard the lady. Let’s go.” The guard yanked Chyna by the arm, roughly.

“Oww!” She winced in pain, as he tried to drag her out of the room.

“You must be tryin’ to die today,” Dame’s deep voice bellowed, commanding the attention of everyone in the room.

Chyna had never seen Dame look so angry. He wasn’t even this mad when he choked out Carlos. It was like his face was balled into a fist. His eyebrows were furrowed, and his eyes were squinted to the point you could only see his dark irises. Not one of his teeth showed because his mouth was so tight. Any good in him was gone. This was no longer the controlled, refined man she knew and loved. This was Dame the beast; the devil that would kill you without blinking an eye.

Despite the pain she was in, the only thing Chyna could concentrate on was the pounding in her chest. She hadn't been this scared since the robbery. When Dame got like this, there was no stopping him. There was no talking him off the ledge. It was either kill or be killed. For her, he'd body a muthafucka and would go on about his day without a care in the world. She didn't want him to come out of character over something so small.

"Baby, calm down."

"Shut up." Dame shot, not taking his eyes off the guard.

"You need to get back," the guard said with an attitude, as he tried to bogart his way past Dame.

Chyna's shoulders slumped, as she closed her eyes. The security guard had just fucked up in the worse way. Before Chyna could reopen her eyes, Dame had hooked off on the guard. He'd punched him so hard in the jaw, he'd fallen back into the door and fell to the ground.

"Fuckin' pussy!" Dame raised his foot and started to stomp the guard out.

The sole of his thousand-dollar, Saint Laurent dress shoes connected to his face, repeatedly. Dame was trying to smash his head in. Soon, the guard's head would look like a deflated basketball. Blood spurted from his nose and mouth like he was the star of a horror film.

"Dame, stop!" Chyna yelled.

Her pleas fell on deaf ears. Nothing or no one was stopping him. No one disrespected Basil Damien Shaw and lived to talk about it. Chyna officially stopped breathing, when several cops ran down the hall ready to tackle him.

"Dame!" She screamed.

"Nephew, chill!" Mohamed appeared out of nowhere and pulled him off the guard.

Furious, Dame snatched away from his uncle, wiped the sweat off his brow and fixed his suit. A sly grin was etched on his face, as he examined his handy work. The guard was a bloody mess. His eyes were swollen over, and bloody spit drooled from his slack jaw. He was now as repulsive as his behavior. Dame had no choice but to make his outside reflect the man within.

"Put your hands up! You're under arrest!" A young, white cop pointed his pistol at Dame's heart.

"Uh ah." An older, black cop gripped his shoulder. "Put your gun down, son."

"Why? He just assaulted an armed guard." The white cop continued to aim his gun at Dame.

"We work for him." The black cop whispered in his ear.

"Who the hell is he?"

Dame walked up and smacked his gun out of his hand.

"I'm the muthafucka that just signed your death certificate." He gripped the white cop by the collar of his shirt.

"He a rookie, boss. He ain't know." The black cop pleaded.

"And now he does. If I ever see this Tom Brady-lookin' muthafucka again, your life will be next. I want this nigga 6F."

The black cop groaned. This was not how he saw his day going. 6F was code for six feet under. His partner would never see another day on earth. He'd made the biggest mistake of his life by pointing a gun at Dame. The rookie cop didn't know that they were all on his payroll.

"And handle this nigga too. He got blood on my fuckin' shoes." Dame kicked the guard one more time.

"A'ight, boss." The black cop grabbed the battered guard by the arm.

"Bring yo' ass on." Dame said to Chyna, as he walked past her - pissed.

She knew he was livid because he didn't even bother to help her to the elevator.

"C'mon, niece." Mohamed tenderly took Chyna by the hand.

"Chyna, I'll talk to you later." Felicia called out.

Chyna was in such a state of shock over the events that had just occurred, that she didn't even respond. On the elevator ride down to her room, neither she or Dame spoke a word to each other. She could feel the steam radiate off him, he was so mad. No matter what she'd done, Chyna had never been the focus of his wrath. Nervous at what he might do to her, she hesitantly walked back into her room with him hot on her trail. Knowing they needed a moment alone, Mohamed stayed outside the room.

"What the fuck was you doing in that nigga room?" Dame glared at her.

"I wanted to see how he was doing."

"I told you that nigga was breathing. What more you need to know?"

"Dame—"

"Dame nothin'." He grabbed her by the jaw harder than expected and looked into her eyes. "What the fuck were you cryin' for?"

"I—"

"Let me find out you still got feelings for that nigga. Yo' ass gon' come up missin'." He gripped her tighter.

"Let me go!" She tried to push him back to no avail.

"You still love him?"

"You know I don't." Chyna's eyes welled with tears.

"Do I?" Dame quizzed, letting her face go.

Chyna's heart dropped. Her day had gone from bad to worse. Never in a million years did she expect that kind of response from him. She thought she'd made it clear that her heart belonged to him and only him. She'd agreed to spend the rest of her life with him for God sake. This was the side of Dame she hated. The devil had an easy way of entering and taking over his soul when he felt his back was up against the wall. Being vulnerable was still something he wasn't used to. Dame only knew how to get his point across by force and aggression. He was so used to being that way in the streets that most times he forgot he couldn't be that way with her.

"Are you fuckin' serious?"

"You walkin' around in this thin-ass gown, wit' yo' ass out, titties bouncing and shit. What the fuck am I supposed to think? You were creeping around with the nigga."

"For the last time, I wasn't creeping around. I was on my way to you. I thought you said you believed me?"

"I did, but now I'm starting to wonder. For all I know you been fuckin' that nigga this whole time."

"Woooow." Chyna tucked her bottom lip inside her mouth, so she wouldn't cry.

Once again, he'd hit her with some shit she wasn't expecting. Dame looked at the tears in her eyes and sighed. He'd gone too far. He was being an asshole, but what did she expect? Chyna unknowingly was playing on his worst fears. Finding out she was with L.A. from Brooke damn near killed him. He just knew that she'd played him and cheated. Once he heard her side of the story and saw her face, he realized that his anxiousness was for nothing and she'd stayed true. Coming back to the hospital and learning that she'd left her room to go see him, reignited his fears all over again. He didn't understand her connection to him. The nigga was lame as hell. Plus, he'd almost gotten her killed. The only thing Dame could think was she still low-key was in love with L.A. and was too afraid to admit it.

"Don't cry." He reached out for her.

"No, fuck you!" She punched him in the chest, repeatedly. "You hurt my feelings and if you grab my face like that again, I'ma fuck you up!"

"Shut up." Dame took her into his strong arms and held her close.

He couldn't go in on her knowing what he'd done behind her back. The secret of his betrayal was making him act out of character. He had to get a hold of himself. If he kept reflecting his own infidelity onto her, he was going to fuck around and lose her for good. If he lost Chyna, he'd lose himself. Falling in love with her was a gift and a curse. She was the love of his life. Because of her, he now knew what it felt to be alive. She made everything in his life right. Without her, he'd go back to feeling lost again. On the other hand, Chyna was his one and only weakness. Thoughts of another nigga breathing the same air as her or thoughts of her leaving him drove him mad. He couldn't handle it if she slipped through his fingers again.

Like the love-sick fool she was, Chyna rested her head on his firm chest and cried silently. Her entire life was in shambles. She could only see out of one eye, Bellamy had tried her life, Dame had almost killed a man, and was now doubting her love. What was next? She couldn't take anything else bad happening. She'd fucked up by getting in the car with L.A. that night, but Dame should've known that she'd lay down and die before she ever stepped out on him.

"I'm sorry. I shouldn't have gone up there without telling you. I just knew you would be mad."

Dame ran his hands through her soft, curly hair and inhaled her scent. In seconds, her body molded into his own. In the center of the room, they stood sharing body heat as easily as they shared their hearts. He could never let another woman get this close to him, but Chyna was like no other. There wasn't a thing about her he didn't love. There was a purity to Chyna, a naivety that made her dumb decisions forgivable. He'd never known a person to always have the right motivations, even when their actions were totally wrong.

"In order for us to work, you're gonna have to communicate with me. No more sneaking around behind my back, Belle. It never works out when you do. Somebody almost dies every time," he chuckled.

"Stop. That's not funny." Chyna laughed, playfully hitting his chest.

"What? You laughing too." Dame kissed her lovingly on the forehead.

"And what the fuck does 6F mean?"

"Don't worry about it for yo' ass be 6F too." He slapped her on the ass, as India, Brooke, Delicious and Asia stormed into the room.

"Mom!" India rushed towards her mother.

"My baby!" Chyna immediately started to cry all over again.

Dame watched on as the love of his life embraced the first love of her life. Seeing her with India for the first time since she was a newborn was mind-blowing. She was an exact replica of her mother. She was beautiful. From the looks of her, Chyna had done a wonderful job raising her.

"This is a fucked-up way for y'all to meet, but India, this is my fiancé, Dame. Dame, this is my beautiful, smart, well-traveled daughter, India." Chyna brushed her hand across the top of India's head.

"Nice to meet you." Dame held out his hand.

"Nice to meet you as well." India shook his hand.

"I ain't seen you since you were a baby."

"Oh, so you the man that was almost my daddy?" She eyed him quizzically.

"India!"

"What? It's the truth. Just know if you mess over my mom, I'ma round up the crew and we all gon' jump you."

"India, what the hell has gotten into you?" Chyna covered her mouth and stifled a laugh.

"I just gotta let him know. You've had your heart broken too many times. We ain't going through that mess again."

"You got that right." Delicious pursed his lips.

"You ain't got nothin' to worry about. I got your mom back." Dame pulled Chyna into him and kissed her forehead.

"Do you?" Brooke quipped, arching her brow.

"He betta." Chyna placed her head on Dame's chest.

"You did good tho', ma. At least he looks better than that ugly-ass Tyreik." India groaned, rolling her eyes.

"India!" Chyna's eyes grew wide.

Her daughter had gone to Australia a young girl and came back a sassy, young woman.

"My bad, Mom, but it's the truth. Any man you get wit' is a step up from that bum."

"You betta speak a word!" Delicious pretended to shout.

"Girl, let me look at you. Are you ok?" Asia wrapped her arms around Chyna too.

"Yeah, girl, we were worried sick." Brooke rubbed her back.

Dame stood back with both his hands in his pockets and stared at her. Everything in him wanted to yank her hands off his belle. Brooke didn't deserve to breathe the same air, let alone be in Chyna's presence. She was as fake as they came. Brooke was nothing more than a scandalous-ass bitch that didn't give a fuck about anyone but herself. He hated that Chyna didn't know what kind of viper she was dealing with. What made him even angrier was that he couldn't tell her Brooke wasn't her real friend without telling her he'd fucked her over too.

"I'm ok." Chyna confirmed, wiping her wet cheeks.

"Damn. That nigga fucked up your face. You might need to go to Dr. Miami to fix that." Brooke said, with repugnance.

It was taking everything in her not to laugh. She knew how much Chyna cared about her looks. Having her face look like Martin Lawrence from the boxing episode had to play on her self-esteem. Brooke would use this to her advantage and play on her psyche.

"Bitch, fuck you." Chyna curled her upper lip.

"Don't listen to her. She a hater, ma. You look good as fuck." Dame kissed her injured cheek to show he didn't give a damn about her trauma.

"Right. Ain't nothing a li'l foundation and concealer can't fix," Delicious agreed.

"What I wanna know is: why are you out of bed?" India asked, with a concerned look on her face.

"I went to see L.A." Chyna looked at Dame, warily.

"How is he? Is he doing ok?" India questioned, concerned.

Despite Chyna and L.A.'s breakup, she still loved and cared about him very much. He was the only father figure she'd ever had. As long as he wanted to keep their relationship going, she would too.

"He's in stable but critical condition."

"Was he awake when you saw him?"

"No. He was asleep."

"Ok. I'm gonna go visit him later."

"I don't know if that's a good idea, sweetheart."

"Why?" India wanted to know.

Before Chyna could answer, her doctor walked in.

"Well, hello, everyone." Dr. Tatum smiled, brightly.

"Hello." The gang spoke back.

"Miss Chyna, how are you today?" Dr. Tatum focused her attention on her vitals.

"I'm feeling a little better."

"How is your head?"

"It still hurts some and my face is still sore."

"The pain meds we have you on will help with that but we're going to have to lower your dosage."

"Why is that?" Dame demanded to know.

"I have some news. Do you mind if everyone steps out of the room?"

"We're all family here. You can tell me now," Chyna replied.

"Ok, well, Miss Chyna, according to your test results, you're pregnant."

"What?" Chyna's mouth dropped.

"Yes, ma'am. You are."

"Oh my god." She looked up at Dame to see his reaction.

A look of bewilderment was on his face. Chyna had never really thought about having another kid, but now that the opportunity had presented its self, she was suddenly overjoyed. She was so young when she had India. She didn't really appreciate the sacred moments of having a newborn. With this new baby, she'd be able to get things right. She just prayed that Dame wanted the baby too. If he didn't, she'd be devastated. She couldn't imagine being a single mother, again; especially, not at the age of 35.

"You aren't mad, are you?" She intertwined her hands with his.

As always, she couldn't tell what Dame was thinking. His face was made of stone. Dame looked down at Chyna's scared face. The apprehension of his response resided in her eyes. He'd gone 40 years without having kids. He refused to get a chick pregnant if he couldn't see her being his wife. Chyna had been wifey material since the age of 16. No other woman could don his last name but her. It was only right that she be the mother of his kids. Dame leaned down and leaned his forehead against her. Chyna closed her eyes and prepared herself for his answer.

"J'espère que notre petit garçon ou fille ressemble à toi." He lovingly kissed the tip of her nose.

"Speak English, Dame." Chyna said on the verge tears.

"He said, 'I hope our little boy or girl looks just like you'," India replied.

She'd taken French her sophomore year in high school.

"You're gonna be a daddy." She placed her lips against Dame's and kissed him tenderly.

"My baby having my baby." He took her face in his hands and placed small kisses on her forehead, eyes, cheeks and lips.

"Congrats, Mom," India beamed. "But I told you, I'm not babysitting," she joked.

"Shut up, girl." Chyna laughed.

"Congratulations, friend." Delicious and Asia hugged her as well.

Brooke tried not to roll her eyes but was unsuccessful. No one caught her reaction because they were so focused on Chyna, except Dame. He never missed a thing. Brooke shot him a heated glare, as he placed his hand on Chyna's stomach. Now would be the perfect time to bust Chyna's li'l happy bubble. She thought her life was so perfect. Little did she know, but her man was a lying, cheating ho. Dame wasn't any better than the rest of these niggas. He just had more money and power to conceal his dirt. If he thought he was going to get away with using Brooke, he had another thing coming. When she was done with him, Dame was gonna regret every, despicable thing he'd ever done.

"You'll say any and everything, so you can keep me in your space tonight. Every little tear drop, you just try to wipe off with one more of your lies." – Victoria Monet, "No Good"

Chapter 6

Gray

Gray sat on her mustard yellow, suede couch with a glass of Chateau Montrose 2005 Boudreaux red wine in hand, reflecting on the thoughts in her head. For the past few years, it felt like she was walking dead. Somehow, she'd figured out how to exist instead of live. Gray learned how to numb herself to the world's pain; but after the day she had, the wall she built came tumbling down. She couldn't keep up her strong face anymore.

To say she was tired of Gunz was an understatement. She was tired of him, the games he played, the lies he told, the broken promises, constant heartbreak and his existence on earth. She was tired of being a pretty liar. For years, she'd kept up the facade that they were this happy family, when really, she was dying on the inside. She'd completely lost herself loving him. In the process, he'd broken her down to nothing. Gray didn't even recognize herself anymore.

When had she become the woman that would put up with a lying, cheating manipulator? Somewhere along the line, she had become Gunz's doormat. After the first few times she'd caught him cheating and she took him back, she'd unknowingly set the standard for their relationship. Any respect he had for her went out the window. He realized she wasn't going anywhere and used it to his advantage. When she had Press, he really knew he had her. Gray came from a broken home. She didn't have a relationship with her father. She never wanted her daughters to suffer the same fate. So, for the sake of her girls, she stayed in a toxic relationship that made her unhappy.

It baffled her how Gunz could be such an amazing father but a shitty-ass mate. Sometimes, she found herself being jealous of the relationship he had with Aoki and Press. He loved on them the way she wished he'd love on her. He treated them like the princesses they were. Meanwhile, she was treated like gum stuck on the bottom of his shoe. Gray had no one to blame but herself. The antagonizing ache in her chest was her fault. No one had told her to stay. She made that foolish decision on her own and was now suffering because of it.

If it wasn't for her kids, Gray would've ended it all years ago. Her life seemed to be consumed with tragedies and losses. Somehow, she'd survived being raped by Aoki's biological father and managed to move on. It was hard sometimes, looking at her daughter, knowing how she was conceived. She always wanted her children to be conceived with love, but that option had been taken away from her. Gray was done with being a victim. It was time she took back control of her life.

Now that her magazine had gone under, she could take the time to figure out what her next move would be. Getting rid of Gunz was the first step in her transformation. Like the coward he was, she hadn't heard from him all day. He was probably trying to figure out the lie he was gonna tell her. There was nothing he could say. She'd seen him with her own eyes in another chick's bed. She didn't give a damn what he had to say. It was over between them. He wouldn't be able to beg or guilt-trip his way out of her leaving him this time.

It was fucked up they didn't work out. They'd built an amazing life together. The 3-bedroom, 3.5 bath, 2-million-dollar high rise apartment they owned was magnificent. It had taken Gray over a year of decorating to get it just the way she wanted it. Every room had an art deco feel. She especially loved what she'd done with the living room. On the wall above the couch was a photo of Scarlett Johansson laying on top of a bearskin rug. Black and white, chevron throw pillows decorated the mustard, suede couch. A vintage, glass, coffee table with books sat on top a gray and white-printed area rug. Grey, suede chairs and a gold and white, modern chandelier finished off the room. Gray had put her heart and soul into decorating the apartment. She and Gunz had planned to live there until the girls graduated high school. Now, she'd be living there alone.

There was no way in hell that she would continue to accept Gunz foolin' around with a bunch of baby bitches that wore 32-inch nails and colored weaves. If he didn't see the value in the woman that had held him down for ten years, then so be it. Gray would find another man that would value her beauty, education, class and success.

Gunz stood in front of the elevator door, bracing himself for it to open. The moment he'd been dreading since that morning had finally arrived. He couldn't avoid Gray any longer. When he woke up to find out that Tia had answered his phone, he went ballistic. The backhand to her face that split open her lip was punishment for not staying in her lane. Gunz wasn't shit, but he wouldn't allow none of these hoes to disrespect the mother of his kids'.

All day he racked his brain on how he was gonna get out of this one. He'd fucked up in the past but never this big. Gray had never physically caught him foolin' around. Once again, he'd have to see the sad look in her blue eyes that he'd caused. He hated disappointing her, but it was her fault he behaved the way he did. She'd put him on a pedestal, no matter how many times he let her down. It had gotten to the point he felt numb when it came to cheating. She'd allowed it for so long that he no longer tried to conceal his dirty deeds.

Gunz was a man and a man had needs. The needs he had, Gray wasn't providing. She put the kids and her career ahead of him. She was always too busy to spend time with him or fuck. That wasn't an excuse for him to seek comfort in another woman, but she made it easy for him to go elsewhere.

Gray talked a big game like she was going somewhere if he continued to do her wrong, but Gunz knew she wasn't going nowhere. They had ten years together, two kids and a house. He'd been there after she killed Aoki's father in self-defense. He was the one that held her at night when she woke up in a cold sweat from nightmares. He was the one that gave her the startup money for her magazine. Gunz had practically raised Gray. When he met her, she was this young, naive girl with big dreams and an even bigger heart. He taught her how to be a boss bitch and how to take that dick. She was never gonna find another man like him.

Gunz was that nigga and had been since his 20's. Gavin "Gunz" Marciano was the former leader of the Marciano Crime Mob. Once he settled down with Gray and became a father to Aoki, he decided to leave all that street shit alone. He had a family to protect. Leaving the dope game behind, he became the owner of seven, five-star restaurants and ten Wingstops. His street money and legal money had him sitting pretty. Him, his kids and grandkids would never have to work a day in their life, if they didn't want to. He had Gray to thank for that. She'd been right there by his side, guiding him and giving him advice.

For that alone, he should've married her, but having legal ties to a woman made him cringe. Gunz couldn't help it. He was a selfish muthafucka. What was his, was his. If things didn't work out between him and Gray, he didn't want her taking half his shit. He'd have to kill her if she did.

Yeah, it was fucked up making her think he was going to make things official. Marriage was important to Gray; and if she knew he had no intentions on ever marrying her, she would've left him a long time ago.

To avoid that, Gunz did what most niggas do and gave her an engagement ring to placate her. While she dreamt of a wedding and them saying 'I Do', he did what he always did and that was whatever the fuck he wanted to do. He might not have sold dope anymore, but the streets kept calling his name. Unfortunately for him and Gray, there was nothing in the streets but temptation. Gunz couldn't keep his dick in his pants. These hoes were getting finer and bolder by the day. They didn't give a fuck if you had a woman at home. They would gladly be your side bitch, as long as you threw them a couple of dollars and laid down the pipe.

Chicks were dying to say they had Gunz's attention. He was a street legend. How could he say no when hoes approached him? Chicks made it too easy to cheat. Plus, he was fine as fuck. Bitches stayed in his face. They couldn't get enough of his Hershey chocolate skin. He was tall with a muscular body that was crafted by spending five days a week in the gym. Spinning waves, succulent lips, a full beard, tattoos and a ten-inch dick adorned his body. There was no way Gray was leaving a nigga like him. No other man was going to pick her up, throw her against the wall and dick her down like he could.

To his dismay, the elevator door opened quicker than he expected. Gunz didn't know what he was about to walk into. When Gray had found out about him fuckin' a li'l young chick name Tanisha a year ago, she'd tried stabbing him. Gunz had to threaten shooting her to get her to calm down. Cautiously, he walked into the foyer. To his surprise, Gray wasn't waiting with a butcher knife, but all his clothes and shoes were in trash bags by the door.

It was after ten, so all the lights were out except the lamp in the living room where he found Gray. Anita Baker's *Fairytales* played softly on repeat, as she sat staring blankly at the city skyline. With one look at her, Gunz remembered why he wasn't going anywhere either. Gray was fucking beautiful. He'd never seen a woman that looked better than her. She was gorgeous. The black and white bustier had her titties sitting up like two, round melons. Thoughts of sucking her hard nipples as she moaned out his name invaded his mind. He wanted Gray in the worst way, but he knew baby girl wasn't having that. She hadn't given him the pussy in eight months.

"Where the girls at?" He asked, placing down his keys.

"Sleep." Gray took another small sip from her wine glass.

"How was your day?" He placed his hands in front of him and looked at her.

Gray scoffed and rolled her eyes. If he thought she was gonna answer that stupid-ass question, he had another thing coming. She wasn't in the mood for Gunz and his silly-ass games.

"So, you gon' act like you don't hear me?"

Gray inhaled deeply and tucked one leg under the other. Gunz wanted to argue and she wasn't having it.

"Why you got my stuff by the door?"

Gray cut her eyes at him. Gunz was fine as fuck but his good looks wouldn't save him this time.

"You know why."

"If I did, I wouldn't be asking."

"Gunz, just take your shit and go back to that bitch house you was at. My head hurt and I just wanna finish this glass of wine, so I can go to sleep."

"So, that's it? You not gon' even listen to my side of the story? You gon' take some bitch word over your man?"

"Gunz, you ain't been my man in years. The more I think about it, I don't think you ever were."

"Word? Then what the fuck is that on your hand?" He pointed to the 20-carat, emerald-cut, diamond ring on her finger.

"Reparations." Gray replied, with a straight face.

Gunz massaged his jaw and tried to conceal his rage. Even though he was the one in the wrong, it took everything in him not to slap the shit out of her.

"That's how you feel?"

"This ring don't mean shit to me just like it don't mean shit to you. Here! You want it back? You can have it." She took it off her finger and slid it across the table. "Lord knows, I don't want the next nigga I fuck wit' to think I'm taken." Gray shot to get under his skin.

"I'll kill you before I let you be with another nigga." Gunz said, sincerely.

"Gunz, ain't nobody thinkin' about you and your empty-ass threats. You don't run shit over here. You and I are so fuckin' through."

"Man, please. Go head wit' that." He waved her off.

"Think it's a game. Yo' ass gettin' out of here tonight." Gray got up and proceeded to grab the bags of clothes and place them on the elevator.

"What the fuck is you doing?" Gunz snatched her up by the arm.

"Puttin' yo' ass out." She tried to reach down for another bag.

"C'mon, man, chill. I'm sorry."

"As fuck!" She flared her nostrils.

"Really, Gray?"

"Yeah. You's a sorry muthafucka. I don't need you or your raggedy-ass apology. What I need for you to do is get yo' shit and get the fuck out."

"I ain't going nowhere and you know deep down inside you don't want me to go either." Gunz gripped both her arms and pulled her close.

Gray could smell his minty breath and Tia's cheap-ass perfume on his shirt.

"Shiiiit. I can show you better than I can tell you. Don't make me call the police. They ain't gon' give your ass as much time as I will to leave," she threatened.

"Call the police and see don't I knock yo' fuckin' head off your shoulders." He squeezed her tightly. "Quit actin' stupid. I know you mad about what you saw, but that bitch don't mean shit to me." He tried to kiss her on the cheek.

"She mean something. You was laid up in the bed with her." Gray moved her face out the way.

"I love you. I don't love her."

"You don't love me. You don't even love yourself."

"Whatever, Gray. How you gon' get mad at me when you been puttin' up with my shit for years? You know how I am. I told you from the jump this relationship shit wasn't for me, but you just kept pressing a nigga."

"So it's my fault you ain't shit?" Gray said, with tears in her eyes.

"You allowed this shit to go down. Don't cry now." Gunz released her from his grasp.

"Wow." Gray stepped back, stunned by his revelation. "So, I'm supposed to sit here like some battered woman and accept what you tell me and ask nothin' more?"

"Every time you get mad, you make a li'l noise to remind me of what a good person you are, but a good person wouldn't be here right now. You stay wit' a nigga 'cause you know ain't shit else out there. You think I ain't shit? Take yo' retarded-ass out there and start fuckin' wit' these other niggas. Yo' ass gon' be beggin' me to take you back."

"Bitch, anybody is the fuck better than you! I can't do no worse than I am right now! Talkin' about I'm gon' be beggin' to be back with you. Bitch, please!"

"I ain't even gettin' ready to go back and forth with you. We both know I ain't leaving, so you can argue wit' yourself."

Looking into his eyes, Gray didn't know who this man was standing before her. Had he always been this cold? Had she made him this way? Was her heart ever safe with him or had she slipped up and fell in love with an iceberg?

"Get the fuck out! Why won't you just leave? Let me have the apartment and go on about your business." She placed her face in her hands and cried.

Gray couldn't take it anymore. One more second around him and she was going to go to jail for murder. Somehow, for ten years, she'd tricked herself into believing he loved her, when in actuality, she'd been in the relationship by herself.

"I ain't giving you shit. We gon' die in this muthafucka together."

"I fuckin' hate you." She cried harder. "I wish I never met you."

"Stop crying, ma. You gon' wake up the kids." Gunz tried to hold her.

"Get your fuckin' hands off me!" She pushed him away with all her might. "I have never hated a muthafucka more than I hate you! Look at what you've done to me! I don't even know who I am anymore!"

"You act like you ain't play no part in this. Nobody put a gun to your head and told you to stay."

"You right. You sholl right. That's why I'm done with your tired-ass. The next bitch can have you."

"I don't want none of them bitches! I want you."

Gunz might've fucked with other women, but Gray had no reason to question if his love for her was true. His actions might've said that he didn't care but he did. Without Gray by his side, he would go insane. In Gunz's mind, what he did with these li'l chicks in the streets was nothing compared to his feelings for Gray. They would never trump her. She was his heart.

"Well, guess what? I don't want you. I'm tired of babysittin' yo' ass. All you do is hurt me. That's all you're capable of. A nigga like you don't belong in the world with normal people. Don't you think I get tired of being my own savior? For ten years, I have fought to keep you. I did everything you like. I cooked, cleaned, took care of our kids, mothered you, sucked your dick and spread my legs, even when I didn't feel like it, and none of it mattered. You had me thinkin' all these years you were the prize. When, in reality, you were never good enough for me."

"Now a nigga ain't good enough for you? I was good enough for you when I bought this expensive-ass apartment, and when I invested in yo' wack-ass magazine. You was all on my dick then, but now I ain't shit? Yeah, picture that. You like saying a bunch of dumb shit."

"No, you like breaking me down. You like to see me weak and crying over you."

"You think I like being this way? It kills me to see you upset behind some shit I did."

"Since it kills you so much, do us both a favor and kill yourself."

"You don't think I've tried?" He got in her face.

"Well, try harder. Nobody likes a quitter." Gray arched her brow.

Gunz stood dumbfounded. Gray had never said no cruel shit like that to him before. Baby girl had went for the juggler. She knew he feared death and barely slept at night from having suicidal thoughts. Maybe she really was sick and tired of his shit.

"What the fuck you say?" He inched closer.

Gray stepped back, scared. His eyes had darkened. She'd hit a nerve and now Gunz was enraged.

"You heard me." She tried to remain strong.

"You gon' wish death on the father of your kids, like I'm some random nigga off the street? You hate me that much?"

"Without question. Now, get out!" She pushed him with all her might.

"You really don't wanna be wit' me no more?" He asked, feeling his heart break.

"No!" Gray yelled. "I can't keep trying to put a crown on a dummy and expecting a king."

Gunz's eyes grew wide. He'd turned his precious Gray into a monster. She'd become a savage, just like him.

"I won't be runners up to no bitch." She mushed him in the forehead.

"You never were." Gunz took her hand in his and kissed the palm of it. "There has never been anyone in my life like you. Just stick with your man and I swear to God one day I'ma be the man you deserve."

"Bitch, you 42! How much more time you need? Pretty soon, you gon' be dead!"

"Chill." He wrapped his arms around her waist. "I fucked up and I'm sorry. Just let me make it up to you."

"No." Gray pushed him away, again. "I told you it's over!"

"Nah, I ain't accepting that. It'll never be over between us. You always come back and so do I."

"Not anymore. I'm done!"

"Mommy! What's going on?" Aoki rubbed her eyes, as she walked down the hallway.

"Nothing, baby. Go back to bed." Gray wiped her face and pushed past Gunz.

"Something is wrong. You and Daddy are fighting, again. Why?"

"'Cause Mommy tryin' to put a nigga out," Gunz answered.

"Why would you tell her that?" Gray damn near snapped her neck to look back at him.

"'Cause it's the truth."

"Mommy, no! Don't make Daddy leave!" Aoki ran over to her father.

Gunz didn't hesitate to scoop her up in his arms.

"Aoki, you don't understand. Mommy and Daddy can't be together anymore." Gray tried to pull her away from Gunz's arms, only for Aoki to wrap her arms around her father's neck tighter.

"Yes, you can! You love each other! Don't you, Daddy?"

"Daddy loves Mommy with all his heart."

"See!"

"Gunz, stop!" Gray stomped her foot.

She felt like she was losing her mind. He always did this to her. He always made her look like the bad guy in their daughter's eyes. It wasn't fair.

"What? You tryin' to take me away from kids."

"Stop lyin' to her! You know that's not the truth. Aoki, I would never keep you away from your daddy."

"Then why are you tryin' to make him leave? Just because you don't want him around doesn't mean we have to suffer."

The lump in Gray's throat almost cut off her air supply. The tears falling from Aoki's eyes made her feel like the worst mother on the planet. How could she make Gunz leave when she saw how much her decision was affecting their daughter? She couldn't. Aoki and Press would hate her forever, and Gunz knew it. That's why he played on their intelligence, so he could get his way. Gray wanted to curl up in a ball and die. He was never gonna let her go. She was trapped with him forever.

"Mommy won't make Daddy leave."

"You promise?" Gunz asked.

Gray glared at him, with tears in her eyes.

"I promise."

"''Cause no one fights to be the #1 contender forever. I want the title." – Xavier Omar, "The Title"

Chapter 7

Mo

"Fuck my life." Mo said, stripping out of her clothes and throwing them in the washer.

Zaire's pamper had exploded and his brown feces got all over her shirt and pants. If this was the first time this had happened to her, she would've vomited; but after four kids, shit like this had become normal. Mo had been pissed, shitted, vomited, coughed and sneezed on more times than she cared to think of. The job was gruesome, but it was all a part of being a mom.

Zaire shitting on her was the last thing she needed. She was already behind schedule with washing clothes, fixing dinner and helping the kids with their homework. Zaire had been cranky all day. He was sick with a cold and didn't want to nap or latch onto her nipple during feeding time. His constant crying and refusal to sleep or eat stopped her from doing the loads of clothes that needed to be washed and baking 100 cupcakes for King's bake sale at school. The twins were at home, but of course they were no help. They thought being suspended for two days was a mini vacation.

Mo woke up to find them wearing her colored wigs, pretending to be Sky and Donna from Black Ink Crew. They'd used their colored markers and drew fake tattoos all over their bodies. Ryan was running around the room, lifting her shirt and pretending to tell an imaginary Teddy to come look at her titties. Meanwhile, Makiah was bent over, twerking to *Bodak Yellow* with a red Solo cup in hand. Mo lost her shit and damn near kicked their backs in.

After spanking them, she demanded that they go wash the fake tattoos off their bodies and sit their asses down somewhere.

She couldn't believe that they were taking their suspension so lightly. It was all Boss and Cam's fault. They thought the shit was cute. Boss wasn't even mad that they were suspended from school. He simply asked the girls if they'd beat the little girl's ass, and when they said yes, he gave them a high five and 100 dollars each. Mo wanted to fuck him up after that. She hated that Boss was so laidback and cavalier when it came to the kids' behavior. His nonchalance always made her look like the bad guy. It wasn't fair that she was labeled the disciplinarian and he was labeled the cool, fun parent. They should've been a united front, but that would've been too much like right.

Mo was always left out in the cold alone. She was drowning, and her husband was nowhere to save her. This last pregnancy had done her in. She'd lost her sense of self. Mo missed who she used to be. Nothing about her was recognizable anymore. After showering, she stood in front of her full-length mirror naked, examining her body. Mo knew she was a good-looking woman, but she no longer felt confident about her looks. Her hair stayed pulled up in a ponytail. She never had time to go to the shop anymore or get her nails and feet done.

She hadn't gone shopping for new clothes in ages. She was no longer in single-digit sizes. After Zaire, she'd ballooned to a size 12/13, which was huge for Mo. She felt like a fuckin' beach whale. Her 5'9 height supported the extra weight, but she wasn't comfortable at all. Mo went from being shaped like a skinny supermodel, to being shaped like Instagram starlet, Maggie Carrie. Boss loved her 32 DD breasts, wide hips and gigantic ass. Thankfully, none of the weight she'd gained had gone to her stomach. It was still flat but covered with stretch marks. She hated that shit. It looked like a tiger had clawed at her stomach. She'd never be able to wear a crop top again in life.

And forget wearing booty shorts. The cellulite in her thighs, and the fact that they rubbed together, was outright disrespectful. The days of having a thigh gap was over. Mo couldn't even remember the last time she'd worn makeup or got her eyebrows threaded. Boss always said he liked her without all that shit on her face, but Mo liked to be beat to the gods. It was a blessing that her smooth, Godiva chocolate skin, whiskey brown eyes, high cheekbones and full, luscious lips didn't need makeup, or else she would've been fucked.

"Umm… Monsieur, your kids are hungry, and your baby is crying." Boss' mother, Phyliss, barged in her bedroom without knocking.

"Do you know how to knock?" Mo shrilled, covering her breasts and vagina with her hands.

"Girl, please, you ain't got nothin' I ain't already seen."

"That's not the point. This is my bedroom. You can't just walk in here like this is your house." Mo slipped on a pale pink satin bra and thong.

"You need to take that thong off with all that ass, and my son's name is on the deed, correct? So, what's his is mine."

"And one day you gon' walk in here and see yo' son's tongue in between my thighs." Mo threw on a one-shoulder, grey sweatshirt, joggers and pink, furry Fenty PUMA by Rihanna slides.

"You kiss my grandkids with that filthy mouth?"

"And I suck your son's dick with it too." Mo mumbled under her breath.

"What was that?" Phyliss followed behind her, as she went into the kitchen.

"Nothin'."

"What up, OG?" Mo walked in on her son, King, dapping up his dad.

Mo was madly in love with her first son, even though he was bad as hell. Like the rest of her kids, he had creamy, mahogany skin, a head full of thick, curly, black hair and an unrelenting mean mug. King may have looked like her, but his mannerisms and attitude came straight from his father. King was a baby thug. He didn't smile unless it was necessary. He had a slight dip to his walk like Boss, stayed listening to trap music and knew how to Crip walk better then O.T. Genasis. Mind you, he was only six.

"What's up li'l man?" Boss dapped him up. "How was school today?"

"It was copasetic. I made ten dollars selling my snacks to a couple shorties."

"You still got your friends on the playground selling for you too?"

"Of course. I'ma businessman." King pulled out a wad of cash from his pocket.

"That's my boy." Boss ruffled his hair.

"What kind of baby drug dealer are you raising?" Phyliss asked Mo, as she took a seat at the kitchen island.

"Why you saying something to me? I ain't got nothin' to do with that. Direct that to your son."

“Quit hatin’, Syphilis.” King stacked his money on the table.

“King!” Mo screeched, taking out a bag of flour.

She was about to fry some chicken.

“What the hell you just call me?” Phyliss looked at her grandson.

“Syphilis; that’s what Mommy calls you,” Makiah replied, opening the refrigerator door.

“Is that right?” Phyliss glared at Mo. “It’s a wonder your kids ain’t on America’s Most Wanted. Who in the hell goes around calling their mother-in-law a venereal disease?”

“Mommy.” Makiah drank the orange juice straight from the carton, and then wiped her mouth with the back of her hand and burped like a grown man.

“Look at your daughter. Ain’t got no damn home training. What are you over here teaching these kids? One’s a trap king, the other is a street fighter and this one ain’t got no damn manners. I’ma stop bullshittin’ and write into Iyanla.”

Mo tried her best to ignore Phyliss’ constant digs at her parenting. If she went toe to toe with her, she’d surely end up saying something she’d regret. Mo wished they could go back to the way they once were. At one point in time, Phyliss was like a surrogate mom to her like Quan’s mom, Nicky. With Mo’s own mother being dead, she desperately craved a mother’s love. She thought she’d have that with Phyliss, and at one point she did. After she and Boss’ little sister, Shawn, fell out over a business decision that resulted in her boyfriend and Mo’s artist breaking up with her, Phyliss took her daughter's side and started to hate her too.

Mo thought they'd be able to salvage their relationship, but after nearly four years of slick comments and degrading from Boss' mother, she gave up hope. She wasn't that beat for the chick to like her anyway. Long as her son did, that was all that mattered. The only problem was, Boss didn't check his mother when it came to Mo. He claimed he didn't want to get in the middle of their mess, but Mo wasn't having it. She would never let anyone in her family disrespect him. It was only right that he show her the same courtesy. She was tired of being a runner up to his mother. She needed to be #1.

"How my baby mama doing?" Boss stood behind his wife and wrapped his arms around her slim waist and kissed her cheek.

Mo could feel his stiff dick in the crack of her ass. No matter the time of day, he was always ready to smash. If the kids and his mother weren't in the room, she would've gladly sat on top of the counter and let him have his way with her. But like always, there were too many things getting in the way of them getting it in.

"What I tell you about callin' me that?" She pushed her butt back into his crotch, which caused his dick to jump.

"What? You're my baby mama and I'm your baby daddy and these are our baby-babies." Boss placed his phone down on the counter.

"I swear, I can't stand you." Mo laughed, as he slipped his hand between her legs and massaged her pussy. "What are you doing? I'm tryin' to fix dinner."

"Fuck dinner. Let's go back to the room so you can be dessert." Boss licked her earlobe, which sent a spark of electricity down her spine.

"Stop. You're gettin' me wet."

"That's the point." He rotated his fingers in a circular motion.

"Boss, your mother is here," Mo whined.

"So." He turned her face and kissed her softly on the lips.

Mo closed her eyes and let his tongue slip into her mouth. The seat of her thong was instantly drenched. Eleven years later and Boss still made her drip wet with desire. The kiss between her and him was so good that she didn't even realize she'd let out a moan.

"Mmm hmm!" Phyliss cleared her throat, loudly. "What is this Pornhub? Don't you see me sittin' here?"

"Didn't you hear your grandson? Quit hatin', Syphilis." Boss eased up on Mo before smacking her hard on the ass.

"Oww! That hurt!" She tried to hit him, but he jumped out of the way.

Mo tried to pretend like she was mad, but Boss knew she wasn't. She loved when he showed her attention. He tried to show her as much as he could. Since having Zaire, Mo needed the extra assurance of his affection. Every time he turned around, she was downing the way she looked, which he thought was absurd. Yeah, she'd gained weight, but it wasn't like she was 500 pounds. Boss liked the extra hips and ass she was carrying around. That shit was sexy as hell to him. Mo had a body like a stripper now.

His only gripe was that she didn't dress up or fix her hair anymore. He missed seeing her all dolled up. Mo used to command a room. Now, it was like she coward in the corner. She didn't like going anywhere because she claimed none of her clothes fit and that she looked ugly. Boss wished he could help her through this battle she'd waged on herself, but no amount of telling her how beautiful she was helped. Mo had to feel it for herself.

Juggling four kids, several businesses, after-school activities, an overbearing mother, Mo's weight issues and a nonexistent sex life had Boss on edge. He and Mo hadn't had a perfect marriage, but it was damn near close. Things were great until she started beefin' with his mother and sister. After that, everything went downhill.

The tension between his wife and mother was real. It had gotten so bad that Mo didn't even want to celebrate holidays with her anymore. Instead of kickin' it with him and his people, she went to her ex fiancé, Quan's, mom's house and chilled with him and his family. That shit was the ultimate sign of disrespect to Boss. He barely liked that she still associated with that nigga's family but tolerated it because his ole bird was like a mother to Mo. It was bad enough that after being together 11 years, she still had that nigga's name tattooed on her wrist. She didn't even have his name tattooed on her and he was her husband.

Mo claimed she didn't have feelings for Quan anymore, and Boss believed her, but his wife having close ties with her ex and his family didn't sit well with him. It wasn't helping that she never wanted to have sex anymore; and when he could get her in the mood, one of the kids were always around or she was too tired.

On top of that, the beef between Mo and his mom was causing a major rift in their marriage. Mo didn't like the way his mother talked to her, and his mother felt it was her job to stick up for her son. Boss was incredibly close to his mother and would vent to her sometimes about his issues with Mo. He didn't think it was wrong to air out his grievances to his mom. When Mo got mad, she ran to Quan's mom, Nicky. The good thing was that he didn't have to hear Nicky's mouth about the shit Mo told her. He didn't fuck with that lady. Phyliss, on the other hand, made it her business to let Mo know how she felt about the way she treated her son.

Boss loved and respected both women. He didn't want to choose one over the other. He couldn't. He'd been his mother's rock since his father's passing. They had an unbreakable bond. Mo was his heart and soul. He'd take the moon out of the sky and give it to her, but he couldn't choose her over his mother and vice versa.

"Mama, we hungry. When the food gon' be ready?" Ryan pouted.

"In an hour, Nemo." Mo kissed her daughter on the forehead.

"When Boss was a kid, I had dinner ready and on the table by the time he came home from school every day," Phyliss bragged. "Ain't that right, baby?"

"Yeah, Mama," Boss groaned.

"Good for you, Phyliss. You want a treat?" Mo snapped back.

"I'm just sayin', a real mother knows how to prioritize her time. Ain't no reason that dinner shouldn't be ready when your kids come home, especially when you're sitting at home on your ass all day."

"Why are you here? Didn't a new Tyler Perry movie come out today?"

"I'm here because this is my son's house and I'm hungry too."

"Why don't you go floss? Maybe you could get a meal out of that." Mo snapped, slamming a cabinet door.

"You tryin' to say my breath stink?"

"Your breath do be kickin' in the front door like the police," King chimed in.

Phyliss leaned over and got into his face.

"Just cause yo' mammy don't kick yo' ass don't mean Granny won't put her foot up yo' ass."

"Chill, Granny, I thought I was yo' boy."

"I'm sorry, baby." Phyliss ruffled his hair. "Sometimes Granny forgets she's saved."

"You crazy as hell." Boss guzzled down a bottle of water.

"All I'm sayin' is: you got to keep your house in order. My mother-in-law always told me keep yo' man's belly full and his balls empty."

"Can we please not talk about balls in front of the kids?" Mo looked at Boss for backup.

"Ma, chill." He took her cue.

"You might not like it but I'm speaking the truth," Phyliss continued. "Like my mama said, 'What you won't do, another bitch will'."

"Oh my god." Mo rolled her eyes.

As far as she was concerned, Phyliss and her dead-ass mama could kiss her ass. She ran her household just fine. If Phyliss didn't like it, she could take her ass home.

Annoyed with her mother-in-law's presence, Mo washed the flour batter off her hands and then reached for a towel. As she dried off her hands, she couldn't help but see Boss' phone vibrate. Normally, she wouldn't check his phone, but when she saw the name Zya flash across the screen with the words, 'Hey Zaire' followed behind, Mo's face screwed up. Nobody called him by his first name. Not even her or his mother. Without hesitation, she tapped his screen to read the rest of the message.

Zya: Hey Zaire… I have a quick question. Hit me back when you can.

If Mo wasn't already mad that she was on a first name basis with her man, the smiling, winking face emoji that she added at the end made shit worse. She didn't know who this Zya chick was, but she had her all the way fucked up.

"Umm… who is Zya?" She held up his phone.

"Why you going through my shit?" Boss walked over and took it from her.

"'Cause I can. Now answer the question." Mo narrowed her eyes at him.

"Calm down. She's the manager at Babylon."

"What is she doing callin' you Zaire?"

"That's my name, ain't it?" He laughed.

Mo was sexy as hell when she got jealous.

"I don't see shit funny. Tell that bitch to call you Boss like everybody else."

"It ain't even that deep."

"Yeah, it is. She's a little too comfortable for my taste."

"You the one hired her." Boss threw up in her face.

Mo stood silent. She'd completely forgot that she was the one that told him to hire Zya based off her resume and application. Mo, however, had never laid eyes on the chick. She'd been at home on mommy duty since Babylon opened.

"I don't give a fuck," Mo yelled, 'cause she couldn't think of anything else to say.

"Watch your mouth. My kids are in here."

"Nigga, yo' mama been cussin' all day long and you ain't said shit to her."

"He bet not." Phyliss shot back.

"Keep playin' with me. Your kids are gon' be fatherless," Mo warned.

"Chill. Ain't nothin' going on between me and that girl. She is strictly my employee."

"Our employee." Mo reminded him.

"You know what I mean."

"Actually, I don't."

"I know you ain't mad when you got a whole other man's name tattooed on you." Phyliss stuck up for her son.

"You need to mind your business. This is between me and my husband."

"You gon' let her talk to me like that?" Phyliss asked her son.

"Man… both of y'all crazy." Boss replied, stuck in the middle.

"Really?" Mo looked at him to back her up.

"What?" Boss shrugged.

He refused to get in the middle of Phyliss and Mo's fight.

"You know what?" She threw up her hands. "Make the damn chicken yourself; or better yet, have Zya or ya mama do it." She spat, before storming out of the kitchen.

"Now she wanna be all up in arms. I told her what she won't do another woman will," Phyliss smirked, dropping a piece of chicken in the hot oil as it popped back on her. "Ouch!"

"That's what you get. God don't like ugly." King grinned.

"Shut up, boy. Didn't nobody ask you shit." Phyliss rolled her eyes.

"I don't satisfy you, apparently. Even though you say I'm the one that you desire. But you're making a fool of me, so I won't hold you back. I hope you do good, my nigga. I hope to find you in love. I hope you do better with her. I hope it's better than us." – TXS, "Do Good"

Chapter 8

Gray

It was Gray's last, official day as a magazine editor-in-chief. With her box of keepsakes in hand, she walked into her building. Normally when she entered her place of residence, a sense of pride bubbled in her chest. She and Gunz lived in one of the best high-rise apartment buildings in Saint Louis. It housed a gourmet grocery store, Panera Bread, bowling alley, book store, boutique and movie theater. That day, however, she felt nothing. She couldn't smile or feel happy if she tried. Her career was over. Owning her own magazine had been a lifelong dream. She'd worked her ass off to give readers a monthly dose of fashion, art, music and literature.

At the height of her success, her self-titled magazine was one of the hottest in the United States but then the digital age hit. People no longer ran out to the stores to pick up the latest issue of their favorite magazine. By the time Gray caught on and made her magazine available online, it was too late. Now, here she was, jobless with no clue of what she would do with her life. Thankfully, she had a nice amount of money saved up, but the money wouldn't last forever.

Gunz would give her anything she needed, but him having financial control over her wasn't an option. Anytime they got into it, he liked to throw in her face what he did for her. He loved tearing her down and making her feel like she couldn't survive without him. Gray had to figure out her next move - quick. The faster she did, the quicker she'd be able to get away from him. Living under the same roof as Gunz was killing her softly. She hated looking at his lying, cheating face.

Gray didn't know how her life got so fucked up. She needed a stiff drink, so she could drown her sorrows. Gray needed to let her hair down and get loose. For years, she felt confined. It was becoming suffocating. Thankfully, her best friend, Kema, had talked her into going out that Friday. Clubs weren't really Gray's thing anymore, but Kema had begged her to go, so she couldn't say no. The only good thing about going out was she'd be able to cloud all her worries with copious amounts of alcohol. The draw back was that they were going out so Kema could link up with her new boo thang. His pot'nah was celebrating his birthday and he wanted her to come through. Kema didn't want to be around a bunch of niggas she didn't know alone, so she begged Gray to tag along.

"Good afternoon, Miss Rose." The doorman, Smith, nodded his head in her direction.

"Hi, Smith." Gray forced herself to smile.

It physically hurt her face to smile full on. She'd been crying all morning. She was sure her eyes were still red and swollen from saying all her goodbyes. She'd truly miss every one of her employees.

Gray pressed the up button on the elevator and waited, as a million and one thoughts swarmed through her mind. One being what she would whip up for dinner. It was after 7:00pm. Cooking was the last thing she wanted to do, but if she didn't she and the girls wouldn't eat. She could order takeout. *Yep, pizza it is,* she thought, as her phone rang. Gray adjusted the box on her hip and dug in her purse to fish it out.

"Hello?" She answered cautiously because she didn't recognize the number.

"Hi, may I speak to Gray, please?"

"This is she. Who is this?"

"Hi, this is Mo. Ryan and Makiah's mom."

Gray rolled her eyes. She hoped Mo wasn't calling her to argue about the fight between the girls. She would hate to have to cuss her ass out.

"I got your number from the parent directory," Mo continued. "Is now a good time to talk?"

"Sure." Gray said dryly, not in the mood.

"Sorry my husband and I couldn't make it up to the school Monday. We were a li'l busy." She reminisced about Boss bending her over the kitchen sink and fucking her brains out. "I heard about what happened between you and my brother. I apologize for his rude behavior. Unlike me, he doesn't have any home training," she joked.

"Yeah, your brother is an acquired taste," Gray agreed, rolling her eyes.

Thoughts of the tattooed thug with the reckless mouth for some reason made her even angrier. He was a complete asshole. She hoped and prayed to God she'd never have to see him again.

"I just want to let you know that my husband and I don't condone fighting," Mo lied.

Boss didn't give a damn.

"Even though my girls didn't start the fight, we're still very sorry about what happened."

Gray let out a sigh of relief. She just knew that Mo was calling her on some rah-rah shit. Mothers could be real bitches when it came to their kids.

"I'm so happy to hear you say that. I just knew this conversation was about to go left. I would've called and apologized myself, but I've been swamped with work and some personal issues." She thought of Gunz, which made her heart constrict.

"Oh, girl, trust me. I understand."

"What Aoki did was inexcusable. She had no business putting her hands on your daughter. I don't play that. Outside of getting suspended, she was placed on punishment. I just hope it works because she's been acting out a lot lately. Her father and I haven't been on the best of terms lately and I think it's affecting her," Gray found herself admitting.

"It's ok, girl. I understand," Mo said, thinking of her own material problems. "Listen, from what I learned, the girls were friends before this. Why don't we get them together for a playdate this Saturday, so we can squash this little, petty beef?"

"I love that idea."

"You have two girls, right?"

"Yes, Aoki and Press."

"How old are they?"

"Ten and asshole," Gray joked.

"Oh, I like you." Mo cracked up laughing. "Your daughter, Press, knows my son, King. I think he has a li'l crush on her," Mo laughed.

"Oh Lord," Gray chuckled.

"Right; but look, bring her too."

"I will, and thanks again for calling, Mo. I really appreciate it."

"No problem. You have a good day."

"I'll try." Gray ended the call, feeling a little better than she had before answering.

Seconds later, she was stepping off the elevator and into her foyer. The smell of her favorite Korean dish, Kimchi fried rice, wafted up her nose. Gray scrunched up her forehead. She wondered who made it. Gunz was too lazy to cook. Kicking off her Gianvito Rossi, lace-up, suede heels, she placed the box down and walked into the dining room.

"Surprise!" Gunz, Aoki & Press yelled.

Gray stood speechless. Silver helium balloons that spelled 'I Love You' were up against the wall. In the center of the table was a bouquet of white roses that signified *I'm sorry*, champagne on ice and several gift boxes wrapped in silver and white paper. In the past, Gray's heart would've melted, but this wasn't the first time Gunz had hit her with an apology dinner.

"You like it, Mommy?" Press ran over and hugged her legs.

Gray looked down at her baby girl's beautiful face. Press had a head full of sandy brown, curly hair, caramel skin and almond-shaped eyes. She looked just like Gray except she didn't possess her blue eyes. Press' eyes were brown, just like her father's. Aoki, however, had her mother's mesmerizing, ocean blue eyes.

"I love it, boo bear." Gray lied, giving her an Eskimo kiss.

She was sick of Gunz fucking up then trying to buy his way out of it.

"You look pretty, Mommy." Aoki gave her a hug.

"She sure does." Gunz eyed her hungrily.

Gray was bad as fuck. Most women that were plus size didn't wear their weight well, but she did. Gray was sexy as fuck and didn't give a fuck about being a BBW. She hated when other plus size women got down about their weight. She was fine and knew it. Men went crazy over her 30 D breasts, wide hips, luscious thighs and fat ass. Gray had more curves than a race track and had no problem showing it off. Usually, she was covered up in designer duds, but on occasion, she would let loose and put her thickness on display.

That day, she wore a Johanna Ortiz silk organza, off-the-shoulder top with a crisscross, wrap bodice and white, Ralph Lauren, wide-leg trousers. The billowy, blush pink and brown top showed off her soft tan skin. Gunz desperately wanted to kiss her collarbone to see if she still tasted like honey.

"Thanks, sweetie." Gray glared at him.

She detested that he used their children to get back into her good graces when he fucked up - which was often. When she was a weaker woman, she fell for the shit, but not anymore. The girls, roses, gifts and dinner wouldn't change that she was done with him.

"Press, did you do your homework?"

"Yes. Daddy helped me," she smiled, brightly.

"Did he?" Gray eyed Gunz, quizzically.

There he was, standing with a big-ass, goofy grin on his face. The nigga helped their daughter with her homework once and was grinning like he'd really done something. Gray wanted to slap the smile off his stupid face. Usually, on school nights, he was nowhere to be found. Gray was left to do everything by herself, while he ran the streets doing God knows what with God knows whom.

"We already ate and took our bath too." Aoki added.

"You ready to go back to school tomorrow?" Gray tilted her head back, so she could have a good look at her.

"Yes."

"No more fighting, Aoki, ok?"

"Yes, ma'am."

"Forsyth is a very prestigious school. If you get in trouble again they're gonna put you out."

"And then you gon' go to jail," Gunz chimed in. "And you know what happen to li'l girls when they go to jail?"

"No, what?" Aoki's eyes grew wide.

"They get fucked."

"Gunz!" Gray placed her hands over Aoki's ears.

"What? It's the truth."

"Mommy, I don't want Aoki to get fucked!" Press cried.

"She won't. See, Gunz, look what you did." Gray bounced her up and down.

“It’s ok, Press. Daddy said I can’t get fucked until I’m 43.” Aoki rubbed her little sister’s back.

“What the hell do you be tellin’ them when I’m not around?”

“The truth.” Gunz took Press into his arms. “Come on, li’l mama. Time for bed. Me and Mommy got some talkin’ to do.”

“Night, Mommy.” Press waved goodbye.

“Night-night, baby.”

“Mommy?” Aoki got her mother’s attention.

“Yes, baby.”

“Be nice to Daddy tonight, ok?”

The eagerness in Aoki’s eyes damn near killed Gray. Aoki wanted so bad for her parents to stay together. Gray would give her daughter the world, but staying with Gunz for the sake of her kids wasn’t something she could do anymore. If she did, the little bit of sanity she had left would disappear.

“I’ll try.” Gray rubbed the side of her face. “Oh, and Saturday you and Press have a playdate with Ryan and Makiah.”

“I know. I talked to Ryan today.”

“Who said you could talk on the phone? You on punishment, li’l girl.”

“Daddy let me use his phone.”

All Gray could do was shake her head. Gunz had no concept of discipling the kids.

“So, y’all made up?”

"Yeah, Daddy said I had to call and say sorry for pushing her."

"Well, at least he got one thing right."

"She asked could I come over and play this weekend. I told her she would have to ask her mom, and then her mom would have to ask you."

"I don't wanna hear about you putting your hands on nobody else, Aoki."

"I won't. I can't be walkin' around with my face all scratched up. She's too pretty for all that." Aoki swept her long, curly hair off her shoulder.

"Girl, bye." Gray laughed.

"Night, Mommy." Aoki ran back to her room.

"You ready to eat?" Gunz approached Gray, with a look of desire in his eyes.

Gray inhaled deeply. Whenever she was in Gunz's presence, a small part of her always yearned for him to pull her hair and bury his dick deep inside her walls. For years, he had her sprung off his swag. Gunz was a fine muthafucka. The three, thin, gold chains, crème, fitted, pocket tee, jeans that ripped at the knees and tan Chelsea boots only enhanced his sex appeal. Even though Gunz was 42, he had a boyish face like the rapper, Nas. The nigga seemed to be aging backwards. His chocolate skin, spinning waves, thick beard, chiseled physique and Creed Viking cologne made her mouth water with desire. Gray had to remind herself repeatedly that she hated him.

"Yeah," she finally responded.

Gunz pulled out her chair. Gray took her seat and rolled her eyes, as he dimmed the lights and turned on

PartyNextDoor's *Break Me Down*. As soon as Party started to sing the lyrics, '*Ain't this what you wanna see; me breakin' down',* Gray rolled her eyes, again. *This nigga really tryin' to act like he hurt,* she thought, flabbergasted. Gunz was more delusional than she thought. Seconds later, he returned with her plate and poured her a glass of champagne. Gunz then took a seat next to her and placed her hand in his. Gray looked at him like he was crazy, until she saw him bow his head to say grace.

"Father God, I ask that you bless this food, my daughters and the most important woman in my life, my beautiful Gray Rose. I don't know what I would do without her and I pray I never have to find out—"

"Keep praying, Satan." Gray cut him off.

Gunz raised his head and looked at her. Not the one to backdown, Gray matched his glare.

"I ain't in the mood for your bullshit, Gray."

"I ain't in the mood for your shit either."

"Whatever, man. In Jesus' name I pray. Amen," Gunz finished his prayer, irritated.

Gray placed her napkin in her lap and began eating. She would be damned if she said amen to that shit. She was praying for God to give her strength to leave his ass, not to stay. PartyNextDoor continued singing about his girl being done with him, as she and Gunz ate in silence. It didn't take long for Gray to finish her meal. Kimchi fried rice was one of her favorites. Finished eating, she scooted her chair back to get up when Gunz stopped her by grabbing her hand.

"So, you ain't gon' open your gifts?"

"Fuck them gifts," she spat, snatching her hand away.

"C'mon, Gray. Chill. I fucked up. Let me make it up to you," he pleaded.

"I'm good."

"The girls helped me pick those out for you."

Gray pursed her lips and sat back down. Gunz knew since he'd involved the girls, she would have no choice but to open the gifts. Angrily, she ripped open the first box, not giving a damn about the expensive wrapping. Inside was the $20,000 Hermes Verrou Chaine mini bag she'd been wanting but was on a wait list for. Gray wanted to run around the room and shout, but she'd be damned if she gave Gunz the pleasure of seeing her happy based off something he'd done. In the second box was a pair of emerald green, Alexandre Birman ankle strap heels. The shoes were bad as fuck. If Gunz didn't know shit else, he knew the type of materialistic stuff Gray liked. He'd bought enough 'I'm sorry' gifts over the years to know.

The last box was medium-sized and from Harry Winston. Gray's blue eyes lit up. Gunz knew the way to her heart was through diamonds. Anxiously, she cracked open the box and gasped when she laid eyes on the diamond, straight-line necklace. The necklace was filled with nothing but diamonds, like a tennis bracelet. Gray ran her fingertips across each sparkling stone.

"You like it?" Gunz asked, seeing a flicker of happiness in her eyes.

"It's exquisite." Gray said, in awe.

"Just like you." Gunz stood and placed the piece around her neck.

Gray wanted to check herself out in the mirror but didn't want to seem too pressed over his good deed.

"Thank you, Gunz. I appreciate dinner and the gifts but that doesn't change anything between us," she clarified, as he stood over her.

"I know. I just wanted to show you how much you mean to me."

"Gunz, I can't mean that much to you. Every time I turn around you got yo' dick in another bitch."

"You know I don't give a fuck about them hoes. You the only one that got my heart. But, shit, what you expect? I ain't smelled the pussy in eight months."

"So, once again, it's my fault that you don't know how to keep your dick inside your pants?"

"You can't leave a nigga out here in the field and expect him not to hunt something."

"If you had a brain cell it would die of loneliness." Gray looked at him with disgust. "Ain't no way you gon' sit up here and blame your infidelities on me. You cheat 'cause you wanna cheat. Even when I was giving you the pussy, you still was out here doing you."

"See, there you go assuming I was just cheating to be cheating. I cheat because you put everything else before me. Like I ain't the muthafucka that's been holding you down this whole time."

"The sad part is: you really believe the bullshit that's coming out of your mouth right now."

"No, the sad part is: you really believe that everything I say is bullshit. Like you perfect or something."

"No, that's just your insecurities, so don't throw that shit off on me." Gray rolled her neck. "Even after all the bullshit you put me through, I stayed faithful to your ignant-ass. You haven't even asked me how my last day at work was. 'Cause, guess what? Everything is about you. You don't give a fuck about me or what the hell I got going on in my life."

"I do." Gunz wrapped his arms around Gray and pulled her up.

"No, you don't." She tried to push him away, unsuccessfully.

"How you gon' say I don't give a fuck when everything I do is for you and our kids? I love you to the ends of the earth and ain't no changing that. Even though your mad at me right now, I know you still love me too."

Gray looked up into Gunz's smoldering eyes. She hated him; but more than anything, she hated herself. She hated herself because everything he said was true. No matter how much she tried to fight it, love for Gunz still resided in her heart. He used to be her anchor and her best friend. She wished they could go back to the way they were. She just didn't know if they could find their way back to happiness. Gray might've loved him, but she no longer trusted him.

"You standing here being quiet lets me know you ain't gon' ever stop loving me. Keep it real. You love me, don't you?"

"Whether I love you or not don't make a difference," Gray argued.

"Bullshit. You too real to be out here lying and fakin', especially to yo'self. Now, in order for us to move forward, we gon' have to be honest with each other. Admit it. You love me."

"We both know I love you but—"

"Nah, ain't no buts. From here on out, we gon' keep it real wit' each other, a'ight?"

"Yeah, Gunz," Gray sighed, weakly.

"A'ight, now keep it real and tell me you love me." He placed a passionate kiss on her lips.

Gray's arms fell to her sides, as he rotated between kissing her top and bottom lips. She tried to remind herself that she was better than this. She couldn't keep lying to herself. Gunz was no good for her. He was incapable of loving her the way she deserved, but the minute his tongue caressed hers, all common sense went out the window. Gray felt like an idiot. She was supposed to be trying to find a way out of this madness not run back into the flames.

"Say it, Gray," he whispered into her lips. "You love me, don't you?"

"Yes."

"See… that wasn't so hard. Quit tryin' to be so fuckin' tough." Gunz deepened his kiss and ran his hands over her ass.

He wanted Gray in the worst way, and judging by the way she moaned, she wanted him too. His plan to break her down was working.

"I love you, Gray. Ain't nothin' gon' change that, ok?" He ran his thumb across her cheek.

"Ok."

"So, since we keepin' it so real. I gotta let you know I might have a baby on the way."

Gray stumbled back. A piercing silence filled the room. No way had he just said what she thought he said. Gray had to be having a bad dream, but the ache in the pit of her stomach told her she was wide awake. It felt like he'd kicked her in the chest. He must've. All the air had escaped her lungs.

"Baby, you hear me?" Gunz shook her.

"What?" She snapped out of her trance.

"Ol' girl claiming she pregnant; but if she can fuck wit' me knowing I got a girl, then who's to say she wasn't fuckin' another nigga behind my back? I can't trust that," he explained like it was nothing.

Gray couldn't even say anything. Instantly, bile rose in her throat. Her stomach contracted so violently that she didn't even have time to run to the toilet or push Gunz out the way. Chunks of food from her stomach propelled into the air and splattered all over his shirt. Gunz stood covered in throw up, as she heaved again. This time, he was able to jump back. Gray sank to her knees and puked until only clear liquid came up. Her throat felt sore from the stomach acid that coated it, and her mouth tasted of vomit and Kimchi. The vile stench of barf filled her nostrils. When she was done vomiting, she surveyed the mess she'd made with watery eyes.

She wished her eyes were only watering because she'd thrown up, but it was also because Gunz had officially killed her. Knowing he'd cheated with other women was one thing, but hearing that he'd probably gotten another chick pregnant was the ultimate betrayal. Gunz had literally taken a knife and stabbed her straight through the heart.

"What the fuck, Gray? This shirt cost $300… damn!" He yelled.

Gunz wanted to throw up too. The sight of her vomit all over his shirt and arms repulsed him. Cautiously, he pulled the shirt over his head and prayed none of her vomit got on his face or hair. Gray wiped her mouth with the back of her hand and brought her knees up to her chest. She would never recover from this.

"You a'ight?" He finally asked.

Gray stared out into space, unsure of what to say or do.

"Gray!"

"You got her pregnant—"

"I said it *might* be my baby."

Thick, heavy tears dripped from Gray's stormy blue eyes. The salty tears she cried were like a hurricane coming through, crushing everything in sight. Not only had Gunz ruined them but he'd ruined her. The walls she'd built to hold herself up and keep her strong collapsed, and now she was dead inside.

"You said you didn't want any more children after we had Press. Your exact words were, 'Two kids is the perfect size for a family'. You begged me to get my tubes tied, even though you knew I didn't want to; and like a dummy, I did it. I did it 'cause I loved you. Now you sit here…" Gray's lips quivered. "…and tell me that you nutted up in that trifling, ghetto-ass bitch and probably got her pregnant. How could you do this to me?" A tear snaked down her cheek and dropped from her jaw.

"Baby, I'm sorry." Gunz bent down before her and tried to brush her cheek with his thumb.

Gray smacked his hand, hocked up as much spit as she could, and spit in his face.

"Fuck you and your apology," she quipped, as her heart continued to break in half.

Gunz looked at her, shocked. The savage part of him wanted to punch her in her shit. Instead, he wiped her vomit-infused spit from his face and walked away. He knew that he wouldn't be able to talk or charm his way out of this. He'd dreaded telling Gray this news. He'd been putting it off for months, but Tia was beginning to show, so he couldn't keep the secret hidden any longer. What he'd failed to tell Gray was there was no doubt the baby was his. He couldn't tell her that after he'd made her get her tubes tied. Her reaction solidified his decision. She wouldn't be able to mentally or physically handle it.

Gunz didn't know what he was going to do. He loved his family, but he loved Tia and their baby too. He was a man tied between two worlds. Sooner or later, he was gonna have to give up one or the other.

Alone on the dining room floor, tears clouded Gray's vision, as she sat comatose. All she could concentrate on was his treachery. Gunz had ruined her life in more ways than one. If this baby was his, she didn't know what she was gonna do. How could she move on knowing he'd asked her to get her tubes tied and then turned around and gotten one of his side hoes pregnant? She couldn't. The mere thought was too antagonizing to accept.

"Long distance in the way of what we could be." – K. Michelle, "Maybe I Should Call"

Chapter 9

Chyna

"Dame," Chyna moaned in her sleep.

She was having a good-ass dream. It was so vivid that it felt real. Biting her lip, she rotated her hips as her pussy walls contracted. A soul-stopping sensation swept across her body, as she dreamt she was getting head.

Dame grinned, mischievously. He had Chyna right where he wanted her. The sound of her silky voice calling out for him made his dick extremely hard. He loved the control he had over her sexually. It had been days since he last touched her. He couldn't go another second without having some part of her on him. She'd been out of the hospital a few days; and no, her face wasn't fully healed, but he didn't give a fuck.

The minute he walked into her room, after taking a business call, and saw her lying on her back dressed in nothing but a white, silk negligee with lace trim, Dame had to have her. Chyna's creamy, honey wheat skin, short, black, curly hair, mouthwatering, melon-shaped breasts and toned legs had him going crazy. He missed hearing his belle moan. It was only right that he bless her with his tongue.

Chyna was so hot and bothered that she didn't know if what she was experiencing was a dream or reality. All she knew was that it felt good. Her long fingernails scrapped across the top of his head, as he toyed with her hardened nipples. Her body was his garden of Eden. There were so many nasty things he wanted to do to her. It was a shame he couldn't take it there with her the way he wanted to. Dame wasn't comfortable fucking her yet. He felt she needed more time to heal; and to be honest, he was afraid to fuck her while pregnant. His dick was so big, he thought he'd hurt the baby.

Despite his worries and Chyna having a messed-up face, she was still sexy as hell to him. She was even sexier now that she was carrying his baby. Dame never pictured himself being a father, but with Chyna he wanted a whole liter. Sucking and licking on her inner thigh, he anticipated her opening her eyes. It was only a matter of time before she realized the pleasure she was experiencing wasn't a figment of her imagination. Until then, he would continue to feast on her lower lips like it was her mouth.

"Damn, baby, you taste good than a muthafucka." He ate her pussy like it was his last meal.

"Dame." Chyna gasped, opening her eyes.

There was no way a dream was making her feel this way. Only one man could bring her to such heights of ecstasy. Chyna looked between her legs and found the love of her life, her fiancé and father of her unborn baby. He was so fuckin' handsome. Every time she looked at him, he took her breath away. Dame could've been Mahershala Ali's twin. They had the same cocoa skin, small, whiskey brown eyes, chiseled jaw and wickedly dangerous sex appeal. Chyna couldn't have been happier that he was going to be her husband and father to her child.

"'Bout time you woke up. I was starting to think I lost my touch."

"Impossible." Chyna spread her legs wider, to give him more access.

She could feel him in all her most intimate places. Dame's lips were wrapped around her clit like a vice grip. Two of his fingers dipped in and out of her sweet pool. Gently, he fucked her pussy with his fingers, while his tongue drew circles around her juicy bud. All Chyna could do was whimper and moan. Her soft groans only egged him on. Dame wanted more. Placing her leg on his shoulder, he pushed his fingers deep inside her abyss, and then curled them as if he was saying come here. Instantly, he located her G-spot. Chyna lost her shit.

"Dame-Dame, wait!" She tried to push his head back.

"Be still." He smacked her thigh, like she was a child, and gripped her tighter.

Chyna wanted to protest but knew better. The more she tried to resist, the longer he would torture her pussy. Plus, the shit he was doing with his tongue had her unable to put together words and sentences. Dame could feel it. Chyna was on the verge of cumming.

"Let that shit go, baby." He flicked his tongue faster.

On the brink of climaxing, Chyna gripped the sheets and braced herself for takeoff. She was moaning so loud, she was sure her neighbors could hear. Chyna tried to quiet her cries but couldn't. Dame was assaulting her pussy with wet tongue lashes. The orgasm that had been building in her pelvis erupted. Chyna arched her back and came into his mouth. Dame being the nasty nigga he was, lapped up all her juices till he was full.

Dame made his way up to her mouth and kissed her fervently on the lips. The smell of his cologne had Chyna drunk with lust. She wanted to hop on his dick and ride him in the worst way. Placing her hands on both sides of his face, she kissed him back with as much intensity as she could muster. It was then that she realized there was something heavy weighing on her left hand. Breaking away from the kiss, she looked at her hand and found an eight carat, oval cut, pave, 14k, rose gold, engagement ring.

"You like it?"

"Yes." Chyna sat up and admired the way it sparkled under the sunlight.

"I know it's not exactly like the one I gave you—"

"It's beautiful." Chyna cut him off and pecked his lips, lovingly.

She didn't want Dame to worry about a thing. Nothing would replace the ring that was stolen, but this one would surely do. Once again, Dame had done an extraordinary job of making all of her dreams come true.

"I love you." She held his face in her hands.

"I know."

"No, like, I really, really love you." She gazed deeply into his eyes. "I don't know what I'd do without you. I thank God every day that he brought you back into my life."

Dame wasn't into all that mushy shit, but Chyna's words of affection squeezed at his heart. He loved this woman more than he thought he was even humanly possible.

"I love you too, big head." He slid his index finger down the side of her face and kissed her sweetly on the lips.

"I can't believe you got me a new ring so fast." She went back to admiring her ring.

"Gotta let these bum-ass niggas know your taken."

"I'm sorry your mom's ring got stolen."

"It's not your fault." Dame swallowed the lump in his throat.

The fact that his mother's ring was out of his possession sickened him. He'd had possession of it since he left home at the age of 13. After sneaking into his father's room and taking it from his dresser drawer, Dame slipped it into his pocket and never looked back. It was the only thing he took when he went to live with Mohamed. No one even knew he had it. Not even his father. For years, he'd kept the ring safe with the hopes that maybe one day his dream girl would wear it on her finger. Dame always knew that lucky girl would be Chyna.

"It is my fault. I should've went with my first mind and called a cab," she said, sorrowfully.

"What's done is done." Dame changed the subject.

He didn't want to talk about that shit anymore. Anytime he thought back on that night, he got angry. Chyna had been through enough. He didn't want to take his anger out on her.

"What you need to be focusing on is when you gon' sell this muthafucka so you can move in with me." He glanced over at her, while massaging her stomach.

It was crazy to him that his seed was in there. Dame wasn't scared of shit, but learning he was gonna be a father, had him shook. He hoped he could live up to the challenge.

"Dame… I can't sell my place until after India graduates."

"And when is that?"

"May."

"That ain't gon' work." He shook his head.

"It's gon' have to work."

"Nah, it ain't," Dame argued.

He was a man that always got his way. The simple solution to their problem was Chyna moving her ass to New York with him.

"You act like you ain't just get robbed. What I look like leaving you here while them niggas still breathing?"

"You said you were gonna find out who did it and handle it. Plus, you got guards watching us all day every day."

"So, you really expect for us to live apart for the next ten months?"

"Babe, I don't have no other choice," she explained, seeing that he was getting upset. "I can't just pack up and leave. India has to finish her last year of high school."

"I get that, but where does that put us?"

"I don't know. Maybe that was something you should've thought about before you proposed," she mumbled under her breath.

"Nah, you need to recognize who I am and the uncertainties I don't deal with."

"And what is that supposed to mean?" Chyna drew her head back.

"What the fuck that means is: what the fuck I said. I don't deal with uncertainties, so you moving yo' ass to New York. End of conversation."

"Noooo… it's not."

"Yeeeesssss, it is. You can keep the apartment for India for when she turns 18; but when it comes to me and my family, y'all are coming with me. Ain't no way we living separate while you carryin' my baby. Fuck you thought?"

"I don't want to but what other choice do we have?" She shrugged.

"You don't have another choice. You moving with me."

"Dame, I have a choice. Why don't you move here?"

"That's highly illogical with all of the things you know I have going on."

"So, fuck what I got going on?" Chyna spat, with an attitude.

"You can write and make videos from anywhere." He got off the bed and loosened his tie.

Dame had never been a fan of long-distance relationships. That's why he'd never had one. Leaving his pregnant fiancée while he worked back and forth between New York, Chicago and Miami wasn't an option. Especially, with Brooke's ho-ass on the loose. There was no telling what she might say or do while he wasn't around. Dame couldn't chance that. He had to keep a close eye on her, Chyna and his baby, as well as build a relationship with India. He couldn't leave the people he loved to the wolves. And yeah, he could hire 24-hour security to watch over them, but Dame needed his own eyes on his family at all times.

"Look, babe." Chyna scooted to the edge of the bed. "I don't wanna be apart from you either, but my daughter is my priority."

"You being separated from India isn't an option either." Dame stood between her legs.

"Then what are we gon' do 'cause I don't want to be away from you either? Believe it or not, I'm actually scared to have this baby." She placed her head on his abs and circled her arms around his waist.

"Why?" He ran his fingers through her hair.

"The last time I was pregnant I was 17. I'm about to be 36 in a week. You know the older you get, the harder it is for you to carry a baby to full term."

"Don't worry about that. You gon' be straight. I'll kick our baby ass if it try to die on us."

"Dame!" Chyna cracked up laughing.

"That's real talk."

"I know. That's the funny part."

"Look at me." He lifted her chin with his index finger. "Everything is handled. Only thing you need to worry about is our baby and your health."

"You sure we'll be able to figure this out?" She pleaded with her eyes.

"What I say?"

"Ok." She surrendered all their problems over to him. "The ball is in your court, baby daddy."

"Tell her check herself 'cause I'm hotter than she ever will think she can be." – Megan Rochelle feat. Fabolous, "The One You Need"

Chapter 10

Mo

Mo cooked breakfast for her and Boss, while trying to calm Zaire down. He cried nonstop, while resting in the baby carrier on her chest. She should've been numb to his screams by now, but each time he cried it was like nails on a chalkboard. Mo couldn't stand it. The longer he cried, the more she wanted to escape. Zaire was by far her fussiest baby. The twins and King were easy to handle. Zaire was a terror. No matter what she did, he was never happy. Even after being fed, changed, bathed and rocked, he always found a reason to cry.

Mo didn't know what she was doing wrong. For some reason, she and Zaire just weren't connecting. The vibe between them was all wrong. He was almost ten months and she still hadn't figured him out. Her mind kept telling her that she loved her son, but Mo was secretly starting to despise Zaire. He acted like he didn't like her, and she was starting to feel the same way about him. When he was with Boss, he was a perfect angel. When he was in Mo's arms, he immediately started acting up. Mo didn't get it. She wanted to feel connected to her baby, but each day she found it harder and harder. She tried talking to Boss about it, but he said it was all in her head.

Speaking of Boss, instead of taking Zaire while she cooked, he sat in front of the television playing the game. He heard him screaming his head off and did nothing to help. Mo was seconds away from slamming her head into a wall. Maybe if she split her head in two she'd get some relief. Mo often thought about running away or ending it all. She'd never had these thoughts before, but they felt natural. Things had gotten so bad that she hated waking up in the morning. Most days, she wished God would reunite her with her mom. Being in heaven would be far better than being here on earth, amidst all this chaos and nonsense.

"Shhhh… shhh… shhh." She bounced Zaire up and down, while patting his back.

In the midst of trying to calm him down, she tried to dodge being popped by the bacon grease in the pan. She'd already been popped twice. After making the bacon, she had to make the Belgian waffles and freshly-squeezed orange juice Boss had requested. Mo was tired already and her day had just begun. Since waking up, she'd made a separate breakfast for the kids, washed the dishes, dropped the kids off at school, picked up Boss' dry cleaning and went to the grocery store. While she did all that, Boss slept soundly in bed until he decided to get up. Mo wished she had the luxury of sleeping in. As she thought about what she'd do if she had a day to herself, the doorbell rang.

"Baby! Get the door!" Boss yelled from the sitting room.

Mo furrowed her brows and looked up at the ceiling. *No the hell he ain't asking me to open the door when he's in there sitting on his ass.* Mo tried her best not to explode. Boss was really trying her sanity and her patience.

"Babe!" He called out, as the doorbell rang, again.

Pissed, Mo threw down the tongs and stormed out of the kitchen. She now understood how a person could go crazy and kill their whole family. She was seconds away from losing her shit on Boss. If she would've known she was getting with a man that was a mama's boy and didn't know how to take care of himself, she would've thought twice about getting into a relationship with a younger man. Mo hoped and prayed that she and Boss wouldn't have one of those relationships where they were together for years, got married and then broke up. It was starting to look that way. They were still into it from the other day and had barely spoken a word to one another.

"Who is it?" She asked, opening the door.

"Zya. Is Zaire here?"

Mo's mouth dropped open, as she took in the chocolate beauty who looked like she could've been her younger sister. The bitch was beautiful. She reminded Mo of herself when she was young and poppin'. It was only 10:00am and Zya was already dressed to the nines. She had her hair up in a sleek topknot and a simple, daytime-appropriate beat. Outside of her stunning good looks, Mo noticed how sexy she was dressed. Zya wore a black, off-the-shoulder top that was mesh on the sleeve and chest area. The chick wore no bra. The only thing covering her silicone titties was the thin, black fabric hanging off her shoulders. Homegirl was serving major under boob. The skin-tight, ripped jeans and black, thigh-high boots had her looking like a whole snack.

Hell, the bitch was so bad that Mo wanted to fuck her. Zya had huge, fake boobs, a small waist and nice, round hips. She couldn't believe this was the chick who was around her man six days out of the week. Mo was slipping. Before Zaire, she would've never let no shit like this go down. Mo wasn't an insecure woman, but she wasn't a fool either. If you put temptation in front of a man, nine times out of ten, he was going to give into it.

"It's Boss," Mo said.

"Huh?" Zya said, confused.

"Zaire, his name is Boss. Nobody calls him Zaire. Now, who are you again?" She played dumb.

"Zya."

"I'm Mo."

"Ohh… you must be the nanny." Zya smiled, brightly.

"No, I'm his wife," Mo scowled.

"Really?" Zya arched her brow and looked her up and down.

As fine and fly as Boss was, she was almost sure that his wife would be a baddie. Mo wasn't ugly, by any means. The woman was effortlessly beautiful, but she looked a mess. Her hair looked like it hadn't been combed in days. Bags were under her eyes. She wore a dingy, oversized t-shirt, leggings and house shoes. She didn't even have any lashes on. Now Zya understood why Boss spent all his time at Babylon with her. If this was what he had to come home to, she would stay away too.

"Excuse me?" Mo said, ready to go off.

"No disrespect. I've heard so much about you. I was just expecting something different."

"And what the fuck is that supposed to mean?" Mo snapped, ready to put her baby down and square up.

Before Zya could answer, Boss rounded the corner. Hypnotized by his animal magnetism, she licked her lips like Mo wasn't even there. Even lounging around the house, Boss was sexy as fuck. He donned a Cardinals snapback, two, thin, gold chains, no shirt, Versace boxer/briefs, black jogging pants, socks and Versace slides. Zya had never seen him without a shirt. The heartbeat in her clit started to thump overtime. Boss was covered in tattoos. There were so many that it looked like one, big mural. From his neck down to his shoulders, arms and chest was ink. She wanted to trace her tongue over each line.

Boss may have looked like a street dude, but he was far from it, which made him even sexier. His brown skin and thick beard was so tempting to touch. There wasn't an ounce of fat on him. Every inch of his upper body was ripped. He was a living work of art. Every move he made gave away to his strength.

"Looks like somebody's been hitting the gym." Zya admired his physique.

"Damn, I forgot you was stoppin' by. What's up?" Boss gave her a quick, polite hug.

"You always forgetting something." Zya giggled like a little schoolgirl.

Mo stood with Zaire on her chest, looking at them like they'd lost their minds.

"Have you met my wife?" Boss placed his hand on the small of Mo's back and kissed her cheek.

"Yeah, she introduced herself." Zya said, dryly.

Mo picked up on her tone and eyed her hard.

"We were busy. What you stoppin' by for?" She cut to the chase.

"Easy, tiger." Boss grinned. "I asked her to drop off the profits from last night, so I can deposit it in the bank. And, I wanted y'all to finally meet. You hungry, Zy? Mo was just making breakfast." He ushered her in.

"I would love to have breakfast with you." She beamed, sauntering inside.

Mo looked at her husband like he was crazy. She barely wanted to cook for him let alone him and their THOT-ass employee, who clearly wanted to fuck him. Anybody with two eyes could see Zya had a thing for him. There was no way Boss didn't know it too. Mo closed the door and realized that Zaire had stopped crying. Looking down, she saw that he'd fallen asleep.

"Thank God." She said to herself.

Mo wanted to put him down but was too afraid he'd wake back up. Instead, she followed her husband and chocolate Barbie into the kitchen. Boss was at the kitchen island, counting the money, as Zya stood close to him looking on. The chick was a little too close for Mo's comfort. She was practically shoulder to shoulder with the nigga. Boss wasn't being inappropriate, but she still didn't like how relaxed he and Zya were together. She was high-key jealous. Not only was the bitch gorgeous, but she laughed and joked with Boss like he was her husband.

"Who does your tattoos? I was thinking about getting one right here." Zya pointed to her left titty.

Boss looked at her breasts and quickly diverted his eyes.

"My pot'nah. He owns a shop off Delmar." He continued to count the money.

"You talkin' about S. Dot?"

"Yeah."

"I know him." She smiled, animatedly and placed her hand on his shoulder. "My homegirl used to mess with him. We should all go out sometime."

Did this bitch just ask my husband out on a date? Oh, this bitch is bold, Mo thought, finishing up the bacon.

"That sound cool. Me and Mo ain't been out in a minute." Boss placed the money back in the bag and zipped it up. "What you think, babe? We should go out this weekend."

"I got a feeling I'ma be tired." She fake yawned.

"That's too bad. Zaire, you can still come." Zya touched his arm.

"No, the fuck he can't." Mo shot. "And again, his name is Boss, like how I'm your boss. Yeah, Boss."

"I'm hungry than a muthafucka. Babe, is the food almost ready?" Boss tried to ease the tension in the room.

"In like 20 more minutes."

"It do smell good up in here." Zya rubbed her flat stomach.

"Mo, you mind if Zya stay for breakfast?" Boss asked.

"Actually, I do," she replied, not in the mood to be polite.

"Damn, Mo, really?" Boss chuckled at her brashness.

"It's ok, Zaire. You know I'm always watching my weight. I gotta keep this body tight." Zya ran her hands down her waist and shot Mo a look.

Mo nodded her head and sneered. She knew Zya's dig was a shot at her weight. She also peeped that she'd called him Zaire, again.

"You keep it up and you ain't gon' have no choice but to watch yo' weight 'cause you ain't gon' have no job," she shot back.

"C'mon. Let me walk you out." Boss escorted Zya to the door, before Mo popped off and hit her.

"Yeah, you better take her ass outside before I pick her up and hit you wit' her!" Mo said, loud so Zya could hear.

"What was that all about?" Boss asked, coming back into the kitchen.

"That li'l bitch likes you."

"No, she don't. She got a man."

"So! Like hoes don't cheat every day. I had a nigga and I cheated wit' you. Remember when you sucked my titty on the sidewalk in front of the diner?"

"Stop bringing up old shit, but yeah… them was good times." He stared off into space, reminiscing. "Let me suck your titty right now."

"Move!" She smacked his hand out the way. "Like, I said. It's obvious that li'l girl like you. She was damn near sucking your dick."

"Now you overexaggerating."

"Whatever. You can deny it all you want to but I ain't stupid. I know when a chick is checkin' for a nigga, and that ho is checkin' for you. So, you betta get her in check before I do."

"Look at you. It's nice to see you jealous over me. I ain't seen you like this in a minute." Boss placed his soft lips on her neck and inhaled her scent.

Mo always smelled like strawberries and honey.

"Oh, you think that's funny?" Mo raised her hand to hit him.

"Man, chill! I was just playin'." Boss ducked.

"I'm far from jealous," she lied. "I'm protective. There's a difference. Now, move yo' ass back. We still into it. I ain't fuckin' wit' you."

"How long you supposed to be mad? I said I was sorry."

"Until you recognize that I should be number one in your life."

"You are number one; but how can I disrespect the woman that birthed me?"

"Nobody asked you to disrespect her, but I don't want you to disrespect me in the process," Mo clarified.

"Alright, Mo. I'll work on it. I just wanna chill wit' you before I go to work." He rocked her back and forth. "And stop callin' my mom Syphilis. That shit ain't funny, man."

As Boss kissed the side of her face, Mo swallowed the tears creeping up her throat. Boss was completely oblivious to the agony she was in. For months, Mo had swept her problems under the rug, but she couldn't any longer. The pile was getting bigger by the day. Trouble was on the horizon and there was no stopping the tsunami coming her way. In the past, Boss would be right there by her side to fight their battles, but now she had to fight all alone. He didn't get that every second of the day she was losing bits and pieces of herself. It was like he no longer saw her anymore, which was hurtful. He looked through her like she was invisible. Mo felt like a ghost in her own household.

She not only felt disconnected from Zaire, she felt disconnected from everyone, including herself. If that wasn't enough, now she had to worry about a pretty, young chick coming after her man. She and Boss barely had sex. It was only a matter of time before he started to look for what he wasn't getting at home elsewhere. Mo couldn't let that happen. She loved her husband too much to just willingly give him up to some thirst bucket. The only problem was she didn't know how to save herself, let alone her marriage.

"You need a real nigga in yo' life." – Bow Wow & Omarion, "Can't Get Tired of Me"

Chapter 11

Gray

The last time Gray went to the club was back in 2015 when Obama was still president. Yet, here she was with Kema walking into Pepper Lounge like she owned the place. At one point in time, Gray used to go to the club every weekend, but throughout the years going out became less a priority. Being around a bunch of young stunners and half naked chicks didn't appeal to her anymore. On top of that, she got tired of hoes looking at her sideways because they were fuckin' Gunz. Every time she went out, there was some big booty bitch giving her dirty looks, rolling their eyes, sucking their teeth or being extra so they could get her attention. She got sick of that shit, so she focused on her business and kids.

Gray often thought about returning Gunz the favor by cheating, but everybody in St. Louis knew she was his. No one would dare take the chance of coming up missing behind fucking with her, so it was pointless to even try. Even if Gray wanted to mess around with another man, there wasn't anybody that was worth giving her time to. Most of these men nowadays were just like Gunz. If she wanted to be lied to, cheated on and sold a dream, she could just stay with his lousy-ass.

Chris Brown said these hoes ain't loyal, but he had it all wrong. No, these niggas weren't shit. You couldn't depend on them if your life depended on it. Gray didn't have time. That's why she focused on the two most reliable things in her life, which were Aoki and Press. They were her anchor. They were the only sense of normalcy she had. Without them, she'd surely lose her way.

Ever since Gunz dropped his bombshell on her, she hadn't been able to get it out her head. She'd been sick to her stomach. All night long she tossed and turned. It was like nothing she ever said or did in their ten-year relationship mattered. She'd given him her love, her time, her trust, her heart, hell her womb and he still had no problem sleeping with another woman.

For years, she chased after a high she'd never be able to get back again. Gray tried to tell herself that she and Gunz could make it, but he always brought her back to reality. She'd given him her all, but it was painfully clear that they weren't meant to be. Gunz getting another chick pregnant, after begging her to get her tubes tied, was the worse thing he could've ever done - and he'd done some fucked up shit over the years. Not only had he taken away her belief in men, but her ability to bear children. It was mind-boggling how one man could wreck so much havoc on a person's life.

Gray just wanted to know if Tia and her baby was worth the demise of their relationship. She hoped it was, because they were done. She and Gunz would never be able to salvage what they once shared. She couldn't wait forever for him to grow up. She wanted a man that she could call her own. She no longer wanted to be unhappy. She was done carrying his baggage. She could do bad on her own. At this point, all he could do for her was leave her the fuck alone.

After getting their hands stamped, Gray and Kema made their way into the club. She would never admit it, but Gray was excited about going out. After the week she had, she needed to take several shots to the head. Kema promised to get her fucked up so she could forget all her troubles. Gray thanked God that she had a best friend like Kema to hold her down. Without her, she'd be lost. Not only was she an awesome best friend and godmother to her kids, she also kept her young and vibrant.

Being a CEO and dealing with Gunz's trifling behind had made Gray guarded and dull. She'd lost the lively personality she once had. The outfit she wore reflected just how much she'd changed. Back in the day, Gray would've hit the club in a tight freak'um dress. Now, here she was, covered up from head to toe.

The black and white Versace print suit, strapless, low-plunging bustier, canary yellow diamond stud earrings, gold, Edie Parker, lizard skin clutch and gold, Christian Louboutin So Kate, six-inch pumps was fly as hell, but way too sophisticated for the club. Gray looked like she was about to lead a board meeting, not shake her ass to trap music. The sleek ponytail and soft beat didn't help much. Kema, however, was club appropriate. An army fatigue jacket hung off her shoulders. On her petite frame was a tan bodycon dress and army green, open-toe, over-the-knee boots. Her blonde weave was parted down the middle and flat ironed straight.

Gray's bestie was too cute. As soon as they stepped foot inside the club, Trina's old-school hit, *Look Back at Me* feat. Killer Mike, started to play. It was almost like the DJ was showing them love, exclusively.

"Bitch!" Kema turned back and looked at Gray with a wild look in her eyes.

"No." Gray shook her head.

"Yes. Yo' ass ain't about to be a Debbie Downer tonight."

"Nah, I don't feel like dancing," Gray whined.

"Fuck that. We dancing to this. C'mon!" Kema dragged her to the dance floor.

Look Back at Me was Gray, Kema and their other best friends, Heidi and Tee-Tee's, shit. Gray wished they could've been there with them. Heidi and Tee-Tee were at home with their kids. Since they couldn't be there, it was only right they turn up for them. Neither Kema or Gray could see the dance floor, as they bogarted their way through the sea of people. Pepper Lounge was packed from wall to wall with partygoers. There was no room for any more people on the dance floor, but somehow when Kema and Gray made their way onto it, space magically appeared.

Kema immediately started twerkin' and biting her bottom lip. Gray, reluctantly, followed her lead. She couldn't remember the last time she bent over and shook her ass in the club. She was a mother of two. She couldn't be giving the kids a full-on, ATL stripper twerk. Instead, she hit 'em with a light, pretty girl bop. Together, she and her bestie rapped along to the lyrics.

I got an ass so big like the sun.
Hope you got a mile for a dick, I wanna run.
Slap it in my face. Shove it down my throat.
Nigga, where your blunt? I can make this pussy smoke.
I know how to fuck. I know how to ride.
I can spin around and keep the dick still inside.

Gray and Kema stood in the center of the dance floor getting their life. A bunch of chicks where looking them up and down 'cause they were new meat in the club, but they didn't give a fuck. If anybody had a problem with their turn up, they could run up. Gray might've been straight-laced, but she had no problem squaring up with a bitch. Being with Gunz had toughened her up.

Gray was so into the song that she had completely forgotten about her problems. She hadn't felt this alive in years. It wasn't until Kema's boo thang, who looked a lot like the rapper, Lloyd Banks, scooped her up, that Gunz's baby drama came flooding back. Gray wished she didn't care that he might have a baby on the way, but she did. The notion was eating away at her insides.

"Gray, I want you to meet my friend, Quan." Kema smiled.

"Friend?" He balled up his face.

"I ain't stutter. You heard me right the first time. You ain't my man," she challenged.

"That's what yo' mouth say." Quan shot her a look, before focusing on Gray. "So, you the homegirl she can't quit talkin' about?"

"That would be me." Gray patted her forehead.

She'd begun to sweat while dancing. Gray hated to sweat. It was so unladylike.

"It's good to meet you. Y'all, c'mon." He turned to lead them over to his section.

"Go 'head. I'm about to head to the restroom," Gray replied.

"You want me to go with you?" Kema asked.

"Girl, go be wit' yo' man." Gray playfully pushed her in Quan's direction.

"He ain't my man."

"When I put this dick up in you tonight we gon' see if you be singing the same tune." Gray heard Quan say, as she made her way through the crowd.

It seemed like it took forever for her to make it to the back of the club where the restrooms were. Gray adjusted her eyes. The hallway was slightly dark. A blue light dimly lit the small space. Gray thought she was alone, until she saw a cloud of smoke waft in the air. Squinting her eyes, she spotted a tall frame leaning against the wall. The closer she got, the clearer the person appeared. Offset & Metro Boomin's *Ric Flair Drip* thumped throughout the club, as she and the tall man connected eyes.

The nigga had an angry scowl on his face, as he looked at her. Gray should've been scared but she wasn't. She'd seen those mean brown eyes before. They belonged to the twins' rude uncle, Cam. As long as she lived, she'd never forget Cam Parthens. He'd made quite the impression on her - and not in a pleasant way. The nigga was crazy, and she wanted no parts of him or his bipolar-ass attitude. But for some odd, demented reason, she found his sinister glare sexy as hell.

His presence was so commanding and alluring. She wanted to keep walking and head to the restroom as planned, but her feet were planted in place. It was like she and Cam were in their own world as they eye-fucked one another. That was until she noticed a girl down on her knees giving him head. The chick was sucking his dick like she was trying out for a spot in the next Booty Talk porn video. Cam gripped the back of her head and pumped his long cock in and out of her mouth, while smoking a blunt. Gray couldn't believe her eyes. No way was he getting his dick sucked in the club. The nigga had no shame. He didn't even care that she was standing there watching him.

"Fuck you lookin' at? You wanna join in?" He frowned, as the girl looked at her out the corner of her eye.

Spit dripped out of her mouth and onto the floor. Gray snapped out of her trance and said, "Fuck nah. Wit' yo' nasty-ass."

Once again, disgusted by him, she pushed open the restroom door and stomped over to the sink. Her heart had damn near leaped out of her chest. She'd never witnessed someone performing a sexual act live in the flesh. Gray was hot, flustered and ashamed. Seeing Cam receiving head disgusted her and turned her on all at the same time. She needed to get the visual out of her head but couldn't. He stood there with no facial expression on his face. She wondered if he was even enjoying it. *If it was me giving him head,* she thought, then quickly deaded the idea. Cam would not take her over to the dark side. He was an arrogant asshole that didn't deserve the air she breathed, let alone space in her memory bank.

Gray touched up her makeup, washed her hands and headed back out to find Kema. Pepper Lounge was so full that she had to squeeze her way through the crowd. Gray hated making body contact with random people. Being a germaphobe, she avoided it at all cost. By the time she made it over to the table, she was hot all over again. She'd started to think wearing a suit to the club wasn't such a good idea. Things went from bad to worse when she realized the table she'd be occupying belonged to none other than thee Cameron Parthens.

"The devil sure knows how to put a package together." Gray's heart rate increased, as they linked eyes.

Cam stood front and center amongst his pot'nahs with a toothpick dangling out the side of his mouth. His infamous scowl was still plastered on his face. Gray couldn't help but think he looked like the' I like it rough' type. The black and gold Versace, silk button-up, black, denim, biker jeans, Versace, Medusa-embellished, velvet smoking slippers, Rolex and gold pinky ring only added to his bad boy appeal. The first five buttons of his shirt were open to expose the ice on his neck and the tattoos on his chest.

Like the Migos, he wore multiple chains. One was a white gold, two-tone white diamond piece with a high voltage emoji pendant. The other was a 65-karat chain with a white diamond letter C pendant. Gray wished she wasn't attracted to him, but she was. The nigga was hot. Her hard nipples solidified the fact.

"There she is!" Kema pointed. "For a minute, I thought yo' ass fell in."

"Nah, I'm good." Gray looked around at all the dudes in the section.

They were poppin' bottles, smoking weed and vibin' to the music. These niggas looked like they woke up with murder on their minds. Gray hadn't been around dudes like this since she was introduced to Gunz's old crew. A slew of females with itty bitty dresses and Ombre weaves were dancing on them like they were in a French Montana video. Gray wanted to kick Kema's ass for having her around a bunch of goons and banshee whores. It was most definitely time for her to go home.

"Let me introduce you to the birthday boy." Kema tried to pull her over in Cam's direction.

"Nah, I'm gettin' ready to go."

"What? Why?" Kema asked, disappointed.

"This just ain't my scene." Gray looked around at the group of savages.

"You can't leave. C'mon, Gray. Stay, please." Kema poked out her bottom lip.

"She ain't gotta stay. Let her bougie-ass leave." Cam ice-grilled her, while walking past.

Gray looked up at him and tuned up her face.

"Nigga, I'm far from bougie. I just don't wanna be around your ADHD-ass."

"You tryin' to leave 'cause you wanna fuck me and I don't wanna fuck you back." He gazed down into her angry, blue eyes.

Cam wished his words were true, but he was lying through his teeth. He wanted to fuck the shit out of her prissy-ass. Gray placed her hand on her chest aghast. She couldn't believe he'd spoken to her that way.

"What?" Kema looked back and forth between them. "You wanna fuck him? Why you ain't just say so, friend? I would've been hooked it up."

"Shut the fuck up, Kema!" Gray snapped, stomping her foot like a child. "Don't nobody wanna fuck his dusty-ass."

"I'm dusty but you in here with this Ashley Stewart blazer on."

Gray's mouth dropped wide open. Cam saying she rocked Ashley Stewart fashions was the equivalent of him calling her a fat ass bitch.

"Close your mouth, ma, before I stick something in it." He smirked.

"Fuck you."

"Maybe later, if you act right." Cam fixed her a drink and handed it to her.

"I don't want this!" She tried to hand it back.

"Sit yo' Asian-ass down and shut the fuck up. You need that drink more than I thought."

"First of all, I'm Korean not Asian, but I wouldn't expect anything else from your public-school-educated-ass."

"Hold up. Y'all know each other?" Kema asked, confused.

"Yeah, my nieces beat her daughter the fuck up," Cam replied, nonchalantly.

"No the fuck they didn't!"

"There you go lyin' again, Korea."

"Kema, I gotta go; 'cause if I stay, I'ma end up killin' his ass."

"You always this uptight? Sit yo' ass down." He forcefully wrapped his arm around her waist and made her sit next to him.

Gray tried to get up, but the hold Cam had on her waist was too tight. It wasn't until she stopped fighting that he let up. Gray fixed her blazer and huffed. She didn't understand how a stranger could have such an effect on her. Cam enraged her but intrigued her. Being this close to him and smelling his Tom Ford Oud Wood cologne had her pussy doing backflips. The scent was rare, distinctive and exotic, just like him. Gray had to stop herself from leaning over and placing her nose up against his neck.

Everything about Cam was sexy. Even the way he took the bottle of Ace of Spades straight to the head was sensual. Over the years, she'd found other men attractive, but none piqued her interest like him. Gray had to dead any thoughts about getting with him tho'. The two of them were like oil and vinegar. Besides, she didn't even know if he liked her too. Every time she encountered him, all he did was say a bunch of slick shit to get under her skin. He couldn't like her.

Plus, once he had her seated next to him, he didn't pay her any attention. He acted like she wasn't even there. Gray returned the favor by pulling out her iPhone and reading a book on her Kindle app. *Cranes in the Sky* by Chyna Black had her mind gone. The book was too good. Gray found herself rooting for Messiah and Shyhiem like they were a real couple.

Cam bobbed his head to the music and took another sip of champagne. After their confrontation in the principal's office, he never expected to see the blue-eyed beauty seated next to him again, but welcomed the surprise. Gray was a firecracker. He liked her quick wit and no-nonsense attitude. Shorty was a rare breed. Most chicks jumped at his command but not Gray. She didn't take any of his bullshit, which he found captivating.

For 38 years of his life, he'd been the fuck 'em and leave 'em type. The only thing these hoes could get from Cam was long dick, and on occasion, a little conversation. He'd tried the love thing once before and got his heart torn to shreds. After that, he chucked love up the deuce and never looked back. There were too many women in the world to be hung up on one chick. Cam was getting pussy in abundance. Women threw themselves at him. They fucked him and sucked him like they needed him. His handsome, good looks, street creed, fat pockets and crude attitude had chicks falling over themselves to get to him.

That night was no different. He hadn't even been in the club ten minutes and had a bitch down on her knees. Shoving his eleven-inch dick in a random bitch's mouth was a normal occurrence for him. The girl thought she was gon' come chill with him and his mans, but Cam left her dumb-ass right there on her knees. If no one else piqued his interest by the end of the night, he might get up with her. Cam was a savage. He hardly ever fucked the same chick more than once. Her pussy had to be grade A for him to double back.

There was no reason for him to change his selfish ways. The only thing he cared about was his family, tippin' scales, fuckin' up the club and running up in new pussy. His life was amazing. He had mad bitches and stayed sauced up. There wasn't a day that went by where he wasn't shining on a pussy nigga. They hated him but wouldn't dare test his gangsta. Cam had a short fuse and no tolerance for disrespect. His trigger finger stayed itching. They didn't call him Killa Cam for nothing.

His plan for the night was to buy out the bar, vibe out, and fuck a bitch in her Louboutin's. Once he saw Gray, his entire night changed. He had no idea that Quan's new flame, Kema, was her girl. It was a welcomed surprise that he had full intentions on exploring. Gray's stuffy-ass needed a real nigga like him in her life. She was too restrained and uptight. While everyone else was drinking and dancing, she sat quietly with her phone in her face. She was so into whatever she was reading that she didn't even notice him staring at her. Cam didn't want to like her, but shorty was bad. Gray was the kind of pretty that would have a nigga stuck on stupid. The whole time he sat next to her, his dick was brick hard. If she played her cards right, she might be the one he chose to go back to his smash spot that night.

"Fuck is you reading, weirdo?" He snatched her phone out of her hand.

"Give me my phone back!" Gray tried to reach for it, unsuccessfully.

Cam held her back with one arm, while reading out loud.

"I want you to cum, Shyhiem. I want you to cum in my pussy." Swiftly, he turned and looked at her in disbelief. "You a fuckin' pervert. What kind of shit is you reading?"

Gray sat mortified. Her cheeks turned a bright shade of pink. The look of disgust on Cam's face made her want to crawl up into a ball and die. No matter how small he made her feel, she wouldn't let him get the best of her.

"No, I'm not! Now, give me my phone back, dick head!"

"What? You got horny from watching me get my dick sucked? You wanna pick up where she left off, perv?"

"I swear to God I'm gon' slap you." She snatched the phone back, aggressively.

"You real aggressive with that hot-ass blazer on. Why the fuck you in the club lookin' like you about to go to jury duty?"

"Nigga, this is Versace."

"I don't give a fuck. You still look like a Republican. Let me find out you voted for Trump."

"You are such an asshole."

"Nah, I'm just speaking facts. You got too much body to be covering that shit up." He tried to peek inside her blazer. "Show them titties off."

"Get yo' fuckin' hands off me, creep!" She quickly slapped his hand away.

"Yo' horny-ass like that shit. Now say you don't?" He dared her.

Gray sat silent and rolled her eyes.

"That's what I thought, and the next time I see you, have your fuckin' hair down. I don't like that shit." He pointed to her ponytail.

"Next time? Nigga, you will never see me again," Gray scoffed.

"You must not even know who you talkin' to, Star."

"Star? Who the fuck is Star?"

"Quit actin' dumb." He stared deeply into her innocent eyes.

Gray had even, luminous skin with small freckles sprinkled about like confetti. Her eyebrows curved in swooping arches over her eyes, as she gazed back at him. Cam tried not to stare too long but found himself incapable of looking away. He could study the features of her face and never get bored. Gray's small, button nose, plump, pink lips and blunt chin were picture-perfect but wouldn't make you look twice. It was her eyes that stopped you dead in your tracks.

They were like the stars. With each blink, they drew you in and made you want to explore. The longer you looked, the more emotion you found hidden in their depths. The black of her pupils were encircled by a ring of jagged, silver fire, swallowed by cobalt blue. At one glimpse, her eyes merely shone, but if you dared to look closer you could see the sadness of heartbreak, the joy of love, the pain of sorrow, and the fire of a woman who wouldn't quit.

Breaking their connection, Gray looked away and resumed reading her book. Cam had her feeling things she shouldn't. She didn't know him from Adam for him to be giving her nicknames and demanding how she should wear her hair. Cam was obviously insane; but maybe she was too, because it was taking everything in her not to yank her hair out of that damn ponytail.

"Don't act scared now," Cam whispered in her ear.

A shiver of electricity shot up Gray's spine, as his lips brushed against her ear.

"Boy, ain't nobody scared of you," she lied, yanking her head away.

She would never let it show, but Gray was scared shitless of Cam.

"You scared of me and this dick." He eyed her, lustfully.

"Is that all you talk about? You must really be overcompensating for something."

Cam didn't even bother acknowledging her remark about him having a small dick. There was nothing little about him. He knew it and Gray knew it too.

"I ain't have time to get you nothin' but I got 50 racks for you, youngin'." Quan came over and handed him a stack of cash. "Spend it how you want to, my nigga."

"Oh word? Good lookin' out, cuz." Cam stood and gave him a one-arm hug.

Then, Stacy and Diggy came over and handed him another 50 racks a piece. Gray couldn't believe that they were handing out thousands of dollars of cash like it was candy. Cam nor his crew seemed to care that everybody in the club was videotaping them. All the attention on them only intensified their turn up. Bottles of Ace of Spades were passed around, as Cam and 15 other niggas rapped along to Meek Mill's *Dreams and Nightmares.* Gray watched on in awe. Cam was in his element. His swag was on a 100, as he rapped liked he was Meek.

Seeing him show-off had Gray feeling some type of way. Like every other chick in the club, she wanted to be his girl. Wasn't nothing sexier than a fine-ass man with power to back up his confidence. When the beat dropped and Meek rapped, *'Hold up, wait a minute, y'all thought I was finished? When I bought that Aston Martin y'all thought it was rented,'* Cam and his people started bouncing and spraying champagne. The club went crazy. Killa Cam made an appearance when he rapped:

> *These niggas tryna take my life, they fuck around get killed!*
> *You fuck around, you fuck around, you fuck around, get smoked!*
> *'Cause these STL niggas I brought with me don't fuck around, no joke!*
> *All I know is murder, when it comes to me!*
> *I got young niggas that's rollin'. I got niggas throwin' B's!*
> *I done did the DOAs I done did the KODs!*
> *Every time I'm in that bitch I get to throwin' 50 G's!*

When Cam said that, he actually threw 50 G's into the crowd. Gray's mouth formed the letter O, as partygoers scrambled to grab the money.

"These niggas are crazy." Kema beamed, getting her life.

Thirty minutes went by before the club calmed down.

"Where the fuck my present?" Cam asked Gray, as they sat back down.

"I didn't even know this was your party; and even if I did, I still wouldn't have bought you shit." Gray tried to be tough.

"You gon' give me something tonight," he assured.

"Yeah, we'll see about that," Gray quipped, as some girl came over and got in Cam's face.

"Happy birthday, Killa." She grinned like an airhead.

Her breasts were damn near spilling out of her dress, as she leaned over and kissed Cam on the cheek. Gray rolled her eyes and resumed reading her book. The THOT coming over reminded her why a man like Cam was off limits. He was no good and came with too much drama. After the first chick told him Happy Birthday, it was like the floodgates opened. THOT after THOT came over to show him some birthday love. Each girl's dress got shorter and their weaves got longer.

One girl, however, made it her business to make her presence known. She strutted over into his section like she was Beyoncé, stomping down the street in the *Crazy in Love* video. Homegirl was stunning and intimidating. There was a hard edge to her that reminded Gray of the Instagram star, Jasmin Jaye. Her hair was parted on the side and pulled back in a bun. She rocked a simple beat and no jewelry. The black, high neck, long sleeve dress she wore hugged her body in all the right places, but didn't leave anything to the imagination. The huge keyhole that exposed the inner part of her boobs and stomach, as well as the high split that showcased the fact that she wore no panties, cheapened everything about the look. Every man in the club, including Cam, was salivating over the girl. *Who is this bitch,* Gray thought, as the chick looked at her like she was trespassing.

"Sorry I'm late." LaLa wrapped her arms around Cam's neck and tried kissing him lightly on the lips.

Cam turned his face. LaLa knew damn well they didn't kiss each other on the lips. He hadn't kissed her since they broke up four years ago. Cam didn't kiss any bitch on the lips. Kissing was far too intimate and special to be doing with just anyone. The next chick he kissed would be his wife. It was obvious LaLa was trying to stake her claim because Gray was by his side. Normally, he would've checked her about being extra, but he wanted to see how Gray would react. He couldn't get down with a chick that was easily intimated.

"Give me some." LaLa took the bottle of Ace of Spades from his hand.

Sitting sideways on his lap, she finished off the last of the champagne, while wondering who the bougie chick was sitting next to her man. No, she and Cam weren't exclusive, but she'd been the only consistent woman in his life for eight years. Whoever this woman was, LaLa didn't like her. Cam wasn't the kind of nigga to have just any ol' random girl around him. Bitches could barely get a hi from him, let alone a seat next to him. This chick had to be special.

Gray tried to concentrate on her book, but out the corner of her eye, she could see the Jasmin Jaye look-alike straddle Cam's lap and begin kissing his neck. Gray was appalled. The girl was practically fuckin' him in the club. She guessed that was the kind of freaky shit Cam liked 'cause he seemed to be enjoying it. His hands gripped her ass like it was a basketball. Gray didn't want to be associated with him or the whore on his lap, so she got up.

Cam chuckled. He knew she couldn't handle a nigga like him. She was too much of a square. Seeing that he had Gray rattled, he signaled for LaLa to get up by patting her butt. She didn't want to get off his lap but knew better than to question his commands. Annoyed, she stood behind him and draped her manicured hands around his tattooed neck. Cam sat with his legs cocked open, while he sipped on a fresh bottle of Ace of Spades. Gray's back was to him, but he couldn't take his eyes off her. His day one niggas, Diggy and Stacy, peeped it too.

"Drink up." Kema passed Gray a shot of Patron.

"Eww… you know I hate tequila."

"I don't care. You ain't drank nothin' all night. Cheers, bitch." Kema clinked her shot glass against hers.

Gray frowned, as she raised the glass to take a sip. Feeling the intense burn on her tongue and throat made her recoil like a squeamish little girl.

"Girl, drink that shit," Kema demanded.

"I hate you." Gray tipped her head back and let the tequila slide down her throat.

The strong liquor burned her chest and warmed her insides. Gray shook her body to get rid of the feeling. Three shots and a Long Island later, she was in the zone. Holding on to the rail, she two-stepped to the beat. Kema had disappeared for a few minutes but came right back. When the DJ queued up the Pussycat Dolls' *Buttons*, Gray knew exactly where she'd gone.

"You didn't." Her eyes grew wide.

"I did." Kema grinned, wickedly.

She knew that when that song came on, Gray couldn't contain herself. She instantly morphed into the seventh member of the Pussycat Dolls. It was her go-to jam when she wanted to feel herself. The tequila in her system had her buzzed, so she was really about to act up. Unable to stop herself, Gray spun around and faced Cam. The feelings she'd been harboring for him had bubbled to the surface. If he wanted a birthday present, she was about to give him one. It was time she showed him how much of a boss bitch she was. All eyes were on her as she slowly pulled the rubber band off and let her hair fall around her shoulders.

"Fuck it up, friend!" Kema cheered her on.

As Nicole Scherzinger sang the lyrics, '*you've been saying all the right things all night long, but I can't seem to get you over here to help take this off*', Gray came out her blazer and let it fall to the ground. The gold shimmer body lotion on her skin glimmered under the dim lights. Cam's eyes traveled from her face to her collarbone, and then to her breasts. He didn't know what was happening but was on pins and needles for more. LaLa quickly became a distant memory, as Gray sauntered over and placed herself between his knees.

Mesmerized by her cockiness, he looked up into her starry eyes. The world could keep its anorexic supermodels and Instagram baddies. Gray's voluptuous, size 18 body was the truth. Her breast looked so warm and soft that he wanted to bury his dick between them. Mouthing the words to the song, Gray placed her index finger up to his lips and wound her hips. Cam watched, as she ran her hands over her breast and neck like she was starring in her own, personal music video. Gray moved like a professional dancer. She whipped her hair, popped her ass, dipped it down low and brought it back up without missing a beat. When she fell to the floor, got on all fours, spread her legs and swung her hair from left to right, Cam almost came on himself. It was the sexiest shit he'd ever seen.

With her hands in the air, Gray moved her body like an uncoiling rope. She had become one with the music. It was her drug. Each lyric and grind of her hips took her higher and higher. Flipping her hair to the side, she spun around and sat her butt on his dick. She could feel his cock harden beneath her. It took everything in him for Cam not to pull her ass off to the side and fuck the Korean out of her.

By the time the song went off, Gray had given him a full lap dance, while LaLa looked on, jealous. She wanted to yank Gray up by her hair. She'd never been more blatantly disrespected in her life. Gray obviously didn't know who she was and how she got down, but if she kept this shit up, she was sure to find out.

With her back pressed against his stomach, Gray turned her head and looked up at Cam's serious face. From the outside looking in, you would've thought they were a couple. His hand was on her stomach, as he held her close.

"Happy birthday," she whispered, before getting up.

Cam didn't want to let her go but allowed her to gather her things.

"You did that, bitch! Now, that's the Gray I know!" Kema snapped her fingers.

"Girl, I'm not about to play with you." Gray placed on her blazer and put her hair back in a ponytail.

"Ol' girl hot. She gon' beat yo' ass." Kema arched her brow in LaLa's direction.

She literally had steam blowing from her ears.

"I wish she would; but anyway, I'm about to get another drink."

"Look at you. This bitch done had three shots and about to burn a hole in her liver," Kema joked.

"Whatever." Gray waved her off and headed towards the steps.

Cam quickly hopped up. After the sexy lap dance she'd given him, there was no way he was letting her jet without getting her info.

"Where the fuck you going?" He took her by the arm and pulled her back.

"None of your business."

"Give me your number," he said, as more of a demand and not a request.

"No."

"Fuck you mean no?" He spoke, in a low, raspy tone.

His voice reminded her of the actor, Evan Ross.

"You blind? I know you see my ring." Gray held up her left hand.

"Fuck that ring. You wasn't thinkin' about that ring when you just had your ass on my dick." Cam got lost in her eyes again.

"That was a birthday gift." Gray bit her bottom lip.

"Nah, a birthday gift would be you bending over and lettin' me shoot up your club, but you ain't ready for that yet; so for now, I'll settle for your number."

Gray hated herself, because despite the crude shit he'd just said, she found herself wanting to feel him inside her.

"I'm sure Miss Fashion Nova will let you squirt all over her, but you don't meet the qualifications to get my number, let alone shoot up this club. Now, if you'll excuse me." She left him standing there.

Cam stood dumbfounded. He couldn't remember the last time a chick had turned him down. Gray playing hard to get only made him want her more. Cam always got what he wanted, and he wanted Gray Rose in the worst way. The only problem was, after he got her, he didn't know what he'd do with her. Falling in love and wifin' her up wasn't an option. All he could offer her was a good time and dick that would change her grey skies blue. Knowing that, he should've left her alone, but Cam never did the logical thing. He always went with what felt right in the moment.

Gray wasn't even at the bar five minutes before a nigga was all up in her face, trying to holla. He was cute, came to her correct and offered to buy her a drink, so she entertained his conversation. Little did she know, but her grinning up in another nigga's face had Cam boiling hot. Gray's disrespectful-ass had him fucked up. She had to be dumb if she thought she was gonna turn him down, and then let some lame muthafucka get at her.

"Where you going?" LaLa called after him.

Cam didn't answer to anyone. He kept walking like he didn't hear her screaming and hollering his name. Gray had him acting completely out of character, but he didn't care. Something about shorty made her worthy of being chased.

"Yo, don't play with me." He spun her around to face him.

"What?" Gray asked, caught off guard by his anger.

"You walked away like that shit was optional. Give me your fuckin' number." He ice-grilled her.

"I don't even know you, and most importantly, I don't even like you!" She lied.

"That's the third time you've lied tonight. I ain't gon' keep going back and forth with you about this. You either gon' give me your number or I'ma take it." He pointed to the phone in her hand.

"What the fuck is wrong with you? Are you insane?"

"Ay yo, don't you see us talkin'?" The dude she was chatting with stepped up.

"This ain't what you want, homey." Cam warned, forgetting he was even standing there.

"Nigga, who the fuck is you?" The guy sized him up like he wasn't shit.

When Cam didn't respond, he said, "That's what the fuck I thought," turned his back and resumed his conversation. Gray stood wide-eyed and speechless. She didn't know Cam well, but she knew he wasn't the nigga to be fucked with. Quietly, Cam came out of his Versace shirt. Gray sucked in a sharp breath, as his shirtless torso was exposed for the entire club to see. Ogling wouldn't quite describe her state. She was dazed, astounded, staggered and wonderstruck by his physique. It was like nothing she'd ever seen before. His body was drool-worthy. He had a chiseled chest filled with tattoos. His abdominals were sculptured to perfection. His six-pack looked like a stack of bricks… and his arms! His biceps were the size of her daughter's head, and his triceps reminded her of the rarest diamonds. Gray wanted to extend her hand and touch him, but it wasn't the right time. Some shit was about to go down. Cam took off his chains, placed them on the bar and slid them over in her direction. After that, he tapped the dude on his shoulder to get his attention.

"Damn, nigga, you still here?" The fool barked, turning around.

Whatever he was about to say next was lost in the wind. Cam pulled his gun out the waist of his jeans and cracked him across the face. The first blow was so hard that it knocked the shit out of him. The guy didn't stand a chance. Gray could hear his nose snap, as Cam pounded into his grill. Blood was all over his hand. Every time the dude tried to fight back, Cam got angrier. Before long, he had the guy on the floor and was stomping him out. Gray watched horrified, as Quan, Diggy and Stacy jumped over the railing and joined in on the fight.

No questions had to be asked. If Cam was whooping ass, then they all were fuckin' a nigga up. Cam tried to break the dude's neck with his foot. Nobody would disrespect him and live to talk about it. The whole club was in disarray, as security made their way through the crowd.

"Cam! Cam!" They yelled, pulling him off the guy.

"Get the fuck off me!" He jerked away and punched one of the guards in his jaw.

Blood, instantly, pooled in the man's mouth. Cam should've felt bad but didn't. They knew not to touch him.

"Cam! My man." The owner pleaded. "We can't have this. You're gonna get us shut down. Can you guys please leave," he begged.

Cam looked over at Gray who was visibly shaken up.

"My nigga! We gotta go!" Diggy got his attention. "Somebody called the police!"

Unwilling to leave until he got Gray's number, Cam snatched her phone out of her hand.

"What the fuck are you doing? Give me back my phone!" She yelled.

"See you later, sweetheart." He winked his eye, as he pocketed her phone and walked out.

Gray tried to run after him, but security was in the way.

"C'mon, girl! We gotta go!" Kema pulled her by the arm.

Remembering Cam's shirt and chains, Gray quickly placed the items in her purse and rushed outside into the midnight air.

"I don't know where your charms end and you begin, but it's all beautiful. You almost have me." – Alex Isley, "Smoke & Mirrors"

Chapter 12

Gray

From the time she left the club, till the time she got home, Gray called her phone. Cam refused to answer her calls, and at some point, powered the phone off. Gray was so mad, she fought the dashboard. She couldn't believe he had the nerve to turn off her shit like it was his. She hated him. She wanted to punch him in his stupid, beautiful face and then bite him, kiss him, fuck him and suck him. He was maddening. That's why she couldn't mess with him. Cam would drive her to drink. She already had one nigga driving her insane. He would push her right over the edge.

The next morning, she called him from her daughter's phone and demanded that he bring her phone to his sister's house. Cam was half sleep when he answered. The sound of his groggy voice caused Gray to lick her bottom lip. The affect he had on her was indescribable. Despite the authority in her tone, Cam told her he'd think about it and hung up. Gray called him back to go off, but he'd turned her phone off, again. It took everything in her not to scream.

Instead, she headed to her walk-in closet to decide what she was going to wear. It was one of those days where it wasn't hot, but it wasn't cold either. The weather was just right. The sun was out and there wasn't a cloud in sight. It was a perfect, August, Saturday in St. Louis.

Since she knew it was a good chance she'd see Cam, Gray decided to wear something laidback but cute. She didn't want to seem like she was doing the most, but also wanted to look like she'd put some effort into her look.

Gray felt stupid for even caring about how she looked around him. The nigga was a nuisance. She had nothing to prove, but after the way he clowned her Versace suit, she had to show him she knew how to dress. She'd built a career based off her taste in fashion.

After way too much deliberation, she took a shower and threw on a crème, cropped sweater, Saint Laurent distressed, mid-rise, skinny jeans, a Gucci fanny pack and crème, lace-up, Yeezy ankle boots. Her brown hair with honey blonde streaks was down in natural, wild, loose curls. A pair of big, gold, hoop earrings and extra glossy lipgloss finished off her 'Jenny from the block' look. Her big hair, exposed stomach, tight jeans and high heels had her feeling hella sexy. Gray hadn't felt this good about herself in a long time. She felt like her old self again.

With the girls in tow, she headed to Mo's house. It didn't take them long to get there. Mo lived in the Central West End which wasn't far from Gray's place. It was a little after 2pm when they got there. Gray rang the doorbell and waited anxiously. Even though she used to run a company, she still hated meeting new people. Having idle conversation with people she didn't know always felt forced. She hoped Mo wouldn't talk her head off, so she could hurry up and leave. Gray had a ton of errands to run that day and planned on being done by the time the girls' playdate was over.

"Hi. Mo?" She smiled, as a tall, cocoa brown woman opened the screen door.

"Yes, and you must be Gray." Mo welcomed her in. "It's so good to finally meet you." She gave her a warm hug.

Makiah, Ryan and King came running behind her to greet their friends.

“Hey, friend!” Ryan greeted Aoki by doing the Nay-Nay and snapping her fingers in a circle.

Aoki responded with the Milly Rock and a hair flip, before doing a secret handshake the girls had created.

“What in the Luther Vandross?” Mo said, amazed.

“Exactly. Now, why were you two fighting, again?” Gray asked.

“It was that time of the month, chile.” Aoki shook her head like a grown woman.

“Yeah, girl, you were PMS’ing like a mug,” Ryan added, pursing her lips.

“You haven’t even gotten your period.” Gray reminded Aoki.

“And what you know about PMS, li’l girl?” Mo quizzed her daughter.

“I know that’s what Daddy say you have every time y’all fight.”

“Ok, y’all go ‘head and play,” Mo replied, embarrassed by her answer.

She’d just met Gray. She didn’t want her knowing all her business.

“What’s good, Press?” King bopped towards her like a grown man and took her by the hand. “Tell me. Is yo’ daddy a beaver... ‘cause goddamn!” He looked her up and down like she was a snack.

“King!” Mo shouted.

“Chill, ma.” He held up his hand. “Now, back to you, beautiful. You wanna go play with my Legos?”

"Yeah, and I brought my dolls too." Press held up a bag full of Barbies.

"Oh word?" King arched his brow. "You wanna play house? You can be the mama and I'll be the daddy."

"Ah uh! Ain't gon' be no playing house." Gray pulled Press back by her shoulders.

King's li'l bad-ass was tryin' to hit on her daughter, and Press' fast-ass had the nerve to be blushing.

"Yeah, y'all two can't be alone. Go play in the backyard with your sisters," Mo ordered.

"You really gon' do ya boy like that? I'm tryin' to bag shorty." King eyed his mom in disbelief.

"Boy, you're six! You can't bag nothin' but groceries. Now, gone!"

Mo and Gray laughed, as King and Press headed outdoors.

"Girl, they are a mess."

"Ain't they? We gon' have to watch them. Press gon' mess around and be my daughter-in-law."

"Girl, I can't take it."

"C'mon, you want something to drink?" Mo led Gray to the kitchen.

"I'll take some water, please." She sat down at the kitchen island. "Your home is beautiful."

"Thank you." Mo smiled, handing her a bottle of water.

She lived in a white and black, English, country-style, 6-bedroom, 4-bathroom home. The entire theme of the house was black and white. Gray especially loved her kitchen. Mo had tons of cabinet space, marble counter tops, industrial lighting and hardwood floors. Gray could tell that she'd put a ton of thought into every design aspect of the house.

"Thank God I like it 'cause I never leave it," Mo sighed, wearily.

Gray recognized the sadness in her eyes, 'cause she too carried the same sadness around. She wondered what problems Mo could possibly have. She was beyond gorgeous. Gray wished she could be as naturally pretty as Mo. The chick didn't have on a stitch of makeup and looked better than most runway models. Gray was low-key jealous of the bitch.

"I love your outfit. You look so pretty." Mo sat across from her.

"Thank you. I can't believe I'm maintaining, 'cause in my mind, I'm sleeping; but in real life, I'm awake."

"Long night?"

"Yes. Me and my girlfriend went out last night."

"Where y'all go?"

"Pepper Lounge."

"That's where my brother had his party at." Mo opened her own bottle of water and took a sip.

"Yeah, I found that out once I got there. My friend, Kema, is dating his friend, Quan. You know him?"

Mo covered her mouth, so she wouldn't spit out her water.

"Do I know him?" She smacked her chest. "He's my ex fiancé."

"Really?" Gray said, stunned. "Girl, St. Louis is so small."

"Tell me about it."

"So, how is he? Should I be worried for her?"

"Uhhhh… let's just say when I was with him, half of Saint Louis was with him too." Mo couldn't help but laugh.

"Hell, he sound like my baby daddy."

"Tell your friend to keep both eyes open. Quan is a sneaky one."

"I'ma tell her, but Quan might've met his match. Kema ain't like these other chicks. She love 'em and leave 'em, just like these niggas."

"That's what his ass need. Somebody that's gon' get his ass in check."

"Why weren't you at the party?" Gray inquired.

"Girl, my going out days are over. Plus, I got a nine-month-old."

"You sound like me. Minus the baby."

"Y'all kick it?"

"It was cool, until your crazy-ass brother beat up this guy that was tryin' to talk to me and took my phone."

"He did what?" Mo exclaimed.

"Yes! He stole my phone 'cause I wouldn't give him my number," Gray giggled.

"That sound like something Cam would do."

"He was supposed to stop by here to bring it to me. Has he been by?" Gray's heart filled with hope.

"Hell nah. That nigga don't get up before five."

Gray let out a long breath and rolled her eyes. If Cam didn't bring her phone, she was going to find out where he lived and kill him.

"So, what's going on between you two?" Mo died to know.

"Absolutely nothin'."

"If my brother stealing yo' phone, there's most definitely something going on. That nigga like you."

"No, he don't." Gray's body tensed up.

The notion that Cam might have a thing for her was too much for her to handle.

"And he got a girlfriend anyway." She waved Mo off.

"Lies you tell. My brother ain't got no girlfriend."

"Well, who was the light skin chick glued to his side like a guard dog last night?"

"You must be talkin' about LaLa. Light skin, shaped like a video vixen with a resting bitch face?"

"Yeah, that's her."

"I can't stand that bitch." Mo rolled her eyes.

"She think she the shit, baby."

"I don't see why. The bitch don't even wear perfume. She just walk around smelling like Hennessy and flat irons all day," Mo joked.

Gray doubled over laughing. She went from not wanting to chat to enjoying every minute of her and Mo's conversation.

"You stupid."

"I'm for real. That ho and my brother ain't together. He been left her bogus-ass alone."

"Well, last night they were all over each other."

"Knowing Cam, he just wanted to fuck." Mo assured, as a black Lambo with heavy bass pulled up in her driveway. "Speaking of my big head brother... There he go right now."

Gray's heart rate spiked, as she looked over her shoulder. She tried to be a big girl and act like his presence didn't affect her, but it did. Whenever she was around Cam, she lost control. Maybe it was the dip in his walk or the slang he spoke when he talked that had her heart palpitating. Whatever it was, she needed to get over it and quick. She was too old to be having a crush.

But how could she not want him? The suicide doors of his Ferrari lifted, and he got out looking good enough to eat. There wasn't much to his look, but he made it look like a million bucks. He donned a black Air Jordan sweatshirt, black, jogging pants that sagged off his butt and Concord 11's. Cam walked towards the house with his hood over his head. She couldn't see his face but would bet money his signature frown was plastered on it. Before he reached the door, she turned her head, so he wouldn't see her lusting after him.

"I told you that nigga like you. Cam don't get out of the bed before five for nothin' except his nieces, nephews and money."

Gray didn't respond. There was nothing for her to say. Whether Cam liked her or not didn't matter. Nothing would ever go down between them. The nigga had trouble written all over him and she was gonna proceed with caution.

"Where you going dressed like an abusive boyfriend in a Lifetime movie?" Mo eyed her brother.

"Meanwhile, you almost 40 and still ain't got no edges," he shot back.

"You see what happens when your parents don't beat you?" Mo looked at Gray. "No, for real. What you doing over here?" She played dumb.

"I came to bring her li'l crybaby-ass her phone." He took Gray's phone out his pocket and tossed it onto her lap.

"Throw something else at me," she warned, reaching inside her fanny pack. "Here." She handed him his jewelry.

"Where my shirt?"

"I decided to keep it for pain and suffering." She smirked.

"You talkin' all that shit but I see you got that hair down." He couldn't help but point out.

Gray, unknowingly, raised her hand and smoothed down her hair.

"It look good tho'," Cam said, with lust in his eyes.

Gray's hair was like liquid sunshine. She had the kind of hair you wanted to mess up and play in all day. Cam wanted nothing more than to wrap it around his fist and fuck her hard from behind. Realizing they'd been staring silently at each other while Mo looked on, Gray rose from her seat.

"And that's my que to leave. Mo, it was so good chatting with you."

"Same here. We gon' have to get together for lunch or something."

"I would love that. How about drinks next week? I'm free," Gray suggested.

"Sounds like a plan."

"Bet. I'll be back in a few hours to pick up the girls. While I'm out, do you need anything?"

"No, I'm fine, but thank you. Cam, isn't she so sweet? You could learn a thing or two from her," Mo snickered.

Cam ignored his sister and watched as Gray switched out the door. He knew she was curvy but he ain't know she was holding like that. Gray's body was crazy. She could've easily graced any billboard or magazine, but she was hotter than those one-dimensional, photoshopped models. Her imperfections made her perfect. There was no other word to describe her besides beautiful. He loved every inch of how God put her body together. Her hourglass shape deserved to be explored with his tongue.

"Yo' scary-ass just gon' let her leave?" Mo squealed.

"What you talkin' about?" Cam peaked inside her refrigerator.

"A blind man can see that you like her."

"And a fat nigga can see that you ain't got no food. Take yo' nosy-ass to the grocery store." He closed the refrigerator door. "I'm up."

"You should get on her! I think she could be good for you! She could be the one to calm yo' crazy-ass down!" Mo shouted, behind him.

Cam ignored his baby sister and kept it moving. He refused to take it there with Gray. She was too soft and sugary sweet for a nigga like him. It was obvious the nigga she was with had already fucked her over. He didn't want to add to her misery. Cam wasn't a one-woman kind of guy. He was the meet a bitch, bang her back out and never see her again type. Monogamy and marriage wasn't his thing. Gray needed a man that was gonna love and adore her. She deserved a man's undivided attention. He couldn't give her that, so it was best he put some distance between them.

With his hand inside his sweatshirt pocket, Cam stepped outside. He thought Gray would've been long gone, but she stood beside her Range Rover looking like she was about to cry. Cam should've kept walking and went on about his day, but seeing her in distress did something to him. He found himself wanting to fix whatever saddened her - in more ways than one.

"Fuck is wrong wit' you?"

"Nothin'." Gray continued to look down.

"A'ight." Cam shrugged.

If she thought he was gonna beg and plead for her to tell him what was wrong, then she had another thing coming. Since she wanted to act tough, she could act like a big girl and handle whatever was bothering her on her own.

"I caught a flat and I don't know how to change it!" She spoke up, seeing that he was about to leave.

Cam stopped in his tracks and faced her. For a second, he and Gray stood silent, staring at one another. She naturally assumed since he hadn't left that he would come over and help.

"Are you gon' help me or what?" She asked, with an attitude.

"I know you can ask better than that."

"Will you help me?" She groaned.

"Say please."

"You know what? Fuck it. I ain't doing all that." She pouted like a little kid.

"Shut… the… fuck… up. Don't you get tired of whining all the damn time?" He pushed her out the way.

"I'm a grown woman. Grown women don't whine. We bitch. There's a difference."

"Not only do you whine, but you lie all the fuckin' time too." Cam popped her trunk. "Instead of Star, I'ma start callin' yo' ass Pinocchio."

"For your information, I'm one of the most honest people you will ever meet."

"You lyin' right now." Cam checked her trunk for a spare tire but instead found a donut. "What the fuck is this shit?" He held up the small tire.

"Oh, I forgot, I already used the spare."

"You and yo' nigga need y'all ass beat. And I'm tellin' you now... If my outfit get messed up, I'm fuckin' you up." He pointed his finger in her face.

"I will bite that muthafucka off." Gray shot daggers at him with her eyes.

"I got something else you can put in your mouth."

"Your mouth is disgusting. Your mother must be so proud."

"I wouldn't know. She's dead." Cam gave her his back.

Gray watched as he took the bolts off her tire, speechless. She felt like a complete and utter fool.

"I'm sorry. I had no idea. If it's any consolation, my mother's dead too."

"What kind of dumb shit is that? Hell nah that don't make me feel good," Cam said, over his shoulder.

Gray couldn't even hit him back with a smart comment. Telling him her mother was no longer living wouldn't make him happy. If it did bring him any joy, that would be weird and creepy as hell.

"Sorry to hear about your old bird tho'." He stood up with the flat tire in his hand. "How she die?"

"Stroke, five years ago. Yours?"

"Plane crash."

"Damn, that's fucked up."

"Tell me about it." He finished placing the donut on. "But that's life, so it's cool."

"Thanks." Gray inspected his work.

"I ain't did shit yet." Cam slammed the trunk shut and hopped into the driver seat. "Get yo' ass in the car."

"What you doing?"

"Takin' yo' ditzy-ass to my repair shop so you can get this shit fixed." He started up the engine."

"You can drive your car. I can follow." She tried to hide the nervousness in her voice.

Nothing good would come from being in a confined space with Cam. Nervous butterflies already filled the pit of her stomach. Whenever she got nervous or upset, Gray threw up. She'd be absolutely mortified if she vomited in front of him. He would never let her live it down.

"Do I look dumb? I know you can follow me, but I told you to get your hardhead-ass in the passenger seat. If not, hop yo' ass in the back. Either way, you ain't driving. Now, what's it gon' be? 'Cause, I'm hungry than a muthafucka and you wasting my time."

Distressed, Gray let out a long breath and stomped around the car. Cam watched with a slight grin on his face. He had the perfect view of her frame. Gray's hips swayed from side to side as she walked. He'd never seen a woman make a crop sweater and jeans look so good. The sliver of skin that peaked out under her top exposed her flat, soft stomach and her waist that dipped in on the sides like the letter C. Her meaty thighs and Georgia peach shaped ass had Cam's dick as hard as a steel pipe.

Once she was inside the Range, Cam pulled off and sparked up a blunt. Gray rolled down the window. Cam had some loud that was sure to get her high if she didn't get some fresh air. For a while, they rode in silence. Gray found herself taking small glimpses of him when she thought he wasn't looking. Cam was so damn fine. His energy was so intense it scared her and made her want to protect her own. He had the ability to be the center of her whole universe. Seeing him whip her car in and out of traffic while smoking made her pussy quiver. She wondered how his lips would taste on her tongue. She guessed like toffee and cinnamon.

"So, you own a repair shop?" She asked, intrigued.

"No. I own three repair shops."

"Excuse me," she replied, mockingly.

Cam ignored her and continued to drive.

"I have to say. I am surprised," Gray admitted.

"Why? You thought I was just out here sellin' nickel and dime bags?"

"Pretty much," she shot, sarcastically.

"So, I guess you own a few beauty supplies and Panda Express? Wit' yo' racist-ass. Fuckin' Trump supporter," he quipped, upset.

Cam never tripped off what people thought of him. He could give a fuck about a person's opinion, but Gray's perception of him hit a nerve. He didn't want her to think he was just some arrogant drug dealer with no goals or aspirations. There was far more to him, and if she took the time to look under the surface, she'd see that.

"I wasn't tryin' to offend you," She spoke, softly. "You just don't look like the type; that's all."

"And what does a business owner look like?"

"Not you. You just seem like you're more into toting guns and smoking blunts." She pointed to the cigarillo in his hand.

"I like that too, but you don't know me so don't assume shit about me. Understand?"

Livid that he'd tried to check her, Gray sat quiet and looked out the window. She couldn't wait to get to the repair shop so she could get away from him. Cam was an egotistical asshole. How could he get mad at her for thinking he was nothing but a thug when that was how he presented himself? From the moment they met, he'd been rude, flashy, abrasive, controlling, angry and violent. In her mind, he was nothing but a handsome hooligan with a chip on his shoulder.

Fifteen minutes later, they pulled up to the repair shop, which was located off Saint Louis Avenue. Cam's Luxury Auto Shop was smack dab in the hood. Despite the repair shop being state of the art, Gray didn't feel safe at all. Gunz never let her go to bad neighborhoods. Even though he was out the game, he still had enemies. He never wanted a fuck nigga to go after her 'cause they couldn't get to him. Cam pulled her Range Rover into the warehouse and hopped out. Gray followed suit and looked around. Cam's shop was huge and spotless. Luxury cars like Mercedes Benz, BMW, Audi and Lexus were up on lifts being worked on. One of his men went right to work, finding her a new tire, while another went under the bottom of her car.

"Damn, she fine than a muthafucka." A light skin cutie traced the curves of her body with his eyes.

"Pussy, divert your eyes elsewhere before you be out of a job and shot," Cam barked, furiously.

He didn't want anybody looking at Gray but him.

"My bad." The worker eased away, slowly.

"Was that really necessary?" Gray questioned, annoyed.

"It's yo' fuckin' fault. I told you to let your hair down and loosen up. Not come out your Lane Bryant blazer and dress like a fuckin' MILF off Pornhub."

"You think I'm a MILF?" She blushed, twirling her finger through her hair.

"That's all you took away from that?"

"What? That's all that was relevant."

Cam shook his head and focused his attention on a worker who'd called his name.

"Come take a look at this, boss."

Cam took off his sweatshirt. The only thing he wore underneath was a white wife-beater. Once again, Gray became mesmerized by his muscular physique.

"Hold these for me." He brought her back to reality by placing his chains around her neck.

Gray looked down at all the ice on her chest and damn near fainted. Gray wasn't very big on expensive jewelry. She barely liked wearing her engagement ring out of the house. Having hundred-thousand-dollar jewelry on her always made her nervous. Cam slid under her car, tinkered around, and then rolled back out.

"You need new rotors, your tires are balding, your brakes are rusty, and you need an oil change." He wiped his hands on a towel.

"Damn, how much is that gonna cost?"

"It's gon' take them a minute to fix it." Cam disregarded her question and put his shirt back on, to

Gray's dismay. "Come take a walk with me." He placed her hand in his.

"Where we going?" Gray lightly jogged after him to keep up.

"Just bring yo' ass on." He let go of her hand, once they got outside.

The sun was on full display, but a cool breeze swept through the air. Cars zoomed past them, as they walked down the street. Gray prayed they were safe. She didn't feel like getting robbed like L.A. and Chyna Black. The incident had been all over the news. She was sure to get shot walking around the hood with platinum jewels around her neck. It didn't help that trash and debris was all over the sidewalk. They even passed a rest in peace memorial filled with lifeless flowers and dirty teddy bears, as they strolled leisurely down the street. Gray was scared out of her mind. She wanted to ask Cam where they were heading but knew he wouldn't answer her. He was rude that way. She quickly realized that no harm would come to them. People kept honking their horns and saying what's up to Cam, as they made their way down the busy avenue.

"You live over here?" She watched her step, so she wouldn't fall.

"Nah, but my people do."

"Question. Why were you gettin' head in the club?"

"'Cause I wanted to."

"Did you even know ol' girl?"

"No."

"And she just sucked your dick like that?" Gray said, in disbelief.

"Yeah. Instead of worrying about me gettin' my dick sucked, you need to be worried about why ya man got you out here wit' bad tires, rusty brakes and needing an oil change."

"Well, damn. You told me."

"I mean, you got your face turned up like me gettin' my dick sucked was a bad thing."

"I could never do no shit like that in public with a random stranger. It's too much shit out here."

"Don't get it twisted. I stay strapped up; and you ain't foolin' me, ma. I know this li'l good girl persona you got going on is all an act. You a freak, Gray."

"I never said I wasn't, but I'm a freak for my man. Not the general public."

"You fuck around wit' a nigga like me and I'll have you fuckin' any and everywhere."

"We are never having sex, so that will never happen. I refuse to be another notch on your belt."

"That's what your mouth say."

"Boy, please, you don't want me. I'm nothin' like the women who chase you and suck your dick in public. I'll make you come get me. Now, back to this MILF thing. You really think I'm Pornhub worthy?"

"You could star in a flick with Brian Pumper," he joked.

"Eww! Nigga, fuck you!" She hit him, playfully. "Why couldn't it be Johnny Sins or something? Black porn is disgusting."

"What? You trippin'."

"It is. Ain't no storyline. Them niggas be fuckin' with they socks on. The girls be lookin' musty. They hair be nappy. It don't blend in with they weave. They got gunshot wounds all in they ass. It's the worse."

"That's some racist-ass shit. How you not gon' fuck wit' yo' own people porn?" He watched as she hopped over a crumpled-up McDonald's bag.

"You don't like that shit either," Gray challenged.

"Nah, I feel you. Them bitches be missing nails and shit. I can't even concentrate on getting my nut. Hold up. How you got a man and up here talkin' about watching porn? That nigga can't be fuckin' you right."

"Not that it's any of your business, but I haven't had sex in eight months."

"No wonder you so uptight. You need me to stretch that pussy out."

"This is as close as you will ever get to me." She side-stepped an old Sprite can.

"What the fuck are you doing?" Cam stopped mid-stride.

"Trying not to get my shoes dirty." Gray frowned.

"I swear you a big-ass baby. C'mon." He gestured for her to get on his back.

"I am not gettin' my big ass on yo' back."

"If you don't get yo' husky ass up here."

"BITCH, I AIN'T HUSKY!" Gray rolled her neck.

"Man, you know I'm playin'. You ain't husky. You fine as fuck and you know it. Now, c'mon. Get on my back, for real."

Cam could see the hesitancy in her starry, blue eyes. He hated that she was always so unsure of herself. Cam was determined to change that. Gray was going to learn the true value of her worth, one way or another.

"You bet not drop me." She wrapped her arms around his neck and hopped up on his back.

Cam's skin tingled from her touch. There were butterflies - no, lions - in his chest, but it felt good. His heart beat so erratically that he thought it would stop all together. Having Gray this close made him wonder if this was what it felt like to have a crush on a chick. It had been so long since he felt any emotion, besides anger or lust, that he honestly didn't know. Whatever was happening between him and Gray was foreign territory.

Surprisingly, Cam was a lot stronger than Gray thought he was. He carried her down the street like she was as light as a feather. A smile a mile wide was etched onto her face. Gray felt like a little girl. An explosion of happiness exploded in her chest, as she held on tight.

"So, you ain't had no dick in eight months? I know yo' ass get horny."

"Every woman wants to be bent over and banged like a screen door during a hurricane from time to time."

"Why you ain't fuckin' yo' man?" Cam asked, with a hint of venom.

He didn't like bringing up her fiancé. It only reminded him that she wasn't his.

"'Cause he's too busy fuckin' everybody else." Gray placed her chin on his shoulder and made herself more comfortable.

She was itching to rub her nose against the side of his tattooed neck.

"He has a baby on the way with another girl." Her voice cracked from the sadness she felt.

Cam heard it and became even angrier.

"Don't let that shit have you all in yo' feelings. If he can dip out on you like that, then he don't deserve you."

"I don't even know why I care. It ain't like I'm exempt. All niggas cheat."

"That ain't true."

"You don't cheat?"

"You have to be in a relationship to cheat."

"So, you don't do relationships?" Gray held her breath.

She prayed to God he said yes.

"Nah, that ain't for me."

If Cam could've seen the disappointment on her face, he might've answered differently. She hated his response. For a second, Gray thought she and Cam might've had a chance at building something. When he wasn't being a cocky prick, he was quite enjoyable to be around. There was something in the way of him opening his heart. She wondered who or what had hurt him. Cam was emotionally closed off. It would take a miracle to get him to let down his guard and stop running.

"I don't get it. Why do niggas want to be eternal playboys?"

"I don't know about other niggas, but I have my reasons." His mind went to LaLa.

He'd loved her more than any man should, and she'd fucked him over in the worst way. Because of her, no other woman on the planet would be able to say she had Cameron Parthens' heart.

"Who was worse, Michael or Vito?" He changed the subject.

"Huh?"

"From the Godfather. Who was worse, Michael or Vito?"

"I don't know. Vito?" Gray answered, without really thinking.

"Wrong. I'ma give you another chance to answer later; and next time, think before you respond," he scolded, turning onto his block.

22nd street was lit. Everybody was out. The smell of barbecue filled the air. Kids were running around. A group of girls were playing double Dutch. His homies stood in front of his Aunt Vickie's house, smoking weed and shooting dice. There was even a game of dominoes going on. Some big, swole-ass niggas were lifting weights in the middle of the yard. Gray peeped that a lot of the guys wore the color red. They were on a Blood set. She wondered if Cam was affiliated. When he threw up a gang sign, she got her answer. Gray was really scared now.

All eyes were on her and Cam. People were stunned that he was giving a chick a piggy back ride. Cam wasn't the sentimental, hearts and flowers type. Everyone knew he didn't show hoes love.

Cam, reluctantly, put Gray down. He'd enjoyed every minute of smelling her clean, sweet scent and having her thick thighs wrapped around his waist. He could tell by the look on her face that she didn't want him to let go of her either. Since they had an audience, he had to put her down. Cam didn't like people all in his business. Quan, Diggy and Stacy couldn't believe their eyes. Not only was Gray wearing their boy's chains, but he was actually holding her hand. They knew he was feeling her, but his feelings were far stronger than they expected, and he let on.

"Fuck y'all niggas lookin' at?" He growled.

"We lookin' at yo' Prince-Charming-lookin'-ass," Diggy shot.

"Hey, Miss Lady. You lookin' good today." Stacy kissed the outside of Gray's hand.

Cam balled up his fist. If it was anybody else, he wouldn't have given a damn, but Gray was special. She was his. Homeboy or not, he didn't want anyone touching her but him.

"Unless yo' fat ass wanna come up missing, don't touch her again," he advised.

"Oh, my bad. This you? I ain't know."

"Don't worry about what the fuck it is. Just make sure you keep yo' fat, crusty, all-you-can-eat lips off her."

Quan and Diggy bugged up laughing.

"You got all the fat jokes today." Gray hid her face and laughed too.

"Oh, word? You gon' laugh too, Miss Lady?" Stacy cracked a smile.

"Ay, go inside and get us a plate." Cam pulled out a wad of cash and peeled off a hundred-dollar bill.

"Inside where?"

"My Aunt Vickie house." Cam pointed towards the house they were standing in front of.

"I'm not just gon' walk up in that lady house."

"You good. Tell her Cam sent you."

"What am I supposed to be gettin'?" Gray asked, nervously.

"Whatever the special is for today."

"I'm scared. I don't want to."

"If you don't take yo' scary-ass on." He smacked her on the ass and watched it jiggled, as she walked off.

"Nigga, what the fuck you gon' do wit' all that ass?" Quan admired Gray's backside.

"Same thing you gon' do with Kema's. Fuck the shit out of it." Cam took the dice from his hand. "And don't look at her ass again. I'll fuck you up too."

Fifteen minutes went by before Gray returned with their food. She'd gotten them macaroni cheese, collard greens, burnt ends and a slice of caramel cake. Aunt Vickie took an instant liking to her and told her to come back soon. Cam thought he was hungry for food, but when Gray sauntered towards him, his appetite for honey-colored flesh took over. There was something about her that made him feel young inside, but not in a childish way. Gray awakened the pure side of him. When she handed him the food and ran to jump double Dutch with the kids, a block of ice surrounding his heart chipped away.

She might've been bougie, bad and thick, but she fit right in. He knew Gray had a li'l hood in her. She jumped rope like a pro. She even bounced on foot in her stilettos. By the time she was done, Gray was out of breath and giggling out of control.

"You have fun, little star?" Cam brushed her hair back, so he could see her face.

"Yeah, I haven't jumped rope in years."

"C'mon, your car is ready." He held her hand and led her over to his black, 1960, droptop Chevy Impala.

"Where this come from?"

"I had one of my employees bring it." Cam opened her door.

Gray got inside and admired the black and white houndstooth fabric. She'd always had a thing for old-school cars. The fact that Cam drove one, made her like him more. When they got back to the repair shop, all of her tires had been replaced, her brakes had been repaired and her car had been fully detailed. Gray wanted to pay Cam for his services, but he wasn't having it.

"Let's just say you'll owe me a favor."

"That means you'll be able to cash in at any moment." She leaned back against the driver's side door.

"Exactly." Cam stepped into her personal space.

Gray could feel his dick on her stomach.

"Nah, I don't know about that. That sound like trouble."

"A girl like you need a little trouble in her life."

"I've had enough trouble." Gray thought of Gunz.

It was then that she realized she hadn't thought about him or felt the agony of heartache all day. She had Cam to thank for that.

"Michael." She said out of nowhere.
"What?"

"You asked me who was worse, Michael or Vito. Michael was worse."

"Why?" Cam folded his arms across his chest.

Her response was cruicial to their future.

"'Cause Michael killed Vito, his own brother. That's when he became a villain. You never sacrifice your family for the life."

A ghost of a smile graced the corners of Cam's lips. It was at that very moment that he fell hard for Gray Rose. Her answer was the equivalent of when Jane popped the lock for Calogero in a Bronx Tale.

"I like your freckles." He traced them with the tip of his fingertip.

Gray had an understated kind of beauty. Maybe it was because she was so disarmingly unaware of her prettiness. There was a shyness to her, hesitation in her body movements and a softness in her voice that drew him to her like a moth to a flame.

"I like yours too." She stared up at him.

When Cam met her gaze, he felt drawn into her eyes. The icy blueness created a feeling like he was being pulled into a lake of frozen emotions. He had to let her go. She'd been through enough. Cam didn't want to corrupt her with his bullshit, but she was so damn pretty, he couldn't walk away. Cam ran his hand down the side of her face.

Gray was a mess of emotions, as her breath hitched. It was finally happening. Cam was about to kiss her. Closing her eyes, she allowed her body to relax. Cam was only inches away from her lips. All he had to do was lean forward and claim what was already his, but his fear of intimacy held him back.

"You should go. It's getting late." He stepped back.

"Huh?" Gray opened her eyes, breathlessly.

"You better go before your food gets cold." He tapped her on the thigh.

Gray blinked twice. She wondered why he didn't go for it. It was obvious that she wanted him to kiss her.

"Oh ok." She quickly unlocked the door. "Thanks for everything, Cam."

"No problem, Star," he said, as she started up the engine. "Don't lose them freckles."

"I won't." She blushed, pulling off.

Cam could see she was embarrassed. He didn't want to play her out like that, but his decision not to kiss her was the right one to make. Gray might be easy on the eyes, have bomb conversation and a heart of gold, but no matter how much he craved her, he couldn't have her. She had a man and he didn't want a commitment. It was best they go their separate ways; but the fact that he'd let her leave while wearing his chains spoke volumes that he wanted to see her again.

“Poor decision-making for the kid and not because you left us for a second.” – 6lack, “MTFU”

Chapter 13

Chyna

"Did I tell you how beautiful you look tonight?" Dame admired Chyna's beauty.

"Yes, five times. Now, stop. You can't be making a black girl blush." Her cheeks turned red.

Chyna was ecstatic to be out of bed. Staying cooped up in the house was torturous. She was used to hitting the streets. Now, her days were spent in the house. The morning sickness she developed only added to her misery. Thankfully, her face had fully healed, and she could celebrate her 36th birthday in style and in good health. Dame had taken care of all the party details. All she had to do was get glam and show up. After walking around in pajamas and sweats, Chyna couldn't wait to get dolled up. Seeing Dame walk around in his thousand-dollar suits inspired her look. She had to pay homage to her man. He'd set up office in Saint Louis while she was on bedrest and waited on her hand and foot. Dame made sure that she and India didn't want for a thing.

His protectiveness only made Chyna love him more. She was overjoyed to have him by her side every day; but after the party, he'd be returning to New York. They still hadn't figured out how they were going to handle being in a long-distance relationship. Chyna didn't want to be apart from him. He'd become her security blanket. She loved snuggling up to him at night and watching his chest rise and fall as he slept. She didn't know what she'd do without him.

They'd gone to the doctor and gotten all her prenatal vitamins. When the doctor had to check to see how far along she was, Dame threatened to shoot him. He didn't want anyone looking at Chyna, let alone touching her vagina. All that went away when they learned she was six weeks and two days with a due date of March 14th. Chyna couldn't wait till she found out the sex. She desperately wanted to give Dame a boy. A miniature version of him would only add to their love. In the meantime, she was going to relish in the fact that she wasn't showing yet. It was only a matter of time before she was as big as a house and couldn't fit anymore of her clothes.

Chyna loved to stunt on hoes. The night of her birthday party would be no different. Her hair was parted down the middle and cut into a blunt, shoulder-length bob. A diamond broach was on the right side of her head. Her makeup consisted of a black, smoky eye and pink, glossy lips. The black, YSL, wide lapel, tuxedo jacket, white button-up , black tie, white, fitted vest and black, wide-leg tuxedo pants took her ensemble to a whole other level. To finish off the androgynous look, she rocked a diamond broach on her tie that matched the one in her hair and a pair of patent leather, pointed-toe, Christian Louboutin, six-inch heels.

When she stepped out and showed Dame her outfit, a rare smiled graced his handsome face. Chyna was always fly, but seeing her dressed like him tugged at his heart strings. It showed how much she adored and respected him. He and Chyna looked like a modern-day version of Bonnie & Clyde. Dame also wore a tuxedo. His was custom-made by Tom Ford. It fit him like a glove. His look was like Chyna's, except he wore a bow tie and a black vest. The hair on his head and face was freshly cut and lined.

Chyna wanted to bathe herself in his Chanel cologne. Dame was simply delicious. She needed a sample of the D ASAP. It had been weeks since they made love. He'd been too afraid to touch her, in fear of hurting her or the baby. Chyna needed the old Dame back. Him treating her with kid gloves was not the business, but she would concentrate on getting her back cracked later. She had to focus on stepping on a few hoes' necks.

An eight-piece band with a horn and trumpet player performed the *Roc Boys* by Jay-Z, as they walked through the door. Chyna couldn't believe her eyes. Dame had gone all out. He'd spent $2,000,000 on a lavish, Great Gatsby-themed party. From the dazzling floral displays, intricate, gold, chocolate cake, floral chandeliers, countless white balloons and dazzling drapes, it was clear no expense was sparred to perfectly embody the spirit of the Roaring Twenties. Behind a dessert table created by celebrity baker, Dylan Monroe, was a huge, black and white picture of Chyna surrounded by flowers. There was also a big flower wall for pictures to be taken in front of.

The star-studded event was being held at a private estate on the outskirts of Saint Louis. Tons of celebrities were there. Diddy, Nas, Mary J. Blige, Chrissy Teigen, John Legend and Pharrell were just a few of the big names in attendance. All of Chyna's closest family and friends were there as well. Photographers and videographers were there to capture all the precious moments.

Everyone was dressed in their finest, after-five attire to fit the theme. Victor, Black and Jaylin stood posted smoking cigars. When they saw Dame and Chyna part through the sea of partygoers, they went up for their looks by clapping and cheering. Asia and Delicious ran up to give her a big hug. Chyna noticed that Brooke lagged back. It was becoming increasingly obvious that she was feeling some type of way towards her. The more Chyna became aware of this, the less she wanted her around.

Brooke was salty as hell that Dame had given Chyna the birthday party of *her* dreams. When her birthday came, Gabe only took her for sushi and bought her a bouquet of flowers from the grocery store. In Brooke's mind, the life Chyna was living should've been hers. She couldn't wait to drop the bomb that she'd had her man's dick in her mouth. Chyna would come off her high horse then.

"Happy Birthday, bitch!" Asia and Delicious shouted.

"Thanks." Chyna beamed, on cloud nine.

Brooke joined the group, with a glass of champagne in hand.

"That nigga got you dressing like him now?" She said, with a snarky attitude.

"Looks like this bitch ordered an extra-large haterade wit' an extra side of hater tots." Chyna glared at her.

"Girl, ain't nobody hating on you. There ain't nothing to hate on." Brooke screwed up her face.

"C'mon, y'all, chill. Not today," Asia pleaded.

"That's her bitter-ass. She needs to open a hatering business 'cause it's clear that she's living in Haterville." Chyna furrowed her brows.

She was sick of Brooke and her mouth. She used to give a fuck about not hurting her feelings, but now she gave a fuck less. If their 26-year friendship didn't mean shit to her, then it didn't mean a damn thing to Chyna either.

"I'm good. You?" Brooke narrowed her eyes.

"I'm more than good. I'm Meagan Good," Chyna clapped back.

"Whatever, Chyna. If it means anything, happy birthday." Brooke finished off her glass of champagne.

Before Chyna could reply, India came rushing over.

"Happy birthday, Mom!"

Chyna's eyes almost popped out of her head. She'd never seen her daughter look so grown up. She wore a black, velvet, slip dress with lace inserts and black, Gucci, ankle strap stilettos with a rhinestone bow on the toe. Her hair was flat ironed straight to the back. Blood red matte lipstick adorned her lips. India looked stunning. Her 5'8 height and slender physique put her on par with any runway model.

"Thank you, baby." Chyna hugged her back. "You look gorgeous."

"It's just a li'l something-something." India bragged.

Going to Australia had changed her daughter in more ways than one. She'd shed her tomboy ways. She was now super girly, outspoken and confident. As a mother, Chyna couldn't have been happier. India was becoming her mini-me.

"Girl, she is your child. We went shopping and she almost bought out the whole mall." Delicious chimed in.

"Y'all gon' make me cry." Chyna fanned her eyes.

"You are so dramatic," Asia teased.

Brooke looked around the room and said, "If I would've known all these fine-ass men was gon' be here, I would've shaved from the knees up."

"Or the chin down," Chyna quipped.

"Ain't you married?" Asia remarked.

"A girl always needs options." Brooke winked.

"Enough about Brooke cheating-ass," Delicious turned to Chyna. "Your man did that, honey. This party is everything! I wish a nigga loved me enough to spend two mill on a birthday party for me."

"Speaking of my man—"

"I'ma go get another drink." Brooke stormed off.

"What the fuck is her problem?"

"Who knows?" Asia said, annoyed.

"Maybe there's trouble in paradise," Delicious guessed.

"Whatever it is, she betta get it together before I punch her in her fuckin' mouth," Chyna fumed.

"Umm… you are pregnant. You cannot be fighting no more."

"Lies you tell. I'll bust a bitch ass."

"And right after you beat a bitch ass, Dame gon' beat yo' ass."

"Have you heard any news on L.A.?" Asia asked.

"I talked to him," India spoke up. "He's finally home."

"That's good."

Chyna didn't say a word. Since the robbery, L.A. had been a sore subject between her and Dame. She'd asked if it would be ok for her to reach out to him, but he'd said no. He didn't want her to have any communication with him. He said it would be a sign of disrespect if she did. Not wanting to argue, she let the conversation go. Chyna was engaged to be married and pregnant with her second child. It was the happiest time of her life. She didn't want any negative energy or bad blood to fuck that up.

"As I was saying before I was rudely interrupted. Let me go thank my man for this fabulous party." She excused herself.

On the way to Dame, she spotted Brooke off to the side, sitting by herself, nursing a glass of champagne. Chyna wanted to say fuck her, after the slick shit she'd pulled, but then remembered all the good times, laughs, trials and tribulations they'd had. She couldn't just throw years of friendship away because they were going through a rough patch.

"What's going on wit' you? 'Cause you been real bitch here lately." She sat opposite her.

"My bad about earlier. I'm just going through a lot right now."

"Talk to me." Chyna placed her hand on top of hers. "I know we've been in a weird space but I'm still your friend."

"Promise me you won't say I told you so."

"Scouts honor." Chyna held up her hand.

"Nigga, we were Girl Scouts, not Boy Scouts." Brooke giggled, taking a sip of her drink. "This whole marriage thing ain't all it's cracked up to me. I think we rushed into it too fast. Gabe isn't the man I thought he was."

"Well, bitch, I tried to tell you!" Chyna couldn't help but say.

"You said you wouldn't say I told you so." Brooke pouted.

"Technically, I didn't; but listen, you still can get out of this thing. It's only been a few months. Just get the marriage annulled."

"I might have to 'cause… there's someone else," Brooke whispered.

"Gabe cheating on you?" Chyna whispered back, leaning forward. "Where that muthafucka at? You know I been wanting to fuck him up."

"Gabe's not cheating on me. Well, as far as I know he's not. It's me who's cheating. I'm in love with someone else."

Chyna's mouth fell open.

"Who you in love with, girl?"

Brooke looked down and chose her words carefully.

"It's this guy. I've had my eye on him for a while. The only problem is… he's in a relationship too."

"Now you know I don't condone fuckin' wit' nobody's man, but if you think you can pull him, take him."

"I think I can. We had a little sexy moment a few weeks ago that let me know he isn't as in love as he claims to be," Brooke said, with a devilish grin.

Chyna had no idea that she was referring to Dame.

"What happened? Spill the tea."

"We made out and I sucked his dick." Brooke added more to the story.

"Yo' ass always suckin' somebody dick."

"Girl, I couldn't help it. My mouth start salivating every time I'm around him." She glanced over and looked at Dame, who was staring right at them.

"I understand. Dame have me feeling the same way. I can't keep my mouth off him. Speaking of suckin' dick, I hear my nigga cock callin' me now." Chyna stood up.

"You silly." Brooke faked a laugh.

"On the real. Perk up, bitch. It's my birthday. Fuck Gabe. If mystery bae makes you happy, then get on him."

"Now that I have your blessing, I most certainly will." Brooke grinned like a Cheshire cat.

Finish talking to Brooke, Chyna found Dame standing by the bar, smoking cigars with the fellas. The visual was like a scene out of the movie Goodfellas. Victor, Black and Dame stood side by side. Victor was the head nigga in charge, also known as the connect. Black was his right-hand man and Dame was their former #1 D-boy. There was so much money between the three men it was impolite. Chyna watched as they did a toast to money, power and crime. All the men looked good in their tuxedos, but none looked better than Dame. He was on his Frank Lucas shit. His air of confidence and swag was like no other. Wherever he went, Dame commanded a room.

"Goddamn my baby daddy fine." She circled her arms around his waist.

"Happy birthday, Chy." Black and Victor patted her on the back.

"Thanks, guys. Where is Asha? I don't see her anywhere."

"She said she didn't feel well but wanted me to tell you she was sorry she couldn't make it."

"Aww damn, that's too bad."

"What was you and Brooke over there talkin' about?" Dame kissed the top of her head.

"Why you care? You never give a damn about girl stuff."

"You looked upset. I wanted to make sure you and my baby was straight."

"I'm ok. Brooke's marriage is on the rocks."

"Are you surprised?" Dame took a swig of whiskey.

"No, but it's still fucked up. I never want to see my friends hurt."

"Some people deserve to be hurt."

"Babe." Chyna hit his chest. "That's so mean."

"It's the truth. Your homegirl got some shit wit' her. I'm tellin' you. Keep a close eye on that one."

Just as Chyna was about to ask what he meant by that, she was whisked away to change into her second outfit for the night. Dame didn't want to let her go. Chyna was his li'l quarterback. He loved seeing her smile, so he spoiled her. After buying her a mansion on Star Island, proposing with a half million-dollar ring and throwing her a two-million-dollar birthday party, no other nigga would be able to compete or come behind him. He had her on lock. It wasn't just because of the material things he lavished her with. It was because of the bond they'd created together. He loved her more than he thought was humanly possible.

He planned on showing her just how much he loved her that night. Drinking his tumbler of whiskey, he went into a private room where his gifts for her were being stashed. He wasn't in the room two minutes before he heard the door close behind him. Dame turned around to find Brooke leaning seductively against the door.

"Turn yo' ass back around and get the fuck out."

"Stop being so mean. You know you don't mean that." She walked up on him.

"I'm not playin' wit' you or your stretched-out pussy. Back the fuck up." He mushed her in the face.

"Why?" Brooke stumbled back. "Chyna gave me her blessing."

"Fuck is you talkin' about?"

"I told her, I was thinkin' about leaving my husband for you."

"No the fuck you didn't." Dame said, repulsed by her presence.

"Well, technically, I didn't tell her it was you."

"I don't give a fuck what you told her. Bitch, I don't want you." He looked at her like she was crazy.

"Why you actin' like this? You know we had something." She tried to touch him again.

"We ain't have shit." He pushed her away.

"Yes, we did. Dame, I love you and I know you love me!"

"Ho, I don't love you! I ain't even love yo' ass in the 90's. I always loved Chyna. I only fucked wit' you 'cause I couldn't get to her. That shit that happened between us was a mistake. It will never happen again. You had me thinkin' she was fuckin' around wit' ol' boy, when you knew damn well she wasn't. You ain't nothin' but a grimy, miserable, broke, funny-lookin', bald-headed bitch that can barely suck dick."

"You just sayin' that 'cause you mad right now. You want me to suck your dick again?" Brooke sneered, running her hands up his chest.

"Bitch, are you dumb? Get your fuckin' hands off me!" He bent her wrist back.

"Oww… Dame, stop! That hurt!" Brooke fell to the floor and winced in pain.

"I don't give a fuck. As a matter-of-fact, get the fuck out. If it was up to me, your dirty-ass wouldn't have even been here in the first place. Fuckin' whore." He forcefully released her from his grasp.

"Now you wanna act like you got morals. You wasn't actin' all high and mighty when I had your dick in my mouth! I wonder how Chyna would feel about that?" Brooke spat, holding her injured wrist.

"Bitch, if you know what's good for you, she ain't gon' find out shit." Dame got in her face, with his eyebrows turn down.

Brooke rose to her feet slowly.

"Either pay me a million dollars or I'm tellin' everything."

"Yo' stupid-ass really think you about to blackmail me?"

"You spending two mill on birthday parties. You can afford it," she replied, sarcastically.

Dame's eyes darkened. Anger boiled deep in his system, as hot as lava. It churned within him, starving for destruction.

"Let me tell you how this shit gon' go." He gripped her by the neck and slammed her against the wall. "You ain't gon' say shit and I'm not givin' you shit. In return… I'ma let you live. Do we have an understanding? Nod, if you agree."

Brooke tried to respond but couldn't. Her head was spinning, as she tried to gasp for air. Dame had a death grip on her neck. Her eyes were wide with fear. Her lungs had started to ache. If she didn't say yes, he was going to end her life right then and there. Dame took delight in her face turning the shade of an over ripe red tomato. The killer in him didn't want to let her go but he had to. It wouldn't benefit him to have a corpse a few feet away from the love of his life and his future stepdaughter. He didn't want to see the look on their faces when they saw Brooke's dead body. That would bother him more than killing her. Brooke wearily nodded her head. Reluctantly, Dame let her go and watched as she dropped to her knees. Brooke coughed profusely, while struggling to catch her breath.

"Baby!" Chyna came into the room and spotted Brooke on the floor in distress. "What is going on here?"

"She drank too much. I think she having a panic attack," Dame lied. "I was just about to come get you."

"Brooke, are you ok?" She rushed over to help.

"I'm fine, girl. You know I can't be dying yet. I still gotta get my new boo." She held her neck and stared at Dame.

Dame eyed her with contempt. The urge to ring her neck, again, consumed him. Brooke had to go. He would be damned if she ruined all the progress he'd made with Chyna.

"C'mon, Belle. It's time for your surprise." He pulled her close.

"Baby, that can wait. I have to make sure Brooke is ok."

"She a'ight. Ain't that right, B?" Dame looked over his shoulder.

"I'm Gucci." She smiled, wickedly.

"See, she a'ight. As a matter-of-fact, Mohamed, escort Brooke home."

"Gladly," Mohamed replied, with a sinister look in his eye.

Dame had finally given him the ok to end her life.

"Nah, I'm good. I can escort myself home." Brooke nervously speed-walked out the door.

She wasn't no dummy. She knew what was up. Dame's goon wouldn't be laying a hand on her that night.

"I really don't think she's ok." Chyna said, worried.

Dame changed the subject by complimenting her dress.

"I thought I loved your first look but this one got me envisioning how you gon' look on our wedding day."

Chyna smiled, brightly. She'd changed into a $18,000, sparkling silver, mesh and Swarovski-beaded,

Yousef Al-Jasmi gown covered in more than 400,000 crystals. She was a vision of beauty. Back inside the party, Dame led her to the front of the room. With the mic in his hand, he got everyone's attention.

"I wanna thank everybody for coming out tonight to celebrate my belle's birthday. Y'all know it's been a rough couple of weeks, but my shorty pulled through and she lookin' better than ever."

Everyone in attendance agreed. Some of the men even whistled.

"And we just found out she's carrying my baby. For real, a nigga feel like it's my birthday 'cause she's giving me the greatest gift ever, which is the gift of life and agreeing to be my wife. So, to show my token of appreciation, I wanna give you this." He pulled two boxes from his pocket.

Chyna opened them up and found a pair of 6-carat, diamond stud earrings and an iced-out, rose gold Patek Phillipe watch.

"Are you serious? Oh my god!" She jumped up and down.

Dame held her close to his heart.

"You know ya man was going to replace everything that was stolen from you." He kissed her lips, as she cried.

"This is the happiest we've both ever been." Dame talked into the microphone. "And because of that, we're proud to announce that we're getting married October 21st."

The crowd cheered, as Chyna gave him a look of confusion mixed with irritation. They hadn't even discussed their wedding, let alone a date. She hated when Dame hit her with news that would change her life without consulting her. Once again, he was being his normal, bossy, inconsiderate self. Chyna quickly pulled him back into the room she'd found him and Brooke in and slammed the door.

"What the hell you mean we gettin' married in two months?" She placed her hands on her hips and rolled her neck.

"Lower your fuckin' voice." Dame leaned against the desk.

"I can't plan a wedding that fast!" Chyna got louder.

"You can, and you will."

"No, the fuck I won't! I can't! That's too soon! What is the rush?"

Dame crossed one leg over the other and glared at her.

"You actin' like you don't wanna marry a nigga."

"Stop putting words in my mouth. If I didn't wanna marry you, I would say that," she shot, sternly.

"You could've fooled me. First, you couldn't move to New York. Now, you sayin' two months is too soon to get married. Sound to me like you having doubts."

"Think what you wanna think. I'll tell you one thing, we ain't gettin' married in no damn two months."

"Is L.A. the reason you don't wanna marry me?" Dame let his infidelity get the best of him, again.

"Why are you so hung up on L.A.? He has absolutely nothin' to do with this."

"He has everything to do with this!"

Chyna jumped back, startled. Dame never raised his voice. He didn't have to.

"I'm startin' to think you still got feelings for that nigga! You been cryin' about seeing 'em ever since you left the hospital!"

"Nigga, I asked you could I see him once!"

"Once was too many fuckin' times." He got in her face.

"Who the fuck you think you talkin' to? I can ask you how many questions I want!"

"The only nigga you need to be worrying about is me. I'm the one that almost lost you," Dame countered.

He really didn't want to fight with Chyna but the decision for them to marry in two months had to be made. After the stunt Brooke pulled, he couldn't risk her telling Chyna what happened without her being his wife. It was fucked up, but if Chyna wasn't legally bound to him, he knew it would be easy for her to leave him. That couldn't happen. He loved her too much to even consider letting her go.

"I get that." She pressed her body against his and wrapped her arms around his neck. "You don't think that bothers me that I almost lost everything. What if I would've died? India would've been parentless. I would've lost my baby and there would be no more you and I. Dame, I love you. I'm just overwhelmed. I haven't even adjusted to the fact that I'm going to be a mother again. Add planning a wedding in two months on top of that and I'm gonna go insane."

"You know I got you. I'ma make sure you have the best of everything. Wedding planner included." He hugged her tight.

"Why a month tho'?"
"'Cause your last name needs to be Shaw."

"It can be Shaw after the baby is born."

"Nah, it need to be Shaw now."

Chyna held her head back and groaned. There would be no winning this argument. Dame always got what he wanted.

"You have a mental illness, but I love you anyway."

"You ain't got no choice but to love me. Now, give me a kiss."

Chyna kissed his lips, intensely, as he spun her around and placed her on top of the desk. No time for bullshit, Dame ripped her dress down the middle. Thousands of beads and crystals spilled onto the floor.
"Dame! My dress!" Chyna tried to salvage what was left of it.
"Fuck that dress. I'll buy you another one." He softly kissed up her neck.
Chyna let out a whimper of gratification, as his hand cupped her exposed breasts. Dame laid her back. Chyna stretched her arms out above her head and parted her legs wide. Dame gazed down into her deep, submissive eyes. All his problems instantly fell away. Being with Chyna sexually always calmed him. Wetness pooled from between her thighs. Chyna had been waiting weeks for this. She'd longed for him to bend her over and pull her hair. He was the only cure for the desires she craved.
Dame wanted to sink his teeth into the roundness of her thighs. Every inch of her naked body, from her hard,

brown nipples to her curvaceous hips turned him on. For weeks, he'd imagined her naked with her legs spread. No words were spoken, as he undressed. Chyna bit her bottom lip, as he unzipped his pants. The 13-inch python he'd been selfishly keeping all to himself sprang forth. Chyna reached between her legs to stroke him. His cock was hard and rigid - just how she liked.

"Open that pussy for me," he demanded.

Chyna spread her lips wide.

"You want this dick?"

"Yes." She purred.

"Put it in." Dame said, in a low, raspy tone.

Chyna grinned and did as she was told. His dominant demeanor intoxicated her. It seemed like hours went by before he was all the way in. Even though they'd been fuckin' for months, she still wasn't used to his size. With her ankles on his shoulders, Dame dug deep. He was dehydrated, and her wetness was the only thing that could replenish him. To get her used to his size again, he started off with long, slow strokes with a rough grind in-between. He could feel the release of her cream, as he stuck his tongue in her ear. Chyna's pussy felt so good. He tried to reach her soul with each stroke of his dick.

"Oh my fuckin' god! Dame!" She screamed.

"You love it, don't you? Tell me you love this dick." He wrapped his arms under her legs.

"I love this big dick! Lord knows, I love it so much." Chyna's eyes rolled to the back of her head.

"Mmmmmmm." Dame growled. "You feel my dick throbbin' inside you?"

"I feel it! I fuckin' feel it! Ooooh… Dame, fuck me! Don't stop! Right there!"

"There you go. Look at my dick as it goes inside of you."

Chyna looked down. The visual of Dame's cock sliding in and out of her wet pussy caused her to cum on sight.

"That's my girl. Look at all that cream." He grinned, proud of his work.

"Oh fuck! Yeah!" She wailed, as he pounded in and out of her, while kissing her lips.

Chyna placed fervent kisses all over his neck and shoulders, as the desk rocked back and forth. Laying on her back, she played with her pussy. Dame licked and sucked each of her toes. It was his duty to explore each part of her body with his tongue. She belonged to him. Till the day he died, no other man would love her like him.

"You driving me fuckin' crazy." Chyna rubbed her pussy faster to match his speed.

"Let me look at you." Dame stepped back and jerked his cock.

Chyna paused, rubbing her clit.

"Nah, don't stop." Dame bit his bottom lip.

Loving that he liked watching her get off, Chyna spread her legs wider and feverishly played with her pussy. Dame leisurely rubbed his hand up and down his shaft. Chyna was so fuckin' sexy. Her body was a masterpiece. Sometimes, he couldn't believe she was his. He couldn't wait to wife her so she could bear his last name.

"Make that pussy squirt," he demanded.

"I can't do it like you." Chyna pouted her puffy lips.

"Yes, you can. Do it like Daddy."

Chyna stuck two of her fingers inside her slit and pumped until her vagina began to gush. All she could think about was his hot semen exploding onto her stomach.

"That's it." Dame eagerly watched her finger fuck herself.

Chyna had the prettiest pussy he'd ever seen. Seeing her masturbate made his dick as hard as a steel pipe.

"Baby, I feel it coming!" She squeezed her eyes shut.

"That's my baby." Dame massaged his dick, as a stream of liquid squirted from her pussy. "Look at me," he ordered, while plunging his dick deep inside her pussy.

Chyna gasped for air, upon entry. Dame wasn't playing fair. His rod was hitting her spinal cord. Weakly, she gazed into his intense eyes. Her toes curled, as he held her by the throat and rotated his hips.

"No one fucks me like you. No one, baby. Nobody," she pledged.

Turned on by her moans, Dame pushed her massive tits together and devoured each of her nipples, one by one.

"Oh my god, I love them." He smacked them both like they were her ass cheeks.

Switching places, he sat down on the desk. Chyna sank down onto her knees and took his ball sack into her mouth and began to suck. Dame jacked himself off, as he watched her tongue juggle each of his balls.

"I can't wait to cum inside you. You want me to cum inside that pussy?"

"I do." Chyna moaned, as she traced the tip of his dick around her mouth like it was lipstick.

"Yes-yes-yes. Holy fuck." Dame grunted, like a caveman.

Chyna was sucking his dick like a champ. Up and down her head went. The slurping noises she was making caused his cock to stir in her mouth. Chyna's head game was lethal.

"I want you to cum on my face," she begged, as spit seeped out the sides of her mouth.

"You want me to cum all over that pretty li'l face?" Dame caressed her cheek.

"All over it. I want you to cum all over my face and tits. I need it, Daddy. I need it." She popped his dick in and out her mouth like it was a lollipop.

Dame wanted to give her what she wanted but wasn't ready to cum yet. Abruptly, he took his dick away and made her lay back. On her back, Chyna spread her legs in a V shape, while Dame fucked her pussy with two of his fingers.

"Yes-yes-yes! Shit, you're gonna make me cum, again."

"That's what I want. Give it to me. Give it to me. C'mon-C'mon-C'mon." He smacked her thigh, causing her to squirt all over the place.

Thirsty, he drank from her well while pumping his dick with his hand. Dame ate her pussy like it was his last meal. Chyna was so wet that he couldn't get enough.

"Open that pussy for Daddy." He spoon-fed her his cock, inch by inch.

With the full force of his hips, he pounded her pussy into submission. It was taking everything in him not to bust. Chyna's pussy was squeezing the life out of his dick. Hungrily, he licked and sucked her nipples, while drilling into her warm pussy. Dame's tongue and mouth was taking Chyna to another dimension. Her fingernails dug into his back, as she sucked on his thumb like it was his dick. She was used to him making her pussy rain, but that night he made it pour. Savoring the feel of his cock, she fucked him back.

"That's my girl." Dame thumbed her clit.

His balls smacked against her ass to the sound of a rhythmic beat. He was sure their guest could hear her screams, as he gave her every inch of his cock. Harder, deeper, faster he stroked.

"I'ma cum all in that li'l pussy. You wanna feel my cum in there?"

"Yes." Chyna rubbed her pussy in a clockwise motion. "Ooooooooooh, baby!"

"Tell me you want it." Dame flicked his finger and pinched her nipple.

"I want it, Dame. I want you to cum inside of me. Please, cum in me and make me cum!" She repeated over and over.

Dame growled and sank his teeth into her shoulder.

"Please, cum in me! I need it!" Chyna begged.

"I'ma cum, baby." Dame pounded into her so hard she thought her spine was gonna break.

"Ooooh, Dame! I can't take it."

"You gon' take this dick." He grabbed a fist full of her hair.

He wasn't going to stop until she squirted for the third time. As his dick slid in and out of her dripping pussy, she showered his instrument with her juices. It was then that he released a load of cum inside her precious womb.

"Fuccccccckkkkkkk!" He roared.

"Oh my god, baby. I feel it inside of me."

"Look at that." He watched, as his semen oozed out her slit.

Out of breath, Dame placed his thumb in her mouth, as he lay his head on her chest. Moments like this reminded him why Chyna could never find out about his infidelity. With her, he'd found home, and no one was going to tear his home apart.

“Frozen in time off one whiff of your perfume.” – Coultrain, “Be A Darling and Pass the Jam (Hold That Thought)”

Chapter 14

Mo

"Yo, you for real right now?" Boss eyed his wife with contempt.

"Boss, don't start with me." Mo slipped on her shoes.

It was Labor Day and she was heading to Quan's mom's house to spend the holiday. She didn't know why Boss was so upset. For the last four years, she'd been celebrating the holidays with them, while he and the kids went to his mom's house. She'd be damned if she spent the day with Phyliss, if she didn't have to. They didn't get along and it didn't look like they would anytime soon.

"You know I don't like you going over there but you going anyway?"

"I sure am." Mo got Zaire's baby bag together.

He was going with her, since she was still breast feeding.

"You can go but you ain't taken my son," Boss shot, heated.

"You got some milk in yo' titty that I don't know about?" Mo arched her brow.

"Think it's a game."

"What is your problem? We go through this every holiday!"

“My problem is, instead of runnin’ yo’ ass over there, you need to be tryin’ to fix this shit with your real mother-in-law.”

“I need to fix this?” Mo placed her hand on her chest, appalled. “Your mother is the one that has a problem with me! She’s the one that stopped liking me because your sister came at me sideways and got checked! She’s the one that constantly butts into our relationship! ‘Cause yo’ ass always running your fuckin’ mouth and tellin’ her shit! So, instead of blaming me, you need to have my back and put your damn mama in her place!”

Mo was so mad, she wanted to throw the baby bag and everything in it at his head.

“First off, watch your fuckin’ mouth when it comes to my mama. Next, since you love that nigga family so much, why don’t you marry him? Hell, you half way there with that nigga name on yo body like you his fuckin’ bitch.”

“So now I’ma bitch?”

“Here you go wit’ that shit.” He waved her off. “If I wanted to call you a bitch, I would call you a bitch.”

“Whatever, Boss. You don’t get it.” Mo’s eyes welled with tears.

“Honestly, I don’t give a fuck about the why of the situation, but humor me. What don’t I get?” He crossed his muscular arms over his chest.

“Nah, forget it.” Mo threw a stack of pampers into the diaper bag.

She could barely see what she was doing. The tears in her eyes were clouding her vision.

"Yo' ass cryin' now? Say what the fuck you got to say," Boss urged.

Mo stood up straight and took a deep breath.

"Your mother stay disrespecting me. I would never let my father or anyone in my family disrespect you. You never stick up for me," she cried. "Why would I wanna be around a person that constantly berates me? I'm already struggling as it is. The shit she says ain't making me feel no better."

Boss stood across the room and looked at her. He saw the sadness and distress in his wife's eyes. He never wanted to see her hurt. It was apparent that Mo had been having a rough time. He tried to do as much as he could to make her happy, but nothing seemed to work. She wasn't herself anymore. She was constantly moody. She stayed crying. She never dressed up anymore. Sex was an afterthought, and she barely wanted him to touch her.

"Come here Li'l Mama." He walked around the bed to console her.

Mo quickly fell into his awaiting arms. She hated to fight with Boss. He was her best friend. Without him by her side, she felt alone.

"Stop cryin', ma." He rubbed her back.

"I don't know what to do," she sobbed. "Everyone hates me."

"Who hates you?"

"You, your mother, Shawn, Zaire. He really hates me. He's never happy with me. He always cries. Maybe if he had a different mother he'd be happy."

"Mo, what are you talkin' about?"

"I should just die. I wanna die."

Boss' heart stopped.

"Chill out. Don't say no shit like that." He rocked her back and forth.

"I'm for real, Boss. I'm tired. I can't do this anymore. If it wasn't for you and the kids, I would've been killed myself."

"Mo, stop!" He held her at arm's length.

Her face was drenched with tears.

"I'ma tell you right now... If you go, I go; and if we both die, who gon' take care of the kids? I know you ain't tryin' to leave them with Phyliss."

"No." She shook her head.

"A'ight then. Stop talkin' that nonsense. You ain't going nowhere. Me and you supposed to be together forever, remember?"

"Yeah." She nodded.

"If that day comes that one of us has to go, I'ma go before you. God knows, I wouldn't be able to survive without you. You're the glue that holds this family together."

"I know," Mo laughed.

"I'll tell you what, since you feel the way you feel, I'll give you a pass today; but after that, we gon' have to work this shit out."

"Ok." Mo wiped her face.

"Stop all that cryin' and shit. You know I hate to see you cry." Boss placed several, sweet kisses on her nose and cheeks.

"Don't make me cry then." She finished packing the baby's bag.

Boss truly didn't want to let her go over Nicky's house, but the argument needed to be deaded for now. Hearing Mo say she wanted to kill herself scared the living shit out of him. With the way she'd been acting, he genuinely thought she might try to do it. From that day moving forward, he was going to keep a close eye on her. Losing Mo for any reason wasn't a risk he was willing to take.

By mid-afternoon, Mo sat outside on Nicky's patio, rocking Zaire to sleep. It had taken him forever to calm down. Mo wanted to pull her hair out. Thank God she had Nicky there to help her. If she hadn't been there, Mo was sure she would've snapped his neck. Thoughts of harming herself and Zaire often ran through her brain. She'd been secretly harboring the thoughts for weeks. She tried praying them away, but they remained in the forefront of her mind. Mo didn't know what was wrong with her. She felt like she was losing her mind. She didn't trust her sanity anymore.

"Mama, I got something to tell you." She ran her fingers through Zaire's soft curls.

"What is it, baby?" Nicky rocked in her chair.

Mo opened her mouth to speak but was cut off by Quan's loud mouth.

"Ma! Who ate all the rib tips?" He stepped outside.

"Boy, if you don't hush all that damn noise. You gon' wake the baby," Nicky scolded him.

As soon as she did, Zaire's eyes popped open and he started screaming again.

"See. Look what you did." She got up and took him from Mo's arms.

"Aww damn. My bad. I ain't know Mo and li'l man was out here." Quan's heart contracted.

He and Mo had been broken up for 11 years, but whenever he saw her, all the old feelings he tried to dead came flooding back. She was, and would probably be, the only woman he'd ever love. There wasn't a moment that passed by where he didn't regret all the dirt he did. He'd broken Mo's heart time and time again. He'd fucked up royally when he lost her trust and her heart. If he could take it all back and be the man she deserved, he would.

She didn't look quite the same as she used to. Over the years, she'd gained a little weight. She no longer dressed in designer duds from head to toe, but none of that took away from her timeless beauty. Mo wasn't beautiful in the classical, European way. She didn't have flowing, golden curls, ivory skin or penetrating eyes of green. She was taller than the average woman and certainly larger than a catwalk model. Her molten chocolate skin, liquid brown eyes, Naomi Campbell cheekbones and full, thick lips was nothing short of striking. Something emitted from within that rendered her enticing to both genders. Men desired her, and women died for her friendship.

Mo sat up straight, as he took her in. She wore her long, black hair in a ponytail, but in his mind, it lay gently over her shoulders, kissing her soft skin. There wasn't a stitch of makeup on her face. She was dressed casually in a grey, short sleeve sweatshirt, fitted joggers and Yeezy Boost 350. Gold, hoop earrings, a gold Cuban link chain and her wedding ring was the only jewelry she wore. It was the most she'd gotten dressed up in months.

"You gon' stare at me and not speak?" She cocked her head to the side.

It took everything in Quan not to stutter and blush when she addressed him.

"What up, big head?" He kissed her cheek and pulled up a seat next to her.

Mo checked out his neck. The tattoo of her name was still there. She didn't want Quan anymore, but it made her feel good to know he hadn't gotten rid of all traces of her. For half her life, he was her lover and best friend. It nearly killed her when she had to let him go. She knew it was wrong, but the reason she kept his name tatted on her wrist was because she wanted to remind herself of who she used to be. The old Mo was spirited, fun, fearless, weak, unhappy and lovesick. Some characteristics she wanted back, some she prayed she'd never see again.

"Where my grandson?" Nicky referred to Li'l Quan, as she bounced Zaire up and down.

He was still fussing.

"In the house with the other kids."

"Let me go kiss my grandbaby. Mo, I'ma put Zaire back to sleep."

"Thanks, Ma."

"I bet yo' greedy-ass ate all the rib tips," Quan joked.

"You know I did," she giggled.

"How long you been here?" He leaned back in his seat and sparked up a blunt.

"A few hours." Mo watched as he puffed on the weed-laced cigar.

She only had eyes for Boss, but goddamn was Quan fine. If she allowed herself, she could get lost in his beauty.

"Yo' mama gon' kick yo' ass if she catch you smokin' out here."

"She'll be a'ight." Quan tried to pass her the blunt.

"I can't. I'm breastfeeding." Mo poked out her bottom lip.

"Sucks for you. How you been?"

"Good, I guess."

"Stop lyin'. What's good wit' you, Mo?"

Mo might've thought her pain was invisible to the naked eye, but it wasn't. Her feelings were not easily concealed on her innocent face. Her agony was evident in the crinkle of her brow and the down-curve of her pouty lips. Her eyes, however, showed everything. An ocean of hopeless sorrow rest deep in her russet-colored irises.

"What you mean?"

"You walkin' around lookin' like a lost puppy."

"You callin' me a dog?" She said, after a pause. "First, my nigga call me a bitch. Now, you callin' me a dog. Ain't that some shit?"

"No, dumb-ass. You just not yourself. If I can see it, I know that nigga you married can see it too."

"I don't think he does."

"Talk to your BD."

Mo grinned, slightly. It cracked her up that Quan was technically her first baby daddy.

"I don't know. I'm just sad all the time. I'm overwhelmed with the kids—"

"You do got four kids, don't you? Damn… yo' vagina been through some shit."

"Fuck you." She pushed him, playfully. "As I was sayin'. I wanna go back to work but I can't 'cause being a manager doesn't fit into my lifestyle anymore. I've gained all this weight." She pointed to her thighs.

"Nah, yo' skinny ass needed that."

"No, I don't."

"You act like you fat. From where I'm sittin', them titties sittin' up, that pussy still fat and them thighs got me remembering how I used to push them muthafuckas back when I was beatin' the pussy up."

"You are such a creep."

"I'm speakin' facts. You gotta get yo' shit together for your ass be lookin' like Cardi B when she found out about Offset and his side bitch."

"You really think Boss would cheat on me?" Mo panicked.

Thoughts of Zya instantly filled her head.

"I'm not sayin' that, but why give him the incentive to."

"What you mean by that?"

"I mean, you look like you about to go midnight shoppin' at Wal-Mart." Quan pointed to her outfit.

"That is so rude." Mo chuckled.

"It made you laugh tho'."

"I know, I been lookin' a mess lately," she responded, somberly.

"Don't get me wrong. You still beautiful as fuck, but when you put yo' game face on you turn into Wonder Woman. At the end of the day, a man is attracted to your confidence more than anything else. Yeah, we do look at your outer beauty. We recognize that, but it's your swag that stands out more than anything else. Now, I don't know where the fuck yours went, but you need to find that muthafucka."

"You're right. I do, but it's hard. I just feel like I can't pull myself together. I feel like I'm drowning, and no one is there to save me."

"Well, with them big-ass titties you should be able to float," Quan joked.

"I can't stand you." Mo bugged up laughing.

"I'm just saying, these muthafuckas out here are savages."

"What, like Sherry?"

"May her ho-ass rest in piss."

"You ain't shit." Mo giggled.

It was funny how they could laugh about his infidelity now. Especially, since Sherry was dead.

"Anyway, I heard you fuckin' wit' a girl name Kema now."

"Who told you my business?" He died to know.

"I'm cool wit' her homegirl, Gray."

"Yeah, yo' brother on her thick ass."

"Y'all bet not fuck them over," Mo warned. "I know y'all still out here fuckin' wit' these nasty bitches."

Quan changed hoes like he changed his drawgz.

"I'ma always do me, but I'm feelin' shorty. I might keep her around for a li'l bit. See what she talkin' about. You know, she kinda remind me of you."

"Oh, really? If that's the case, marry her ass now."

"Marriage ain't for me. You gotta have a heart and a soul to commit yourself to a person."

"You have a soul."

"No, I don't; 'cause if I did, I wouldn't have fucked you over."

"The past is the past. You got a soul. You just keep it hidden under a layer of bullshit. You'll wake up one day and find it."

"I guess." Quan shrugged, unsure.

"Since me and you broke up, you can't tell me you haven't met a woman that can make you happy?"

"I done met tons of bitches that can satisfy me, but none I can see spending the rest of my life wit. You fucked that up for everybody," he spoke truthfully.

Quan wanted to add that he couldn't give his heart to another woman because he was still madly in love with her. Mo would always and forever be the one that got away.

"Don't put that shit on me. You the one that can't keep yo' dick in yo' pants."

"Quit bringing up old shit." He chuckled, standing up. "Come fix a nigga a plate. I'm hungry than a muthafucka."

"Nigga, you ain't my husband. I wish I would fix you a plate." Mo pushed him out of the way and opened the screen door.

"But that tat on your wrist make you something like mine so chop-chop."

"Five times, five times I call your phone. 3:00am and you not home. Got me thinkin' something wrong. Got me startin' to believe you think you're better off alone. Maybe I should give you what you want." – TXS , "Lay Down"

Chapter 15

Gray

I swear to God, I'ma fuck him up, Gray fumed, tapping her foot against the floor. Gunz had practically begged her to cook and have everyone over for Labor Day. She didn't want to. She had other things to worry about - like what she was gonna do with her life. She'd been out of work for a month. Sleeping in and sitting on her ass wasn't her plan when she'd closed Gray Rose magazine. She'd become so wrapped up in Gunz and his maybe baby that she'd lost focus. After Gunz's latest stunt, she was determined to get her life back on track.

That morning while she slaved in the kitchen, he got dressed and headed to the store to buy soda, ice and alcohol. Hours later, after numerous phone calls, Gunz was nowhere to be found. All their family and friends had arrived, ate, had seconds and he still hadn't returned home. Gray was furious. It was one thing to feel stupid, but to look stupid in front of his Uncle Clyde, his wife, Candy, her daughter, Dylan, her husband, Angel, their son, Mason, her best friends, Kema, Heidi, Tee-Tee, their spouses and children, was another story.

Gunz had her lookin' like an absolute idiot. No one would dare say it, but they all knew why he wasn't home. They all knew he was with his other bitch. Everybody laughed and talked like nothing was wrong, but Gray couldn't hide her disdain. She was pissed. She didn't care that he was with Tia. He could stay with the bitch for all she cared. She was mad because he'd been begging her for weeks to give him another chance. He swore up and down that he was gonna change. He put it on their kids that he wasn't going to deal with Tia anymore. He said that if the baby was his, he'd take care of it, but that was it. Gray knew he was full of shit, and once again, he'd proven her right.

The only thing Gunz knew how to do was lie, sell a dream and give out dick. She was so over him and his bullshit. Gunz would never get it together. He'd say any and everything so he could have his cake and eat it too. He would never do right by her. He'd been a liar and a cheat from day one. She had no idea what she was in for the night that they met. The first time he cheated she should've left. She should've known he wasn't shit when he cheated on her with Devin and all the other bitches he slept with. She'd wasted ten years investing her time and love into a man that could care less. She'd been loyal to him and he didn't even play on her team.

Gray was tired of feeling this way. No person should have so much power of her emotions. Gunz had the ability to make her feel like she could kiss the sky and in the next breath make her feel like absolute shit. She needed to get away from him before he destroyed what was left of her sanity.

Aoki had been crying for her daddy all day. Every five minutes, she begged for Gray to get him on the phone. When he didn't answer, Aoki walked away with a sad look on her face. Gray wanted to crack Gunz's skull. She grew up without a father and always longed for one. She never wanted Aoki to go through the same thing. She was so relieved when he stepped up to be her father. A weight was instantly lifted off her shoulders. Aoki would be raised in a two-parent home and have all the love a child could absorb. One day, she'd have to learn the truth that Gunz wasn't her real father. Gray wanted to shield her from the truth for as long as possible. There was no telling how Aoki would react to learning she was the product of rape, and that her mother had killed her biological father in self-defense. If Gray had it her way, she would've buried the secret right along with Truth.

Things in her life had to change ASAP. She thought staying with Gunz for the sake of the kids was the right things to do, but now she was starting to think that was a horrible decision. Gunz's fuck ups were starting to trickle down to their kids. She wouldn't allow him to hurt them like he'd hurt her. Picking up her phone, she tried calling him for the fifth time. Like all the other times she called, his phone rang until his voicemail clicked in.

Gray went to text him when a text from Cam came through. A sly grin graced her face, as she bit down into her bottom lip. Since the day he'd fixed her car, they'd kept in contact. Not a day went by where they didn't communicate. Cam made it his business to check to see how she was doing. Gray found herself looking forward to his calls and texts. At first, she had no plans on keeping in touch with him. She never wanted to see him again. Especially, after he tricked her into thinking he was gonna kiss her. She was humiliated, to say the least.

She was so embarrassed that she planned on keeping his li'l funky chains as payback. That was, until she went to her photo album and saw a video of him jacking off. The video was taken that night after he left the club. Gray couldn't believe that he'd videoed himself masturbating with her phone.

Cam pulled his eleven-inch, swollen cock out his Balmain jeans and said, "Look at what you did." A cold sweat washed over Gray, as he stroked up and down. She wished her lips were the ones sliding up and down his shaft. Cam's dick was abnormally big. It was long, thick, veiny and curved to the right. He groaned a bit, as the speed of his hand increased. It didn't take long before a stream of white cream oozed out the head of his dick. Cam being the nasty nigga he was, massaged his cum all over his dick and started all over again.

Gray enjoyed every second of the explicit video. Pretending to have an attitude, she texted him and asked why he left something so vulgar in her phone. Cam responded, 'After an eight-month drought, you need to be tellin' a nigga thank you'. The freak inside of Gray wanted to a sing his praises, but she could never let him know how much his little video turned her on. Gray wished she didn't get so excited when he reached out to her. Any contact with him made her day ten times better. Eager to see what he had to say, she opened the text and found a naked pic of him. His hard dick was on full display. After the pic, he texted, 'Happy Labor Day, big head'. Gray burst out laughing.

"Whose dick is that?" Dylan said, louder than she should have.

"Move yo' nosy-ass back." Gray quickly closed the message.

"Ah uh. Pull that dick back up. That muthafucka was beautiful."

"Don't get yo' ass beat." Dylan's husband, Angel, threatened.

"I can look, as long as I don't touch."

"Get fucked up."

"Speaking of fuckin'," Tee-Tee popped his lips and nodded his head towards Candy and Uncle Clyde.

They'd come out of Press bedroom disheveled, fixing their clothes. Uncle Clyde was a sight for sore eyes.

The old man was always extra as hell when it came to his fashions. It was like he was stuck in the 1970's. He rocked a Jerry curl, pencil-thin goatee, black shirt with ruffles on the chest and a shiny, gold, metallic suit. The suit was so bright it looked like gold leaf paper.

Candy's attire wasn't any better. While Uncle Clyde couldn't leave the 70's, Candy was the only person on the planet that still wore Baby Phat. She rocked a strapless, dirty wash, blue, jean dress with a wide belt around her waist and sneaker wedges.

"Did they just fuck in my baby bedroom?" Gray said, in disbelief.

"They sure did."

"Uncle Clyde? Really?"

"What's the problem, baby girl?" He wiped his forehead with a paper towel.

"Y'all couldn't wait until y'all got home to have sex?"

"What? My wife wanted me to beat the pussy up, so I had to beat the pussy up!" He humped and slapped Candy's behind.

"Ooh, Daddy, you so nasty." Candy giggled.

"On some real shit, I'm about to throw up. That's nasty as fuck." Dylan covered her mouth.

"It's bad enough my house stink from making them funky-ass chitterlings! Now you gon' have my baby room smelling like bussy!" Gray whined.

"What is bussy?" Candy asked.

"Butt and pussy," Tee-Tee replied.

"My ass don't stink! This OG puss. Nothing but water and vinegar splash on this thang right here."

"My wife keep it right and keep it tight," Uncle Clyde clarified. "You young hoes could learn a thing or two."

"Gotta fix his meal for him right." Candy patted the face of her pussy. "What it taste like, baby?"

"Like… an… ice-cold… bottle… of… Fiji." Uncle Clyde growled in her ear.

"You two are disgusting. I'm ashamed to call you my mother," Dylan snarled.

"I don't see why? This ocean brought yo' ass into this world and it will take you back out," Candy remarked.

"That pussy is lethal!"

"I drown you. Don't I, baby?"

"Er'single night. Good thing I swim like a Navy SEAL." Uncle Clyde bit her earlobe.

"Just be deep sea diving in the pussy."

"There are children in here!" Heidi covered her son's ears.

"Them li'l niggas a'ight. If they can listen to Drake, they can listen to me. I'm the one that taught Plies about sweet pussy Saturdays," Uncle Clyde informed the group.

"That's enough. Flag on the play!" Angel waved his hands, surrendering.

"Nah, class is in session. You wanna know what I call his love muscle?" Candy looked around the room.

"I don't know why, but I'm actually dying to know." Tee-Tee placed his hand under his chin, intrigued.

"I call his dick Captain Jack and his balls the Pirates of The Caribbean. See, you gotta put a name to the dick."

"You know what I call ya mama honey pot?" Uncle Clyde asked Dylan.

"No! I don't!"

"Well, I'ma tell you anyway. I call it… Ponderosa 'cause it's all I can eat."

"Nigga never get full. *It taste like candy,"* she sang.

"I can feel it when you walk. Even when you talk! It takes over me," Uncle Clyde joined in.

"Don't y'all start that shit. I hate when y'all sing that damn song." Dylan rolled her eyes.

"Uncle Clyde, you talkin' about eating Candy pussy again?" Gunz questioned, coming through the door.

Gray's entire body stiffened, as Aoki ran into his arms.

"Where were you?" She asked. "Mommy been callin' you all day."

"Daddy had to go check on one of his restaurants."

"You a damn lie." Gray blurted out loud. "I called the restaurants, and yo' black ass was nowhere to be found."

"Ahhhhhhhh… shit. Somebody 'bout to get fucked up. Guess it's time for me to go. Candy, grab my to-go plate. Told you 'bout playin' dirty pool. You playin' the game wrong, nephew," Uncle Clyde advised.

"Who playin' games? I got too much money to make, while you out here callin' somebody a liar." Gunz mean-mugged Gray.

"Ok, Gunz, so your employees just out here makin' up shit?"

"I don't know what the fuck they told you, but I know where the fuck I was at."

"And I do too. You was wit' that bitch," she countered.

"Wasn't nobody wit' no damn bitch."

"Then where are the drinks and the ice? I don't see shit in yo' hands, nigga."

Gunz shook his head, feeling dumb. He'd completely forgot to drop by the grocery store on the way home from Tia's house.

"Yeah, that's what the fuck I thought. You were with that bitch."

"I told you, I wasn't, but I guess your insecurities got you convinced, huh?"

"Insecurities?" Gray drew back her head.

"Come on, kids! Time to go!" Dylan and the rest of the crew started gathering their things.

"Insecurities my ass!" Gray shot up from her seat, outraged. "You had me cook all this damn food, invite everybody over and then you go M.I.A. for the day! The only place you could've been is with her!"

"It's funny 'cause I never hear you talk this bullshit when the checks come in." Gunz placed Aoki down.

"What the fuck does that have to do with anything?"

"It means, I work too muthafuckin' hard for you to be accusing me of dumb shit. Grow the fuck up, Gray. You makin' a scene in front of company. Now, everybody all uncomfortable and wanna leave because of you. You happy now? You've embarrassed yourself, yet again, and don't even know what the fuck you talkin' about."

Gunz knew he was wrong for blaming their argument on Gray but all he knew how to do was fuck a good thing up. Admitting that he was with Tia would only make things worse. Their so-called relationship was barely hanging on by a thread. He couldn't possibly tell her the truth. The lines were so blurred that he didn't know what the truth was and what was a lie. For years, Gray was his #1. He dipped off and did his thing, but with her was where his heart lie. Now, things had changed. Tia had somehow creeped in and took her spot.

Gray was a remarkable woman. Any man would be lucky to have her. She was gorgeous, smart, independent, responsible, loyal and a great mother. Wife was written all over her, but she required too much of him. Gunz got sick of her constant nagging. She stayed in his face, cussing and rolling her neck. He could never just chill without hearing her mouth about something he did to piss her off. She didn't want him to go to the club. God forbid he stay out past 1:00am. He'd never hear the end of it.

The subject of marriage stayed on the tip of her tongue. She didn't like him spending his money on frivolous shit. She clocked his every move and got mad when he asked her to loosen up and show some skin. Gray was all about her career and their kids. She'd completely forgot that she had a nigga at home that needed her attention too. All she cared about was changing Gunz into this cardboard cutout of the man she wanted. She tried to strip him of his hood behavior.

With Tia, everything was easy. She was wild, sexy and fun. They smoked trees together, got drunk together, popped pills together, hit the strip club together, and fucked bitches together. A day didn't go by where she wasn't dressed in some tight, ho shit that showed off her body. She loved when he spent racks on clothes, jewels and cars. The only thing she required of him was shopping money and long dick. Tia allowed him to be himself. He didn't have to pretend to be someone he wasn't. She encouraged his savagery.

Gunz tried leaving her alone, but he enjoyed her company. She made him laugh. He could relax around her. When he was with Tia, his life was stress free. It didn't hurt that her sex was toe-curling good. There wasn't a hole on Tia's body he hadn't fucked. He and Gray had been together ten years and she'd never even let him put his finger in her butt. Not to say her sex was wack. What she had between her legs could be bottled up and sold for millions, but new, young, pussy was life-altering. On paper, Gray was the logical choice. Tia could never compete with her, but Gunz was selfish as fuck. He wanted them both.

"I embarrassed myself?" Gray continued. "You the one that just got here! These muthafuckas been here all day."

"Now why I got to be a muthafucka? I ain't even did shit," Tee-Tee's husband, Bernard, spoke up.

"Shut yo' dumb-ass up and come on." Tee-Tee walked towards the door. "Princess Gaga, grab my purse."

"Fuck I'ma be embarrassed for? Everybody in here knows you ain't shit!" Gray shot, heated. "Everybody in here know you ain't good for shit but payin' bills, making up lies, gettin' minors pregnant—"

"She 20," Gunz cut her off. "And I told you that's not my baby!"

"Put your shoes on, Aoki and Press. Y'all coming home with me," Heidi instructed.

She knew Gray wouldn't want the girls to see them arguing.

"Fuck that! I ain't stayin' here with this nigga! I'm coming with you! He can stay here and have dinner by his damn self! FaceTime that bitch, I'm sure she'll eat wit' you." Gray placed on her shoes.

"So, you gon' leave 'cause you got an attitude and I wasn't even doing nothin'?"

"You lie so much you don't even know when to stop." Gray gave him one last look, and then slammed the door shut.

"They say love is overrated. Somebody lied, I'm faded." – YFN Lucci feat. Marissa, "Run It Up"

Chapter 16

Asha

Asha nursed her fresh glass of orange juice and gazed out the window. Cielo Restaurant offered breathtaking views of the Arch and Downtown St. Louis. It was one of her favorite restaurants. Creator and Executive Chef, Gian Nicola Colucci, a native of Italy focused on homemade, Italian classics made with local ingredients. Although known for their Italian cuisine, Cielo had also made a name for themselves with their scrumptious brunch menu.

They offered unlimited Bloody Mary's and mimosas, as well as a build-your-own omelet station, raw seafood bar and her favorite, French toast with whipped chocolate cream. She and Chyna were supposed to meet there at noon, but it was ten minutes after and she hadn't arrived. Asha hoped she'd arrive soon because she was starving. The tiny baby in her stomach had her constantly craving food.

Asha rubbed her round belly and checked her watch. Chyna was now 15 minutes late. She had another five minutes and she was going to order without her. When she noticed heads in the restaurant turn, she knew Chyna had arrived. Asha turned to get a good look at her future sister-in-law. She understood why her brother was so enamored with her.

Chyna was the kind of woman that chicks loved to hate. She had that movie star look, not overly tall and stick figure thin, but more like Dorothy Dandridge in her prime. She walked with the confidence of someone who had been here before. Chyna wasn't just flawless in her bone structure; her skin was like silk over glass and she exuded a sultry beauty. It was obvious that before settling down with her brother, she was a man-eater.

It didn't even look like she'd been viciously beaten weeks prior. She strutted through the restaurant with her signature, black curls, shaved sides, cat eye shades and black, quilted, Chanel bag. Her outfit consisted of a crisp white, puff sleeve shirt that was tucked inside a black, strapless dress that hit mid-thigh with a deep split. A gold and black layered necklace with a cross pendant hung from her slender neck. Black, patent leather, pointed- toe, The Row ankle boots clicked against the floor, as she switched her hips.

"So sorry I'm late." Chyna air-kissed her cheeks. "Your brother wouldn't get off the phone." She sat across from Asha and took off her shades.

"I can barely get his ass on the phone, since he got wit' you."

"You want me to tell him to call you?" Chyna pulled out her phone.

"No, I'm actually tryin' to dodge that nigga."

"Thanks for inviting me out. I love brunch. Your brother loves it too. He told me mimosa pussy is top five, so you know when I get home he gettin' all this bottomless throat."

"TMI." Asha chuckled.

"Hello." A waitress interrupted their conversation. Can I start you off with a drink?"

"A mimosa, please. Aww shit, I forgot I can't drink." Chyna smacked herself on the forehead. "I'll have a virgin daiquiri instead."

"You're pregnant too?" Asha quizzed, excited.

"Yeah, and what you mean by too?"

"I'm four months pregnant. That's why I didn't come to your party. I've been avoiding my brother."

"Ohhhhhhhhh… ok." Chyna nodded her head.

"That's why I wanted to meet with you."

"And here I thought you wanted to get to know me better. I thought I was about to get the li'l sister interrogation."

"Oh, don't get it twisted. I'ma get all in yo' business," Asha chuckled. "I just wanted to pick your brain on how you think I should tell Dame. He hates my boyfriend."

"Dame hates everybody."

"Exactly. Add his normal hatred and times that by 100. That's how much he hates Gerald."

"Why?"

"He thinks he's using me. Dame thinks I can do better. Gerald made the mistake of asking Dame to put him on, and let's just say things didn't go too well, which only made shit worse. Dame never wanted me to mess wit' a street nigga, but I can't help it. I love Gerald and now I'm carrying his baby. Gerald isn't going anywhere anytime soon, and I need for my brother to accept that."

"You're just gonna have to be honest with him and tell him how you feel. It's your life, at the end of the day.

The only thing Dame can do is respect your decisions; but knowing him, he'll probably just kill Gerald and raise your baby as his second child," Chyna half joked.

"That's what I'm afraid of. My brother is crazy."

"Girl, tell me about it."

"No." Asha said, seriously. "Like, you have no idea just how nuts Dame really is. I've seen him in rare form and it still haunts me to this day." She thought back on Yayo's death.

"Well, hopefully this baby will calm his ass down some 'cause I refuse to be a single mother, again."

"He doesn't even know we live together," Asha admitted.

"Hold up. Don't Dame pay your rent?"

"Yeah." Asha placed her head down, ashamed.

"Oh, you really tryin' to get yo' ass kicked."

"I've been meaning to tell him. I've just been scared."

"Now I know we don't know each other that well, but I have never been one to bite my tongue. You either gon' love that about me or hate me for it. How you got a nigga stayin' wit' you and yo' brother still payin' yo' bills? If he can lay down and stick his dick in you every night, then he should be able to pay yo' bills too," Chyna schooled her.

"He's been steppin' up a lot more lately. He came into some money that will keep us a float for a while, once Dame cuts me off."

"Then after that, what are you gonna do?"

"I was gonna beg Dame to hire me back at 1998."

"What about Gerald? I know you ain't gon' be the only one workin'."

"We decided that he would stay at home with the baby."

"Chile, this a mess." Chyna took a sip of her drink, wishing it had alcohol in it.

She wanted to tell Asha she was dumb as hell, but it wasn't her place. Dame was right about Gerald. He was a loser and he was using Asha. Any man that would live off another man wasn't shit. Asha was a damn fool to get pregnant by him. Chyna was dying to tell her that she was making a big mistake, but she would have to learn that the hard way.

"Is being a mom hard? I'm low-key scared to give birth." Asha changed the subject.

"Childbirth is no joke. It's like the worst menstrual cramps ever, but when it's over you're like oh, I can do this again. Being a mom is the best experience ever. My daughter, India, is my best friend. The bond we have is unbreakable. She's literally my greatest accomplishment. You have nothin' to worry about, Asha." Chyna reached her hand across the table and placed it on top of hers. "You're gonna be a great mother. Now, like your brother, I'm antisocial. I don't really fuck with people, but as your future sister-in-law, I will be there for you every step of the way."

"Thanks, Chyna. I really appreciate that." Asha smiled.

For hours, she and Chyna stuffed themselves with brunch food and alcohol-free drinks. Asha took an instant liking to her soon-to-be sister-in-law. Chyna was the big sister she never had. Her half sisters, Amara and Alecia, never tried to build a relationship with her. She didn't know if it was because they were so much older, or because their father got remarried to her mother. Whatever the reason, Asha no longer cared to have them in her life. She now had Chyna. She hoped moving forward that they're relationship would only grow stronger.

Full and ready to take a nap, Asha unlocked her apartment door and kicked off her shoes. Her feet were killing her. When she heard YFN Lucci's *Run It Up,* her aching feet didn't matter anymore. It was her and Gerald's song. He only played it when he was trying to set the mood.

Rounding the corner, she entered her living room and found a gorgeous, romantic display. Fifty, red, heart-shaped balloons filled the ceiling. White candles and matching rose petals made up a makeshift aisle. In the center of the aisle was a huge, red heart made of red rose petals. Gerald rested on one knee with a ring box in his hand. Behind him were gold balloons that spelled out 'Will You Marry Me'.

Asha's body immediately began to shake. Tears dripped from her eyes, as she cupped her mouth to conceal her screams. She couldn't believe it was happening. She and Gerald had discussed marriage, but she had no idea that a proposal was coming so soon.

"You gon' marry a nigga or what?" He grinned.

Asha looked down at the ring. A 3.78 carat, vintage, pear-shaped, diamond, pave, halo, rose gold, engagement ring shined bright. It was the most beautiful thing she'd ever seen. She didn't know how Gerald was able to afford such an expensive ring, but she didn't care. Her man was a hustler. He would get what he needed by any means necessary. That's what she loved most about him. He would do anything to make her happy. Whether Dame liked it or not, she was going be Gerald's wife and the mother of his child. If she had to lose her brother to gain her happily ever after, then so be it.

"Yes!"

"I can tell that by the look on your face, you really like her that way." – Toni Braxton, "Long as I Live"

Chapter 17

Gray

"Hello?" Gray answered the phone, groggily.

"You sound like a whole nigga."

"Who is this?" She asked, with her eyes closed.

"Your worst fuckin' nightmare."

Gray turned over onto her back and smiled. The sound of the caller's voice made her heart flutter.

"Cam, what do you want?"

"You, but you ain't ready for that yet," he flirted.

"Seriously, I was sleep."

"I don't care. Wake yo' punk-ass up." He took a pull off the blunt and inhaled the smoke.

"What is it?" She groaned.

"Get up and put on some clothes."

"Why?"

"'Cause I fuckin' said so," he shot.

Cam hated to be questioned.

"That bully shit don't work over here, homeboy. You gon' have to come better than that."

"Fuck what you talkin' about. Be at Chaifetz Arena by two o'clock. I got some tickets waiting for you at the door," he said, before hanging up.

"Dickhead!" Gray threw the phone down.

She had every mind to call him back and go off, but Cam beat her to the punch by texting:

Cam: Don't be on no bullshit. I will come lookin' for you.

Gray responded with the middle finger emoji and sat up. She would never admit it, but she was dying to see him. Two weeks had gone by since they'd last saw one another. Why he wanted her to meet him at Chaifetz Arena was beyond her. Perplexed, she called Kema to see what was up. She was informed that the 6th annual Loose Cannon Entertainment Celebrity Basketball Game was that day. The whole city would be out because not only were Cam, Quan and the rest of their crew participating, but celebrities like Floyd Mayweather, Lil Wayne, Chris Brown, Jacquees, Lil Yachty and Adrien Broner were too. There would also be a halftime performance by the Migos. Kema had received the same phone call from Quan, so she was going too.

Amped to get out of the house, Gray snatched the covers off her body and went to find Gunz. She'd been with the girls all week, while he ran the streets doing whatever he wanted. After their blowup on Labor Day, she'd been giving him the silent treatment. Gunz was public enemy #1. Hate was a strong word, but she was truly starting to hate the nigga's guts. Just looking at his sorry face sickened her. As soon as she figured out what her next career move would be, she was moving out. She'd miss her apartment, but he could have it. She was already tied to him through their kids. The apartment was just another tie that bound them together.

Gunz used it to control her. He knew if they lived under the same roof that he'd have access to her always. He could keep track of her whereabouts and know what was going on in her life. Meanwhile, she had no idea what he did or who he was with when he left the house. All that shit would be over soon. Not bothering to knock, she walked into his room. She just knew he'd be sleep but he was up getting dressed.

"Where you going?" She paused, after getting a whiff of his cologne.

Gunz was always a good-smelling nigga. The scent of his cologne made her pussy lips quiver.

"To work. I got some shit to do at the restaurants."

"How long you gon' be gone? I need you to watch the girls."

"I can't, but after I get through, I was thinkin' me, you and the girls could go to the movies on some family shit."

Gray held onto the doorknob and tried to hold onto her resolve. This was why she had to get away from him. She hated when he tried to act like he wanted them to be a family. He always used this tactic to weaken her and it worked every time. Gunz walked over to her and took her free hand into his.

"Look, I know things been fucked up between us but on God, I love you, Gray. You and the girls are my life. This baby shit got us in a crazy space, but I need you to know that I'm gon' fix this shit. It's me and you till the day I die. I ain't tryin to be wit' nobody else but you. I just wanna spend the night with you and my girls. Make you laugh." He caressed her cheek with his thumb. "It's been hella's since I saw you smile."

Gray became a puddle of mush under his gaze and touch, but she was determined to remain strong. She wouldn't allow herself to self-destruct. She'd been here one too many times before. In the past, she made decisions with her heart, but she was older and wiser now. She wouldn't let Gunz infiltrate her heart with the game he was tryin' to spit. What he was proposing sounded good as hell, but her heart no longer desired to be shattered into pieces. Gray had her mind made up. She'd rather go to war with a man than to ever fight for a boy.

"If you're serious about the movies, then you and the girls can go. I, on the other hand, want no parts of you or your family night out." She smacked his hand away.

"Damn, that's cold-blooded. Hopefully, you change your mind 'cause I really wanna spend some time wit' you."

"I won't. You can't never do nothin' when I ask you. Aoki and Press are your kids too."

"I know that. Why you think I'm tryin' to spend time with y'all?"

"Whatever, Gunz." Gray waved him off and left the room.

She was over him and his bullshit excuses. Needing a babysitter, she hit up Tee-Tee to see if the girls could come over and play with Princess Gaga. He, of course, said yes. With that out the way, the next agenda on the list was figuring out her outfit. Loose Cannon events were always star-studded and ghetto fabulous. She wouldn't be surprised if there was a shootout.

It was a little after 3:00pm when Gray and Kema stepped into the building. Damn near every seat in the arena was filled. The city had truly come out to show love and support. The radio station 104.1 The Beat was in the house. Hitman Holla, Stevie J and Young Thug were in the building. Team TMT was on one side of the court and Team Loose Cannon was on the other. They even had cheerleaders for each team. Quavo and Take Off were on the court, warming up, in their TMT basketball uniforms. Gray wondered which team Cam would be on. She tried searching the crowd for him but too many niggas kept coming up in her face trying to holla.

I knew I shouldn't have worn this shit, she thought. Kema had talked her into wearing her hair half up and half down. A blue smoky eye, pink blush and pink, glossy lipstick decorated her face. Around her neck was a diamond tennis necklace, as well as Cam's chains. Wanting to fit in to her environment, she rocked a black and white, graffiti print, Versace motorcycle jacket, black, mesh bralette, denim, booty shorts, blue, Vetements heel-sock ankle boots and a neon yellow, YSL, crossbody purse. Gray hadn't shown this much body in years. No less, during the daytime. Niggas was on her like moths to a flame.

Her butterscotch skin, mouthwatering tits, heart-shaped ass and voluptuous thighs had men's tongues wagging. Gray was a prime example that you didn't have to be stick figure thin to be considered desirable. Men loved her thickness just as much as she did. Cam seemed to love it more because he'd been eyeing her the whole time and she didn't even know it.

He was supposed to be concentrating on warming up, but Gray commanded all his attention. Other men might've flocked to her, but he was her biggest fan. They wouldn't know what to do with a woman like Gray. She was flawless, like the VVS diamonds shining around her neck. Cam still didn't want to be her man, but he didn't want anyone else to have her either. All he wanted was a bit of her time and a slice of heaven from between her thighs. He couldn't give her his heart or a commitment, but he could offer her a good time and some fire dick that would put an arch in her spine.

Placing his fingers in his mouth, Cam whistled loud to get everyone's attention. He had to let muthafuckas know she was off limits. They should've known because his chains were around her neck. Gray and the nigga in her face spun around. Cam ice-grilled the dude and said, "Back the fuck up… and you." He pointed at Gray. "Bring yo' ass over here."

Happy as hell to see him but scared by the angry look on his face, Gray steadied her breathing and walked over. She prayed to God that her excitement was being contained. She didn't wanna come off thirsty, even though she was parched.

"Ok, I'm here. Now what?" She placed her hand on her hip.

"You tryin' to get another muthafucka killed?" Cam shot, heated.

"What you talkin' about?"

"Fuck you got on?" He scowled.

"Clothes." She looked down at her outfit.

"You got yo' nipples and yo' coochie out. What the fuck was you smokin' when you got dressed? Go sit yo' ass down."

"You do realize you ain't my man." Gray rolled her neck.

"Did I ask you that? I don't give a fuck about being yo' man. You still gon' do what the fuck I say."

Speechless, she stood trying to contemplate a comeback but came up short.

"Exactly. Now go sit the fuck down."

Cam was genuinely mad that she had the nerve to come out the house in some ho shit. He didn't want niggas to see what she was holding. Gray's body was for his eyes only. He hated he ever told her to stop dressing like a square. Her physic was too dangerous to be on full display.

Confused by his attitude, Gray walked off hurt. Just when she thought she and Cam had reached common ground, he'd gone back to being rude and mean. She'd made it her business to look good for him and he'd shitted on her. Gray had never been more mortified in her life. Her confidence had been completely shot. She felt like a cheap whore now. Why ask her to come see him if he was going to be an ass? She was honestly over tryin' to figure his bipolar-ass out.

Cam knew he was out of pocket for coming at her crazy, but he couldn't help it. Whenever he was in Gray's presence, he lost all sense of self. Her bright, blue eyes sent him into a tailspin of rage, lust and doubt.

"You ain't have to do her like that." Quan watched her ass jiggle, as she walked.

"Fuck outta here. Got all these wack-ass niggas in her face like her pussy a soup kitchen or some shit."

"Let me find out my nigga choosin'. You actin' like she yours."

Cam looked over at Gray as she sat down. In his mind, she was his.

"Man, ain't nobody got time for that shit right now." He flicked his wrist.

"That's what yo' mouth say," Quan called his bluff.

Cam couldn't concentrate on Gray, her barely-there outfit or his feelings for her. He had a game to play. Back to warming up, he made a quick layup. Little did he know, but over in the stands some shit was brewing. LaLa and her homegirls, Alexzandria and Lynn, were going in on Gray. They'd watched their entire encounter go down. LaLa was pissed. Her whole reason for being there was to solidify the fact that she was still Cam's #1 bitch.

For four years, they had a whirlwind relationship. He fell in love with her, instantly. Every man that came in a 50-mile radius of LaLa wanted her. She was a drop-dead gorgeous redbone with a slick mouth and ass so fat it made you wanna cry. The day they met, she was coming out of a 7/11. After that, they were inseparable. She was a baddie that was down for whatever. She supported his illegal street dreams and allowed him to launder money through her beauty salon. In return for her loyalty, he paid for her breast implants, veneers, bought her a car and a house.

When it came to LaLa, money wasn't a thing. There wasn't a bag or a pair of shoes that she couldn't cop. She had unlimited access to his Black Card. He took her all over the world and showed her how a real nigga treated his woman like a goddess. Before Cam, no nigga had ever spoiled her or showed her the finer things in life. He constantly showered her with affection. She was his world. He stayed buying her cards and flowers, so she would never doubt his feelings for her.

Cam loved her so much 'cause she held him down. When he had brushes with the law, she never turned her back. If he had to lay a nigga down, she burned his clothes and hid the gun. LaLa was the definition of a ride-or-die bitch.

They had the perfect hood romance, even though his family disliked her. They saw through her good girl persona. Mo and his aunt, Vickie, warned him to leave her alone, but Cam thought they were just being overprotective and petty. Nobody could tell him shit about LaLa. She was wifey all the way. When she got pregnant with their first child, he was overjoyed. Cam was well into his 30's and was ready to become a father. He'd fucked mad bitches and lived selfishly. It was time for him to settle down, so he bought a ring and proposed. LaLa, of course, said yes.

Cam couldn't have been happier. His life was perfect. He had his girl, a baby on the way and more money than one man could spend. Everything came crashing down when the streets started buzzing that the baby LaLa was carrying wasn't his. Cam didn't wanna believe it. LaLa was his baby. She would never step out on him. She had no reason to. He gave her everything she wanted, including his heart. Cam chalked the talk up to gossip and kept it moving.

Niggas was always hating on him 'cause he was the man. Everybody wanted what he had, including his bitch, so why not try to tear his empire down? Besides that, LaLa refuted the claims vehemently. She assured him of her love and loyalty and told him not to focus on the lies being spewed.

Six months into her pregnancy, Quan dropped a bombshell that he knew for a fact she'd cheated and had been cheating with local club owner, Kingston. Cam confronted Kingston and like a man he confessed the truth. Not only had he been LaLa's side nigga, but he'd been knocking her down without a rubber for almost a year. Cam wanted to set him and LaLa on fire. He didn't play around when it came to having unprotected sex with multiple partners. He swore up and down if she gave him anything he was going to kill her.

Loyalty meant everything to him. The fact that she'd betrayed his trust and blatantly lied to his face damn near killed him. It took everything in him not to slice her throat when he asked her for the last and final time if the baby was his. When LaLa saw the tears in his eyes and the tremble of his lip, she couldn't deny it anymore. It was a 50/50 chance that the baby could be his or Kingston's. The day she gave birth to an eight-pound, chocolate baby boy, the answer was clarified. The baby wasn't his.

Within a blink of an eye, she and Cam's four-year relationship was over. If it wasn't for their business dealings, he wouldn't have ever given her the time of day again. Cam hated her guts. To him, she was the scum of the earth. He would not and could not forgive her for what she'd done. And yes, she was poisonous, but because of the emotional pull she had on him, Cam dipped back and fucked her from time to time. In LaLa's feeble mind, she mistook him fuckin' her as meaning he still cared.

Unwilling to let him go, she made it her business to get back in his good graces. Cam was the love of her life. She'd fucked up and took him for granted. After all these years apart, she realized that no other man would ever love and take care of her like him. Now, she had this big, Blasian-lookin' bitch trying to take her man. She'd let the chick slide at his birthday party, but to see her walk in with his chains around her neck and grinning up in his face was the last straw. She was making LaLa look bad in front of her girls. She'd made them believe that she and Cam were working things out.

"Who is that fat bitch with Cam's chains on? I thought he was your man?" Lynn interrogated LaLa.

"He is. That's why I'm about to go check his ass, 'cause he got me fucked up." LaLa rose to her feet and pulled her booty shorts out the crack of her ass.

She could feel her friends' eyes on her, as she stomped down the steps. LaLa had no right being upset, but she had to keep up her charade. Her homegirls couldn't know she was a fraud. LaLa was so committed to the role of the mistreated ex-girlfriend that she'd started to believe her own lies. Her hips swayed side to side, as she sashayed across the court. All eyes were on her.

LaLa's name was known all around St. Louis. People knew her for being super pretty, Cam's ex girl and one of the baddest hairstylist in town. Whenever you saw her, she was dripped in the latest fashion. That day was no different. She wore a black, sleeveless bodysuit, black and white, fitted Chanel joggers, lace-up Dsquared2 booties and a MCM book bag. The iced-out Patek Phillipe watch that Cam bought her gleamed from her wrist.

Knowing she had an audience, LaLa used the tip of her stiletto nail and tapped Cam on his shoulder. As he turned to face her, Cam wore an exasperated expression on his face. He knew LaLa like the back of his hand. She wasn't coming over to speak. She called herself being mad 'cause Gray was there.

"What's up?" She cocked her head to the side, with an attitude.

"Nothin'. Fuck you mean?" Cam looked at her like she was crazy.

"So, you fuckin' with bitches that look like Roseanne now?" She pointed at Gray, who was staring right back at her.

"Yo, here." Cam passed the rock to Quan, and then grabbed LaLa by the back of her neck and pulled her off the court.

"What is you doing? Let me go!" She tried to keep up with his pace, as he stormed towards the exit.

Once they were alone, Cam pushed her forward and backed her up against the wall. He was so close to her face that their lips almost touched. Squeezing her jaw, he pointed his finger in her face and said, "I don't know what part of this yo' retarded-ass don't understand, but let me make this shit clear. Just because I stick my dick in you, don't mean that I fuck wit' you. You ain't my girl. The only thing you good for is puttin' your mouth on my dick and cleaning my fuckin' money through your shop. So, the next time you come out the side of your neck about her… ain't gon' be no talkin'." He shot her a look of disgust and went back into the arena.

Embarrassed by the way he handled her, LaLa watched him storm off, with tears in her eyes. She assumed that since he hadn't gotten serious with anyone since their breakup that he still loved her. It was obvious that he had feelings for the beached whale with the aquatic eyes. LaLa couldn't have that. Cam had life fucked up if he thought he was going to trade her in for a bitch that was shaped like a wide-body Benz. If she wasn't the woman on Cam's arm, then there would be no one by his side.

"Girl, what happened?" Alexzandria asked, as she retook her seat. "He looked a li'l upset."

"Nah, he looked like he was about to break her fuckin' neck," Lynn chimed in.

"Y'all know Cam. That nigga does the most. He ain't do shit but pull me out there and start coppin' a plea."

Lynn inhaled deeply and shook her head. She didn't believe a word that was coming out of LaLa's mouth.

"Yeah, I bet," she said, sarcastically. "But that fat bitch still wearing his chains."

"Girl, bye. Don't yo' nigga got life?" LaLa hit back. "I bet he got somebody wearing his chain too. The nigga name probably Ced."

"Bitch, please. My nigga ain't gay and don't try to turn this shit around on me. We talkin' about you, boo-boo."

"That's all you do is talk about me. I can't help it I'm that bitch." LaLa flipped her Peruvian Natural Wave weave over her shoulder.

"Yeah, you that bitch a'ight. The same bitch that's getting played in public," Lynn wisecracked.

"Whatever, girl." LaLa focused on the start of the game.

Cam and his homeboys were playing for Loose Cannon's team. The first two quarters they dominated the game. He and Quan were on their Michael Jordan and Scottie Pippen shit. Cam's tall-ass was a natural on the court. He'd dunked twice and was hitting three-pointers left and right. By the end of the second quarter, he'd racked up 30 points. Cam made sure to give the performance of his life. He had to show Gray his skills; but every time he looked her way, she had her eyes elsewhere.

She was either focused on her phone or talking to Kema. When their eyes did connect, she'd roll hers as hard as she could. Normally, Cam wouldn't give a fuck about a chick being in her feelings, but with Gray, things were different. He didn't like her being mad at him. The shit didn't sit right in his spirit. That nigga she had at home could give her the blues. With him, he only wanted her to experience joy. When the buzzer for the halftime show sounded, instead of going to the locker room, he went directly over to Gray. She had her head down, scrolling through Instagram, while eating a stick of pink cotton candy.

"Gimme some." He squatted down before her.

"I ain't giving you shit. Go back and play your game."

"It's half time, nigga. If you would've been paying attention, instead of rolling them blue-ass eyes, you would've known that." He ran his hand up and down her bare leg.

Gray's skin felt like the rarest silk against his fingertips.

"Don't touch me." She jerked her leg away.

"Quit actin' like that. You know yo' ass ain't mad for real." He gripped her leg and pulled it back to him. "You too damn pretty to be so fuckin' mean." He placed a soft kiss on her knee.

Gray's ice blue eyes linked with his and the anger she harbored evaporated into thin air. The crush she had on him was getting out of control. Gray felt like an idiot for even having a crush. She hated the word. She didn't have a crush on Cam, she adored him with a passion that burned hotter than a thousand suns. He was the one. She knew it deep down in her soul. He was all that in her mind, her true North Star, her everything.

Unable to tell him no, she plucked a piece of the pillowy candy and placed it inside his warm mouth. Her index finger glided across his wet tongue, as he took the opportunity to suck on her finger. Gray watched, intently, as he took each of her fingers one by one and licked the sweet residue of candy off. Her head was telling her to stop him but the heartbeat in her clit kept her lips sealed.

"Sweet." He kissed the pad of her fingertip. "But I bet your pussy taste better."

"It does," she slipped up and said out loud.

A wicked grin graced the corner of Cam's lips. This was the side of Gray he loved to see. When she didn't overthink things, and let her guard down, she was at her best.

"You hurt my feelings," she whispered, as he kissed the palm of her hand.

Cam hung his head low. Hearing her confession fucked his whole mind up. He wanted to tell her that he was sorry for hurting her feelings, but Cam never apologized to anyone. He was the kind of nigga that pulled with one hand and pushed away with the other. It was a fucked-up thing to do, but he couldn't help it. His feelings for Gray scared the shit outta him. For years, he'd closed himself off to emotions, because when he loved, he loved too strong. To hide the way he felt, he gave out mixed messages to disguise his feelings. These were all the things he should've told her, but his selfish pride kept his emotional state at bay. "I know," was all he could muster to say. The somber look on his face let her know that he regretted his actions. That alone was enough of an apology for Gray.

"Aww… hellllllllllllllllll naw!" Kema stood up and started taking her earrings off.

Gray took her eyes off Cam to see what all the ruckus was about. When she spotted Gunz and Tia walking hand in hand, she swore her eyes had to be playing tricks on her. For weeks, he'd denied having any romantic feelings towards her. Hell, the last she'd heard, he'd left her alone; but there they were, looking like Idris Elba and the dark skin version of Kehlani.

From the outside looking in, Gunz and Tia were the perfect couple. Gunz might've been 20 years older than her but you couldn't tell. He was still young-looking himself. Their hands were perfectly intertwined together. He held onto her like she was his lifeline. Seeing Tia's round, pregnant belly was like a kick to the stomach. Because of Gunz, she'd never be able to bear children again, and here he was prancing around his pregnant side bitch like her tubes being tied - at his request - didn't mean a thing. Shaken by his latest betrayal, Gray handed Cam her cotton candy and went to confront Gunz.

"Are you fuckin' kidding me?" She got his attention.

Gunz's eyes damn near popped out of their sockets, when he saw her.

"I must be trippin'. I gotta be, 'cause ain't no way you standing in front of me with this bitch. You couldn't be. This ain't nothin' but a bad dream and I'ma wake up any second now."

"Gray, chill. Let me talk to you outside." He tried to take her by the elbow.

"No, you gon' talk to me right here." She yanked her arm away. "I thought you said you didn't fuck wit' her?"

"Oh, you don't fuck with me, 'cause I thought you didn't fuck with her?" Tia challenged.

"No, sweetie, correction, I don't fuck with him. This lying, sack of shit however stay up my ass, beggin' to be back with me. Ain't that right, Gunz?" Gray folded her arms across her chest.

"I ain't talkin' about this shit here. You got all these nosy muthafuckas staring at me and shit. Nah, I'm good," he fumed, heated.

"What the fuck you mean you good? Answer the question, nigga!" Tia spat.

"I told her that I wanna be a part of my kids' life. That's it."

"Really? So, you wasn't beggin' me to take you back so we could be a family? Nigga, you was just askin' me to go on a family movie night this morning!"

"Yeah, so I can spend time with my kids. It ain't have shit to do wit' you," Gunz lied.

"Wooooow... Word? Ok!" Gray clapped her hands. "I see what this is. You tryin' to make me look like I'm crazy."

"Girl, fuck all that. Who ass you wanna kick first? His or hers?" Kema interjected, ready to thump.

"Neither one of y'all gon' touch her." LaLa joined the conversation.

Lynn and Alexzandria were right behind her.

"Who the fuck are you?" Kema looked her up and down.

"That's my niece. Who the fuck are you?"

"The bitch that's gon' drag you and your niece. Now, what's up?" Kema stood in a south paw stance. "Any one of y'all can get this work." She eyed LaLa's homegirls too.

"I'm in the fuckin' Twilight Zone." Gray ran her hands up her neck and then placed them behind her ears.

It was official. Either God or the universe hated her fucking guts. No way was the two women who were the bane of her existence some kin. Gray wanted to just throw her whole life away.

"So, who tryin' to catch these hands, 'cause I don't know who raised this prosti-tot, but she need her ass beat," Kema said, on go.

"She don't need shit. It ain't her fault your nigga can't be kept." LaLa aimed her words at Gray. "You sittin' up here cryin' over a nigga that don't want you and got my niggas chain around your neck. Fuck kinda shit is that?"

"Whose chains are those?" Gunz's nostrils flared.

"None of your fuckin' business!" Kema shouted.

"Yo, let me holla at you for a second." Gunz walked up on Gray, who still was unable to speak.

So many thoughts were flooding her brain that she was experiencing a system overload.

"She don't wanna talk to you." Kema blocked his path.

"If you don't move yo' big-head-ass out the way."

"What you need to talk to her for?" Tia grabbed him by the arm. "I know you don't care about her messing with another nigga?"

"I don't care what she do. As long as she don't have that muthafucka around my daughters."

Gray blinked her tears away. All she ever wanted was Gunz's love, but he gave her his money instead of his heart. No matter how many times he said he was sorry for hurting her, all his apologies ended with lies. Gray wondered had he ever really cared about her. He never met any of her needs. He didn't give her his everything. Like a fool, she still stuck by him. Gray was no different from any other woman. She made the mistake of thinking if she loved him enough, he'd make the effort to change. Years of hoping, wishing, praying, setting aside her pride, ignoring her woman's intuition, sharing his affection, idolizing him like a god and wasting her time landed her here with her face on the floor.

"I can't believe I wasted ten fuckin' years of my life on you. You are the worst type of nigga there is. You would've been better off swallowed. You told me you couldn't watch our girls 'cause you had to work, but here you are, holding hands with a toddler whose pregnant with a baby you claim ain't even yours."

"You said my baby ain't yours? Please, tell me she lyin'? You ain't say that." Tia studied his face for confirmation.

"Man, get outta here wit' that. You know damn well that's my baby." Gunz pulled her close and planted a kiss on the top of her head.

"Then you need to check her."

"Only thing he gon' be checkin' is them paternity test results when they come back, loose puss." Gray smirked.

"Yo, you doing too much. You not gon' keep disrespecting my girl. Off the strength of our kids, I'm tryin' not to take it there wit' you, but you starting to piss me off," Gunz warned.

"Nigga, I don't give a fuck about pissing you off? Fuck you! As a matter-of-fact. Fuck you, fuck that bitch and her AID's, yeast-infected-ass pussy! I hope y'all baby come out retarded—"

"See, that's why I don't fuck wit' you now." Gunz pointed his finger in her face. "Only a miserable bitch would say some shit like that."

"Aye, you ain't gon' step in? He just called her a bitch." Quan looked over at Cam.

Like the rest of the spectators, he stood back and watched the drama unfold. He thought he was angry before, but now he was livid. Cam didn't know Gunz personally, but he'd seen him around town and heard his name. The nigga tried to portray himself as a stand-up guy, but seeing him playout the mother of his kids for Tia's ho-ass was some straight sucka shit. Cam wasn't an angel by a long shot. He'd done as much dirt as the next man, but he'd never disrespect Gray the way this nigga was. He truly felt bad for her; and as much as he liked her, it wasn't his place to step in. He just hated that she was wasting her breath on such a trash-ass nigga.

"As long as he don't put his hands on her, I ain't got nothin' to do with that." He finally spoke up.

"You foul as fuck, Gray." Gunz barked. "That's why I'm starting a whole new family without yo' dumb-ass."

"And this one won't be no rape baby." Tia rubbed her stomach.

Words left Gray. She placed her hand on her chest to stop herself from dying. Lifeless, she stared into Gunz eyes, which burned with anger, and her heart fell silent. Gray's mind began to shut down, unwilling to think anymore. The coldness of her heart blurred her vision, rimming everything in red. Her eyes could still see, yet the world around her seemed so far away. Hyperventilating, she waited for Gunz to realize the gravity of Tia's words. She desperately searched his eyes, waiting for him to come to her aide, but he never came.

Gray swallowed hard. It was then that everything became crystal clear. Tia wasn't just some fly-by-night side piece. Gunz actually had feelings for her. He liked her so much that the disrespect she'd shown his child went unchecked. Gray would never forgive him. Any love she ever had for him disappeared.

Gunz saw it when it happened. Gray's entire demeanor changed. He hadn't told Tia the truth about Aoki's paternity with the intent of being messy or hateful. He loved his daughter with every fiber of his being. He'd accidentally spilled the beans one night when they were on some drunk and high shit. Gunz was about to put Tia in her place, but it was too late. Gray was already repulsed by him. Blacked out, she threw her body weight behind the punch that struck Tia's jaw with so much force it knocked out her front tooth. Down with the shits, Kema grabbed LaLa by the hair and brought her face down sharply onto her bent knee. Blood flowed from her broken nose, as she staggered backwards.

Alexzandria and Lynn tried jumping in, but Quan yanked them back and tossed them to the ground. Scared of what he might do to them, they stayed back. Nowhere done with Tia, Gray went to hit her again but was stopped by a forceful push from Gunz that sent her flying onto her butt.

His protection of Tia only infuriated her more. Rising to her feet, she went to attack him, but Cam got to him first.

"Nigga, you don't put yo' hands on no fuckin' female. Fuck is wrong wit' you? That's bitch nigga shit."

"Nigga, mind your fuckin' business! This between me and my wife!" Gunz barked, ready to rock his ass to sleep.

"Wife?" Tia screamed.

"My nigga…" Cam scoffed. "You don't want no smoke. This ain't what you want."

"Nah, I do. What's up?"

Cam balled his fist, ready to strike, when Gray snatched him by the arm and pulled him back.

"Fuck him. He ain't even worth it." She placed her hand on his chest to calm him down.

She'd seen Cam in action. She didn't want him to go jail behind her, but when Cam was set off, there was no stopping him. His temper was like TNT. Once the sparks started to sizzle, there was very little time to duck and cover.

"You fuckin' this nigga?" Gunz demanded to know.

"Don't worry about who I'm fuckin'. Worry about your toothless baby mama."

"Fuck this shit. C'mon." Cam took her by the hand and escorted her out the building.

He could give a fuck about a basketball game now.

"Cam, are you serious? You gon' leave with this bitch? Look at what the fuck they did to my face!" LaLa yelled, holding her broken nose.

"I bet you'll mind your business next time!" Kema got in one last dig.

Outside, Quan placed her feisty-ass in the car, while Cam comforted Gray, who was on the verge of tears. Slow like a volcano, a wail rose in her chest that tore at her heart. When it hit her ears, she unconsciously fell into Cam's awaiting arms. A weight of sorrow flowed from her eyes. Gray's mind clouded with pain. Her heart grew cold and numb with pent up emotion. For so long, she'd been clogged up with anger, hurt, and fear. She'd been so scared to step out on faith and leave Gunz that now she had no choice. After what happened, she never wanted to see his face again. Crushed by the day's events, she sobbed into Cam's chest. The pain came in waves, minutes of weeping broken apart by short pauses for recovering breaths.

"How could he do this to me? Do you know this muthafucka had me get my tubes tied 'cause he said he ain't want no more babies?" She cried.

"Damn, for real?" Cam's heart ached for her.

"This nigga out here gettin' hoes pregnant after he took the chance of me ever having another baby away. Why would he do that?"

"Aye, look at me." He cupped her cheeks.

Gray's heavy lashes blinked with tears, as she tried to pull herself together.

"Listen, Star. I ain't one to be doing a bunch of talkin' but don't worry about none of that shit. It's his loss. Don't ever let no fuck-boy-ass nigga have yo' mind fucked up. Don't let that nigga take you off yo' square and have you showing out in public. Fuck that nigga. Fuck him, fuck his baby and fuck his bitch. I got you. He's nothin', my nigga. You see what that nigga and his bum-ass bitch is about. You're the one. Them other hoes ain't worth the ground you walk on."

Gray sniffled and continued to cry.

"Pick yo' fuckin' head up. What the fuck you cryin' for?"

"'Cause… I can't believe he told her our fuckin' business. Aoki doesn't even know he's not her father and that she was the product of rape."

"I don't mean no harm when I say this, but… you probably causing her more harm by keeping his bitch-ass in her life. Don't think she ain't seeing the way he do you. She gon' grow up and date a nigga just like his punk-ass and be cryin' about the shit to you. So, ultimately, it'll be your fault if it happen."

"What you mean? Gunz is a shitty boyfriend but he's a good father to her."

"You don't think she see all the dumb shit he do? You don't think she hear you cryin' at night when you waiting up for that nigga to come home? You don't think she know about him fuckin' other bitches and see you sittin' back and accepting the shit. C'mon, Star, you smarter than that. Honestly, you can't even blame him for doing it. You lettin' the shit happen."

"I don't want that nigga no more, and who the fuck are you to judge me?" Gray became enraged.

"'Cause I was you at one point! That bitch had me thinkin' I was about to be a daddy! Had me buying bassinets, strollers, picking out names, and all along it was some other nigga's baby. So, before you start runnin' off at the fuckin' mouth, read the whole story instead of judging a book by its cover."

All the air in Gray's lungs got caught in her throat. She had no idea Cam had been through so much. No wonder his heart was made of ice.

"Damn, Cam, I'm sorry." She hugged him tighter. "You know what? You're right."

"I'm right?" He drew his head back, surprised.

"Yeah." She looked up at his face.

"You know that's rare when a woman says that?"

"Says what?"

"You're right."

Gray dropped her head and laughed.

"I can't stand you."

"Let me look at you." He lifted her head.

Gently, he wiped her tears away and studied the features of her face. All he could think was she was one of a kind. Her pale, pink lips reminded him of a rose bud. Her top lip was thinner, but not too thin, and it had a natural Cupid's bow. Her bottom lip was larger and plusher. He wanted to lean forward and kiss her so bad, but Cam hadn't placed his mouth on a woman in four years.

"Don't ever let me see you cryin' behind that nigga again. Ya dig?"

"Yeah." She nodded.

Gray felt like a complete idiot for crying over Gunz in front of the man she was feenin' for. It was already clear Gunz wasn't on Cam's level. He paled in comparison, when it came to him. Cam was her knight in shining armor, he was heart-stopping gorgeous. There wasn't one, single feature on his face that made him so handsome, but his eyes came close. From them came an intensity, an honesty and a gentleness.

"Here, I think these belong to you." She took off his chains.

Cam kept his eyes on her, as he tucked them inside his pocket.

"Next time I see you, yo' mood better reflect your worth."

His words sent a jolt of electricity down to her clit.

"You tryin' to fuck me now or later?" She partly joked, turned on by his authority.

"Man, get yo' ass in the car." He opened the door for her.

Gray hopped into the driver seat and put on her seat belt. Cam leaned his head into the window.

"You calm now, Mohamed Ali?" He asked Kema.

"I'm Gucci," she laughed.

"A'ight, li'l Jean-Claude Van Damme. You up here kneeing bitches in the face like you the Karate Kid."

"You stupid."

"Straight up. You and Lil Scrappy got hands."

"Don't let the pretty faces fool you." Gray flipped her hair and smiled.

Cam licked his lips and held back the urge to stick his tongue down her throat.

"Take yo' sexy-ass home, Star." He stood up straight and adjusted his dick. "And I know you wore that cute-ass outfit for me. You ain't low." He said, as she started up the car.

"I did, but you ain't like it, so it don't matter."

"I never said that. Stop puttin' words in my mouth."

"Bye, Cam." She blushed, twirling her fingers.

Hating to see her go, he watched as she pulled off, with a scowl on his face.

"I thought you said you ain't got time for that shit right now?" Quan arched his brow. "Looks like somebody schedule opened all the way the fuck up."

"Get the fuck outta here." Cam laughed, as they walked back into building.

Little did Gray know, but he'd stacked his claim on her. Setting aside his past heartbreak, Cam made a solemn vow to make her his girl.

"Autumn in New York is often mingled with pain." – Frank Sinatra, "Autumn In New York"

Chapter 18

Chyna

All of Chyna's life, she'd dreamt of the day she'd get to go wedding dress shopping. After her disastrous break up with Tyriek, marriage was the furthest thing from her mind. The notion that she was unlovable had sunk into her brain and took up permanent residence. Love and commitment no longer existed in her world. Chyna reverted to ho Chyna with the quickness and never looked back. The only energy she invested into a man was a drunken, one-night stand or a meaningless date. All a man could offer her was dick and an entrée. Anything more, she knew came at the price of a broken heart.

When Carlos and L.A. came into her life, she tried to open her heart to loving them fully, but no matter how hard she tried, parts of her were still left on reserve. Then, a blast from her past named Basil Damien Shaw re-entered her life and turned everything upside down. He was like a tornado. He came in like a wrecking ball. He took no prisoners and made it his business to capture her heart. He made it impossible for her to run away from him or herself. He showed her what real love looked and felt like, and for that, there would never be a day that she wouldn't want him.

He was her lover, her confidant and her best friend. She never wanted to live without him. He brought out a softness in her that she didn't even know she possessed. Nothing with Dame was hard. Loving him was easy. Chyna was truly under his spell. The day she walked down the aisle to be his wife would be the best day of her life, even though she didn't get a say so in choosing their wedding date.

When Dame announced that they'd be getting married in two months, she lost her shit. The day Chyna Danea Black said 'I do' had to be a grand event. No one, including herself, ever thought she'd get her happily ever after. Everything had to be perfect. No expense could be spared. The shit couldn't be thrown together all willy nilly. The special day would not only be monumental for her, but India, her family, friends and readers as well. They'd read all the books based on her life and rooted for her to finally win in love. This wedding was as much for them as it was for her.

Wedding dress shopping had to be epic. Most brides dreamed of wearing Vera Wang on their wedding day, but Chyna always envisioned herself in Monique Lhuillier. When she'd tried to get an appointment and learned that there weren't any openings until spring 2019, her heart sank. Chyna broke down into a heap of tears. She still hadn't found her venue; the caterer hadn't been picked and the flowers she wanted were on back order. Thank God her husband-to-be was a well-connected man.

Dame was able to get her on the books with one phone call. He never wanted his belle to be upset. He would do anything to make Chyna smile. Which was why he flew Asia, Delicious and Brooke out to New York on his private plane to go dress shopping with her. He didn't want to invite Brooke but knew Chyna would be suspicious if he didn't. India was already in town with her mother, and Selicia lived in New York, so she was going to meet them there.

Chyna could hardly contain her excitement. She slept a total of three hours the night before her appointment. When it finally came time for her to get up, her day instantly went from joy to shit. Morning sickness kicked into overdrive and started kicking her ass. Chyna was huddled over the toilet for nearly an hour, puking her guts out. Once the vomiting subsided, she was so weak she could barely stand. She wanted to go back to bed and reschedule her appointment but couldn't. She had to find a dress that weekend. The wedding was only a month and a week away.

Chyna was so fatigued, she didn't even take pleasure in picking out an outfit to wear. She wished she could bury her face in Dame's chest and have him rub her back and tell her everything would be ok, but he had already gone to work. Things went from bad to worse when it came time to leave and Brooke was nowhere to be found. When she finally got ahold of her, she said she'd overslept and would arrive late. Chyna hadn't even stepped out the door and was ready to throw the whole day away.

Dressed in a gold Chanel necklace, white, long sleeve, wrap around top, black, leather, pleated skirt, Christian Louboutin strappy heels with a bow on the toe and a black Chanel bag, Chyna and her crew entered Monique Lhuillier's New York flagship store. As soon as they walked in, they were given the five-star treatment. Champagne was served to everyone except Chyna and India. They both had a glass of Ginger Ale.

Chyna felt like crap, but her mood brightened once she was surrounded by tulle, satin and lace. The ethereal, expensive gowns were nothing short of stunning. There wasn't a dress in the store she didn't want to try on. A consultant guided them all around the store, explaining the collections. Chyna was in couture heaven, but she was also overwhelmed. There were so many options and so little time. She literally had to pick a dress that weekend because it would still need time to be altered.

Chyna tried to stall trying on dresses because she wanted her so-called best friend to be there; but after 45 minutes of waiting for Brooke to arrive, she became fed up. Everyone else had showed up on time. There was no excuse for her to be late. Refusing to wait a second longer, Chyna picked out several gowns and headed to the private dressing room.

The first dress she tried on was a scalloped, lace, off-the-shoulder gown. When she stepped out, everyone smiled and admired the dress but there was a consensus that it wasn't the one. Ten dresses later, she tried on a flutter sleeve, embroidered, ball gown. She didn't even need her friend's opinion. She knew for a fact the dress wasn't it. It was so ugly, she didn't want to leave the dressing room. She looked like an old woman. There was so much fabric that the dress was swallowing her whole. Still reeling from morning sickness and feeling lightheaded from not eating, Chyna was ready to give up and go home but everyone insisted that she come out. Drained, she stepped out the dressing room and noticed Brooke strutting in like she was fucking Queen Elizabeth.

"That is super cute! Love it! Bag it up, bitch! That's the one!" She applauded.

Chyna eyed the dress then Brooke. She had to be kidding. The dress was matronly as hell. It was hideous on her.

"Are you high off bath salts?" Asia eyed Brooke, suspiciously.

"No. Why?" She sat next to her.

"Ain't no way in hell you think that dress is cute."

"I don't think it's cute. I think it's *fabulous, darling*. Garcon!" She snapped her fingers. "Champagne, please."

She smiled, and then focused her attention on Chyna. "I'm sure Dame will love it too."

"I wouldn't be caught dead gettin' married in this dress." Chyna frowned.

"No tea, no shade but you look like a bag of nickels in that getup," Selicia commented.

"Girl, Dame would fuck you up if you walked down the aisle in that bullshit," Delicious joked.

"Don't listen to him. I'm tellin' you, that dress is fly as hell." Brooke tried to convince her.

"Well, you wear it then 'cause I ain't buyin' it." Chyna picked up the hem of the gown, with an attitude.

"Maybe I will," Brooke smirked, devilishly.

The plan to break Chyna and Dame up was still in full affect. After Dame threatened to have her killed the night of Chyna's birthday party, it was obvious he didn't want Brooke like she wanted him, which infuriated her more. Never one to give up, she rethought her plans. Blackmailing Dame wasn't going to work, so the next best way to destroy his and Chyna's relationship was by making her wedding planning experience miserable as hell. If she could get Chyna so stressed out that she called off the wedding, Brooke's dreams would come true. It would be a cold day in hell before she and Dame walked off into the sunset, after how they'd done her. Loyalty and respect meant nothing to those two snakes. They had to pay for mistreating her and disregarding her feelings.

Starry-eyed, Chyna stepped out of the dressing room with a bright smile. The sleeveless, lace, trumpet gown she wore was a huge leap in the right direction.

"Nope! Wrong! Take it off! That is ug-ly! You look like a cake topper, girl. No!" Brooke made a spectacle.

"Well damn, tell me how you really feel." Chyna looked down at the dress.

She liked it, but now was having second thoughts.

"Girl, you trippin'. That dress is bomb as fuck." Delicious screwed up his face.

"Yeah, Mom, you look gorgeous," India said, with a glimmer of pride in her eyes.

She'd never seen her mother look more beautiful.

"Lies, fairytales and fallacies! You too damn short for that dress. All you see is titties and tulle. Nope!" Brooke argued.

Chyna's confidence, once again, plummeted. She was over dress shopping. At any minute, the tears she'd been trying to conceal would come rolling down her cheeks. Shopping for a wedding gown was nothing like she imagined it would be. The only thing that would make her feel better was some Chick-Fil-A, a warm bed and Dame's arms wrapped around her waist.

"Where did y'all find this bitch?" Selicia fumed.

She hated Brooke's guts.

"Selicia, stop." Asia urged.

"Nah, she been rude since she got here."

"Umm… who the fuck are you? I been friends with her for 26 years. I think I know what looks good on her and what don't," Brooke argued.

"And, bitch? I've known her 26 minutes and have been a better friend to her than you!" Selicia took off her jacket, ready to fight.

"Girl, you better put that skeet-ass jacket back on. You don't want it with me. Fuck around and get yo' big ass punched in the mouth," Brooke warned.

"Bitch, what's up?" Selicia rose to her feet. "I will beat yo' long-neck-ass the fuck up!"

"I don't know, Selicia, girl. She kinda big. She might can take you," Delicious instigated.

"I don't give a fuck. This bitch don't want no smoke!"

"Chyna, you better get her." Brooke eyed her.

"No, bitch. You get me!" Selicia pulled off her earrings.

"I'm sorry. We're going to have to ask you all to leave," the consultant said, in a nice, calm tone. "Chyna, it was a pleasure to meet you. We have made donations to the Black Lives Matter movement, but we cannot have ghetto buffoonery in our store."

"Ghetto?!" Chyna and her friends said in unison.

"Bitch, I'm far from ghetto. Do you know how rich I am?" Asia snapped.

"SECURITY! One of them is getting belligerent!" The consultant screamed for help.

"Let me get the fuck out of here before I go to jail." Chyna stormed back into the dressing room.

"That's Humpty Dumpty over here actin' like she ain't never been nowhere. Ghetto bitch, ain't got a lick of home training." Brooke grabbed her purse.

"Meet me outside! We about to slap box! Let's see if your mouth match your hands!" Selicia held the door open for her.

On the way home, Chyna gazed out the window, sadly. New York was such a vibrant city, but she couldn't even appreciate its splendor. Stress filled every inch of her body. There was no way she was gonna be able to pull off a wedding of this magnitude in a month and a week. So much had to be done, and she'd just gotten started. Chyna was starting to think that running off to Vegas and cloping would be the key to all her problems. Fuck a big wedding. As long as Dame became her husband, that was all that mattered.

A sense of calm washed over her, as they pulled up to Dame's house. She couldn't wait to fall into her beloved's arms. Mohamed opened her and India's doors and escorted them inside. When Chyna walked in, she was met with what looked like a firing squad. Dame had the entire staff lined up, as he cussed them clean out. She didn't know what they'd did but he was pissed. All she could see was his back muscles expand as he went off.

The navy blue, checkerboard-print blazer he wore was cut perfectly to fit his broad frame. Dame looked like a delicious tyrant that she wanted to devour. Her hormones started working into overdrive. Her pussy was aching to sit on his dick but all that had to wait. She had to figure out what was wrong with her man. Chyna wasn't surprised by his anger. She'd seen him on ten too many times to count, but India had never witnessed the wrath of her soon-to-be step-father. The last thing she wanted was for her to get the wrong impression of him.

"Dame." Chyna spoke, softly.

The sound of her velvety voice soothed the anger that roared inside of him. Chyna was the antidote for everything fucked up in his life.

"I'ma go up to my room." India scurried away, afraid.

To her, Dame was the big bad wolf. He was totally different from L.A. He never smiled. He didn't joke and play around. He was always serious. She could never tell how he was feeling. India liked Dame, but she honestly didn't understand what her mother saw in him.

"Get back to work." Dame excused his staff with a flick of his wrist.

He didn't like that India had seen him that way. His main priority was shielding her, her future brother or sister and their mother from any harm or discomfort, and he was already fucking up.

"Hi, baby." He walked over and took Chyna into his arms.

Dame placed his face in the crook of her neck and inhaled her heavenly scent. This was what he'd been craving all day. He hated to be apart from Chyna. When she was next to him, life seemed perfect. When she left, she took the best parts of him with her. Without her, he wasn't himself anymore. He reverted to his cold, callous ways. Dame was merely a broken shell of a man without her. He wished that he could extend the minutes in the day just so he could stay close to her, longer. He was safer in her embrace. With her, he started to believe that there was nothing in the world he had to fear. In Chyna's arms he found a peace he'd never known before.

"What's wrong?" She asked, caught off guard by his vulnerability.

Dame was holding onto her like if he let go she might disappear.

"Nothing." He answered, truthfully.

Dame didn't even know what he was mad about it. Ever since the night of the robbery, he'd been on edge. The weight of his betrayal was eating him alive. With each day that passed, his fear of losing Chyna grew greater. Brooke wasn't making it any better by constantly acting up. Dame detested when Chyna had to be around her alone. He never knew if when she returned she'd come back knowing the truth. Brooke was a loose cannon that needed to be put out of her misery. The only reason he hadn't put an end to her life was because it would raise too many questions and her death would destroy Chyna.

"I just missed you. That's all." He squeezed her tighter.

"I missed you too." She rubbed the back of his head and kissed his neck.

A few minutes went by where they just stood savoring each other's embrace.

"How my baby doing?" Dame placed his hand on her flat stomach.

"That li'l demon seed a'ight. He or she had me throwing up all this morning."

"Don't call my damn baby no demon seed. This baby is the second coming of Jesus."

"Between you being a murdering, ex drug lord and me being a reformed ho, ain't shit about this baby gon' be holy." Chyna cracked up laughing.

"You got my baby fucked up." Dame chuckled. "Nah, for real. You find what you were looking for?" He placed small kisses on her shoulder.

"No." Chyna burst into tears.

"Belle… what's wrong?" He held her at arm's length.

"It was horrible. Everything I tried on was ugly. I felt sick all day. Then Brooke showed up late and was tryin' to be funny. I'm just over it. I don't wanna do this anymore."

"You don't wanna do what no more?" Dame furrowed his brows. "I know you ain't sayin' you don't wanna marry me."

"Noooo… I don't wanna plan a wedding. It's too stressful. Why don't we just go to the justice of the peace or Vegas. That'll be much easier."

"Nah, we not doing that."

"Why?" Chyna whined.

"Cause, I know you. You would hate me if I didn't give you the wedding of your dreams."

"You don't know my life." She poked out her lip.

"I know yo' ass better than you know yourself. Besides, you ain't taking away the blessing of me seeing you walk down the aisle."

"You're really lookin' forward to that?" She sniffled.

"Yeah, I am." He wiped her tears away. "And our first dance too." He turned on Frank Sinatra's *Autumn In New York*.

Chyna loved when he played Old Blue Eyes. It always put him in a better mood. Dame pulled her close and swayed to the music. Dame was a big man, but he was as light as a feather on his feet. Cheek to cheek they slow danced around the living room. They were so wrapped up in each other that neither of them knew that India stood in the doorway watching. She'd never seen her mother happier. Dame might've been a brutal man with menacing eyes, but the love he had for her mom was abundant and clear.

Now she understood their dynamic. Her mother brought out the best in him. With her, Dame was a happier, more easy-going person. He could confidently let down his guard without fear of being judged. Around her, he was a teddy bear. Chyna was his anchor. India didn't have to worry that his love for her mother wasn't true. They were soulmates. They saw each other's flaws and accepted them. Nothing would change the way they felt about one another. He loved her in a way she'd never seen a man love a woman. It wasn't perfect, but it was pure and unconditional. The way love should be.

"I been feelin' a way about the way you make a way for all them other girls but me. You said I was the one, and you would ride until we die, but now you actin' differently." – Victoria Monet, "Freak"

Chapter 19

Mo

Growing up, Mo used to hate sitting underneath the dryer at the hair salon. It was always hot as Satan's ball sacks and it seemed like the stylist always made her sit longer than required, so they could finish up other clients. Now, as an adult woman with four kids, sitting under the dryer was a welcomed treat. It was like a mini vacation. She got to catch up on Instagram, read magazines and catch a few Z's. She loved it. If Mo could, she'd never return home. She never got to be away from the house anymore. It was like she was a prisoner in her own home.

Mainly, it was her fault why she felt that way. Her insecurities, infant son and suicidal thoughts caused her to imprison herself. She was trapped in her own mind. For the first time in months, she wasn't in her own head. As the heat from the dryer blew down onto her face, all her worries washed away. Mo was relaxed. Not an ounce of anxiety rushed through her veins. It felt good to be around her friends. She didn't realize how much she missed them until she stepped inside the salon.

Mina Gonzalez had been her best friend since 4th grade. They'd been through hell and back together. As they got older, the tides began to change and they couldn't spend as much time together anymore. Mina was busy running her hair empire. Over the years, she'd transitioned into selling hair care products and her own line of virgin, human hair. She also held it down as the wife of the top mob boss in the country. Between her hectic schedule and Mo's, it was hard to link up.

But true friendship wasn't defined by how many times a week you spoke or how often you saw one another. Mina and Mo could go days or even weeks without speaking and their bond was still there. When they did get together, it was always an event. They'd spent half the morning catching up on each other's lives, while Mo's other best friend, Delicious, added his two cents to the conversation. Gray showed up an hour into her appointment to get her hair done as well. She'd needed a new stylist and asked Mo if she had any suggestions. Mo, of course, told her about Mina's Joint Hair & Spa Salon. It was the best shop in town and one of the most exquisite.

The ceilings were made of mirrored tile. A $200,000 crystal chandelier hung from the center of the ceiling, giving the salon an opulent appeal. The walls were gold and white. Each station had white, oval-shaped, ceiling-to-floor mirrors. All the salon chairs were white, sleek and chic. The black, slick floor set the entire, rich space off.

On Fridays, the shop was always buzzing. Mo couldn't keep track of all the people that came in and out the door. Everybody was trying to get snatched for the weekend. The young girls around her seemed so happy to be alive. Their energy was palpable. Mo wished she could bottle it up and submerse herself in it. She missed getting her hair and nails done, and then hitting up the mall for a dope outfit to wear to the club. Her Friday nights now consisted of pumping breast milk, folding laundry and trying not to kill herself. Feeling herself going back into a dark place, she turned and looked at Gray.

She looked just as miserable as she did. Since she'd arrived, she'd had this faraway look in her eyes. The look was all too familiar 'cause it reminded Mo of her past and her present. Since the girls' playdate, she and Gray had gotten pretty cool. She liked her vibe. Gray was a down to earth chick who was about her business and her kids. Mo respected that.

Gray and Cam had also gotten close. Cam hadn't come out and said it, but he was feeling her. Anytime Gray's name was mentioned, his antennas perked up. Being the overprotective, li'l sister she was, Mo had to make sure another man wasn't occupying the heart her brother was trying to infiltrate.

"You ok, girl?"

"Girl… nah." Gray sighed. "I got so much shit going on it ain't even funny."

"Talk to ya girl. What's up?"

Gray hesitated, before speaking. She wasn't one to tell her business. She didn't want anyone judging her. She, especially, didn't want Mo to assume the worst of her. They'd just started their friendship. She didn't want it to end when it had just began.

"My baby daddy got a baby on the way with another girl."

"That's it? I thought yo' ass was dying or something. Girl, been there, done that and bought the t-shirt." Mo laughed.

Gray's eyes grew wide by the revelation.

"Join the 'I Got Fucked Over by A No-Good-Ass Nigga Club'. Quan had a baby on me too, girl."

"For real?"

"Girl, yeah. When we were engaged and after I had already had three miscarriages. Now, put that in your pipe and smoke it."

“Are you fuckin’ kidding me? That is so fucked up. How that nigga ain’t dead?”

“By the grace of God and the fact that I had the strength to move on.”

“Wooooow.” Gray said, astonished.

“Let me ask you a question.” Mo crossed her legs.

“Shoot.”

“You still love him?”

“As the father of my kids, yes, but nothing else. The love I had for Gunz been faded away. Only reason I stuck around this long was for my daughters. I ain’t want them to grow up in a single-parent home like I did; but now, I’m like, fuck it. I can’t sit around and take his bullshit no more. Me and my girls deserve better, and since he won’t move out, I started looking for me a new place.”

“I’m happy to hear you say that. Your happiness and your sanity comes first, ‘cause these niggas will drive you crazy if you let ‘em. They will literally have you in the hospital behind some shit they did, and be fucking the same nurse that’s tryin’ to take care of you. They don’t give a damn.”

“Ain’t that the truth.”

“I just don’t understand why he won’t leave me alone. I have asked him numerous times to leave but he won’t. Our relationship is done. He knows I don’t want his ass anymore, but he will not give up the apartment.”

“And he ain’t. That apartment ties y’all together. He knows that if he leaves, he won’t have anything besides the girls to keep y’all bonded. Yo’ baby daddy sound like the rest of these niggas. He don’t want you but he don’t want nobody else to have you either. He wanna be free to fuck around and get bitches pregnant and keep you tied to a leash. Don't you let that muthafucka take away all your good years. I was you once. I wasted years of my life, thinking I could change Quan and that shit didn't work. All I got out of it was three miscarriages and a dead baby. A muthafucka will only change if he wants to, and a nigga like Gunz is too stuck in his ways to change for anybody."

"You betta speak a word!" Delicious praise danced.

"You ain't said nothin' but the truth," Gray agreed.

"Do my brother know?"

"He was there when I found out the baby was his."

"And that nigga still breathing?"

"I told him he wasn't worth it. I care about your brother too much to have something bad happen to him on the strength of me."

"So, you do care about him?" Mo arched her brow.

"I don't care about him. I mean… I just… care about him." Gray blushed. "And you bet not say shit. He already cocky enough."

"I stay out of grown folk's business."

"Lies you tell!" Mina interjected, holding her daughter Savannah Marie. "You stay in my damn business."

"'Cause your business is my business." Mo shot back.

"Gray, what you gettin' all dolled up for? You going out tonight?" Mina quizzed.

"Nah. Me and the club don't mix."

"I kinda miss it." Mo admitted.

"You do?"

"Yeah, I feel like I'm an old lady now. I don't do shit besides complain and barely fuck my husband."

"Now that's a problem." Gray replied, stunned. "Looking the way you do, I would think your husband would be all over you."

"Boss stay wanting to fuck, but have you seen me? Girl, I look a mess." Mo scoffed.

"Mo? Stop playin'. You are a freak of nature. You are like scary beautiful. When I first met you, I was like, 'damn this bitch gorgeous'. I ain't even gay and I wanted to fuck you," Gray giggled.

"I ain't even have shit on when you came to my house."

"Have you looked in the mirror lately? You don't need a bunch of bells and whistles, like the rest of us, for people to notice you. Hell, I thought yo' ass was a former model or something."

"Now you bullshittin'."

"I put that on my kids." Gray swore, holding up her right hand.

"Wow… and here I was jealous of you 'cause you came over during the middle of the day lookin' all pretty with your hair, makeup and outfit on point, and I looked like some fat heffa that just rolled out of bed."

"Ma'am." Gray cocked her head to the side. "Fat where?"

"Gray? Look at this." Mo tugged at her stomach and thighs. "I'm big as hell."

Gray held her head back and laughed.

"Girl, bye. I'm fat. I'm a size 18. What are you, like a 12/13?"

"Yeah." Mo said, clearly uncomfortable with the number.

"Mo, you are not fat. You are thick, sis. There is a difference. Your body is banging. I wish I was shaped like you."

"I keep tellin' her dumb-ass ain't nothin' wrong with her." Delicious smacked his lips. "She act like she over there shaped like Miss Trunchbull." He referenced the principal from the movie *Matilda*.

Everybody laughed, including Mo.

"Girl, you betta get like me. I look in the mirror every day and I talk to every part of my body. I'm like, I love you, eyes. I love you, nose. I love you, stomach. I love you, thighs; and of course, I gotta thank my li'l kitty cat 'cause she takes that D like a champ." Gray patted her puss.

"You are a mess." Mo shook her head. "Ooh… let me call Boss and remind him to pick up the kids from school before I forget." She located her phone and dialed his number.

"Hello?" Zya answered, in a seductive tone.

Mo took the phone away from her ear to make sure she'd dialed the right number. Sure enough, she'd called her husband, so who was the bitch answering his phone?

"Who in the fuck is this?" Mo pushed the dryer off her head, so she could hear clearly.

"May I ask who's callin'?" Zya asked, like Mo's name didn't come up on the caller ID.

"His fuckin' wife. Now, who the fuck is this?"

"Oh… it's you." Zya rolled her eyes. "This is Zya. What can I do for you?"

"You can put my fuckin' husband on the phone before I put my foot up yo' ass!" She seethed with anger.

"His hands are wet right now. I'ma have him call you back later." Zya hung up, before Mo could get out another word.

"Did this bitch just hang up on me?" She held the phone in awe.

"Uh ah! Whose ass we gotta beat?" Delicious put his flat irons down.

"I'ma kill 'em." Mo shot up from her seat and paced the floor.

She felt like a complete fool. Here she was giving Gray advice about her cheating-ass man, when it seemed like her husband was cheating too.

"Calm down, Mo. What happened?" Mina rushed over to her friend.

Before she could answer, Mo's phone rang. It was Boss calling her back.

"Hello?" She answered with an attitude.

"Fuck is wrong wit' you?" Boss said, caught off guard by her anger.

"Why the fuck was that bitch answering your phone?"

"'Cause my hands was wet. She told you I was gon' call you right back."

"Why the fuck where your hands wet, Boss? Was you playin' in that bitch pussy?"

Boss bugged up laughing.

"What is wrong with you? Why would you ask me some shit like that?" He continued to laugh.

"Uh ha-ha, hee-hee! Do you hear me laughing? Ain't shit funny! Answer the question, nigga. Matter fact, put your fingers up to the phone, so I can smell 'em."

"You fuckin' crazy. I'm not doing this shit wit' you today," Boss replied, amused by his wife's antics.

"FaceTime me right now so I can see your hands. If I see anything glistening, I'm beating yo' ass! Everybody is dying!"

"Man, finish gettin' your hair done so I can go pick up my kids from school. I'll holla at you later, li'l crazy-ass girl."

"Zaire, don't you hang up on me!"

"Bye, Mo. I love you." He hung up anyway.

"Hello? Hello?" She looked at the phone to see if the call was still connected but it wasn't. "Y'all about to see me on the five o'clock news."

"What happened?"

"I think that nigga is cheating on me."

Everybody in the shop cracked up laughing.

"Bye, Fe'Mo! First of all, that nigga ain't crazy. He knows we will jump him," Mina argued.

"Nah, this li'l bitch he got working for him name, Zya, is pushing up on my man."

"Dark skin Zya?" One of the stylist named Neosha chimed in.

"Yeah, you know her?"

"Yeah, I know she a ho. You might have to kill that bitch. She goes hard."

"Aww hell nah! See, I'm about to be on the five o'clock news and on the front of the newspaper."

"No, bitch, it's time for you to come out of retirement. You gotta remind these hoes who the fuck you are and get yo'self together." Delicious pointed at her outfit.

"What's wrong with the way I look?" Mo glanced at herself in the mirror.

"Umm, bitch… you walked out the house wearing a fuckin' onesie. A onesie," he stressed.

"So, I'm just at the shop."

"You look like a homeless Ghostbuster."

"I hate to say it, friend, but you look a mess." Mina chose her words carefully.

She knew Mo was in a fragile state.

"Is it really that bad?"

"YES!" Everybody in the shop said at once.

"Well, damn."

"We giving you a makeover," Delicious concluded.

"Ooh… I love makeovers! I used to do them all the time, when I had my magazine." Gray clapped her hands, excited.

"Bet. I'ma do your hair and makeup and Gray you can help with her outfit."

"I'ma start looking for some stuff now."

"I appreciate it, you guys, but a makeover isn't necessary." Mo shook her head.

"Yes, the fuck it is, if you wanna keep yo' man. We gon' hook you up and you takin' yo' ass up to that damn bar tonight. Remind yo' husband what he got waiting for him at home and set that bitch straight face to face. Okkuuurrr!"

"You're right! I'm about to go up there and fuck up some shit!"

“Bless your soul. You got your head in the clouds.” – Adele, “Rumor Has It”

Chapter 20

Mo

"I get it how I live it.

I live it how I get it.

Count the muthafuckin' digits.

I pull up wit' a lemon.

Not 'cause she ain't living.

It's just your eyes get acidic."

N.E.R.D's hit song, *Lemon,* bumped throughout Babylon, as Mo sashayed her way through the crowd. The music was so loud that it made her skin tingle and her lungs feel like mush. The bass thumped in time with her heart beat, as though they were one, filling her from head to toe with bass. She hadn't stepped foot inside the building since the renovations were done. She had to admit, she and Boss had created something magical.

The vibe throughout the bar was Egyptian. Amber, dimmed lights, black, satin curtains, black, tufted, leather couches, along with numerous hookahs filled the space. They had a fully-stocked bar and a kitchen that served the best Thai chili wings and mac & cheese balls in town. The atmosphere was hype as hell. The crowd was made up of 20 somethings. They rubbed shoulders, forgetting that their toes were often stepped on or that they were in closer proximity to strangers than they were their own family and friends.

Hundreds of conversations were spoken in elevated tones, all competing with the rap music being played. The stagnant stench of tobacco swirled in a dirty cloud of smoke above Mo's head, as she looked for her husband. Gray was right by her side. She'd practically begged her to tag along. Thank God, she had. Mo didn't know what she'd do without her. After the makeover she'd been given, she needed all the support she could get. She couldn't wait to see the look on Boss' face when he saw her.

A nauseating smell of alcohol wafted her way, as she dipped through the sea of partygoers. The place was so crowded, it took forever to find Boss. When she did, she found him by the DJ booth, talking to Zya. Mo couldn't make out what they were saying, but laughter rang in the air. *What the fuck could she have possibly said that was so fuckin' funny? That nigga knows his laughter is reserved for me,* she thought. It really pissed her off that he looked so good while engaging in conversation with her.

A San Diego Padres hat rested low over his eyes. He donned a black, graphic tee, black, fitted, ripped jeans with an orange and black lumber jack shirt wrapped around his waist and Shattered Backboard Air Jordan 1's. Diamond stud earrings and several, gold chains gleamed under the recessed lights. Boss looked good. He looked damn good. His thick beard and tattooed arms had all the bitches salivating over him, including Zya. Mo wanted to slap fire out of her dick-sucking mouth. She was doing that touchy-feely shit again; and once more, Boss hadn't stopped her.

Ready to regulate, Mo told Gray she'd be back. With the spirit of 2006 Mo, she walked up on Boss and shot him a look like,' nigga, really?'. Boss was shocked to see his wife standing before him, looking like she'd stepped fresh off the runway. He barely recognized her. Mo looked good. No, fuck that. She looked good as fuck. The sassy girl with enough confidence she could bottle it up and sell it was back. From head to toe, she was perfection.

A black, leather, Moschino, newsboy cap rested on top of her 30-inch hair. Wispy eyelashes enhanced her doe-shaped eyes, while a deep burgundy lipstick painted her full lips. Three, gold chokers and a gold Jesus piece chain decorated her neck. A black fur covered the maroon, lace-trimmed, spaghetti strap, slip dress she wore underneath. Black, Dsqaured2, snake skin, Riri heels and a Chanel bag completed her hood and bougie look. A pride like no other filled Boss' heart, as he lusted after his wife. He didn't know what brought on her new look, but he was here for it all.

"Well, look at what we have here," Mo said, with contempt, as she eyed Zya.

"To what do I owe this surprise?" Boss grinned, happy as hell to see her.

Without hesitation, he left Zya's side and extended his arms for Mo to hug him.

"I came to check on my investments. A girl has to make sure her assets are still in place." She referred to him and Babylon.

"Whatever it is, I'm just happy to see you." Boss' tattooed hands roamed her backside. "You look good as fuck, ma." He squeezed her bare butt cheeks. "You ain't got on no drawgz?"

"Nope." She smiled, mischievously.

"Oh, you tryin' to give a nigga some ass tonight."

"If you play your cards right."

"Hold up." Boss stepped back. "Who at home with the kids?"

"The twins and King are at my dad's and Zaire is with Mina."

"You know I don't like my kids around just anybody."

"Since when did my dad and Mina become just anybody?" Mo quipped.

"Babe, yo' dad is old as dirt. He ain't got no business watching the kids. They gon' be over there practically takin' care of themselves."

"God forbid I have a night off. I'll just stay in the house, while you come and go as you please."

"That's not what I'm sayin'!"

"Then what the fuck are you sayin'?" Mo yelled back.

"I'm sayin', let me take a look at you." Boss cracked a smile and spun her around.

Boss' dick was brick hard, as he stared at his wife's long, cocoa legs and pretty feet. Their wedding day was the last time he'd seen her so bold and confident. He wished she could be like this every day. The smile plastered on Mo's face was mesmerizing.

"Yeah, we going for baby number five tonight." He smacked her hard on the ass.

"Ahem!" Zya cleared her throat, to get his attention.

He'd completely forgotten she was standing there.

"My bad." Boss held Mo by her waist. "Zya, you remember Mo, don't you?"

Zya bit her bottom lip and pretended to think.

"Aww… yeah. I remember you. You're his sister, right?"

"No, li'l bitch. I'm his wife, and you gon' quit playin' wit' me, ok?" Mo tried to attack her.

"Baby, chill." Boss held her back by her waist.

He didn't know what had gotten into Mo.

"Nah, she keep tryin' me like I won't fuck her up! Now, I don't know what you thought, but this one right here..." She pointed at Boss. "…is off limits. He is a married fuckin' man with four kids and a wife that will stomp a mud hole in you!"

"I am so sorry. I meant no disrespect. I honestly thought you were Zaire's sister." Zya played innocent. "I am not tryin' to push up on your man. Zaire is my employer. It is strictly professional between us. I would never cross the line."

"See, you tryin' to be funny right now. Didn't I tell you to call him Boss?" Mo tried to get at her, again.

"Zaire said it was ok." Zya conjured up some fake tears. "Like, I don't know what I did wrong, but I'm honestly not tryin' to cause any drama. I would never go after a married man. Maybe I should just leave?"

"Yeah, maybe you should."

"I'm gonna go." Zya cried, walking off.

"Hold up, man. Wait." Boss pulled her back, to Mo's shock and disappointment. "Both of y'all need to chill. I think this is all just one big misunderstanding."

"Misunderstanding my ass! I know when a bitch is tryin' to fuck my husband," Mo spat, irate.

"Zya, go to the back and get yourself together, and then go make sure we ain't running low on liquor," Boss ordered.

"Ok." She sniffled.

Once she was out of ear shot, Boss turned to Mo with an angry scowl on his face.

"Yo, what's up wit' you? You come in here wit' ya Puff Daddy fur on, tryin' to be funny on some pop-up shit, I guess to see if I'm fuckin' wit' ol' girl."

"No lie has been spoken," she agreed, rolling her neck.

"You really think I'm fuckin' her?"

"Yeah," she responded, to see how he'd react.

"Really, Mo?"

"If the voices in my head say you cheatin', you cheatin'. Fuck I'ma lie to myself for?"

"Yo, you are nuts." Boss bugged up.

"No, for real. I don't think you're cheatin' but homegirl tryin' to fuck you."

"Even if she was, what the fuck am I gon' do wit' that li'l girl? She can't do shit for me. I don't want her."

"Well, she wants you."

"And? You know how many bitches wanna fuck me? I curve pussy left and right. I ain't tryin' to fuck up my home for no minimum wage pussy."

"You bet not, 'cause if I ever find out you cheated on me, I will go and get some tinfoil, make a cone out of it, fill it up with water, freeze it, make an ice pick, stab you and the bitch, let the ice pick melt, throw the tinfoil away and no one would ever know how you were murdered; 'cause guess what? There's no murder weapon."

"The fact that you have thought about killing me in such detail, low-key scares me, but umm… straight up. Zya is a good manager. She ain't did nothin' out the way, and if she does try somethin', I'ma dead that shit."

"No, you better fire her ass," Mo ordered.

"That's already understood. But you can't be coming up here tryin' to fight the employees. They haven't even met you yet."

"You betta show them muthafuckas a picture or somethin'."

"For real, Mo?" Boss cocked his head to the side.

"I'm just sayin'." She shrugged.

"Really?" He glared at her.

"Sorry," Mo apologized, feeling bad.

She didn't want their employees to think she was some ghetto, deranged, insecure wife, but her woman's intuition was telling her that Zya was up to no good. She wished Boss could see that she was a snake in the grass.

"Now, can we please stop talkin' about this shit. I'm tryin' to see what you got on under this big-ass wolf pussy you call a fur." Boss slid his hands down the curves of her hips.

"You ain't said nothin' but a word, Daddy." Mo slipped out of the coat and gave him a 360 view.

Boss let his eyes slide over her body. He gazed upon her perfect, mahogany form and thanked God she was his. The next thing Mo knew, his lips crashed into hers, nearly knocking the wind from her lungs. She barely had a second to process what was happening, before he pushed his tongue into her mouth. She eagerly granted him access and twirled her tongue around his. Mo's arms circled around his tattooed neck. The kiss was sloppy and wet, just how she liked it.

This was what she'd been missing. It had been ages since she last felt connected to her husband. Wrapped in his arms, she held on tight, as he carried her to his office. Boss slammed the door shut with his foot. There would be no waiting till they got home. They were about to fuck now. He missed pulling her head back by her hair and sinking his teeth in her neck while she clawed at his skin. At one point in time, he used to have Mo's pussy for breakfast, lunch and dinner.

They were long overdue for a fuck session. On the couch, he lay beside her. Mo gazed up into his chocolate brown eyes, as he lifted the hem of her dress and pressed his fingers on her clit. 'Round and 'round his fingers went, as he breathed life into her lungs with his kisses.

"Oh fuck." She moaned.

"Mmm hmm," Boss egged her on.

The more he played with her pussy, the wetter she became. Turned on by her arousal, he dipped his fingers in and out of her canal, and then smeared her cream onto her hardened clit. Boss was strumming her center like it was a guitar. All Mo could do was buck and moan. He was about to make her cum. Boss could feel her legs begin to shake, as he quickened his pace. The faster he rotated his fingers, the more she wound her hips – until, suddenly, she came.

Panting heavily, Mo bit into her bottom lip, as he pushed her dress up and exposed her cinnamon-colored breasts. Mo's erect nipples pebbled underneath the touch of his soft lips. Boss couldn't wait any longer. He had to feel her. As he licked and sucked her breasts, he unzipped his jeans and pulled out his hard dick. Mo pressed her thighs together, in anticipation of feeling him inside her. She missed her chocolate cocaine. Licking his fingers, Boss resumed massaging her pussy. He wanted to make sure she was nice and wet when he entered her.

"I need you, baby." Mo wrapped her hand around his thick, veiny cock and started stroking his dick.

"You do?"

"I need you inside of me," she whined, as his dick hardened with each jerk of her wrist.

"You wanna cum again, don't you?"

"Yes."

"You wanna cum on Daddy's fingers or on Daddy's dick?"

"Both."

"Then do your thang. Cum for me, baby." He circled his fingers clockwise until her body spasmed.

Mo was shaking and screaming like a lunatic. Pleased with himself, he rose to his feet. Silence filled the room, as he stripped down to nothing. His corded muscles rippled, with each movement of his limbs. Boss looked like a man who had picked up heavy objects and put them down, and then did that again a few billion times. The hours he spent in the gym had done his body good. Mo lay with her legs spread, eagerly awaiting his return. On his knees, Boss held his 10-inch dick in his hand and rubbed it up and down her slit.

"Mmmmmmm." Mo closed her eyes.

"Shit." Boss groaned, as her pussy juices coated his dick.

Slowly, he inched his way inside her warm pussy. Mo's right leg was draped over his shoulder, as he leaned forward and kissed her lips. She could barely breath but somehow was able to inhale and exhale. Boss had completely filled her up. Sweet moans danced in circles around their silhouettes. Together, they rocked to a steady rhythm. Boss' cock grew bigger with each stroke. Mo's moans of gratification were driving him crazy. Eleven years later, and her pussy was still the best he'd ever had.

"Oh fuck! Mmmmmmm." She tried her best to keep up.

"Fuck." Boss pressed her right thigh against her left.

Hitting it sideways, he gripped her titty and slapped her ass cheek.

Mo's bottom would be red and stinging when they got through, but it didn't matter because it felt so good.

"Give it to me. Give me this pussy." He rubbed her clit, while deep stroking her pussy.

"Ooh… yeah."

"That dick feel good, don't it?"

"Yes." Mo purred.

Mo could feel him all the way in her cervix. Ready to bust it wide open, she pinned her legs back with her arms and watched as his dick slid in and out of her slit. Mo's sopping wet pussy was on full display, as Boss licked his thumb and began attacking her clit, again. The combination of his meaty cock hitting her spot and him playing with her nub had Mo calling out for Jesus. If the music inside the club wasn't so loud, she was sure everyone would've heard her screams. Gripping her neck with both his hands, Boss stared into her sparkly eyes, as he quickened his pace.

"Ooh, baby, it feels so good. Don't ever stop fuckin' me," Mo begged.

A low, visceral growl roared from Boss' chest. Back and forth he pumped his cock. His balls slapped against her ass, as he flicked his finger across her clit.

"Ooooh fuck! Yes-yes-yes! Oh my god. I'm cumming, Boss! I'm cumming!" Mo squealed, as her juices poured onto his hand.

"Goddamn, I missed this pussy."

"And I missed this dick. Let me taste you."

Doing as he was told, Boss eased his way up her torso and planted his fat dick in front of her face. Mo raised her head and took his balls into her mouth, and then licked her way up his shaft to the tip of his dick. She loved the sweet and sour taste of his precum on her tongue. Never once breaking eye contact, she sucked on the head while Boss looked back at her in distress.

"There you go. Suck that dick, baby." He ran his fingers through her soft hair.

The more he encouraged her, the further she slid him down her throat. While she sucked his dick, he reached behind him and played in her wet pussy.

"You about to cum again?"

"Yes." Mo devoured his dick.

Spit drooled down her chin, as his cock hit her tonsils. Mo was a freak. Boss loved when she got nasty with it. Every time she licked it, he lost it. A young bitch wouldn't know how to satisfy him like her.

"Mmmmmmm! Yes! Oh my god." She jerked him off with her hand, as he assaulted her pussy.

A cold shiver ran up her spine, as he took her by the neck and lightly restricted her airway. The sensation of his hot breath on her ear and his fingers around her neck in a chokehold
sent Mo over the edge. Her entire body quacked, as she came for the third time. Boss couldn't get enough of his wife. Stopping for a second, he grinned. Mo looked like she'd passed out. Nowhere near done with her, he lay behind her. Lifting her leg, he plunged his manhood deep inside her walls and fucked her from behind.

"You like that?" He sucked on her earlobe.

"Yes, baby. Give it to me. I love this cock."

"My pussy wet. Look at her. Look how she actin' up." Boss placed his finger in her mouth; then, without warning, buried his face in between her legs.

Locking both his arms around her thighs, he placed a kiss on her clitoris that left her aching for more. Mo was speechless. Her entire body was on fire. Boss' tongue circled her clit, as two of his fingers explored her warm tunnel. A thunderous climax built in her groin that she tried to fight but it was a losing battle because Boss refused to let up. When his lips closed around her clit, she tried to run, but he held her hostage. Viciously, he sucked and kissed her center 'til she came. Mo's body convulsed until she went completely numb. Coming up for air, Boss lay behind her and resumed fucking her savagely.

"I want you to cum," he whispered, repeatedly, into her ear.

"I don't think I can cum again."

"You can and you will." He slapped her ass cheek.

"Oooooooh, baby, give me that big dick."

Boss continued to zero in on her G-spot.

"Right there, baby! Ooooh yeah, you hittin' my spot! I can't take it!"

"You gon' take this dick. You gon' take it like a big girl, ain't you?"

"I'ma take it like a big girl. I'ma take it. Ooh… it feel so good. Oh my god, I'm cumming!" Mo whimpered, as tears fell from her eyes.

Boss could feel her pussy tighten around his rock-solid shaft, as she came.

"Ass in the air," he demanded.

On all fours, Mo tooted her butt in the air and tried to steady her breathing. It felt like she was having an asthma attack. Boss walked across the room. When he came back, he tied her wrist together with a piece of cloth. Then, he tied her right thigh to her right leg and her left thigh to her left leg, so she wouldn't be able to extend them. Boss had full control of her body and could do with her as he pleased. He and Mo had never fucked this way before. He didn't know how she would respond to being bound, but she seemed to like it.

Boss held onto her waist and pounded her pussy doggystyle. Not being able to run or stretch her legs as he put her in a choke hold from behind had Mo spiraling out of control. He was her addiction. She couldn't live without him. Their sexual chemistry was intoxicating and crazy addictive. Eleven years ago, he turned her out and she'd been sprung ever since. She was obsessed with him. Once again, her creamy cum coated his dick. This was why they had four kids together. This was why he had that chocolate cocaine. Only Boss had the ability to make her cum over and over again without even cumming once. His dick game was insane.

"Ooooh… yes, Daddy. Fuck me-fuck me-fuck me! Give me that dick."

"I love this pussy, Mo. You bet not ever give my shit away."

"I won't, baby, I swear."

Stroke after stroke, they made sweet love. Roughly, Boss pressed her face into the couch cushions, as he hit it hard from the back. Mo's ass cheeks rippled with each thrust of his hips. Boss' eyes rolled to the back of his head, as the endorphins in his body rushed to his dick, and then his head. He was about to ejaculate. He could feel it building, as he fucked Mo deeper, harder and rougher. Balls deep, his cock swelled and then a burst of creamy, thick cum shot into her womb.

Outside the door, Zya watched as he placed sweet kisses all over Mo's back and butt cheeks. They were so into each other that they had no idea she'd been watching them the whole time. Seeing Boss fuck the air out of Mo's lungs only made her want him more. Zya imagined him taking turns fucking her ass, and then her mouth, as Mo watched on enviously. In her mind, it should've been her he was fucking. Mo didn't deserve or appreciate him.

Anybody that popped up dressed like a Fly Girl from *In Living Color* was nowhere on his level. Boss needed a boss bitch by his side. A chick that wasn't afraid to make money moves. Zya was that girl. She'd been the one by his side every night running Babylon while his dumpy wife sat at home all day on her fat ass doing nothing. Sooner rather than later, Boss would come to his senses. He would soon see that Zya was the only woman he needed.

"Purple in the sky. Cruisin' highway 85. Thought I saw a shooting star beaming in your haunting eyes." – Ari Lennox, "Night Drive"

Chapter 21

Gray

I heard that pussy for the taking.

I heard it got these other niggas goin' crazy.

Rihanna sang, as Gray Dutty Wine to the beat of DJ Khaled's summer hit, *Wild Thoughts*. Everybody in Babylon was going crazy. The song was everyone's jam. Mo was even on the other side of the room, grinding her ass on her husband's dick. She was getting her life and Gray was here for it. Mo and Boss were a stunning couple. She was beautiful, and he was fine as fuck. They were madly in love, which made Gray slightly jealous. It was sickening how much they loved each other. Every time Mo smiled, Boss' eyes lit up. No other woman in the room existed to him but her.

Seeing them together made Gray wish she had someone in her life that loved her just as much. She thought at one time she and Gunz had the same kind of love, but now nothing seemed concrete. She didn't even know who he was anymore. Maybe he'd always been a fucked-up individual and she'd overlooked it. Gray couldn't dwell on the past. After learning the baby was definitely his, she was moving on like Mya. Gunz and his child bride could have each other.

Gray was focused on her future. After giving Mo her makeover and seeing how much confidence it gave her, she realized she might have come up with a new business idea. She'd truly enjoyed helping Mo pick out looks that fit her post-baby body. If more women had someone like Gray who knew fashion to help them after giving birth, maybe, so many women wouldn't find themselves in a rut. Not only did she want to help women who had just given birth, but women in general who didn't know how to shop for their body type. The idea she'd come up with could be lucrative. Her next step would be mapping out a business plan.

Pulling out her phone, she decided to Snapchat her turn up. It had been ages since she last posted something to social media. Panning the camera around the room, she videoed everyone dancing. When the camera landed on Cam, she immediately stopped recording. There he was, leaning up against the bar, talkin' to some chick. Gray's heart rate slowed. Her face burned green with envy. It was becoming increasingly hard to deny her feelings for him.

His butterscotch skin, almond-shaped eyes, bad boy persona and 'I don't give a fuck' attitude sent her emotions through the roof. It was damn near disrespectful for a man to be so alluring. The diamond-encrusted Cuban link chain, Supreme t-shirt, black jeans with rips on the knees and Air Jordan 1's had her pussy doing cartwheels. His wrist dripped with diamonds. Each finger on his right hand had a blinged out ring on it. She wondered how much ice he owned and why he hadn't mentioned going out.

They'd talked earlier that day and he hadn't said anything. She hadn't either, so she couldn't be mad. It wasn't like she was his girl. He didn't have to tell her his whereabouts. Knowing this, she shouldn't have been upset but she was. Seeing Cam all in another chick's face had her tight. He was hers and she was about to make that known. Cam didn't have a problem actin' up when he saw her talking to other men, so he couldn't be mad when she returned the favor.

"Cam!" She placed her hand on her hip.

Cam took his eyes off the girl trying to throw her pussy at him and looked at Gray. She was the last person he thought he'd see. Gray hated going out. Once he got over the initial shock of seeing her, he took in her outfit. The fact that she'd came out the house wearing nothing but a gold, Chanel choker, white, Givenchy t-shirt dress with a black, leather belt tied around her waist and black, Francesco Russo, caged heels infuriated him. If she bent over, her whole ass would be out.

"I know you seen me callin' you!" She got in his face, which shocked him even more.

"What?" He looked down at his phone, confused.

Gray hadn't called him.

"Ray-Ray, Shameka, Ta'Rhonda, Cam-Cam and Tyliv, been askin' for they daddy. You said you was gon' take us shopping for school supplies today! What happened to that, nigga? What about the kids, Cam? What about the kids? What about us?" Gray spoke like a true, ghetto baby mama.

"You said you ain't have no kids." The girl looked at Cam for clarity.

"I don't. I don't know what the fuck she talkin' about."

"Oh, now you ain't got no kids? You wasn't sayin' that when you was beggin' me not to put you on child support. Nigga, I'm pregnant wit' yo' sixth baby right now. Ain't that right, Quan?"

"Yeah, how my god-kids doing?" He played along.

"They a'ight. Just missing they no-good daddy. I'm so sick of you lying to me, Cameron. I don't even know why I stay wit' yo' ass. You forever cheating and giving me shit. I'm tellin' you now, girl, run while you still can. This nigga got a dirty dick. He gave me the clap and gon' lie and say he got it from sitting on a public toilet seat. Ain't that about a bitch?"

"Yo, you buggin'." Cam laughed.

"I'm good. I ain't got time for this." The girl shot him a look of revulsion, before storming off.

"Aye! She lyin'! Come back!"

When the girl was out of sight, Gray burst out laughing.

"That's some bullshit. I should beat yo' ass. I was baggin' that pussy up for later." Cam pretended to be mad.

"Not on my watch, sir."

"I can't believe you just did that. Now muthafuckas gon' think I'm runnin' around here with the clap."

"You'll be a'ight." Gray patted his firm chest.

"I swear to God, you ain't shit." Cam shook his head.

If anybody else had pulled that shit, they would've ended up in a body bag, but Gray held a small piece of his heart. She could get away with pretty much anything.

"What the fuck you doing out? Let me find out you here with another nigga." He frowned.

"I'm actually here with your sister." She pointed across the room in Mo's direction.

"You got my lame-ass sister to come out the house?"

"It's the opposite. She asked me to come out tonight."

"Where my baby at?" Quan questioned.

"You talkin' about Kema or Mo?" Gray quizzed.

"Damn. Really? Why you gotta do me like that? I just had your back."

"I'm just fuckin' wit' you. Kema's on a date."

"A date?" Quan frowned.

"Yeah."

Quan gulped down his glass of Henny and put his emotions back in check. Kema wasn't his girl. She could fuck with who she wanted. That still didn't stop him from feeling some type of way. Chicks stayed on his dick, but Kema kept giving him the cold shoulder.

"Where the girls at?" Cam asked.

"Over their cousin's house."

"So that mean you stayin' wit' me tonight?"

"It depends."

"On what?"

"If you give me a reason to want to stay wit' you," Gray challenged.

"I like this li'l ponytail thing you got going on." Cam toyed with a piece of her hair.

She had it up in a messy ponytail with a single French braid going down the center of her head. He didn't like that she was practically naked, but her beauty couldn't be denied.

"Thanks." Gray played it cool.

She wasn't about to play herself by fawning all over Cam. He ran hot and cold. One minute he acted like he wanted her, then the next he put her in the friend zone.

"What you drinkin'?" He turned towards the bar.

"You buyin'?"

"Not if you keep askin' stupid questions."

"I'll have a Patron Margarita with no salt."

Three drinks later, Gray was nice and tipsy. Her, Cam, Quan, Boss and Mo kicked it the rest of the night. The tension between Quan and Boss was thick. Whenever Quan would speak to Mo, Boss would catch an attitude. Gray sympathized with him. It had to be tough being around his wife's ex fiancé. Especially, with all the history they had. Gunz would never hang around any of her ex's.

Turnt off Patron, Gray danced in front of Cam. He blew smoke from the hookah and watched her ass bounce as she twerked. Gray knew exactly what she was doing. She was putting on a show just for him. The shit was sexy as hell. Gray could dance her ass off. Every time she wound her hips, he caught a glimpse of her ass cheeks. For weeks, he'd been lusting after her. No other woman, since LaLa, held his attention this long. Cam wanted to put their friendship on the back burner and cross over to lovers, but was hesitant. He knew himself.

He'd been playing a game of peek-a-boo with her since they met. He'd flirt and get close, then the closeness would trigger a panic in him, causing him to turn cold as ice. Cam would become afraid of his feelings and retreat. Then, when the fear of being hurt subsided, he'd go back to being flirty and affectionate. So far, he'd been careful not to cause any damage to Gray's heart, but if he took it there with her, he might.

"Come here." He wrapped his arm around her shoulders and pulled her close.

Cam was cross-faded and ready to sample a taste of Grey's honey-colored flesh. The second she landed in his arms, he felt whole. Cam bathed in her warmth and the clean, magnolia scent of her Kilian perfume. In his mind, he thanked God for her existence, and hugged her tightly. Despite the heaviness in Gray's stomach, it fluttered at the feeling of her body being pressed against his. She sunk into the heat of his embrace, appreciative of the romantic gesture. Cam was finally letting it be known that he saw her as more than a friend.

With her back to his chest, Gray ground her ass into his hard cock, as he held her close by the waist. 21 Savage's *My Choppa Hate Niggas* played as Cam rapped along. Wanting to document the moment, Gray pulled out her iPhone and recorded him. Cam blew a cloud of smoke into the camera, as he rapped:

Hang around a lot of gang-bangin'-ass niggas.
Crip, Blood, blue or red, what you bang, nigga?
You might gotta pistol but this stick is way bigger.
I call it KKK, 'cause my choppa hate niggas.

Muthafuckas was gon' be mad when they saw them boo'd up together but neither of them cared. Cam and Gray looked good as hell together. The video ended with his tattooed arm wrapped around her neck, as he kissed her cheek and she smiled.

Together, they vibed to the music and shared a hookah pipe. When the DJ played TXS ' *Good 2 U,* Gray lost herself in the melody. The song was the perfect representation of her feelings towards Cam. She couldn't help but lip sync the words to him.

See you posted at the bar.
She know how to spot 'em out.
She know what that money 'bout.
You know what I'm talkin' 'bout.
Got a lotta bitches in yo' pocket you don't like it tho'.
I can see the two of us together like a psychic tho'.
I know what to say to make your mood change.
I'm thinkin' that I should be your boo thang.
I'm thinkin' that me and you can do thangs.
Fuck that old shit, this a new thang. Oh and I.

Can't blame you for havin' your wall up,
Can't blame you 'cause that's what that taught ya.
(That's the one bad thing about men with money)
Everybody wants something.
They don't wanna give nothing.
It's probably why you can't trust 'em.

I just wanna love him. Oh baby.

I can be so good to you.

Cam watched her mouth the words with a cocky grin on his face. He liked seeing Gray so animated. With each lyric she rocked her neck and danced seductively. Cam was stuck between a rock and a hard place. The song put everything on the line for Gray. She was so sure about her feelings for him, when he was still stuck. He wondered if he should allow his heart to open up to another woman. Gray might've seemed innocent and sweet, but girls like her were silent killers. They were the ones that caused the most damage to a man's heart. Cam knew he should back away and go back to being the cold-hearted asshole she'd become accustom to but couldn't.

All the chatter and loud music went silent, as they gazed into each other's eyes. Cam swore he saw a shooting star beaming in her haunting eyes. Gray tried to keep her wall up and remain indifferent. It wouldn't help any to let a nigga with an ego as big as Cam's know how much power he had over her. Never one to backdown from what he wanted, Cam leaned in slow and caressed her neck. Gray could already feel the warmth of his lips on hers and he hadn't even kissed her yet. She'd been yearning for his touch. Finally, he was ready to fulfill her desires.

Gray, desperately, wanted to taste him. Her insides craved his touch. The agony of him making her wait was killing her softly. She was fed up with all the games. She wanted his lips on her now. With her eyes closed, she held her breath and cherished the feel of his hands. Then, she felt his hot breath on her neck and the tender brush of lips. As soon as Cam's plump lips imprinted on her collarbone, Gray lost all rational thought and became consumed with the idea of being his girl.

Enthralled by her taste, Cam tugged on her ponytail, as his kisses became harder and more intense. His tongue thrashed against her neck, as a wave of pleasure shot through his veins. Just that quick, he'd become addicted. Cam didn't give a damn about her wack-ass baby daddy or any other fuck nigga in the room lusting after her. Gray was his.

He made that clear, by placing sloppy kisses all over her neck, while palming her ass. The way he was handling her, he was sure there was a flood in her panties. He was right. Gray's thong was soaked. The lips of her pussy began to swell, quaking with desire. If they were alone, she would've been pulled her thong to the side and let him slide his steel pipe inside her wet slit.

"I hate to break this up." Mo tapped Gray on the shoulder. "But, umm... we about to go. You want us to take you home?"

"Nah, she ridin' wit' me," Cam answered.

"Gray, is that what you want?" Mo ignored her brother.

"Yeah, he can take me."

"Ok. Make sure you call me tomorrow, girl. We got a lot to talk about."

"I will." Gray giggled.

"I'm gettin' ready to head out too." Quan dapped Cam up, and then gave Gray a quick hug goodbye.

"You good?" Cam gazed deeply into her eyes.

What had transpired was a lot for him to digest, so it had to be hard for her too.

"Yeah." Gray swallowed the lump in her throat.

She was still reeling from his passionate kisses, even though he still hadn't kissed her lips.

"A'ight. We gon' leave as soon as I come back from the restroom."

Gray nodded, and used the time while he was gone to touch up her makeup. She felt like a giddy schoolgirl. She couldn't believe she'd been afraid to open herself up to Cam. He'd been nothing but a gentleman all night. Maybe fucking with him was the confidence boost she needed to further separate herself from Gunz.

Ten minutes went by and she found herself still waiting for his return. She didn't know what the holdup was. Babylon wasn't even that full anymore, so the line for the restroom couldn't have been long. Tired of waiting, she went looking for him. When she turned the corner, she spotted him talking to the same girl that was in his face earlier that night. Cam's back was to her, so he had no idea that she was ducked off in the cut, listening to his conversation.

"Nah, that ain't my girl. She just the homey. I'm single as fuck," he told the chick.

"Friends don't kiss each other on the neck."

"Don't trip off that shit. That was the Hennessy that had me actin' up."

Crushed by his confession, Gray tucked her tail between her legs and marched off. She didn't need to hear anymore. Once again, she'd been made to look like a sucker by someone she cared for. Gray thought the pain she experienced by the hands of Gunz was bad, but Cam's betrayal was far worse. He had actually fooled her into thinking he was different.

"You ready?" He asked, pulling out his car keys.

Gray started walking without responding. Cam led her to his candy red LaFerrari. If she wasn't so pissed, she would've taken the time to admire the car's splendor, but she didn't give a fuck about Cam or his car. Snug in the passenger seat, she snatched on her seatbelt and sat with an attitude. The sooner she got away from him the better. Cam was so preoccupied with finding something good to listen to that he didn't even notice her mood had changed. After minutes of deliberation, he settled on SiR's *D'Evils* and sparked up a blunt. Cam inhaled the smoke into his lungs and sped off. Doing 90 down the highway, he bobbed his head to the music.

"*One spliff a day'll keep the evils away,*" he sang along to the beat. "*Tell me who that nigga if it ain't me.*"

Cam was in the zone and feeling great. He'd gotten shorty's number and planned on hittin' her up the following day. She was an easy lay, so he was guaranteed to get his dick wet.

"You want somethin' to eat?" He asked Gray.

Cam's stomach was growling out of control. He was hungry as fuck. Gray stared out the window and acted as if she didn't hear him.

"Gray? You hungry?"

Silence.

"You hear me? Nigga, I know you hungry?"

I know he ain't tryin' to say since I'm plus size that automatically means I always want something to eat, she thought.

"A'ight. When I pull up at this White Castle, yo' quiet-ass bet not ask for shit." Cam gripped the steering wheel.

Gray cleared her throat and continued to ignore him.

"Aye!" He slapped his hand against her thigh. "You tryin' to get some food or what?"

Gray pulled out her phone and started scrolling through Instagram.

"I know damn well you hear me," Cam said, becoming irate.

He hated to be ignored.

"Aye… Aye! Hellooo!" He waved his hand in front of her face.

Gray still didn't respond.

"You are a fuckin' weirdo. What's wrong wit' you?"

Gray clicked on her camera and checked to make sure her lipstick was straight, as Cam tried to get her attention by gripping her thigh.

"So, all of a sudden you deaf? Fuck is yo' problem?"

Gray politely removed his hand from her thigh and turned her body to face the door.

"Oh, you big mad," Cam scoffed. "You got me fucked up if you think you gon' sit here and ignore me." He put out his blunt and turned down the radio.

"Look, I don't know what yo' problem is, but you ain't gon' keep actin' like you don't hear me. I ain't no fuckin' kid. If you got an issue, say what the fuck it is."

Gray rolled her eyes and let out a heavy sigh. Cam's li'l speech didn't intimidate her.

"You keep rollin' yo' eyes them muthafuckas gon' get stuck."

Silence.

"Gray!" He placed his hand on her jaw and made her face him.

"Leave me alone! Damn!" She smacked his hand away.

Caught off guard by her response, Cam sat silent - hurt.

"I'll leave you alone when you tell me what the fuck is wrong wit' you."

"It's obvious, I don't wanna talk to you, so shut the fuck up and take me home!"

"Who the fuck is you talkin' to?" He looked at her like she had two heads.

"You!" Gray refused to backdown.

"Ok." Cam nodded.

Furious, he snatched her phone out of her hand and threw it out the window.

Gray's jaw dropped. She couldn't believe he'd actually thrown her phone out the window.

"Why would you do that?" She screeched, as they whizzed down the highway.

"'Cause yo' ass was fuckin' ignoring me!"

"But you ain't a kid?

"I don't give a fuck. You gon' talk to me."

"Oh my god! I fuckin' hate you!" She groaned.

"You brought that shit on yourself. You should've answered me."

"Let me out." Gray took off her seatbelt.

"Man, sit back."

"No! Let me out!" She hit him, repeatedly.

“Is yo’ ass on medication?” Cam looked at her like she was insane.

“Dealing with niggas like you, I should be! Now, let me the fuck out!”

“No!” He held her back by one arm.

“A’ight. Two can play that game.”

Since he didn’t want to let her out, Gray swiftly grabbed his phone and tossed it out the window too. Blinded by rage, Cam pulled over onto the shoulder of the highway. He’d officially reached his breaking point. It took every, last bit of home training he had not to choke her.

“You better hope I find my fuckin’ phone; ‘cause if I don’t, yo’ ass dyin’ tonight.” He pointed his finger in her face like a gun.

Gray stared back at him, without saying a word. She didn’t know Cam well enough to test his limits. He was so mad, he might haul off and hit her. Cam hopped out the car, pissed. It was pitch black outside. Cicadas and crickets made noises all around him. Trying to find his phone without a light was like searching for a needle in a haystack. It took him forever, but he finally located it. Thankfully, for Gray’s sake, it had landed in the grass and wasn’t broken. Relieved that he had his precious phone, he headed back to the car only to find Gray gone.

They were on the highway, so she couldn’t have gone far. Once he got in the car and turned on his headlights, he spotted her stomping down the side of the rode. He didn’t know what her problem was, but he was too drunk and high to be chasing after her. If Gray was any other chick, he would’ve left her childish-ass there but since he cared about her well-being, he drove slowly alongside her.

"Gray, get yo' ass in this car!"

Gray kept walking, with her arms folded across her chest. Walking alone at 3:00am wasn't a good idea, but her pride wouldn't let her get back inside his car. Fed up with her bullshit, Cam turned on his hazard lights and got out.

"Yo, I ain't got time for this shit. What the fuck is wrong wit' you?" He pulled her by the arm, aggressively.

"You! You're my problem!"

"I ain't even do shit to you!" He got up in her face.

"Oh, you ain't do shit to me? Ok."

"What the fuck I do, then?"

Cam wanted a fight, but she wasn't going to give him one.

"It don't even matter. Just leave me alone." She resumed walking.

"Obviously, it matters to you or you wouldn't be out here actin' stupid. One minute we was chillin' and the next you actin' like a fuckin' psychopath!"

Gray spun around on her heels, halting him in his stride.

"I'm just the homey, right? Me having an attitude shouldn't matter to you."

"Speak English. What the fuck is you sayin', my nigga?"

"Whatever. Just leave me the fuck alone." She waved him off.

"You ain't gon' keep walkin' away from me."

"Watch me!" Gray threw up the middle finger.

Done going back and forth, Cam ran and blocked her path.

"Move!" Gray unsuccessfully tried to push him out the way.

"Shut the fuck up. You don't run shit." He swung her over his shoulder like she was a rag doll.

"Put me down!" She kicked and screamed.

"Didn't I tell you to be quiet?" He swatted her hard on the butt.

The pounding of his footsteps against the gravel road made Gray feel helpless. She needed to get away from him. Tears were starting to well in her eyes. She couldn't let him see her cry. If he did, he'd know how much his words affected her. Back at the car, he placed her down and pinned her up against the passenger side door.

"Now, I'm gon' ask you one last time. What the fuck is your problem?" Cam's chest heaved up and down.

Gray defiantly stood with her arms crossed and her eyes locked on him. She wanted to continue being mute but needed to get her feelings off her chest.

"That ain't my girl. She just the homey. That was the Hennessy that had me actin' up," she mocked him.

It took Cam a minute to realize what she was talkin about, and then his words came flooding back. Instantly, he felt like shit. When he'd spewed that nonsense to ol' girl, he regretted it immediately. Gray wasn't just his friend and they both knew it. She was the chick he daydreamed about being his wife; but how could he give her his heart when he didn't know if he had a heart to give?

"Yo, I ain't mean that shit." He panicked.

"Yes, you did."

"If I said I didn't, I didn't." He shot her a look of annoyance.

"Then what the fuck are we doing? What is this, 'cause I'm tired of being in limbo with you."

"I don't know. What do you want it to be?"

"Stop answering my questions with a question."

"Why? Does that bother you?" He did it again anyway.

Gray glared at him, and then rolled her eyes. Everything with Cam was a game.

"What should I say when people ask me about us?"

"Tell 'em what you wanna tell 'em."

"So, I'm your girlfriend?"

"Do you wanna be my girlfriend?" Cam countered.

Gray was too self-conscious and ego-driven to say yes. She refused to look like a fool in front of him.

"Are you gon' fuck that girl?" She asked, instead.

"Yeah," he answered, truthfully.

Gray's heart split in two.

"But I'm willing to make adjustments if you open yo' mouth and say what the fuck it is you want."

"I want you to want me like I want you. I want us to get past the bullshit and be together."

"This ain't no damn Disney movie. I ain't no prince that's gon' come save you. This is real life. We grown as fuck. I don't believe in fairytales and I most certainly don't believe in love."

"So, you've never been in love?" She placed her hand on her chest in disbelief.

"Once."

"With who?"

"Do you really want me to answer that?"

Gray quickly realized the girl he was referring to was LaLa.

"No, I don't." She turned her head, defeated.

Cam hated to see her that way. He never wanted to let her down, but knew if he let her in he'd kill her bit by bit. That's what he did to everyone who tried to love him. The only problem was that Gray wasn't like everybody else. When he was around her, it was as if space and time never existed. His universe began and ended with her. Cam could search the world a thousand times, but in the end, whatever path he took would lead him back to her.

Gently, he traced her lips with the tip of his finger. The urge to bite them, kiss them and suck them overwhelmed his senses. Cam gazed thoughtfully at each indentation of her lips, as if he could map out prehistoric seas and future plans. He was so wrapped up in her touch that he didn't wanna look up. If he did, he might find himself at the mercy of interrogative eyes, wondering what he was doing. Cam wished he was at liberty to say, but the truth was he honestly didn't know. His feelings for Gray were an enigma wrapped in fear but there would be no letting her go.

"You mine. You hear me?" He said more as a command than a request.

Gray's lips stretched wide into a smile that reached her eyes. This was how Cam liked to see her. She had the kind of smile that made a man feel happy to be alive. Cam was going to do everything in his power to keep that same smile on her face every day.

"I've been yours." Gray stood on her tippy toes and tried to kiss his lips.

"Uh ah." He dodged her attempt.

"What?"

"I don't kiss."

"Why?" Her heart constricted.

"'Cause I don't wanna feel. I just wanna fuck." He pushed up her dress.

Right there on the busy highway, cars rushed past, as they lost track of space and time. Gray didn't hold anything back and neither did Cam. They both wanted to feel every inch of each other's skin. The onlookers and stream of traffic faded away. It was just the two of them. Gray circled her arms around his back, as she felt his minty breath upon her neck. Cam ran his fingers down her spine. They were so close that there was no space left between them. Gray could feel his heartbeat against her chest. Nothing else had to be figured out or explained. She was his and he was hers. If Cam lost her, he'd lose pieces of himself. Gray was the half that made him whole.

At his crib, Cam carried her inside and gently lay her down on his king size bed. Usually when he brought chicks to his apartment, it was all about rough sex and busting a nut, but with Gray things were different. He didn't just wanna fuck her. He wanted to devour her. She was the match and he was the fuse. Even with all the confusion in both their lives, he had faith in her. For weeks, she'd been piercing his thoughts with her caerulean eyes. Lying on her back, Gray's lips poked out in a pout, as her eyes begged him to take it easy on her.

Almost a year had passed since she'd last had sex. She needed him to be gentle - for her heart and pussy were tender. Quietly, with a stern look on his face, Cam peeled her shirt and panties off. Her voluptuous body caused his cock to stir in his jeans. Gray's curvaceous frame might've been intimidating or too much for a lesser man to handle, but for him, it was perfect. She had an hour glass figure. Her coconut-sized boobs, soft, flat stomach and bountiful hips made his mouth water.

Naked, his long body hovered on top of hers. Gray was a seductress to his soul. He would gladly cross an ocean just to taste her. Eagerly, he lusted for the taste of her flesh, as her body enthusiastically writhed from the feel of his tongue. Cam planned on spending the rest of the night fucking her pussy and eating her ass. He savored her from head to toe. Gray could feel his desire through the earnestness of his touch. An unbridled craving crept in his fingers, as he searched every inch of her physique.

A slight whimper escaped Gray's trembling lips, as his hand found her center. It was at that time that she gave him all she had. Her body was his and under his control. Cam's fantasies and desires played out across her frame, as he was nourished by the sugary sounds of her voice. Every sigh and moan enthralled him. In a circle, he rubbed her nub, as he sucked on each of her budding nipples. Cries of passion danced in the air. Cam used her own juices as lotion to massage her clit. Dizzy with lust, Gray closed her eyes and rode the wave of pleasure that was coursing through her veins.

Cam loved seeing her fall apart just from the touch of his hands. Needing to taste her, he buried his head deep between her thick and floral-scented thighs. She was already sticky and wet from his finger strokes. Cam's tongue invaded her succulent trap, lazily licking and exploring the depths of her walls. In the 69 position, Gray's ravenous mouth lined up with his throbbing cock, ready to satisfy him. Cam tried his best not to cum, as the heat from her tongue hit the base of his swollen rod. Clenching his ass muscles, he fucked her mouth like it was her pussy.

"Ahhhhhhh." Gray moaned, drunk off his taste.

She craved every pump of his instrument. Cam's body shook with distress, as he avoided exploding in her insatiable mouth, which awaited the overflow of his seed. He was at her mercy and she was at his. Deliberately, he licked, bit and sucked her pussy, making sure her clit became so sensitive that she begged him to stop. But Cam would never let up. His intent was to drive her mad. He had to let her know he was in control. Chivalry was dead. He could kill her with kindness or murder it.

Never one to back down from a challenge, Gray swallowed his dick whole. Soon, it became a race to see who could bring who to ecstasy first. Neither of them was going to stop until the other was fatigued and gasping for air.

Going in for the kill, Cam slipped her aching nub into his mouth and flicked away with the tip of his tongue.

Gray lost her breath and bit down into her bottom lip. Moans filled the room, as he tongue kissed her pussy. At the peak of her final groan, Cam's tongue readily awaited every splash of her creamy stream, as it trickled across his lips. Loving her sweet essence, he bathed himself in her ivory liquid.

"Cam." Gray sighed, breathlessly.

Gunz had never ate her pussy so good. Cam had her seeing the sun, moon, stars and distant galaxies. Reeling from her first orgasm, she gasped as he spread her legs apart. His hard rod brushed against her tender wetness. Slowly, Cam slid into her warm pussy, stretching her wide.

"Ahhhhh... it's too big. Take it out. It's not gonna fit," Gray cried, as a single tear dripped from her eye.

"It will," he assured.

"Mmmmmmmm... it's so big. It fills me up."

Cam's cock deep-dived inside her canal, as he pressed his firm body against hers. Gray let out a long, thunderous moan, as her eyes rolled to the back of her head. It amazed her how good he felt. With each stroke of his cock, Cam watched her. Desire burned between them. Thrust after thrust, Gray writhed in agony, wondering if her pussy was that good. Cam had been fuckin' her for hours. She could feel his knees sink into the mattress. Cam was fucking her so hard and deep, he nearly split her in two. Gray's head tossed and turned, as he pounded into her pussy.

After having her, Cam never wanted to feel another woman. All he wanted to do was please, kiss and fuck her. Stroking her middle, he made it difficult for her to breathe, by lightly choking her. He was hitting her spot so good, he could feel her pussy liquify. He and Gray both gazed down at her pussy. She'd started to cream all over his dick. White streaks of passion coated his cock letting him know he was hitting it right. Gray could tell by the determined look on his face that he wanted her to cum, but before she bust another nut, he had to fuck her from behind. Gray's ass cheeks smacked against his pelvis, as he continued to drill into her.

"Oh…my…fuckin'…god," she wailed, squeezing her inner walls. "Ooooh… it's so deep. Mmmmmmm."

The more she moaned, the faster he drove his cock into her middle.

"That's it, baby."

"Fuck me like you love me!" She pleaded.

"See what you do to me when you say shit like that?" He yanked her hair.

"Fuck me harder.

"This pussy is mine." Cam growled, pressing his face against hers.

His breath on her ear sent Gray's body into overdrive. He wanted to destroy her resolve, as she fought the electric currents building in her belly. Cam's fingers dug into the sides of her waist, as she rocked back and forth on his cock.

"Tell me it's mine," he commanded.

"It's… it's—" Gray stuttered.

"Say it!" Cam smacked her ass cheeks.

"It's yours! This pussy is all yours!"

"Goddamn right." He growled. "Fuck, this pussy tight."

"Don't stop. Keep fuckin' my tight, li'l pussy."

"You like the way I fuck this pussy?"

"Oh yeah," Gray whimpered. "You have the best fuckin' dick. Don't ever stop fuckin' me. It feels so good."

"C'mon, baby. Throw that pussy back." Cam pumped his cock.

"Like that?" Gray did as she was told.

"That's my girl."

"Am I doing good, baby?" She Dutty Wine on his dick.

"That's it. Dance on my dick," Cam encouraged her.

"Ooh, baby! I want you to cum!"

"Is that what you want?"

"Yes."

"You want my cum inside you?"

"Yes. I want all of it."

Cam held on to her waist and pulled her hair, as he hit her with long, deep strokes. Gray grinded in place, squeezing her pussy muscles. Hot and wet, she milked his cum. Cam rode the creamy wave of her orgasm, as they both came for each other... together… at once. He watched his cock go in and out of her dripping hole. The scent of their sex filled the air, as he pumped copious amounts of cum inside her. Skin to skin, they lay side by side under the threshold of breathless moans.

The next afternoon when, she returned home, Gray was on cloud nine. She and Cam spent the entire night laying in bed, fucking and sucking. When they came up for air they swapped childhood stories, hopes and dreams. By the time they fell asleep, the sun had come up. Her heels were in her hand, as her bare feet clapped against the cold, marble floor. She was so into her own thoughts that she had no idea Gunz was waiting on her in the living room.

"Where the fuck you been?"

The sound of his booming voice caused Gray to jump back ten feet.

"Oh my god. You scared the shit out of me." She held her chest.

"Why the fuck you ain't been answerin' your phone? I've been callin' you all night."

"I lost it," she answered, stepping into the room.

Something was wrong. Gunz never sat in the living area. The smell of liquor permeated the space, burning her nose. Gunz gazed absently at the wall with a far-a-way look in his eyes. His clothes were disheveled, and it looked like he hadn't slept a wink. Gray even swore she saw dried up tears on his cheeks. Her staying out all night had really fucked him up. She wished she felt bad for him but didn't. He didn't care when he left her home alone wondering about his whereabouts, so why should she?

"You lost it, but you was all on Snapchat hugged up with that nigga." Gunz took a swig from the bottle of Cîroc.

"Jealous?" Gray delighted in his misery.

"Honestly, I don't give a fuck."

"Then what the hell you got an attitude for?" She plopped down in the seat opposite him.

"Uncle Clyde died."

"What?" Gray damn near fainted.

"I tried callin' you but you ain't answer. I guess that nigga you was fuckin' was more important." Gunz gulped down the bottle of vodka. "Thank God it wasn't one of the kids," he shot to make her feel bad.

It worked.

“Here we go. Climbing the stairway to heaven.” – The O’ Jays, “Stairway to Heaven”

Chapter 22

Gray

"You doing ok, Candy?" Gray rubbed her back.

She was worried sick about her. Uncle Clyde dying on top of her during the middle of sex had to have taken a toll on her. The autopsy report said the cause of death was a stroke. If it were Gray, the visual would forever be stuck in her head. She didn't know if she would ever be able to have sex again.

"I'm fine, chile." Candy flicked her wrist.

"You sure?"

"Girl, she a'ight. She already plottin' on her next victim," Dylan replied.

"Don't be tellin' all my damn business." Candy swatted her hand.

"Just 'cause you're my mama don't mean I won't fight you."

All Gray could do was shake her head and laugh. Dylan and Candy were always arguing and fighting. Most people found it weird the way they communicated; but once you got to know them, you realized that was their way of showing each other love. Gray looked around the room. All Gunz's family had gathered at their apartment for the repast. His mother, Vivian, grandmother, Emilia, and his uncle, Ronnie, were all there. Despite her feelings towards Gunz, she felt it was necessary to support him during such a trying time.

Uncle Clyde's sudden death not only affected him but the girls too. They loved their uncle. He was like the grandfather they never got to have. Clyde had practically raised Gunz, since his father, Joseph, wasn't around due to his drug addiction. After Joseph passed from AIDS, they became even closer. Gray had never seen Gunz take a death so hard. His father and best friend had died, but neither of those deaths affected him the way Clyde's had.

The man was a wreck. All he did was cry and tell Gray how much he needed her. She didn't want to be an asshole, but Uncle Clyde's passing didn't change how she felt about him. As far as she was concerned, he was dead to her too.

But Gray being the loving, kind woman she was kept her true emotions bottled up. Instead of focusing on Cam and their budding relationship, here she was, once again, catering to Gunz and all his needs. Since he and Candy were too distraught to handle the funeral arrangements, Gray was the one to step up to the plate. She'd done everything from picking out to casket to writing Uncle Clyde's eulogy.

She missed Cam like crazy. The same day he'd dropped her off, he had a new phone and a huge teddy bear made out of pink roses sent to her house. Gray loved the gifts, but whenever he called or texted, she didn't respond. Gray felt bad for brushing him off, but her family came first. Gunz might not have been shit, but his family took her in when she had none of her own. It would be disrespectful and a slap in the face if she wasn't there for them. *Stairway to Heaven* by The O'Jays was on repeat, as Gunz and his Uncle Ronnie had their own mini concert in the living room.

"Put yo' hand on my shoulder! Lean closer!" Uncle Ronnie crooned.

Gunz placed his hand on his shoulder and sang, *"Don't you wanna go? Don't you wanna go? Don't you wanna go?"*

"Hea-ven!" Uncle Ronnie sang backup.

"Ooooooh-whoo-whoo-whoo-whoo-whoo-whoo!" Gunz channeled his inner Eddie Levert.

"It's just me left." Uncle Ronnie took a bottle of Crown Royal to the head.

"Pass me that." Gunz reached out his hand.

He'd been drinking nonstop but didn't care. Alcohol was the only thing that numbed the pain.

"We all we got, Unc." He sat back with his legs spread wide apart.

"Me and Clyde had just booked some studio time, so we could record the remix to *Smokin' Weed Wit' the Windows Up*."

"He was excited about that."

"Clydeascope and the Ill Street Band is officially over. Unless—"

"Nope." Gunz cut him off.

"Aww… c'mon, nephew! We gotta continue the legacy."

"Nah, I'm good," he responded, while watching Gray's every move.

She was across the room talking quietly on the phone. Gunz didn't know what he'd do without her. She'd been a godsend to him and the girls. He didn't deserve her kindness, after everything he'd put her through. Tia had tried being there for him but Gunz only wanted to be around Gray. She knew him inside and out. She'd been there through all his trails and tribulations. Tia would never be able to understand or relate.

"What the fuck is yo' problem?" Cam barked through the phone.

"What you mean?" Gray went into the laundry room and closed the door.

"You been duckin' and dodgin' a nigga."

"No, I haven't." She lied.

"I see you back lyin' again."

"Look, can we talk about this later?"

"Fuck no. Bring yo' ass downstairs."

"What? You at my apartment?" Gray panicked.

"Why the fuck would I tell you to come downstairs if I wasn't?"

"Oh my god." She covered her eyes with her hand.

"And if you wanna meet him, keep playin' wit' me. Meet me in the garage."

"No. I can't." Gray's palms began to sweat.

"No?" Cam drew his head back. "A'ight, I'll see you in a minute."

"Ok. Wait! Here I come."

"Don't make me come knock on your door. You know I will."

"I'm coming." Gray hung up.

Her heart was pounding in her chest. She knew Cam was crazy, but she didn't know he was certifiably insane. If Gunz caught him at their home, Gray was sure to come up dead. Exiting the laundry room, she steadied her breathing. She couldn't let everyone see how on edge she was.

"What you doing?" Gunz came up behind her.

Gray jumped.

"Boy, you scared me. About to take out the trash." She tied up the bag.

"Since when you start taking out the trash?"

"I didn't wanna bother you with it 'cause I know you got your family here."

"Man, watch out. I got it." He tried to take the bag from her.

"No, go be with your family. I'll be right back." She ran out the door before he could stop her.

Gray dumped the trash down the shoot and took the back staircase down to the parking garage. Cam was standing at the bottom of the steps awaiting her arrival. When he laid eyes on her, he momentarily lost his breath. He'd seen Gray look sophisticated and sexy, but that day she looked royal. There was a regalness to the black choker that adorned her neck and the black, velvet, Valentino, strapless, hoop dress and six-inch, pointed-toe heels she wore. She looked like a black Grace Kelly. That still didn't stop him from getting her ass together.

"You really gon' make me fuck you up."

"What are you doing here? You can't just be poppin' up at my house." Gray stomped down the steps.

"Last I checked, I could always check up on what's mine."

"Cam, we together but—"

"But nothin'. I told you, you was mine, right?"

"Yeah." She sighed, not in the mood for his bully tactics.

"So, whatever I say is mine needs to check in and follow the rules accordingly."

"Last I checked, I was your girl not yo' pet." Gray curled her upper lip.

"Fuck all that. Where you been at?"

"Gunz uncle died and I had to make the funeral arrangements."

"So, that gave you the audacity to grow a pair of balls and disappear?"

"It wasn't even like that. I had to take care of my family."

"Fuck that nigga and his dead uncle. You belong to me. That means when I call, you fuckin' answer," he scowled.

"You don't get it. His uncle meant a lot to me."

"Just because you over here wit' his piece-of-shit-ass family, don't mean you gotta say fuck me in the process."

"You really need to stop. I would never say fuck you—"

"Yeah, but family comes first, right?" Cam arched his brow.

Gray paused for a second and looked into his eyes. There was something there that she didn't recognize. Anger, lust or mischievousness normally resonated in his irises, but that day, there was a flicker of sadness there as well.

"Oh, I see what this is. You in yo' feelings." She smirked.

"Get the fuck outta here." Cam clenched his jaw.

"No, you are." Gray placed her hands on his shoulders. "Your feelings are hurt but you too much of a nigga to admit it."

"Fuck all that. You know what type of time I'm on."

"Your male pride is gonna fuck you up one day," she remarked, kissing his face.

Cam stood silent. He'd never say the words, but his feelings were hurt. Just when he decided to let his guard down, she went M.I.A. on a nigga. What kind of shit was that? Gray talked a good game, like she was over her baby daddy, but her actions said otherwise. He prayed for her sake she was, 'cause if she wasn't, Cam was gonna make it his business to end her life.

"Listen… it was never my intention to hurt you. I just had a lot going on and I didn't know how to handle it. All of this is new to me. But you have to understand. That quote unquote family that you made fun of is the only family that I know. I'd be less than the person you think I am if I didn't show up for them when they needed me."

"Yeah, I hear you," he responded, nonchalantly.

"I need you not only to hear me, but I need you to feel me too. I'm sorry. I truly am." She kissed his lips, passionately.

Cam should've stopped her when he saw her lean forward but didn't. Gray had him wide open and there was no hiding it. The taste of her tongue had him dazed and confused. He was consumed by slow, steady kisses, as she quenched her thirst upon his lips. Kissing her was better than he imagined. Gray had him moaning and groaning. Kissing her was like reliving his first steps. Gray pushed her lips in more firmly. The wave that ran through Cam was so intoxicating it made his head swim. She was his champagne and he was her hazelnut latte.

Gray's hands gripped the back of his neck, pulling his head tightly into hers. Cam held her in his arms, locking lips, kissing passionately. Gently, he bit her bottom lip and tugged on it a little bit. His hands slid over her dress till he felt the curve of her breast. The next thing Gray knew, their kisses morphed into her legs being spread and her panties being pulled down her thighs. A weakened sigh escaped her lips, as his hand grabbed hold of her derrière.

Seductively, he kissed her thighs, while looking upwards with hard, staring eyes. Gray's pants echoed throughout the garage, as she drove her hands through his hair. Ready to dive in, Cam parted her legs wide enough to fit his head in between, and then dove in. He licked Gray from her ass crack to her middle. Methodically, he licked her labia, tenderly, making sure to not miss an inch of her precious spot. With each stroke, he could feel her wetness seep onto his tongue.

Gray's back scrapped against the concrete steps, as he feasted on her kitty. What she was experiencing was utter madness. She wanted to tell him to stop. Anybody could come down the steps and catch them, but Gray didn't care. Her creamy center had betrayed her. She needed this release.

Cam's tongue swirled around her pearl like he was kissing her mouth. The sensation was magnificent. Gray threw her head back and gazed at the sliver of light peeking through the window. Cam had her legs locked, so she couldn't escape. Gyrating her hips up and down, she spoon-fed him the pussy. Feasting on her kitty, Cam drug his nails up her inner thighs, sending shockwaves through her core.

Gray's clit started to swell. Cam's tongue licked her swollen bud, as he fingered her vagina. Hot, wet liquid dripped down his hand, as his fingers thrusts in and out of her. Wanting to taste every inch of her pussy, he folded her knees back, and then thrust two of his fingers inside her walls. Quick, then slow, he went. The faster he finger fucked her pussy, the louder her moans became. Cam enjoyed watching her squirm and pant. Gray's body was his to do as he pleased. Unable to fight the orgasm building in her pelvis, she screamed to the high heavens, as her sweet fluids squirted into his hungry mouth.

Coming up for air, Cam kissed up her neck, as her right hand caressed his ball sack in a clockwise motion. On his feet, he stood, so that he towered over her. Cam's lips gently pecked her lips, as his large hands cupped her butt cheeks. Passionately, they kissed until her lips started to move over to his cheek and then his ear. There, she nibbled and kissed down his neck and shoulder until she made her way to his dick. Gray's eyes were filled with dark lust, as her hand gripped his shaft. Leisurely, she began to suck. Cam took a deep breath, as she intensified her tongue strokes until he could no longer contain his groans.

After an eternity of nonstop pleasure, Gray unlocked her lips from his cock and smiled. Then, she slid her mouth down his dick, taking him deeply within her throat. Cam could feel the pressure building up. He was about to cum. His grunts and groans deepened, as her soft hand stroked his cock. Gray released her swollen lips, as her thumb ran over the tip of his dick. Cam was about to erupt. With one last explosive moan, he ejaculated all over her hand. While looking up into his eyes, Gray lapped up every, last drop.

Forgetting the world even existed, Cam rubbed the tip of his cock over her stiff clit. He loved teasing her. It had become his favorite thing to do. Under his spell, she came apart. Cam had to teach her a lesson. She'd been a bad girl. After he was done with her, he could bet money she would never not answer his phone calls again. Showing her pussy no mercy, he slid his dick into her center, penetrating her vagina. Gray gasped for air. Thrusting deeply, Cam relished the feel of her insides, as she gripped his back and they rocked steady.

Switching positions, he sat on the steps and allowed her to bounce on his dick in a soft but hard motion. Gray's hot lava flowed down his shaft, lubricating his cock, as she thrust down on his dick. Cam's mouth covered her nipple, as she wound her hips. Firmly, he wrapped his arms around her waist, flipping her onto her back. Gray's left leg found its way onto his left shoulder. Cam's cock thrusted hard and fast, as his sack repeatedly tapped her butt cheeks. Gray's breath picked up. Cam watched, as her chest rose and fell with each lick of his tongue on her breasts. Gray could barely keep up, let alone take his size. She came hard, causing her pussy to squeeze the life out of his dick. The erotic sounds they made filled the garage. Slowing his pace, Cam pumped in and out. He was about to cum. He couldn't wait to fill her up.

"Fuck!" He snapped his eyes shut.

Cam's milky, white semen shot up her pussy. Normally, he wouldn't nut in a chick; but since Gray's tubes were tied, he didn't have to risk her getting pregnant. Plus, he wanted his cum to sit inside her for the rest of the day, so even when he was gone, a piece of him would still be there. Spent, he leaned forward and kissed her lips. A satisfied yet exhausted expression was plastered on her face.

Once her clothes were fixed, Gray kissed Cam goodbye and returned to her apartment. She hoped and prayed to God that no one noticed she could barely walk straight.

"You get lost? What took you so long?" Gunz eyed her, suspiciously.

"Mrs. Williams nosey-ass stopped me on the way back up. She practically talked my ear off," Gray lied.

Gunz didn't say anything else so he must've believed her. Either way, it didn't matter. She was well fucked and having Cam's nut oozing inside of her made her day even better.

"Girl, it was nice seein' you but I gotta go home to my baby boo." – Dave Hollister, "One Woman Man"

Chapter 23

Boss

"A'ight, y'all have a goodnight." Boss told his staff, as they headed home.

It was the end of the night and Babylon was officially closed. Boss was exhausted but happy as hell. They'd had another successful night. It was so packed that they ran out of hookahs for everyone. Babylon had only been open six months and he'd already made back all the money he'd invested. Business was so good that he and Mo were talking about opening a second location.

Boss loved being a business owner. He thrived on creating something from nothing. The night Mo had blessed him with a surprise visit had been one of the best nights he'd had in a while. Their marriage was crumbling right before their eyes. It had been hard to get things back on track. Sometimes, Boss found himself finding reasons not to go home. The energy there was fucked up. Mo was sad and depressed all the time. Nothing he said or did helped.

It had become extremely hard to be around her. Boss hated that he felt that way about his wife. At one point, they were thick as thieves. They used to do everything together. Now, he could hardly stand to spend five minutes alone with her. Mo wasn't the same woman he'd fallen in love with.

He thought her quitting her job and being a stay-at-home mom would bring them closer, but somehow, they'd drifted further apart. The night she popped up on him, however, was a welcomed surprised. It was the first time in ages he'd seen signs of the woman he met back in 2006.

She was wild, sexy, and uninhibited like she used to be. Boss felt like the luckiest nigga in the world to have her on his arm. His wife was a bombshell. It was good to see her delight in her beauty again. Mad niggas had their eyes on her all night, but she was his. Boss felt truly blessed that she donned his last name. He prayed their fun night together was a step towards them heading in a positive direction. For the first time in a long while, Boss looked forward to going home.

He and Zya stood behind the bar, counting down the money. Mo had already called and said she was waiting for him to walk through the door. Despite it being 2:00am, she'd cooked dinner and waited to share her meal with him. The kind gesture warmed Boss' heart. With him being gone all the time, they hardly ever got to eat together. Most nights, by the time he came home, she was knocked out asleep. The fact that she was waiting up for him meant that she was putting forth an effort to work on their relationship.

Boss had to figure out a way to return the favor. Mo deserved the world. If he could give it to her, he would. Tried as fuck, his eyes filled with water, as he yawned.

"You tired?" Zya massaged his right shoulder.

"Yeah, a li'l bit." Boss eased his arm away.

"Oh, you are tense." She stepped behind him and started massaging both his shoulders.

Boss dropped his head. He knew he shouldn't have enjoyed her touch, but Zya's hands were working magic.

"Damn, that feel good," he confessed, caught up in the moment.

"You should always be treated like a king and taken care of." She massaged her way down his back.

Boss' eyes drifted closed. Zya's fingers kneading into his muscles stimulated his senses and released all his tension.

"Let me make you feel good." She eased her way in front of him and unbuttoned his jeans. "I want you to cum in my mouth." She looked up at his face and unzipped his pants with her teeth.

Coming back to reality, Boss' eyes snapped open.

"Yo, what the fuck?" He pushed her head back.

"Ain't nobody around." Zya pulled off her shirt and revealed she wore no bra. "Nobody has to know. C'mon, I want you to cum right here." She cupped her breasts and jiggled her titties.

"You trippin', cuz." Boss quickly jumped over the bar. "I don't know what you thought, but this ain't that." He fixed his jeans.

"Stop lyin' to yourself. I see the way you look at me. You been wanting this pussy for a long time."

"I don't want that shit!"

"How could you not want me?" Zya came around the bar and walked towards him, seductively.

She wanted him to get a good view of her body. The lines of her body were long, clean and symmetrical. To most niggas, Zya was a dime; but to Boss, she was nothing but an inflatable toddler. He liked his women natural. He wasn't feeling her or her fake body parts.

"Real shit. Put your fuckin' shirt on before I shoot you." He pulled out his gun.

Zya stood frozen with fear. She'd never seen Boss so mad.

"Are you deaf?" He pulled the hammer back.

Zya scurried back around the bar and threw her shirt on. Boss couldn't believe Mo was right about her ass.

"Let me make this shit crystal clear. I don't want you. I've never wanted. I ain't never even looked at you in any other way than an employee. There ain't shit you can do for me besides get me locked up. I don't fuck wit' hoes and you on some ol' ho shit. I love my fuckin' wife. That's the only bitch my dick get hard for. Get some fuckin' dignity. Get some self-respect. Go home tonight and reflect. Matter-of-fact, don't even come back tomorrow."

"I'm fired?" Tears stung Zya's eyes.

"Hell yeah. Fuck you thought?"

"No, please. I need this job."

"You should've thought about that before you tried to stick my dick in your mouth and jiggle them titties."

"I'm sorry. I just like you so much and I see how good of a husband and father you are. I wanted a piece of that too, but now I get it. You don't want me. I swear, I will never cross the line again. Just, please, don't fire me."

Boss saw the look of dread and despair on her face. He should've kept his word and fired her, but Zya seemed to have gotten the picture.

"Check this out. Stay ten feet away from me. Only speak to me when spoken to. Other than that, don't say shit to me. And if you ever try this shit again, yo' ass is the fuck up outta here and I'ma tell my wife. If she find out, she gon' beat you the fuck up and have yo' ass in the ICU."

"You won't have any more problems out of me. I will be strictly professional from here on." Zya crossed her fingers behind her back.

"He ain't always right but he's just right for me."– Jazmine Sullivan, "In Love With Another Man"

Chapter 24

Gray

"Come on, girls!" Gray grabbed her car keys and headed to the door.

The pitter patter of Press' footsteps bounced off the walls, as she ran down the hall in her Mary Janes. Aoki popped a piece of gum and walked behind her slowly. She was too busy watching a YouTube video to rush. A small smile graced the corners of Gray's lips, as she looked at them. They looked so cute in their Gucci outfits. Their hair was freshly washed, so their natural curls bounced with ease. Aoki and Press were so pretty they could've been models. Gray had gotten tons of offers throughout the years but turned them all down. She wanted her girls to remain kids. Modeling would cause them to grow up too fast.

"We're ready, Mommy." Press said, out of breath.

"Where y'all going?" Gunz asked, coming down the hall.

"My boyfriend birthday party today." Press twisted her torso from side to side.

"You ain't got no damn boyfriend." Gunz snarled.

"Ah huh! His name King and he asked me to marry him and I said yes and we gon' get married at Legoland."

"What is she talkin' about?" Gunz looked at Gray.

"Her classmate, King, is having a birthday party today and we're about to go, so we'll see you later."

"Hold up." Gunz took Gray by the elbow. "I think I'ma roll wit' y'all."

Gray screwed up her face. Gunz hated going to children's parties. He avoided them like the plague; but since Uncle Clyde's death, he'd been doing a lot of things different. He walked around like a sad, lost puppy. He hadn't been out the house much. Most nights, he slept at home. When he wasn't working, he spent all his time with the girls. They'd go bowling, skating and to Sky Zone. On more than one occasion, he asked Gray to accompany them, but she always said no. Gunz had actually been bearable to be around, but that didn't change anything. Her guard was still up. The beast inside of him was still there. It was only a matter of time before he re-emerged.

"Ooh... can Daddy come?" Press looked at her mom for permission.

"Umm." Gray tried to think of a way to say no.

She felt bad for Gunz. She really did, but she'd given him enough of her support. He was no longer her concern. Therefore, he couldn't come. She wasn't trying to spend the day with him. That would only send the wrong message to the girls. She didn't want them to think they were getting back together. Plus, Cam would be there. If she showed up with him, Cam would have a fit. The last thing she needed was for there to be a shootout at a seven-year-old's birthday party.

"You ain't gotta ask if I can come. What type of time y'all on? I'll be back. Let me go put on my shoes."

Gray ran her hand through her hair. Her day was already ruined and it had just begun. This was about to be a whole shit show and she had no way of stopping the train wreck that was about to occur.

The weather was perfect for an outdoors party. Mo had gone all out. She'd thrown a modern, superhero-themed birthday jam. From what Gray knew, she'd made the invitations, building backdrop, place cards, toppers, superhero masks, food, drinks and cake all by herself. Gray didn't know how she did it. From the looks of the bags under Mo's eyes, she'd stayed up all night getting everything done.

Gray felt bad for her. Mo was supermom and didn't seem to get any credit for it. She ran around the party like a chicken with its head cut off, making sure that everyone was comfortable. Boss pretty much chilled with his homeboys and played the background. Gray hadn't seen him offer Mo a helping hand once. She couldn't put her finger on it, but something was up with him. His energy was off. Mo was too preoccupied to notice, but whenever she came around, he tensed up like a child who was awaiting an ass whooping.

If she and Mo were closer, she would've put her up on game; but they weren't, so she kept her mouth shut. Plus, she also didn't want to have to cuss his rude-ass mama out. The whole time she'd been there, she'd done nothing but complain. Syphilis, as Mo liked to call her, thought the food was too salty, the drinks were too bland, and the music was too loud. Nothing Mo did was good enough. Gray had never wanted to fight an old person more in her life.

An hour and a half into the party, Cam still hadn't arrived. Gray knew it was just a matter of time before he did. While she waited, she watched as the big kids swam in the pool. The little kids jumped in the bouncy house, while the parents sipped on mint-colored lemonade infused with vodka. Gray stayed away from the drinks and focused on the dessert table. She had a serious sweet tooth and Mo had made all her favorites. There were brownies, Oreos, macarons, superhero cookies, vanilla cupcakes and a chocolate chip cookie cake.

The dessert table was also a great distraction. It kept her mind off the tsunami brewing around her. Thank God, Gunz had been on his best behavior. He'd basically been rappin' to Boss and his peoples, instead of being all up in her face. But just as Gray took a bite of her third macaron, Cam came walking through the door. She could feel him before she saw him. His presence was that strong. Gray turned around and stared in his direction.

The heartbeat in her clit thumped like a bass drum. Every time she saw him, he looked better and better. His sex appeal was entirely too much to handle. The designer clothes he donned only added to his mystique. His hat was turned to the back and he wore nothing but a few gold chains, a black, denim jacket, Versace boxer/briefs, fitted jeans and Balenciaga sneakers. His tattoos and washboard abs were on full display for everyone to see. Gray wanted nothing more than to drop to her knees and give him head.

On the other side of the lawn, Cam gave his brother-in-law and his homeboys dap, when he noticed Gunz sitting off to the side.

"What the fuck is he doing here?"

"He came wit' ol' girl." Boss nodded his head in Gray's direction.

Cam looked over his shoulder at her. She could tell from where she stood that he was pissed. Gray didn't know whether to run or pretend as if she was invisible. She was scared shitless. She damn near peed on herself. Cam was crazy, so there was no telling how he was gonna react. The sad part was she had no reason to fear his wrath. She'd done nothing wrong. She hadn't cheated on him or lied. She'd simply attended his nephew's birthday party with her kid's father.

"Oh, word? Say no more." He nodded his head and walked over to the gift table.

Cam had come to the party with the intentions of kicking it with his family and his girl. Little did he know, but his new lady would arrive with her old flame. He'd feared that Gray was on some bullshit when it came to Gunz. It was one thing to go M.I.A. after the nigga's uncle died, but to bring her cheatin'-ass baby daddy to his nephew's party was something he couldn't forgive. She'd crossed the line and disrespected him in the worst way. Cam didn't know what type of man Gray thought he was, but she had him all fucked up. He'd killed niggas for less and she was pushing him over the edge. All he could do was thank God that she'd shown him her hoish ways before his feelings got too deep.

With her shoulders back and her head held high, Gray made her way over to the gift table. Cam was already surrounded by a slew of thirsty bitches, as he placed down King's present.

"*Hi.*" She waved, awkwardly.

Cam glared at her with contempt in his eyes. Gray was delusional as fuck if she thought she was gonna come speak to him like it was all good.

"Back the fuck up." He shooed her away. "What y'all want to drink?" He asked the bevy of beauties salivating over him.

Flabbergasted, Gray stood looking stupid. He'd played the shit out of her and could give a damn about it. Gray thought about saying something else but didn't want to risk playing herself anymore than she already had. Humiliated, she strolled back to where she'd come from. Cam had every right to be upset, but he should've let her explain. If this was how he was going to act during conflict, then maybe they were better off not dealing with each other anymore.

"Do I look dumb to you?" Gunz walked up on her.

"Yeah, and you always will, but that's neither here nor there." She turned her back to him.

"That's that same nigga from the basketball game whose chains you had on and the same nigga I saw you hugged up wit' on Snapchat. What the fuck is up wit' y'all? You fuckin' him?"

"Yeah," she replied, like it was nothing.

Gunz stood, dumbfounded. He never expected her to say yes.

"You that comfortable? You ain't gon' even lie about the shit?"

"What the fuck I gotta lie for? I ain't you and we ain't together."

"You see, I been tryin' to do better by y'all. I been trying, and this how you gon' do me? You gon' bring me around this Big Bird-lookin' muthafucka?"

"Gunz, get out my damn face." Gray waved him off. "Just leave me alone. Why ain't you with Tia? Go be with the teen mom."

"I don't wanna be wit' her. I wanna be wit' you."

"Gunz, what we had been over. Just let me have the apartment and go on about your business. 'Cause I'm tried of you fuckin' up my life."

"I'm fuckin' up yo' life?"

"Yes! You holding me up. I'm tryin' to move on with my life."

"That nigga got you that in a hurry?"

"I been in a hurry. When is this gon' be over? When are you moving out?"
Gray was physically and emotionally tired of him and Cam.

"See, this nigga got yo' mind fucked up. He got you thinkin' you can be happy without me, but that nigga ain't nothin' but a clown. Truth be told, I ain't happy wit' you either, and if I ain't happy, I don't want you to be happy either."

"You know how dumb you sound?"

"Ain't nobody gon' love you right. Not like me."

"You really think you the only nigga that's gon' love me?"

"Yeah."

"So, nobodies gonna love me like you do?"

"Like I do now," Gunz clarified.

"Nigga, you don't love me. You don't even love yourself, so stop tryin' to drive me crazy by giving me the runaround. Ain't no more Gunz and Gray. It's over, nigga. Deal wit' it."

"Gray, don't play wit' me. I will shoot this whole fuckin' party up, kids and all," Gunz warned.

"Well, pow pow, muthafucka. Do what you gotta do. I'ma be right over there when you start shootin'." She pointed to an empty chair.

Like she figured, Gunz didn't do shit but sit and pout. He was the least of her worries though. The tall, cocky muthafucka with freckles that matched hers was the one that had her on cardiac arrest. Hours had gone by and the sun had gone down. Cam still hadn't said a word to her. Gray sat alone, nursing a drink, while he grinned up in some light skin bitch's face. She wanted to slap the black off his ass but played it cool. She knew he was doing it to piss her off, but it still got to her anyway.

Her feelings were already invested in Cam. And yeah, she could've gotten him back by making him jealous as well, but Gray was too old to be playin' games just to try and cover up her hurt feelings.

"I'm ready to go." Gunz blocked her view of Cam.

"Ok… leave."

Damn, she really don't fuck with me. He stared at her with hurt in his eyes.

"The girls ready to go too."

"They can leave with you then, 'cause I'ma stay and help Mo clean up." She told a half truth.

She planned on helping Mo, but she also wanted to try to talk to Cam again. It wouldn't be Gray if she didn't try to mend things. Cam being mad at her was the worst feeling ever. He'd slowly become one of her closet friends. Him giving her the silent treatment was a cruel form of punishment.

"Come tell ya mama bye," Gunz called out to the girls.

He was furious and couldn't wait to get out of there. It was becoming clear that Gray was truly over him and Gunz didn't know how to handle that. He never thought she would stop loving him. It was selfish of him to think that he could have her and Tia too, but Gunz was narcissistic that way. In his mind, Gray was his and always would be. He would be damned if he let her move on with another man. He would make her life a living hell before he let that shit go down.

Gray hugged the girls and kissed them goodbye. They'd had a ball and exhausted themselves. As soon as Gunz and the girls were gone, she swallowed her pride and headed back over to Cam. He was sitting next to Mo, who looked like she was struggling to stay awake.

"You done being a brat? You ready to talk to me now?"

Cam's nostrils flared, as his fingers curled around the beer bottle in his hand. Every time Gray opened her mouth and said some dumb shit, he became angrier. If he didn't get the fuck away from her, he was sure to snap her neck.

"I'm about to head out." He disregarded her and tapped Mo on the thigh.

"Thanks for coming, big bro, and King loved the PlayStation 4 you bought him too."

"That's my li'l man. You know I got him. I'ma holla at you later." He bypassed Gray and walked inside.

And just like that, he turned her safe haven into hell. Gray's mind became its own prison, as she tried to figure out why he was treating her this way. His cruelty wasn't warranted or deserved. Gray's shoulders slumped, as she struggled to breathe. She wanted to run after him, but her mama hadn't raised no fool. If he wanted to be mad, then so be it.

"What's going on between you two?" Mo questioned, with her eyes closed.

It was the first time she'd gotten a chance to sit down in 24 hours.

"Y'all haven't said two words to each other all day."

"Your brother is a fuckin' psycho. He's mad because Gunz was here. I guess, he thinks I invited him, but I didn't. He asked to come, as we were leaving. Since the girls wanted him here, how could I say no? I would've explained that, but your hardheaded-ass brother didn't wanna hear shit I had to say."

"Cam is pigheaded. Once he gets something in his head, it's hard to change it. He's been that way since we were kids. Cut him some slack tho'. He's been through a lot. That skank whore, LaLa, really did a number on him. He ain't been the same since he stopped fuckin' wit' her. The nigga already had trust issues, but after she cheated on him, the shit got ten times worse. Just give him a minute to calm down and then try to talk to him."

"Nah, fuck that. He gon' talk to me now." Gray dialed his number.

"I wouldn't do that if I were you," Mo advised.

Gray took heed of her warnings but didn't hang up. She needed to dead this beef before things got out of hand. Three phone calls later, Cam still didn't pick up the phone. Gray knew she was doing the most by calling him back to back, but she couldn't stop herself. The fact that he wasn't answering her calls infuriated her. It was the equivalent of him spitting in her face. They were too new to be going through shit like this. Things were way too intense. Maybe it was a sign that they weren't meant to be.

"What the fuck you keep callin' my phone for?" Cam barked into the phone, causing her to jump.

Gray was so wrapped up in her thoughts that she forgot she'd called him for the fourth time.

"Cam, let me explain," she stuttered.

"Explain what? You made your decision. Go ahead and be wit' that nigga. Wit' his ten baby moms and his eleven kids. Oops, my bad. I mean, ten, 'cause he don't even claim one of yours."

Words flew out of Cam's mouth that he never thought he'd even think, let alone say out loud. Disgusted with himself, he hung up before she could reply, but Gray didn't have anything to say. Her heart had just exploded in her chest. Cam's words had literally killed her. Only a man she truly respected and adored could be her assassin. Gray could be hurt by anyone else and bounce right back, but Cam did more damage to her psyche with those few, small words than Gunz ever had. She knew deep down he didn't mean it; but in a way, that's what made it worse.

She'd trusted him with her emotions and the first chance he got, he used it against her. Gray shot up. She'd officially reached her breaking point. At that moment, she was blinded by a five-course serving of rage that tasted bitter, yet surprisingly sweet. No one, including Cam, was going to disrespect her and get away with it. Within minutes, she pulled up on 22nd street.

It was pitch black outside. Only the street light was on. The whole neighborhood was out. Cam and his pot'nahs were posted up in front of Aunt Vickie's house, shootin' dice and smokin' weed like the ring of bandits they were. LaLa was there too. Furious at how he'd spoken to her, Gray hopped out of her car.

"What was that shit you was talkin' over the phone? Say that shit to my face!"

Surprised by her presence and her outburst, Cam drew his head back.

"Don't get quiet now, bitch!" Gray mushed him in the forehead.

Cam quickly caught her by the wrist and pulled her close.

"You will be disabled for the rest of your life. Don't ever put your fuckin' hands on me. I will break your shit." He released his grip and flung her hand away.

"Nah, nigga. Keep that same energy you had over the phone. He don't claim my daughter? So, you gon' throw that shit up in my face? Do I throw up in your face that this cum guzzler had a baby on you wit' another nigga? No, 'cause I actually give a damn about your feelings."

"Hold up, bitch. Who you talkin' to?" LaLa rolled her neck.

"I'm talkin' to you, so unless you wanna get your nose cracked again, I would advise you to shut the fuck up and mind your fuckin' business."

"Cam, you gon' let her disrespect me like that?"

It was then that Gray took in the spectacle before her. Cam had the nerve to be standing in between LaLa's legs, as she sat on the hood of his car.

"So, this what we doing now?" She pointed at LaLa with her index finger and thumb.

"Now? This what he been doing, so you can back your big ass up, Baby D."

Cam turned around and grabbed LaLa by the throat, while holding Gray back with his free arm.

"Didn't I tell you not to disrespect her? Go the fuck home before I let her beat your ass." He pushed her back so hard she slid off the car with a squeal and fell to the ground.

LaLa got up and dusted off her jeans.

"So that's how it is? This bitch come around and it's just fuck me? You not gon' keep puttin' me on the back burner and then pick me up when it's convenient for you."

"Bye, loose puss." Cam focused his attention back on Gray who was still going off.

"You gon' remember this, Cam! Mark my word! Yo' ass gon' pay for this!" LaLa jumped in her car and sped off.

"Now, back to you. The fuck is your problem?" He mean-mugged Gray.

"What the fuck is my problem? You the one with an attitude. I tried to tell your dumb-ass that I didn't invite him. He came on his own. I didn't want him there, but I can't tell that man where he can't go when his kids are involved. You see I wasn't even around his ass, but nooooo… you wanna walk around like an ol' sensitive thug, instead of hearing me out."

"Damn, Cam, I ain't know you was the emotional type," Stacy joked.

"Stacy, shut yo' fat ass up."

"I'm just sayin'. Don't shoot the messenger, nigga."

Scowling, Cam glared at Gray.

"First of all, what I tell you about doing all that rah-rah shit?" He tapped her forehead with his index finger, continuously, as each word left his mouth. "You still gon' let people bring you out of your character even after the conversation we had?"

"Tap my forehead again—"

"No, you done talkin'!" He cut her off. "At the end of the day, you knew that shit was wrong. That's why you ain't give me no heads up. You knew I was gon' be there. You could've kept it a bean and let a nigga know what was up, but *nooooo*... you wanted to be scary and hide 'cause you still fuck wit' that nigga!"

"I swear to God. Y'all niggas is Bobby and Whitney for real. Cam, you might've met your match with this one." Stacy cracked up laughing.

"Shut the fuck up, Stacy!" Gray shot, annoyed.

"Damn, what I do now?"

Gray gazed up into Cam's coffee-colored eyes with disappointment in her own.

"You really think I'm still messing wit' him?"

"I don't know what you do. I just know you ain't about to play me."

Fuck you-fuck you-fuck you, Gray said, repeatedly, in her head. She was done with Cam and his insecure bullshit.

"Bet. You got it. Y'all, have a good night." She turned to leave.

As mean and tough as Cam was, the thought of her leaving and never returning paralyzed him. Somehow, Gray had snuck into his heart. He didn't know if he loved her, but it was damn near close. She had a hold on him. Their dynamic might've been crazy and chaotic, but he wouldn't have it any other way. Gray challenged him. She didn't let him trample all over her the way LaLa did. He couldn't lose her. His life was nothing without her in it.

"Where the fuck you think you going?"

"The fuck away from you and Stacy goofy-ass," she snapped, opening her car door.

"I wish you would jump in your shit and pull off. I will have every nigga on this block flip this bitch upside down and you won't be having shit to drive tonight."

"Well, heave-ho, nigga." Gray called his bluff by taking her car out of park.

"Think it's a game." Cam stood back, as several of the homies neared her car.

"Are you fuckin' for real? You gon' flip my car over… with me in it 'cause you don't want me to leave?"

"You heard what the fuck I said. Either get the fuck out or go to the emergency room. It's up to you."

Gray hesitated. Her unwillingness to cooperate caused Cam's goons to surround her car.

"Ok! Wait! Wait!" She panicked, turning off the ignition. "I can't believe you. You really was gon' try to kill me?" She got back out.

"Don't blame that shit on me. That decision was in your hands. You was gon' kill yourself."

"You are fuckin' insane."

"You just now figuring that out?"

"Whatever. I'm out the car. Now what?" Gray placed her hands on her hips.

"You already know what it is. You coming home wit' me." He took her by the hand and led her to his car.

"What about my car?"

"I'ma have one of the homies drop it off."

"On God, I don't know why I fuck wit' you."

"You know exactly why you fuck wit' me." Cam placed his dick in the crack of her ass and kissed her cheek.

"Nobody wins when the family feuds."– Jay-Z, "Family Feud"

Chapter 25

Mo

Mo didn't look forward to much, but attending her favorite author and friend, Chyna Black's wedding was a big deal. Anybody that was somebody was going to be there. It was the wedding of the century. People would be talking about it for years to come. She'd heard that Chyna's fiancé, Dame, had spent a half a mill on the flowers alone. She couldn't wait to see the decor and Chyna's gown.

Gray had helped her pick out a dope dress of her own for the event. Mo had already gotten her hair done and was now at the mall getting her eyebrows threaded. Next up was her nail appointment. Mo laid her head back and enjoyed being pampered. She needed the rest and relaxation. She'd gone far too long without taking care of herself. After King's party, she needed it. She'd worked herself to the bone, trying to ensure that he had the party of his dreams.

It hadn't gone unnoticed that Boss hadn't lifted a finger to help. She was honestly tired of him and his chauvinistic ways. Phyliss had raised a man that thought it was the woman's job to take care of all the domestic duties. Boss really thought all he had to do was pay bills, discipline the kids every blue moon and keep her filled with his hard dick. Things had to get better before they got worse. If their marriage stayed the way it was, she and Boss would be heading for divorce soon.

"Bitch, what's the tea 'cause you did not call me back?" Some loudmouth girl entered the brow bar.

“My bad, girl.” Mo heard a familiar voice say.

“So, what the hell happened? Did Boss finally let you suck his dick? What he workin’ wit’, bitch? I know that muthafucka big.”

“Girl, I tried, but that nigga wasn’t having it. I know he out here fuckin’. I don’t know why he keep playin’ wit’ me and don’t wanna give me none.”

Mo realized it was Zya speaking and abruptly rose from her seat.

“What the fuck you just say about my husband?” She lost all decorum and got in her face.

A rush of fear shot through Zya’s core. She had no idea Mo was even in the room. If she would’ve known she was there, she would’ve added more spice to the story just to piss her off.

“You know this bitch?” Her friend asked.

“This his pathetic-ass wife.” Zya rolled her eyes.

Mo didn't know who threw the first punch, but suddenly her fist was slamming into Zya’s face, while hers thrust against her throat. Blood pooled in Zya’s mouth, as Mo gasped for air. Surprised by each other’s strength, both women paused before ripping each other’s head off.
Mo avoided Zya’s fist and hit her with her own. Zya’s eyes grew wide with shock, as she reared her head back and slammed it into Mo’s forehead. A kaleidoscope of stars orbited before her eyes, as she blindly threw out a kick. Cockily, Zya stepped back, dodging her attack.

"You talked all that shit. Bitch, you can’t even fight,” she taunted Mo.

Mo channeled her inner Deion Sanders and tackled her like a football player. She and Zya fell into one of the chairs. Venomous words spewed from Mo's mouth, as she grabbed Zya's hair and hit her continually. All of Mo's pent up frustration was taken out on her face. She'd told Zya over and over to stop fuckin' with her, but the bitch just wouldn't listen. Zya got in a few good licks but was no match for Mo. All she could do was kick and scream.

Mo could hear the rush of heavy footsteps coming her way. At any minute, the police would be there, but she didn't care. Mo had to teach this little whore a lesson. Grabbing her by the foot, she yanked Zya to the ground, causing her head to hit the floor with a thud. Bruised and winded, with her skull in agony, Zya screamed for help. Her head was pounding. She was sure she had a concussion. Using her foot, Mo kicked her in the stomach. Zya's guts smashed together in agony. The Christian thing would've been to stop kicking her once Zya started spitting up blood, but Mo couldn't stop. She was in the zone. The one thing that stopped her was the police, as they placed a set of cuffs on her wrists.

The car ride home from the precinct was quiet. Neither Mo or Boss said a word. Mo was too mad to speak, and Boss was flat out terrified of what she might do to him if he said the wrong thing. She couldn't even look at him, she was so mad. Mo looked in the rearview mirror. She needed to see if there was any damage done. There was blood on her knuckles and a bruise above her right eye, but other than that, she was good. Her physical wounds might not have been bad but the emotional scars she harbored would be there for life.

The one person she counted on and believed in had let her down. For months, she'd looked past a lot of Boss' nonsense, but this was unforgivable. He'd left her out in the cold and betrayed her trust. She no longer knew what to believe when it came to her own husband. The fact that he'd kept Zya coming onto him a secret spoke volumes. It told her that his feelings for her might not have been as one-sided as he portrayed them to be. The bitch had tried to suck his dick, and instead of firing her ass, he kept her around. As far as Mo was concerned, Boss and Zya could rot in hell.

It didn't take long for them to pull up to the house. All Mo wanted was a hot bath and to be around her kids. They were the only ones that loved her wholeheartedly. She didn't have to worry about them letting her down. The car hadn't even come to a complete stop before she tried to hop out, but Boss quickly switched the child safety lock on.

"Let me out this muthafucka." Mo pushed on the door.

"Nah, man. I know it's a million things going through your head. Let me explain to you what happened."

"Now you wanna tell me what happened? Say what you got to say, nigga." Mo sat back in her seat, heated.

"Well, umm… remember that night I came in the house wit' a real bad headache?"

"Yeah. And?" Mo shrugged.

"That was the night it happened. I had been drinking with the staff. Everybody had left. It was just me and her counting down the drawers. We was talkin' and shit, and the next thing I know, she was on her knees tryin' to suck my dick."

"So, she just dropped to her knees to suck you off and you ain't do nothin' to make her think she had the go ahead?" Mo quizzed.

She might've been out of the game, but she was far from a dummy.

"I mean… before that… she was massaging my shoulders and shit."

"What?!" Mo jumped up in her seat.

"Before you get to trippin', calm down and let me explain!"

"Nah, you gon' have to talk a li'l faster, my nigga, 'cause in a second, I'ma start throwin' hands!"

"I was sayin' how tired I was, and the bitch got to massaging my shoulders. I ain't gon' even lie, I let that shit rock for a minute 'cause I was trippin'. But once I realized what she was doing, I curved the situation," Boss clarified. "She ain't even get to see the dick. She did show me her titties tho'."

"You're not serious! You're lyin'! You ain't that fuckin' stupid," Mo said, in disbelief.

"On our kids ain't shit happen."

"Nope. No-no-no-no-no." Mo covered her ears and rocked back and forth.

"Nah, hear me out." Boss took her hands into his. "On everything. I didn't touch that girl. I don't wanna be with that girl. I wanna be wit' you and that's all that matters."

"Yo, you're buggin'!" Mo slapped his hands away.

"C'mon, Mo. You know I would never cheat on you."

"Do I? 'Cause you got me out here lookin' hella stupid! Have I ever had you lookin' crazy? No!"

"I know I fucked up but you gotta let me fix this."

"The hell I do! You got bitches out here tryin' to suck your dick and show you their titties like you ain't gotta wife at home. I told you that bitch wanted to fuck you but you ain't wanna listen. Now look at ya dumb-ass. You about to lose your wife 'cause you wanted to jeopardize what you have with a gem for garbage!"

"Look, Mo, I can't lose you."

"Fuck you! Let me out this fuckin' car!" She yanked on the handle.

"I ain't lettin' you go nowhere until you calm the fuck down." Boss stood firm on his word.

"You made your decision. Why can't I make mine and go?"

"'Cause I love you. You're my wife. Ain't no leavin' me."

"Boss, just let me out," Mo said, in her regular tone, so he'd think she'd calmed down.

Boss stared at her for a second. Once he thought she'd relaxed a bit, he undid the child safety lock. Free, Mo jumped out the truck and slammed the door so hard the window shattered.

"Are you fuckin' for real?" Boss jumped out and assessed the damage. "I told you ain't shit go down! I ain't even touch that girl!"

"And I don't fuckin' believe you!"

"This shit ain't even this fuckin' serious, yo." He charged towards her, causing her to trip over her feet, but Mo caught herself. "That's what yo' ass get."

"If I would've fell, I would've fucked you up! Bird-ass nigga!" She mushed him in the head then stormed into the house.

Boss stood there for a second, trying to calm himself down. Mo was on some ol' other shit, but she had every right to be. He'd fucked up and he had to take his punishment.

"Yo, Mo! Hold up! We need to talk about this." He followed behind her.

"Go talk to that bitch! You lyin' sack of shit!" Mo slammed the door in his face.

"I might've omitted the truth, but I never lied to you." He tried to keep his cool.

"Omission is the same as lyin', dickhead!"

"Hey-hey-hey! Cut all that damn noise out!" Phyliss rocked Zaire in her arms.

She'd come over to watch him while Boss went to go pick Mo up from jail.

"You in my fuckin' house! You don't tell me to be quiet. You be fuckin' quiet and give me my baby." Mo tried to take him from her.

"I'm not giving him to you. Look at you." Phyliss blocked her attempt by turning to the side.

Mo was a mess. There was dried up blood all over her.

"Give me my damn son," Mo said, outraged.

"You are not fit to be around him right now. You need help. Up here fighting some li'l girl in the mall like you ain't got no damn sense. Zaire, I told you her ass ain't got no home training." Phyliss looked at her like she was crazy.

"I'm tellin' you now." Mo turned and looked at Boss. "If your mother doesn't give me my son, I'm going to slap the shit out of her."

"See! She's crazy."

"I'm crazy?" Mo placed her hand on her chest. "No, I am sick and tired of your lonely, miserable- ass butting into my marriage. Boss is not your husband. He's mine. You can't fuck him, Phyliss. I know you might want to, but you can't. I can, and I do it quite well. Your husband is dead! He died almost 20 years ago—"

"Yo, chill! You going too far," Boss interjected.

"No! I haven't gone far enough. I have been puttin' up wit' y'all shit for way too long. You stay sticking up for her rude-ass, but when it come to me, yo' ass is on mute. Let me find out you wanna fuck yo' mama, 'cause I swear you love her more than you love me! Every time I turn around, she up in our business; and why, because you stay runnin' and tellin' her shit. I don't know if you forgot but, nigga, you married me! Not her. The Bible says therefore shall a man leave his father and his mother and shall cleave unto his wife: and they shall be one flesh. Memorize the shit and live by it, my nigga!"

"What the fuck are you talkin' about? I put you before everything."

"Did you put me before that bitch? 'Cause if I remember correctly, she tried to suck your dick, and afterwards was still able to keep her job. Let me be in the same vicinity as Quan and your period come on. Meanwhile, you don't do shit around here! You don't help me cook! You don't help me clean! You barely help me raise the kids! All you wanna do is worry about another nigga that ain't worried about you!"

"Yo, don't even bring that nigga's name up, 'cause trust me, ma, you don't wanna go there."

"Nah, let's go there!" Mo challenged.

"You still ain't covered that nigga's name up! Every fuckin' holiday you over there with him and his family. How you think that make me feel? Seem to me you still holding onto something. We married, and we don't even spend holidays together. What kind of shit is that? Meanwhile, you worried about bullshit that I stopped. It didn't happen. But you bringin' up a nigga that cheated on you 50 million times, had a baby on you and let's not forget the nigga used to put his hands on you. Fuck outta here, Mo. You on some dumb shit. I put up wit' all types of bullshit when it come to you."

"Oh, so now you put up wit' me?" Her voice cracked.

"Don't get in yo' feelings now! You wanted to go there, so let's get down to what's really going on. You still fuckin' that nigga? 'Cause you ain't fuckin' me. Every time I turn around, you *so tired* and always talkin' about *I don't like the way I look.* But on Labor Day yo' ass got dressed up to go see that nigga. You could put on some clothes then, but I gotta see you walk around this muthafucka lookin' like you don't give a fuck. And I still ain't fuck that bitch!"

"So, you want brownie points for keepin' yo' dick inside yo' pants?"

"Hell yeah! You need to be happy my son ain't been fucked somebody else. You walkin' around lookin' like you done gave up on life!" Phyliss hissed, with hate.

"Bitch, mind your fuckin' business. This ain't got shit to do with you." Mo got up in her face.

"My son is my business. I told him to leave yo' ho-ass alone a long time ago. Didn't you fuck Quan and his friend? I know your mother is ashamed of the way you turned out. She probably turning over in her grave right now."

Mo blacked out, forgetting that her baby was in Phyliss' arms and backslapped the living shit out of her. The slap was as loud as a clap and stung the outer part of her hand. Under Phyliss' eye was a small cut from where Mo's wedding ring had scratched her.

"Don't you ever say shit about my mother!" Mo screamed, like a madwoman.

Her lungs felt as if they'd been given an acid bath. Whatever was in her brain that had been holding her together had officially snapped. The need to kill consumed her. No one talked about her mother unless they wanted to die. Phyliss staggered backwards, clutching the baby and her face. She couldn't believe that Mo had actually hit her.

"You see, Boss! She's not fit to be a mother, let alone a wife!"

"Mama, shut the fuck up!" Boss bear hugged Mo from behind and body slammed her onto the couch.

A fury like no other ran through his veins. His rage bristled like wildfire. Mo could practically see the flames roaring in his eyes.

"What the fuck is wrong wit' you? Why would you hit my mother?" He pinned her hands down.

"Did you not just hear what she said to me?" Mo tried to buck him off her and break free.

"So the fuck what! That don't mean you put your hands on her!" Boss shook her violently.

In the 11 years they'd been together, he'd never had to put his hands on his wife.

"You know what, Boss? Fuck you! Dealing wit' you, I should've stayed wit' Quan's ass. You ain't no better than that nigga. You ain't worth shit and you ain't gon' be shit." Mo's bottom lip trembled.

Boss stared down into Mo's eyes and no longer saw his wife. She was now his enemy. Fuck sparing her feelings. Maybe his mother was right. Maybe they should've ended their relationship before it ever began.

"You know what? I wish I would've fucked that bitch. I thought about it on several occasions. I could've came home and fucked you right after and your dumb-ass wouldn't have known shit. For real, for real. I still could fuck her if I want, so keep on actin' stupid if you want to."

Mo tried to steady her breathing but couldn't. Boss' eyes held a coldness she'd never seen before.

"You wish you would've what? After all the shit I do for you?" Tears welled in Mo's eyes to the point she couldn't see.

"All you do for me? I'm the reason this house stay afloat. You sit around the house lookin' like who did it and what the fuck for and you got the nerve to complain about everything you do? I work my ass to the bone for you. Just to get home for you to bitch at me nonstop."

"I bitch at you 'cause you don't do shit, nigga. I take care of everything in this muthafucka including your ungrateful-ass and your kids. You wouldn't survive a day without me, nigga. I put up with your naggin'-ass bitch of a mother and all you wanna do is strut in here with the same tired-ass line - *let me put my dick in you.* I got four kids, nigga! What the fuck makes you think that I want any parts of you or your dick? You lounge around here like you King Tut and I'm one of your fuckin' slaves. I'm your wife, nigga. Well, for now anyway."

"Well, you one hell of a slave with Chanel flip flips on. You delusional, spoiled-ass wretch. You bitch, gripe and complain about doing something that's your responsibility. It's called doing your part. It's called being a wife. Hell, I can do your job and mine."

"Aww… ok. You can? Say no more. Take the wheel, captain." She pushed him off her and grabbed her purse and car keys.

"Oh, you leaving? You know what, Mo? I don't give a fuck. I'm over this shit anyway. This been the worst 11 years of my fuckin' life, and you wonder why it took me so long to marry yo' ass."

Hurt covered Boss like a cloak he never wanted. With each word Mo spewed, a new scar was etched into his heart. He had to make her feel what he felt. She'd cut him down to size. It was only right that he returned the favor. And yes, he saw the endless tears that dripped from her eyes, but he had to remain cold. He couldn't let it show that he was on the verge of crying too. He refused to cry and grieve for her. She'd taken away her love and locked it inside the cage she called a heart.

Mo gazed helplessly at her husband, praying he would set aside his pride and save her, but once again, she was on her own. They'd gone through a lot together, but Mo was starting to realize some shit couldn't be fixed. She would've rather Boss took a knife to her throat than speak the words he'd spoken. He talked to her as if she were a stranger. He stared into her eyes, saying whatever he knew would hurt her the most. Knowing her as well as he did, he knew it wouldn't be hard to split her heart into two. Mo pretended to be hard, but she was as soft as baby shit. That still didn't give him the right to treat her like she was beneath him. Without saying another word, Mo walked out the door and never once looked back. Boss would have to learn the hard way that she was not to be taken for granted.

“We will not be disturbed by the fussin’ and fightin’.”– Kanye West, “White Dress”

Chapter 26

Chyna

The time had finally arrived. It was the day before Chyna said I do. A happiness like she'd never known filled her spirit. She was void of all negative emotion. She thought she would've been a ball of nerves but only excitement consumed her. The time for her to walk down the aisle couldn't come fast enough. With the help of celebrity wedding planner, Mindy Weiss, she was able to plan the wedding of her dreams. Once again, Dame hadn't let her down. He'd said she could get it done with his money and resources and she had. They'd just finished the wedding rehearsal and now Dame and their wedding party sipped on chilled champagne.

It was a glorious Friday afternoon. The weather was perfect. Fall was always one of Chyna's favorite times of year. The air hadn't chilled yet. Heat from summer often lingered over well into October. Chyna couldn't have asked for a better day. Outside had the sweet scent of freshly cut grass. The birds chirped in the trees. The sky was sapphire with a few clouds making their unhurried way south. The sun was a welcoming ray of yellow, promising more heat as the day went on.

The rehearsal dinner setup was glorious. Blush-colored drapes billowed over the dinner tables, protecting the guests from the sun. Miniature, crystal chandeliers that would light up the area when nightfall hit, hung from hooks. Centerpieces made of pale pink roses and white hydrangeas sat on top of black, lacquer, S-shaped tables. Tall gemstone candle sticks lined the tables as well. Guest could sit in black, suede, armless chairs or on pink, velvet couches. Everything was immaculate. People were shocked that the rehearsal dinner was so extravagant. It hyped everyone up even more for the wedding ceremony and reception.

Chyna stood next to her handsome man, nursing a glass of sparkling champagne. Dame hadn't let her leave his side. She didn't mind. She was her happiest when she was next to him. Chyna wasn't oblivious that when she wasn't around Dame he was unhinged. Anyone that wasn't her or India could get it. The killer look she'd come to know well would be in his eyes. It would take hours of her hugging and kissing him for him to return to his normal self.

At first, she thought it was just his nerves about the wedding and the baby, but he'd been acting this way since she'd been robbed. Dame was a man that had control over everything in his life. He'd promised to shield her from all harm, and that one night he'd failed. No matter how many times Chyna told him it wasn't his fault, Dame still blamed himself.

"You ready to tell me what's been bothering you?"

"What you talkin' about, shorty?"

"You've been spazzin' on everybody for weeks. At first, I thought it was just you being your normal grumpy self, but it's more than that. Something's going on wit' you. I just need you to keep it a buck wit' me and tell me what's up. I don't wanna go into this marriage keeping secrets from each other. Is everything alright with us? Are you having doubts about marrying me?"

Dame hated that she thought his mood swings had something to do with his feelings for her. That was the furthest thing from the truth. He didn't wanna lie to her, but telling her the truth wasn't an option either.

"It's business, Belle." The lie slipped out, smooth and easy like melted butter running down toast.

Chyna narrowed her eyes at him. She was far from a fool. She knew he was lying.

"We're about to take vows tomorrow to share everything. Tell me what's going on with you."

"I'm scared, Chy," he confessed, when he saw she wasn't going to let up. "I'm scared for you. I'm scared for the baby, and this is how I am when I'm scared. It's unfamiliar to you but not to me."

"But why? I'm fine. We're fine." She placed her hand on her stomach.

"I don't know. I can't explain it."

Chyna wished she could believe him, but uncertainties still lingered in her spirit.

"Come here." He palmed her cheeks with his hands. "I'm sorry for being busy in my head."

"It's ok."

"No, it's not. Today is your day. You're supposed to be happy. Not worrying about me."

"As long as you're by my side, I'll always be happy." She gave him a short but sweet kiss.

"Did I tell you how beautiful you look today?" Dame pulled her close and placed his lips against her forehead.

Chyna closed her eyes and blushed. Only Dame could make her feel like she was the prettiest woman on the planet.

"Don't think I didn't peep how you been jockin' my style." He ran his hand over her bountiful ass.

Dame loved everything about her outfit. Chyna wore her hair parted down the middle with a halo braid wrapped around it. Her makeup was immaculately done. Her eyebrows were arched to perfection. ColourPop Cosmetic's Ultra Matte Lipstick in the shade *Avenue* decorated her lips. Drop, pearl earrings dangled from her ears. Her Dame-inspired outfit consisted of a Viktor & Rolf, sleeveless, mesh top with pearl appliqués that covered her breasts and white wide-leg trousers. An over the top, exaggerated, satin bow tied around her tiny waist. If it were left up to Dame, he would've married her right then and there. Chyna didn't need a wedding gown to make her beautiful. The male-inspired look she wore was more than enough.

"What can I say? I learned from the best." She gently leaned in and kissed his pillowy lips.

"Eww... get a room," Asia teased.

"Now you see how I felt watching you and Jaylen all these years." Chyna came up for air.

"You two love birds ready for tomorrow?"

"I have been waiting 36 years to say I do. I am beyond ready." Chyna smiled.

"I know that's right." Asia gave her a high five.

"Babe, did you finish your vows?"

"Nah, not yet," Dame lied.

"Dame, you bet not recite no bullshit to me tomor. I'ma beat yo' ass if you do."

"You worry about you. I got this."

"Chyna, you staying at your house or the hotel tonight?" Delicious joined the conversation.

"Neither," Dame said, simply.

"You do know she can't stay with you tonight? It's bad luck for the groom to see the bride before the wedding."

"I don't believe in all that superstitious shit. She coming home with me." Dame shut the conversation down.

It wasn't up for discussion. He would awake next to his belle on his wedding day.

"You heard the man. What Daddy wants, Daddy gets." Chyna stuck out her tongue.

"Y'all backwards as hell." Delicious pursed his lips.

"Just breaking all the rules," Selicia agreed.

"First you get engaged, then pregnant and now you gettin' married and sleeping together the night before the wedding. Well, I de-clare." Delicious fanned himself with his purse.

"Y'all know I have always marched to the beat of my own drum. I don't give a damn. Ain't shit fuckin' up this wedding. If it's just me, him, India and the priest, we gettin' married. Hell, I didn't even need all this shit. I told him we could go to Vegas and elope," Chyna professed.

"You know damn well I didn't believe that shit." Dame took a swig of his champagne.

"Right! Chyna been talkin' about her wedding since we were ten," Asia added.

"Yeah, and wit' ten different niggas." Brooke laughed at her own joke.

"C'mon, yo. Not today." Asia's shoulders dropped.

"You better listen to your girl. I'm not in the mood," Chyna advised.

Brooke had already ruined dress shopping. She wasn't about to ruin her rehearsal dinner or wedding. She'd kill her before she allowed that to happen.

"Girl, bye; you know you was a ho. You been around the block more than a few times." Brooke bugged up laughing.

"And, bitch, you was in the passenger seat riding around the block with me. So, what?"

"Ok, and I'm married now. Nobody ever thought you would get married. You need to be happy Dame saw something in you 'cause none of the other hundreds of niggas you fucked would ever wife you."

"Hundreds?!" Delicious spit out his drink.

"Yes, hundreds. Just shy of a thousand," Brooke confirmed.

"You know what, bitch?" Chyna quipped. "I have had enough of you. Get the fuck out! You ain't even gotta be in my fuckin' wedding, so don't even bother showing up tomorrow."

"Ooooh… you actin' like you hurting my feelings or something. Don't nobody wanna be a part of your li'l funky-ass wedding no way." Brooke sat down her glass.

"Awesome! You can see yourself out. As a matter-of-fact, Mohamed! Please, see to it that she's escorted off the premises!"

"No problem, niece." Mohamed gladly followed behind Brooke, as she left.

A satisfied smile crossed Dame's face. He was so happy that Chyna finally got rid of that snake-ass bitch. He just hoped she would stay gone, so he wouldn't have to put her six feet deep.

"What is her problem?" Asia questioned.

"It's obvious. She's jealous." Chyna's nostrils flared.

"Well, duh. The bitch had on some Target flats with a JC Penny pencil skirt. Of course, she's jealous of you." Selicia threw shade.

Chyna pretended not to care about kicking Brooke out of her wedding, but on the inside, she was hurting. She never imagined that she would get married without her by her side, but kicking Brooke out of the wedding had to be done. Dame had been trying to warn her about her for weeks. She'd seen the hate in her eyes and tried to ignore it for as long as she possibly could. Chyna just couldn't do it anymore. No matter how much she cared for Brooke, some friendships weren't meant to last.

"Yo, where my li'l sister at?" Dame changed the subject. "She should've been here by now."

"Oh, babe, I forgot to tell you. She said she wasn't coming 'cause she was still at the salon getting her hair done," Chyna lied.

The real reason, Asha wasn't there was because she wanted to reveal her pregnancy to Dame at the wedding. Chyna felt bad for her man. His older sisters, Amara and Alecia, didn't respond to their invites at all. Dame wouldn't have any family at their wedding accept Mohamed and Asha.

"She'll be at the wedding tomor," she assured.

"I don't like that shit. Since when she start callin' you before she hit up me? That's my li'l sister."

"Oh, hush up, you big crybaby." Chyna playfully hit his chest, as his body went rigid.

Trepidation set on Dame's face like rigor mortis, his teeth locked tight like a Pit bull. Dame was as dark as night, but somehow, he'd become pale. On the outside, no one knew he was in distress, but Chyna could feel the slight tremor in his hand. Searching the crowd for the source of his discomfort, she spotted an older man and woman she didn't know.

"Who is that?"

"My father… Ahmed," Dame's voice croaked.

"Fuck is he doing here?"

"I invited him."

"Why?"

Chyna would never understand his need to prove to his father that he wasn't the piece of shit he'd branded him. No matter how much he did for Ahmed, he never got the recognition or apology he deserved. Dame figured if he invited his father to the rehearsal dinner, he'd see how good of a man he'd grown up to be. He wasn't the same little, meek, boy Ahmed used to taunt, abuse and control. Dame was a strong, confident man that didn't take shit from anyone, but as his eyes connected with Ahmed's, the vulnerable little boy inside of him re-emerged.

It had been years since he last came face to face with his dad. Flashbacks of him punching, kicking and whipping him with an extension cord danced in his head. Dame could physically feel the lashes all over his body again.

Chyna swallowed the bile in her throat, as the older, grumpier, fatter, meaner version of Dame approached. She'd never met the man, but she didn't like him. The demonic spirit in his soul resonated all over him.

"Basil."

"Père," Dame addressed his father and held out his hand.

"Je préférerais que tu m'appelles Ahmed." His father disregarded his hand, telling him that he'd prefer him to call him Ahmed.

"May I have everyone's attention?" Mindy Weiss said, into the microphone. "You may be seated. Dinner is served."

By the third course, Chyna couldn't wait for dinner to be over. It was awkward as hell sitting across from the man that caused her soon-to-be-husband so much grief. Dame was quieter than usual. He barely said a word or even acknowledged Chyna's presence. It was like his father had him in some sort of a trance. She'd never seen him so withdrawn.

"Lovely dinner that you have here." Ahmed wiped his mouth. "I guess your drug-dealing salary can afford you the finer things in life."

Dame sat quiet for a second, and then cleared his throat.

"I don't know what you're talkin' about, but thank you for the compliment." He continued to look down at his plate.

"You don't know what I'm talkin' about? Look at all this décor. If your pay matched your education, we would be in a hut."

"What is he talkin' about?" Chyna's brows dipped.

"Oh, your American bride doesn't know you didn't graduate from high school? Add another ghost to this demon's life." Ahmed chuckled.

Chyna waited for Dame to respond but he didn't. He just sat there staring at his plate.

"It don't matter to me no way. I didn't graduate either." Chyna placed her hand on top of his.

"So, she's uneducated, ignorant and American. You sure do know how to pick 'em."

"Father... we are here to enjoy this lovely occasion and celebrate my new beginning. Can you please refrain from disrespecting my wife?" Dame finally spoke up but never gave his father eye contact.

"It's Ahmed and you disrespected yourself with this lower class of a woman. So, don't tell me what I need to refrain from!" He pounded his fist on the table.

"This was a mistake." Dame flushed with distress. "I should've never invited you here."

"I'm the mistake? No, you are sorely misinformed, you little ingrate. The mistake has always been you. The very air you breathe is a mistake. You have been the biggest hinderance in my life every since I found out you were alive. Truthfully, the only regret I have is you surviving when you're whore of a mother cowardly took her own life."

An eerie silence swept over the table. No one said a word. You could hear a pin drop. Everyone knew how bad of a temper Dame had. They all braced themselves for his reaction, but nothing happened. Dame wanted to fight back but couldn't. He'd morphed back into his younger self. It was like he was in a catatonic state. He was paralyzed with sadness and fear. His father was the only person on the planet that could make him feel so small. He thought when his father saw how well he was doing, and the woman he was about to marry, he'd find some compassion. But it was becoming painfully clear that no matter what he did, he'd never be good enough.

Chyna, on the other hand, wasn't afraid of him. She was downright pissed. No one would disrespect her man and live to talk about it.

"Let me tell you something." She raised from her seat.

"Excuse me?" Ahmed said, surprised by her boldness.

"You heard what I said."

"Chyna, just let it go." Dame tried to pull her back down.

"No, it's my turn to speak. This man right here might not have a high school diploma, but let's be clear, he's smarter and more successful than most muthafuckas I know who have a college degree. How many dropouts you know got they own private plane and casino? I'll wait…" Chyna placed her hand up to her ear. "Yeah, that's what I thought. You don't. You talkin' all this shit, meanwhile, he paying all your bills wit' ya broke-ass. And since you wanna be so muthafuckin' ungrateful, this American woman your son is about to marry gon' make sure to put a stop to all that shit. So, get ready to go back to work. Cab driver!"

"You are a fuckin' disappointment." Ahmed eyed Dame, with contempt.

"Pussy, them hush puppies you got on is a fuckin' disappointment. Y'all ain't gon' keep playin' wit' me and my nigga. I'm with the shits today. Mohamed, escort this muthafucka out!" Chyna threw her napkin in Ahmed's face.

"Anybody else wanna get some shit off they chest? 'Cause I got time today!" Chyna looked around.

"Belle, you've proved your point. Come sit down."

"Nah, I'm already on go!"

Seeing that she wasn't going to calm down, Dame pulled her off to the side, so they could be alone. Chyna held her head back and exhaled.

"I'm sorry, babe. I didn't mean to embarrass you, but I just couldn't sit back and let him talk to you like that."

"Thank you." He buried his face in the crook of her neck and began to cry.

He didn't want to. Dame had never cried in front of a woman before. He especially didn't want to cry in front of Chyna. She'd only seen the strong, dominant side of him, but he couldn't help it. He felt alone and helpless. He needed her strength and support to pull him through. Chyna held him close. The sound of Dame's heartbreak caused a part of her heart to break too. Moving forward, she knew he'd never be the same. If he wasn't the same, then neither would she be. That's what happens when you love someone, right? Their happiness becomes a part of your own.

"It's ok." Chyna rocked him in her arms and broke down and cried herself.

Seeing Dame cry was almost too much to handle. It killed her to see him so weak. He was her rock. She never thought there would be a day she'd have to hold him up. But the day was here and she wasn't going to let him down.

"You don't have to thank me. You're my husband and I'ma always make sure you're straight. Look at me." She made him stand up straight.

Dame, hesitantly, stood to his full height. Chyna gazed lovingly into his eyes and thumbed his tears away.

"Fuck him. Look at your life. We good and we gon' always be good. You don't need his fuckin' approval. You got me. You got India. You got this baby. You fine as fuck. You rich as fuck. You about to be my husband. You ain't gotta prove shit to him. He's the one that don't deserve you. He's an abusive, miserable fuck. You are beautiful, kind and sweet. That shit he drilled into your head as child - that you wasn't shit - were lies. You are not a failure. You are a successful, black man. You taught me more in five months than I've known my whole, adult life. It is a blessing to be in your presence. Don't ever let a muthafucka like him make you feel less than. You are perfect in my eyes and ain't nothin' gon' change that."

Dame didn't know he could love Chyna anymore, but in that moment, his love for her grew ten times stronger. No one, besides Mohamed, had ever had his back so tough. She didn't judge him or make him feel like he was less than a man because he showed weakness. She loved him through it, like a wife was supposed to.

"I love you, Basil Damian Shaw. I can't wait to marry you and have your child."

"I love you too, ma."

"Even though I met you in the club in a tight dress, at first sight I could picture you in a white dress. Thirty-foot train, diamond from Lorraine, just to make up for all the years and the pain."– Kanye West, "White Dress"

Chapter 27

Chyna

The rapid beat of Chyna's heart was drowned out by the sound of a six-piece orchestra playing Pachelbel's *Canon*. The classical wedding song set the mood for the ceremony. Delicious, Asia and India filed down the aisle, one by one, in blush-toned, beaded, 1920's, Gatsby, flapper style dresses. Asia was her matron of honor and India was her maid of honor. Chyna had never seen her friends and daughter look so angelic. She thought not having Brooke there to celebrate her big day would hurt, but she'd mourned that friendship enough.

Brooke wasn't the same girl she met at Harrison Elementary in the 4th grade. She'd changed for the worst. Jealousy, bitterness and envy had taken over and replaced the kind, supportive woman she used to be. Chyna would miss the friendship they once shared, but her life was moving in another direction. In a matter of seconds, she was about to marry the man of her dreams. The palms of her hands started to sweat because she was so anxious. She wanted to yell at her bridesmaids to run, so she could get down the aisle faster to Dame.

Their star-studded wedding guest included Jay-Z, Beyoncé, LeBron James, Chrissy Teigen, John Legend, Victor Gonzalez, Mina Gonzalez, Meesa Black, Dylan Monroe and Heavy Weight Champion Angel. Everyone that was near and dear to Chyna was there, including her mom, brother and Selicia. Chyna had a huge family, so they took up most of the room.

Finally, the priest came out and asked everyone to stand. It was Chyna's turn to walk down the aisle. All eyes would soon be on her. Mindy Weiss' assistants opened the doors and revealed a floral wonderland. Hundreds of fragrant, pink and white roses, along with Edison bulbs, dripped from the ceiling. White, organza fabric cocooned around the guest, as they sat on white chairs that held court on each side of the white, lacquer, S-shaped aisle. She and Dame would exchange vows at an alter filled with candlelight and an archway made of roses, peonies, hydrangeas and precious orchids. The flower girl lined the path she would walk on with white rose petals, as the music started. Chyna took two steps out before she was greeted by her father.

"You ready, baby girl?" He held out his arm.

"As ready as I've ever been." She linked her arm with his.

Chyna's father escorted her down the aisle, which seemed much longer than she remembered. Like always, when she needed him most, her father became her strength; for without him, she would faint. The guests looked at her, taking pictures of her dress, waving and smiling. Up ahead, she saw him. Dame, her future husband, the love of her life, her everything. He stood taller than ever before, with his shoulders back and his eyes fixated on her.

Dame stood next to the officiant in an understated yet bold, white, Noose and Monkey, skinny-fit, three-piece suit with a white, shawl collar. The suit was crisp, clean, edgy and cutting edge, just like Dame. His fresh and precise haircut, clean-shaven face, broad shoulders and muscular physique reminded Chyna of a chocolate angel. She normally didn't like men in white suits, but Dame made the shit look fly as fuck. If anybody else was going to wear white on her wedding day, it would be him.

Unlike Dame, her nerves kicked in ten-fold. For the first time in her life, the attention on Chyna was too much to handle. Good thing she only had ten more steps to go. At the end of the aisle, her father hugged her and said, "I'm proud of you," then presented her to her groom.

"You tryin' to take a nigga's breath away?" Dame gazed lovingly into her eyes.

Chyna looked like a modern fairytale princess. A long veil covered in crystals and star appliqués cascaded past her shoulders. She wore her hair pulled back to show off the soft beat on her face. The off-the-shoulder, Ziad Nakad, haute couture, full embellishment, ball gown had a sweetheart neckline, open, V back and a royal train.

As a couple, she and Dame stood in front of the priest. Before Chyna's father walked away, he patted Dame on the shoulder. It was his way of welcoming him into the family. A bundle of nerves, Chyna inhaled deeply, and then exhaled. Was this really happening? Was she really marrying Dame?

"You can now be seated," the minister said to the guests.

Chyna and Dame's friends and family followed his request.

"Dearly Beloved, we are gathered here today in the presence of these witnesses, to join Basil Damian Shaw and Chyna Danae Black in matrimony commended to be honorable among all; and therefore, is not to be entered into lightly but reverently, passionately, lovingly and solemnly. Into this - these two persons present now come to be joined. If any person can show just cause why they may not be joined together - let them speak now or forever hold their peace."

Chyna glared over her shoulder, daring a muthafucka to say something. She had no problem whooping ass on her wedding day. Everyone in the crowd cracked up laughing.

"Friends, we have joined here today to share with Basil and Chyna an important moment in their lives. Their time together, they have seen their love and understanding of each other grow and blossom, and now they have decided to live out the rest of their lives as one. Basil and Chyna have prepared their own vows. Basil, you may begin."

Dame retrieved his vows from his breast pocket and cleared his throat. Chyna thought he hadn't taken writing his vows seriously, but he'd been working on them for weeks. Dame wasn't usually a very vocal or emotional man, but it was very important to him that he find the right words to convey just how much she meant to him. There wasn't much that he believed in, besides God and the love he had for her. After he said his vows, the world would know that. Gently, he took her trembling hand into his.

"Gather 'round, one and all… and join me in my rejoicing. As the lover of my soul takes my last name. Bone of my bone, flesh of flesh, indeed this is the queen of me. Join me and my belle as we celebrate this thing our God has done today. I'm marrying my best friend, my heart. Loving you feels like a song that God wrote especially for me. You are the melody he chose to soundtrack my dreams. This is the sound of his faithfulness. Let us sing of how it all began. Sing of how we met. You were a 16-year-old, loudmouth girl with wild, curly, black hair and I a chocolate, D-boy with a cocky attitude."

Chyna and the guests smiled and giggled at his description of them.

"Sing of how your beauty danced in my eyes. How God took his time knitting our hearts together. Using both of our past like needle and thread to weave our stories into one that will glorify Him. The chorus of everything in me, singing 'I do', as God orchestrates the question. Can you hear Him applauding Himself for a job well done? With the same hands that made us one, for it was His story that put us on the same page. Can you hear me now? The sound of my heart calling for yours. The way that Christ calls for His church, I am to love you that way. For I am not perfect. I vow to give this marriage my best shot.

Before this romance can bloom and your roses blush red as my violets turn blue, may we be best buds. May our love blossom in the type of Eden that welcomes Him. With a bounty of our thanks as we spread rumors about this faith until the whole world gossips about His faithfulness. I will love you. I will love you." Dame covered his eyes and began to cry.

Once the first tear broke free, the rest followed in an unbroken stream. Seeing him so vulnerable caused Chyna to tear up as well. Tears burst forth like water from a dam, spilling down her cheeks. Dame took a deep breath and pulled himself together. He hated feeling weak, but for Chyna, he'd be that and more.

"I will love you," he continued.

"The way that God intended for a husband to love a wife. I will remind you every day of just how amazing you are. That God used your heart to reveal the gospel to mine. When I was blind, you allowed His light to shine through you and I have been so blessed by this miracle that you are. So, when things get hard, know that I will fight for you even harder and wage war against anything that will try to separate us from each other or God. I will welcome those scars proudly and wear the bruises of falling in love with you. This, I vow. To be yours and yours alone. I vow to fall in love with you daily. Joy shall race through my heart every time my tongue sprints towards your name. We shall walk by faith. We shall celebrate the working of His hands. For what man can separate what He has called one? I am yours, my love, and you shall be mine and we shall be His." He pocketed his vows, wanting desperately to kiss her.

All the guests clapped, with tears in their eyes. They were blown away by Dame's declaration of love for Chyna.

"Well, I don't know how you're gonna top that, but, Chyna, it's your turn."

Dabbing her inner eyes with a napkin, she tried to calm her nerves, but Dame's words had her rattled. Never had she felt more loved. For the longest, she thought that God hated her, but the man standing before her was a gift sent to her from Him. Chyna took a deep breath. She'd been rehearsing her vows from the moment she'd accepted his proposal. No other words would describe her feelings but a piece written by Jannette IKZ entitled *I Waited for You*.

"Did you know that I'm not her? And I partially agreed to the wait because I didn't believe you existed in the first place. But in the slight, rare possibility that you did, you would definitely not want me. Because I'm not *'her.'* I choke on soft words like *'want'* and *'need'*. I hate flowers, red boxes of unpredictable, strangely-textured chocolate, balloons that take months to die and everything Valentine's Day. I'm sorry, but to me, *The Notebook* and *Love Jones* were just okay. I am the one that fairies tell you to stay away from. I was never *Cinderella*, I was the evil stepmother. I was never the princess, I was the fire-breathing dragon. I was *Ursula*, I was The *Wicked Witch of the West,* yet you still chose to knock on the door of this castle - my heart - unaware that an invisible fortress had been built due to much more experienced pain than a sting.

Unbeknownst to you, there'd be six more doors you'd have to get through before you ever even saw a glimpse of me. I was still wounded. Conditioned to live with a knife lodged in between my third and fourth intercostal margin, which collapsed my left lung, so I never left due to you being out of my comfort zone and shortness of breath. Besides, I was already in a relationship with… pain and I hated him, but I loved him because pain had been faithful for years. I could rely on a past history that he was sure to come. My first love on earth… cheated on me, visiting me on holidays, bearing beautifully-wrapped gifts of empty promises tied with bows the color of wishful thinking and then leaving me.

And although Mommy said I was beautiful, and that it wasn't my fault, it still felt like incarcerated incidence; so, beauty, to me, was incomplete. Like having only five heartbeats with no reason to stand up, there was no heart in the house tonight, nights like this I wish, and I'd pray:

"Our Father who art in Heaven, Hallowed be Thy name, please allow the clouds to gather and the sky to turn to grey. Lead us not into temptation. Oh, how I wish that it would rain, so when I look in the sky I can see my reflection."

"Yassssss!" Selicia waved her hand in the air, dramatically.

Everyone in attendance caught the Holy Ghost too.

"I got nervous when you got to door six, but surely when you saw the auction off art on the wall no one else wanted, re-describing each and every one of my wounds, you'd see the ugliness of pain. That I'm not the beauty you thought me to be when I was 16. So confidently, I stepped outside to bask in the sun. He's the one that knows me. He loves me. He has the ability to foresee and still loves me. So, I stepped outside only to find you sleeping night after night in front of the door of my cold heart. *"Who led you inside?"* I was terrified. No one has ever been this close, but all you wanted to do was show me that we shared the same, old wounds. There were no butterflies, just extreme discomfort because comfort is uncomfortable to someone more acquainted with pain than love."

Dame bit his bottom lip and nodded his head in agreement to prevent himself from crying.

"I was a relentless, unpredictable storm. And I guess those other men were made of straw and hay because I huffed and puffed but the spirit that your brick body house wouldn't go down. *Why couldn't I admit that your hand placed gently on the back of my neck calms me?* Instead, I accused you of trying to control me. I hated the way my heart became a defiant teenager and began listening to you instead of me. And even after you kept giving me your **'I LOVE YOU's'**, I couldn't stop them from replaying in my mind when my spirit, my spirit bore witness to the Christ that I saw in your life. I started getting tired of the fight. I decided to give it a try, just to prove to you that you too would leave, just like my seed and die before petals, stems and leaves. My trusting heart had been attacked. I didn't know the difference between accepting abuse and being the peacemaker. I'm left with a pacemaker, nobody wanted me. My rhythm is abnormal."

Chyna held her head low. The muscles of her chin trembled like a small child, as she tried to keep it together but failed. Salty tears dripped from her eyes, staining her dress.

"I lost my footing and I kept asking myself *'who are you?'* While climbing the attractive mount Everest of your mind, I attempted to hike a little higher to take a peek at your soul. I lost my footing on that trail, dangled off the cliff of your condition of unconditional and that is where I fell… in love, skydiving on the wings of your patience. Thank you for catching me. But this love, it's too much. This love is just way too much because your smoldering volcano erupted upon my arrival. Smothering lava, I mean, hot lava chasing me down, burning the pain of my past. Scorching heat on the back of my heels, a fire that screams *'just let me love you!'* I fell, I am consumed, I am overwhelmed. *Did you know that I am crazy?* It's hard to breathe when anyone gets close. Stand close. And just let me inhale your exhale. Stay close. Even when I punch you with my words, stay close. Even when I cut you with my fears, stay close. Look into my chilling eyes and remember, look at my chilling eyes and remember, look at my bleeding knees and remember, look at my bleeding lips and remember, I fell for you. And it took me 36 years to let that pain die so that new hope and new life could resurrect.

You caught my tears like wilted, worn Bible pages, stored them up in bottles and let the collection remind me that as long as I stay close to Him, I'd never thirst again. And when God removed the scales from my eyes, I remember… looking at you for the first time and finally understood the meaning of the word *'Behold'*."

Dame wiped the tears away from his eyes.

"I remember the first time I looked into your eyes, it was like staring at the back of the moon, only to find that it shines too. You wear patience like a tailored suit," Chyna grinned.

"And all I could do was thank God and Mohamed for raising the man I never believed could exist. You begin to see me transforming by the renewing, I was so comfortable cocooning, as you studied my dimples like ocean waves crashing upon shore. *How sweet it is to know that I'm with someone who would still find me beautiful with stretch marks?*

We are not Romeo and Juliet. We are just Basil and Chyna. We too are a beautifully written tragedy. We too fought in the beginning like Capulets and Montagues. And although we know the world considers this poison, we will continue to drink truth.

And I know they told you, *"Good luck with her."* Many have tried. 'Cause not even Charlie could Parker, but your consistent love would make Ella stop having fits and put down her dukes. You have me willing to walk and hop on cold trains even on a holiday. Inspire the desire to not be headstrong but arm strong, you had me in a sentimental mood, willing to walk miles to get to you. You became my black coffee and I couldn't move on. I felt dizzy because I was out of my element, like an uncovered monk, but you've been a good man for more reasons than I could count. May the Lord continue to orchestrate this beautiful, lifelong, complex cord progression.

I could make a million promises with a long list of what I could vow, but we are flawed human beings. So, today, I will let my yes be my yes, my no be my no and today my I do my I do. I vow that at times I will fail you. I vow that at times I will fall short, but in failures and shortcomings, I won't tap out, I won't give up. I vow… not to buy into false romanticism, saying things like, *"you complete me,"* because, in reality, you don't. In Christ, I have already been made complete, the head over all."

The crowd roared with applause, as Dame smiled at his bride.

"So, I vow not to attribute glory to you that only belongs to God. To you and only you… today, I commit; to you and only you, I submit, with an attitude. I've learned that God loved me enough to give me you, and so I vow to you my last breath." Chyna looked up into Dame's eyes and smiled.

"My God!" The priest exclaimed. "With the power invested in me, I now pronounce you man and wife. Basil, you may kiss your bride."

Dame leaned in and kissed Chyna, softly, like he'd never done it before. Everyone cheered for them, however Chyna barely noticed; her full attention rested on Dame, as it would for the rest of her life.

“A man that don’t take care of his family, can’t be rich .”– Jay-Z, “Family Feud”

Chapter 28

Chyna

"Can we get the happy couple on the dance floor. It's time for them to share their first dance!"

Dame searched the room for Chyna, but there was no need to look far. A spotlight shined down on her, as she sauntered towards the middle of the monogramed floor. Chyna was on her third outfit of the night, and this one literally stole Dame's breath away. She was practically naked, but he didn't care. The beaded, see-through dress with a split so high it reached her waist, poured over her bronzed body. Eagerly, he made his way to her as Keke Wyatt hit the stage to sing *Lie Under You*.

Tears filled the brim of Chyna's eyes. Keke Wyatt's velvety voice twirled like thread around her and Dame. Chyna rested her head on his chest and let him sway her body 'round and 'round. She had no idea that he'd hired her to serenade them live. Determined to live in the moment, she closed her eyes and let her happiness soak into her bones. She was over the moon in love and overjoyed that God had blessed her to experience such a wonderful day.

After saying 'I do', she and Dame jumped the broom and took pictures with their entire wedding party. Dame had wanted to get a few picks with him and Asha, but she'd dipped to the reception, without saying a word. He didn't know what was up with her. She'd been acting hella funny lately. When he got back from his honeymoon, he was gonna holla at her. Until then, he couldn't worry about Asha. No one was going to ruin his and Chyna's day. Once they got to the reception, he had a few drinks and let loose. He was proud of his belle. She, along with Mindy, had put together a gorgeous venue.

In the middle of the Botanical Gardens they created magic. Four rows of rectangle-shaped tables with white, linen cloth and Hermes table wear lined a brick ground for the guest to sit and feast. Hanging vines, orchids and chandeliers floated above them. Copious amounts of champagne, caviar, oysters, blue lobster risotto, Lyme Bay Crab and Australian lamb chops were consumed. Celebrity baker, Dylan Monroe, had designed a dessert bar that consisted of honey ice cream, salted caramel, chocolate parfaits and Dame's favorite Senegalese desserts, Thiakry and banana glace.

The music spun around them; lifting away gravity. Chyna couldn't count how many times she'd smiled. This was perfect. The lights were twinkling with every step, as she spun in delicate circles, her sparkling dress flowing behind her. When the song ended, she and Dame kissed each other fervently and thanked Keke for coming. Numerous guest approached them with envelopes filled with money. Chyna couldn't wait to get home to count it all.

Asha had avoided her brother for as long as possible. It was time to face the music. She'd attended the ceremony alone, but Gerald had arrived for the reception. Together, they would tell Dame the news about their baby and their own, impending nuptials. Dame was in a pleasant mood until he saw Asha and Gerald's broke-ass coming his way. He'd been smiling and laughing all day, which was a rarity in itself. As soon as he laid eyes on Gerald, his signature scowl returned.

"Congratulations, big bro." Asha hesitantly hugged him.

"Thanks," Dame responded, dryly.

"Congrats, OG." Gerald tried to give him dap, but once again, Dame played him.

"You are so rude. Stop being so mean. It's our wedding day. You have to be nice." Chyna chuckled.

The sound of Chyna's voice shook something in Gerald's spirit. That same voice had been haunting him for months. He hadn't been able to get it out his head. Once his eyes landed on Chyna's face, memories from the night he robbed L.A. and his girl flooded his mind. It was her. She was the girl he'd stuck up. *Fuck,* he thought. He had to get out of there.

"You know what, baby. I ain't feelin' too good. How about we talk to your brother later?" He tried to pull Asha away.

"Nah, this conversation long overdue. We gon' talk right now. So, you got my li'l sister pregnant?" Dame tried to control his anger.

He didn't understand what Asha saw in Gerald. He was a loser. A coked-out loser at that. He wondered if she knew he was getting high. The signs were all there. His pupils were dilated. He kept sniffling and rubbing his nose. The nigga was practically bouncing off the walls. He was tweakin' bad for his next hit.

"Dame, it takes two people to get pregnant. I knew what I was doing. I wanted to have this baby," Asha spoke up for Gerald.

"So, you got pregnant on purpose?"

"Yes, this baby was planned."

"Let me get this straight. You got pregnant on purpose by a coke-head-ass nigga that can't even take care of you? Last I checked, y'all was staying in the crib I put you in."

Asha's eyes grew wide.

"You should know me by now, little sis. I got eyes and ears everywhere. You think I ain't know you had this muthafucka stayin' wit' you?"

"Dame—" Chyna tried to intervene.

"Nah, she need to hear this." He stopped her from speaking. "You sound dumb as fuck. It's my funds that maintain all of your bills and utilities. You are held afloat by a monthly stipend that I provide. You would be another dependent of Uber and Metro Bus if it wasn't for me. And not to mention, your outlandish addiction to designer clothes is maintained by yours truly. So, you have the audacity to tell me that this pregnancy was planned when this low-budget, low-life can't provide for anything except his nose habit. I should smack the shit outta you."

"Aye, you don't know what I got. I take care of mine." Gerald grew a set of balls.

"He does, Dame," Asha cosigned his statement. "I haven't touched the money you give me in months because Gerald has been stepping up to the plate. We love each other, Dame. He's my baby's father and..." She slipped her hand inside her purse. "…he's gonna be my husband as well." She placed her engagement ring onto her finger.

Chyna was stunned. She had no idea that Gerald had proposed. Asha had kept that part of her life a secret. Dame looked down at Asha's hand. The same 3.78 carat, vintage, pear-shaped, diamond, pave, halo, rose gold ring he'd given to Chyna when he'd proposed sparkled under the amber-colored lights. It felt like all the wind had been knocked out of him. No way was Asha wearing Chyna's engagement ring.

"Where you get this from?" He snatched the ring off her hand.

"Gerald gave it to me!"

"Where you get my mother's fuckin' ring from?" Dame yanked him up by the collar of his shirt.

"Listen, I can explain!" Gerald panicked, as Mohamed and the rest of Dame's goons surrounded him.

"Dame, let him go!" Asha cried.

"You shut the fuck up and stay in a child's place. Now, you… answer the fuckin' question!" Dame slapped Gerald with so much force his nose began to bleed.

"Nephew, let's take this inside." Mohamed gripped his shoulder.

All the guests were watching. Remembering where he was, Dame let Gerald go, but he wasn't in the clear. Mohamed and a few of the security detail escorted him inside the building. Dame, Chyna and Asha were hot on his trial. Behind closed doors, Gerald was strapped to a chair. An uncontrollable wail escaped from Asha's lungs. The last time her brother had someone tied to a chair he was killed.

"If this is about the pills, I'm sorry." Asha sobbed. "I should've told you sooner. I just didn't know how. I swear to you, Dame, as soon as I found out it was him, I deaded it."

"What?"

"Dame, don't kill him! He was just tryin' to make some money, so he could take care of me and the baby!"

"So, it was you that was moving that shit through my club?" Dame growled.

"Wait a minute. That's not what this is about?" Asha panicked, realizing she'd told on herself.

"You knew it was this nigga the whole time and didn't tell me?" Dame backed her up against the wall.

"I'm sorry, Dame. I just couldn't let you kill him!"

"But you could let me kill an innocent man tho'?"

"What was I supposed to do? He's the father of my child!"

"AND I'M YOUR FUCKIN' BROTHER!" He yelled so loud, spit flew out of his mouth.

Asha coward underneath his wrath. Chyna covered her mouth and cried. Not because she was afraid of what Dame might do, but because, once again, he'd been hurt and betrayed by someone that shared his own blood. Now, she understood why he didn't trust anyone. The very people he tried to take care of and protect constantly took advantage of him. As his wife, she had to shield him from all evil, even if that evil came in the form of his sister.

"I'm your fuckin' blood! I should always come first!" He pounded his fist against his chest.

"I'm sorry." Asha cried, as if her brain was being crushed from the inside.

"You know what? Fuck you." Dame mushed her face. "I'm done talkin'. Mohamed, take that nigga to the back. 6F that nigga."

"Dame, no! Please!" Asha, hysterically, grabbed his arm.

"You still tryin' to save this nigga after he violated me and robbed my wife?" Dame pushed her off him.

"What are you talkin' about?"

"The ring Gerald gave you was the ring stolen from me in the robbery. Gerald robbed me." Chyna jumped in.

"On everything I love. I didn't even know that was your bitch. I got called to do a job last minute! Had I known it was your wife, I wouldn't have even done the shit," Gerald pleaded.

"Nigga, shut the fuck up!" Dame slapped him, again, like he was a li'l bitch. "You fucked up my wife face while she was pregnant. Ain't no coming back from that. Chyna, before I kill this nigga, come get your shit off."

"Babe, just calm down." She intertwined her fingers with his.

"Nah, fuck that! He could've killed you and my baby!"

"I understand that but look at your sister."

Asha was balled up in the corner, weeping. Nausea swirled, unrestrained, in the pit of her stomach. Her head swam with regret.

"You don't wanna do this to her. I know you. You're gonna regret it."

Dame didn't want to spare her any sympathy. He wanted to hate her. She'd destroyed their relationship. He'd never be able to look at her the same, but his wife was right. He couldn't kill Gerald, because if he did, it would be the equivalent of killing Asha too.

"Look at me." He grabbed her chin, forcefully.

Asha's lips shivered, as she gazed up into her brother's demonic eyes.

"I'm only gon' say this shit once. Stay the fuck away from me. You cut off. You ain't my family. Don't say shit to me. If I ever see you or this nigga again, you're both dead. I won't give a fuck about your tears or that baby. You understand?"

"Yes." Asha's heart shattered into tiny, microscopic pieces.

She didn't want to lose her brother. Dame didn't want to lose her either, but without trust, they had nothing.

"Now, get the fuck out."

"I don't deserve you. Please pick up the phone. Pick Up the phone." – Jay-Z, "4:44"

Chapter 29

Boss

"I want my mama!" King tugged on his father's pants.

"I want yo' mama too." Boss struggled to feed Zaire.

The baby was screaming his head off and wouldn't calm down. He was used to drinking milk from Mo's breasts. The stored-up breast milk from a bottle just wasn't his thing. Zaire's high-pitched screams were driving Boss insane. At any second, his eardrums were gonna rupture. The scream was primal. All Zaire knew was that his mother was nowhere close, and he was scared. A baby needed its mother; and although Boss could give his children the world, he couldn't give them Mo.

A week had gone by since she'd grabbed her purse and car keys and walked out the door. Boss figured she'd leave for a few hours and blow off some steam, but boy was he wrong. Mo had completely shut down and gone M.I.A. He hadn't talked to her once. He'd called her phone, repeatedly, but she'd turned it off. The only reason he knew she was alive was because he'd spoken to Mina. She'd told him she'd spoken to Mo and that she was taking some much-needed time to herself.

Thinking that she was at Mina's house, he went beating on her door only to find she wasn't there. She wasn't at Delicious' house either. Boss couldn't find her anywhere. She'd taken five-grand out of their account and that was it. There was no online trace of her whereabouts.

Boss didn't know what to do. He didn't know if she was leaving him for good or what. The kids were freaking out. All day long, they cried and begged for their mother. The twins kept asking him were they getting a divorce. He assured them that they weren't, but deep down inside he honestly didn't know.

He and Mo had arguments in the past but none like the one recently. Accusations were flown every which way. They'd both gone for the juggler, unwilling to backdown. The pent-up frustrations and hurt they'd been trying to suppress finally bubbled to the surface and blew like a volcano. Now, here he was with four kids by himself with no clue what to do. Boss never knew how much shit Mo had to do daily. Raising four kids without any help was hard as fuck.

He'd thought her job was easy, but he was losing his mind. Zaire hardly ever slept more than a few hours at a time. He constantly cried. One of the kids was always whining about something. A fight would break out at any given moment that he'd have to break up and mediate, continuous cooking and cleaning had to be done, and then there was homework, after-school activities, grocery shopping and taking care of their businesses. Mo juggled all these things daily with hardly any help from him. Boss felt like a complete dick.

Here he was thinking her job was easy. He'd grown up thinking it was the woman's duty to take care of the home and the man's job to provide and take care of the bills. He thought that when Mo whined and complained about needing help that she was just being overdramatic. A week alone with the kids made him see things differently. Thank God, his mother was there to help. If she hadn't been, Boss would've flipped.

"Daddy, the food burning." Makiah pointed.

Boss quickly spun around to find smoke coming from the stove. Turning the oven off, he fanned some of the smoke away and pulled out a burnt, crisp pizza.

"Fuck!" He tossed the pizza in the trash.

"Ooooooh… Daddy, you said a cuss word." Ryan stood back on one leg and shook her head.

"Now what we gon' eat?" Makiah rolled her eyes, with an attitude.

"Where is my mama?!" King threw his race car across the room.

"Throw something else and see if I don't go upside yo' damn head." Boss glared at his son. "I know you miss Mommy, li'l man. I miss Mommy too, but you can't be actin' like that. Ok?"

"You're right. My bad, Pop." King nodded his head.

"You need to beat his ass. Mo got these kids acting like goddamn heathens," Phyliss griped.

"How you blaming this on Mo? She ain't even here." Boss ransacked the fridge for something else to eat.

"Exactly! What kind of mother abandons her kids? I'm tellin' you, Boss, you need to leave that girl alone."

"That girl is my wife."

"Only on paper."

Boss paused and took a good look at his mother. It was like he was seeing her for the first time.

"What's really good wit' you?" He placed his hands on the kitchen island.

"Excuse me?"

"Why don't you like my wife?"

"She's not good enough for you. She's a liar and a manipulator. She ruined Shawn's relationship, which caused her to move away. She don't have no home training, and from the looks of it, your kids don't either."

"That's the last time you gon' disrespect my wife. Mo might be a lot of things but she a damn good mother. She hold shit down around here. Way better than what the fuck I been doing." Boss looked at the chaos around him. "I should've listened to my wife. The problem ain't her, it's you."

"What the hell you mean it's me?" Phyliss placed her hand on her chest. "She left you… and your kids. I'm the one here helping you. Like I always do."

"You ain't did nothin' but help me out of a wife. I was so busy defending you 'cause I ain't wanna hurt your feelings, but in the midst of all that, I was hurting my wife. I let you get way too comfortable with disrespecting my marriage and Mo."

"I ain't get away with nothin'. I'm your mother. I can say what I want to say. I come first."

"Now see, that's where you got the game fucked up. My wife and my kids come first. You ain't my girl. You're my mother, and I think somewhere along the lines you got shit misconstrued. Hate to tell you, but you don't run shit over here. When Dad was living, he never put his mom in front of you. You always came first in our house and it's the same for Mo. She ain't some bitch off the street. She's the mother of my kids and my wife. I ain't been treating her like it lately, but she comes before everything."

"Including me?" Phyliss said, horrified.

"Hell yeah! If you wanna be put first, you need to find somebody that's gon' do that, 'cause I'm not your man. I'm your son. Mo is my number one priority."

"Well, you ain't hers. Look around, son. The heffa is nowhere to be found! You don't even know where your fuckin' so-called wife is! Knowing her ass, she probably somewhere laid up with Quan. You betta get a DNA test 'cause Zaire might not even be yours."

Boss stood speechless. His mother was truly the devil.

"You know, sometimes I wonder, did my dad really die or did he run away, and you just said he died to save face 'cause you don't wanna admit how fucked up you are?" Boss looked at her with hatred in his eyes.

"Zaire!"

"Nah, you gotta go, ma. You foul as fuck. Mo was right. You ain't nothin' but an old, bitter bitch."

"Who the fuck are you talkin' to? I am your mother!"

"Only on paper." He hit her back with her own response. "Raise the fuck up." He gripped her by the arm.

"I know you ain't puttin' me out."

"Yes, the fuck I am." He lifted her out her seat. "Your old-ass gettin' the fuck up outta here. You ain't gon' keep talkin' crazy around me. You gon' fuck around and make me put my hands on you. Mo ain't fuckin' Quan. Quan got more respect for my marriage than you do. Yo' negative-ass got too much time on your hands. Don't worry about me and the kids. I got it. I don't want your negative energy rubbing off on them." Boss pushed his mother out the door.

"Boss!" Phyliss spun around.

"Nah, gone! You got yo' own house! Get the fuck away from over here!" He slammed the door in her face and dialed Mo's phone.

The kids needed their mother. He needed his wife. He couldn't go another day without her.

"Mo, I need you. Please, come home. I miss you. The kids miss you. Shit ain't going right. I'm burning pizzas. The kids been eating McDonald's and shit all week 'cause I can't cook. I think King might be constipated. I'm fucked up, Mo. For real. I need you here with me. I can't sleep without you by my side. I need my best friend back. Please, come home. I'll do whatever it takes."

“Just tell me you’ll hold my heart
‘cause them other ones left it only.” –
Teedra Moses, “That One”

Chapter 30

Gray

"I can't believe you got me out here on this gay-ass shit." Cam groaned.

"Don't get mad at me. You the one that wanted to do a picnic in the park." Gray giggled.

"I only suggested the shit 'cause I knew yo' soft-ass would like it." He opened the picnic basket.

Inside was Rosé Sangria with cranberries and apples, Idaho potato chips, shrimp and noodle salad, pulled pork sandwiches and Hazelnut-Nutella sandwich cookies. The rich aroma of the food wafted up Gray's nose. She was starving, and the food looked delicious.

"Oh, hush. You ain't gotta be a thug all the time." She placed a soft kiss on his lips, and then slipped her tongue in his mouth.

Cam cupped the back of her neck and kissed her fervently, passionately and then, lovingly. His lips pressed against hers with passion, love, and affection, as his warm hands roamed her body.

"Keep it up. Yo' ass gon' end up wit' yo' back broke, legs wide wit' hickeys on yo' neck."

"I would love nothing more." She grinned.

Cam poured them both a drink.

"Here. Be a good girl. Swallow." He placed the glass up to her lips.

"You so nasty." Gray took a sip and let the fruity liquid slide down her throat.

It was their first, official date. The day was postcard perfect. The sky was blue. There was no wind and the temperature was a warm 70 degrees. Cam had gone all out to make her feel special. Outside of the picnic, he even bought her two dozen, white, stemmed roses. Gray had no idea that he could be such a romantic.

For hours, they sat engrossed in conversation, barely noticing anyone else. Cam pulled Gray on top of him and gently brushed her hair from her face. Just the right hint of softness creased at the corners of his eyes, as he lost himself in her blue ones. There was so much that could be said for his silence. Gray could see by his expression there was a lot going on in his mind. And she was right. Cam did have a lot on his mind. It was her. She had become his one, stable force. His one stability in a world filled with chaos. He loved her and it was then that he realized it. The feeling was foreign. It overwhelmed him but also made him feel complete. His love for her had no bound, no length nor depth. It was concrete.

"What's on your mind?" She traced her index finger across his freckles.

"You."

"Me?" Gray said, surprised.

"Yeah, you."

"What I do?"

"Marry me," he whispered, so she could feel his warm breath on her ear.

"What?" Gray pulled her head back.

"You heard what I said."

"Stop playin'. You don't wanna marry me."

"Have you ever known me to say some shit I don't mean?"

"No."

"Ok then."

"How you go from not wanting a girlfriend to wanting to marry me? That don't even make sense."

Cam understood her plight. She had every right to question his motives. He was never the type of man to put his feelings on public display. He'd gone from detesting relationships to wanting her to be with him forever. Asking her to marry him was crazy, but Cam always lived his life on the edge of insanity. They didn't have shit to lose but themselves in each other. Why not take the leap?

"You love me?"

"Huh?" Gray said, caught off guard.

"If you can huh, you can hear, nigga. Answer the fuckin' question and you bet not lie to me."

Gray hesitated. She didn't want to tell him that she'd been aware of her love for him since the day they met.

"Do you love me?" She countered.

Cam wasn't madly, deeply in love with Gray but he loved her. He'd grown possessive over her in a way he couldn't control. He had to have her near, in his possession, always; and if marrying her was the only way to keep her by his side, then so be it.

"Yeah, I do," he replied, honestly.

Gray's lips stretched wide into a bright smile.

"Really?" She blushed.

"A li'l bit." He joked.

"I love you too." She kissed his eyes, nose, cheeks then lips.

"Then marry me."

"Cam, we barely know each other. I have kids—"

"And?"

"I can't just run off and marry you. We need to get to know each other first."

"We grown, right?"

"Yeah."

"Tomor ain't promised, sweetheart. Let's just say fuck it and live in the moment. I love you. You love me. We ain't got shit to lose."

"But marriage? We just started going together."

"Look…I always said the next person I get wit' ain't gon' be just my girlfriend. She was gon' be my wife. I'm too old to be bullshittin' around. A nigga like me like to go all in or nothin'."

"But why you wanna marry me—"

"'Cause I want something from you that nigga ain't never had." He referred to Gunz.

"And what is that?" She asked, shocked by his response.

"The honor of callin' you my wife."

Gray's heart skipped a beat. A new relationship was the last thing she needed, but Cam wasn't taking no for an answer. She honestly didn't want no to be her final answer. When she wanted to cry, he made her woman up and face shit head-on. When she wanted to shut the whole world out, he made her get out of the house and have fun. When she tried to push him away, he didn't put up a fight, but every time she fell he picked her up with no "thank you" required.

There was nothing to question or ponder. Cam was the one. She didn't have to be with him for years on end to be his wife. She'd come into his life like a hurricane, raw, hurting and fed up, but he was patient, caring and loving. There was no need to pretend like loving him was a whatever thing, when in reality, loving him meant everything to her.

"Yes. I'll marry you."

"Really?" He flashed her the smile that had her tied up tighter than a banker's money.

"Yeah."

"Don't be on no bullshit, Gray. If we gon' do this, we doing it for real."

"I know."

"A'ight, let's make this shit official then. Put your shoes on. We going to the Justice of the Peace right now."

"It always took her less to say more. I always thought she was an angel, now I'm sure." – Jay-Z, "MaNyfaCedGod"

Chapter 31

MO

Two weeks away from Boss and the kids had damn near killed Mo, but the time apart was necessary for her sanity. She couldn't continue to live her life the way she had been. If she would've continued down the path she was on, Mo would've ended up putting hands on more than just Zya and Phyliss. She genuinely feared harming herself, Boss or her children. After telling Mina about her suicidal thoughts and sadness she'd been experiencing, it was suggested that she might be suffering from postpartum depression. The thought had never crossed her mind. She'd been perfectly fine after giving birth to the twins and King.

Mina explained that all pregnancies were different and that she needed to seek medical help. Mo went to see her doctor, and after being evaluated was diagnosed with postpartum. She was ordered to see a mental health provider. Since she'd been gone, she'd been in therapy daily. The sessions had saved her life. She was able to get everything that plagued her off her chest. Therapy had been such a lifesaver that in order for her to return home, she demanded that she and Boss attend couples therapy together. The issues they had could no longer be ignored.

20,160 minutes had passed since Boss last laid eyes on his wife. The time apart had been hell on him but done wonders for Mo. She looked relaxed and refreshed. Her long hair was filled with bountiful, pageant curls that cascaded down her back. She wore a simple yet colorful Versace print shirt and patent leather, YSL booties with the company logo as the heel. Her long, lean legs were covered in body butter. Boss wanted nothing more than to glide his tongue from her ankle to her hip bone.

Mo sat next to her husband, trying to pretend like he didn't exist, but the smell of his Creed cologne had her pussy on overdrive. She hated the affect he had on her. No matter how mad she was at him, she couldn't deny his sex appeal. He had the kind of face that stopped a girl in her tracks. He was handsome, but inside he was beautiful.

The black, Pittsburg Pirates cap he rocked rested low over his almond-shaped eyes. The short sleeve, matching jersey showed off his well-built arms and tattoos. On his legs were a pair of distressed jeans and he wore black and white Air Jordan 1's. Her husband was fine as fuck but being good-looking didn't stop her from being disappointed in him.

"So, why are you two here today?" Dr. Bennet crossed her legs and placed a notepad on her lap.

"We're in a marriage that's going downhill," Mo replied.

"What are your main issues?"

"My husband and I recently had a huge fight that resulted in me leaving our home."

"Was the fight physical?"

"Fuck nah," Boss snapped. "I would never put my hands on my wife."

"I'm just making sure. These are questions I have to ask," Dr. Bennet explained.

"Well, ask something else 'cause that question was dumb as fuck."

"See, that's his problem. He gets defensive. He never wants to listen."

"I'm not gon' listen when it pertains to bullshit." Boss frowned, with a sigh.

"What caused the fight?"

"I learned that one of our employees came onto him in a sexual manner, and instead of telling me, he kept it a secret and didn't fire her."

"What kind of sexual manner?"

"She tried to suck my dick but I ain't let her," Boss said, nonchalantly.

"And why didn't you tell your wife?"

"Because I thought I handled it and I didn't want to upset her. She hasn't been the happiest lately and I didn't want to make things worse."

"Is that the only reason why you didn't tell?"

"What other reasons would there be?" Boss became agitated.

"Maybe you were attracted to this woman. I am assuming it was a woman." Dr. Bennet probed.

"Yo, hold up! What the fuck? Bitch, I ain't gay!" Boss barked, heated.

"Yeah, girl. You trippin'. Don't ever come to my husband like that," Mo defended him.

"Let's refrain from name-calling. I apologize, Boss. I meant no disrespect."

"Where the fuck you find this bitch at?" Boss looked at Mo.

"I found her on Groupon," she replied, under her breath.

"Groupon? Mo, what the…" Boss scratched his forehead and let out a deep breath. "You know what? I'ma chill. I ain't gon' even go there. We here now, so… it's whatever."

"Back to the subject at hand," Dr. Bennet interjected. "Mo, continue."

"As I was saying. Boss is stuck in his ways. He doesn't wanna listen. He doesn't acknowledge my feelings. His mother constantly disrespects me, and he doesn't do anything about it. He never helps me around the house. He's always at work, so I'm left alone all the time to take care of our four kids. He—"

"Damn, how much more you got to say?" He cut her off.

"A lot."

"Listen, you ain't even gotta say no more. I fucked up. I should've told you what the bitch did."

"Then why didn't you?"

"'Cause I knew you would flip and I didn't wanna risk losing my family over no bullshit. I ain't wanna put that kind of stress on you. I love you. I ain't tryin' to fuck up what we have. You, Makiah, Ryan, King and Zaire mean the world to me. Y'all are the loves of my life. I never meant for shit to get so out of hand."

"You know, the man I married would've kicked your ass all over that living room for speaking to me the way you did." Mo's eyes glistened with tears.

"Whatever the fuck I said, I ain't mean that shit. I was just tryin' to hurt you 'cause you hurt me."

"Mo, what affected you the most about the incident?" Dr. Bennet asked.

"I've had a lot of time to think about this 'cause I really want you to understand how I feel." Mo chose her words carefully. "What happened between you and Zya isn't what hurts. I can forgive that 'cause I know you didn't do anything with her. What hurts is the lie. You failed to trust me. The lie tells me two things. The first, is you underestimate what I can forgive. The second, is that you underestimate my ability to detect your untruthfulness. Two hurts for the price of one, not bad for a minor indiscretion, right?"

Mo's words marinated in Boss' brain and punctured his soul. It wasn't until she put it in those terms that he realized how much damage he'd done.

"Do you and Boss still love each other?"

"Of course, we do. Yo, this chick is retarded. Didn't you just hear me say I love my wife a minute ago?" Boss looked at her like she was stupid.

"The trick is to keep falling in love with each other. What I want you and Mo to know is that marriage is about choices. You gotta keep choosing each other. Even when you're not sure it's the right choice. Marriage is a lot like dancing. You should never break eye contact. You're partners, so you must stay connected. You're the man, Boss, which means she's following your lead. If you don't keep her in your gaze, she might get lost. Once your wife no longer feels protected and cared for, your whole marriage is doomed," Dr. Bennet enlightened him.

"Do you want a divorce?"

"Hell no!" Mo and Boss said, in unison.

"We got too much to lose to walk away from each other. I'll kill myself if I ever lost my wife. Don't none of this shit mean nothin' if I ain't got you. Fuck these businesses, the cars, the house, fuck it all. I need you. On my mama, you're the air I breathe," Boss proclaimed.

"Same here; ain't no living if I ain't got you. Hell, I could barely function these past two weeks. Shit, I damn near had the blade to my wrist," Mo professed.

"This is clearly a text book case of codependency and it's keeping you both from reaching your full potential." Dr. Bennet analyzed them.

"Thank you for the ground-breaking diagnosis that we're codependent. You act like we ain't know that. Where the fuck you get your degree from? The University of Phoenix?" Boss shot, sarcastically.

"We know we're codependent. I mean, we text each other every time we have a bowel movement. That's how close me and my husband are."

"You know what, fuck this." Boss turned and faced Mo. "I know I fucked up. I take full responsibility for what happened. I should've been honest and told you what happened from the jump."

"You humiliated me," Mo replied, somberly.

"And I apologize for that."

"Why did you even let it go that far?"

"I felt disconnected from you and I liked the attention she was giving me, but that's all it was. I swear."

"You sure?"

"Yeah. I ain't never even looked at another girl in the past 11 years."

"Now, that's a lie."

"Yeah it is, but you know what I'm saying."

They both cracked up laughing.

"But nah, for real. I hear everything you sayin'. I should've listened to you about Zya, and you were right about my mother as well."

"Oh really? Now that's a surprise." Mo folded her arms across her chest.

"I finally see what you been talkin' about this whole time. That's my mother and I love her, but she fucked up and until she can get her shit together, she can't come around."

"When did this revelation happen?"

"It don't matter. Just know she's checked now and you ain't gotta worry about that shit moving forward."

"Well, thank you. I appreciate that."

"Now, what I need from you is to understand how I feel about you and that nigga, Quan."

"Already handled. I won't be going over there for the holidays no more, and..." She pulled back her shirt sleeve. "…I covered up his name like you asked me to."

On her wrist was an anchor with a vine of roses wrapped around it. Surrounding the anchor was his and the kids' names written in small cursive.

"That shit dope as fuck, ma. I love it." Boss kissed her with as much intensity as he could muster. "On everything I love, I will never hurt you again. I'm sorry we even had to go through this shit."

"Just remember, sorry is nothing without change."

"Facts and I'ma do that."

Mo pulled out a stack of papers. Boss' heart dropped. If she was tryin' to divorce him, she had another thing coming.

"What's that?" He eyed the papers like they were a disease.

"This is a contract that you will verbally sign. At the end, if you agree, say hell yeah; and if you don't, say get the fuck outta here," she mimicked Kiyanne, from Love and Hip-Hop New York, whom she'd gotten the idea from.

"One… if you wouldn't do it in my presence, don't do it at all. Two… you know that women are gonna deliberately try to get at you 'cause you fine, got a big dick and can fuck, so always have your guard up. Three… too much friendliness will result in you gettin' stabbed and that bitch shot. Four… there's no such thing as a small lie. No matter the situation, come to me. Five… you must agree to us getting a maid and a nanny. I cannot take care of a household, you and the kids on my own. So, you agree or nah? Let me know what's up."

"I got some conditions of my own," Boss replied.

"Shoot."

"You gotta start keeping yourself together, babe. Like, your beautiful regardless, but today you look fine as hell. Got my dick on brick. And I know you be tired and shit, but we gotta start fuckin' more. I'm a man, Mo. You gotta let me hit the pussy at least three times a week," he bargained.

"I can handle that."

"For real?" Boss said, hopeful.

"Yeah. Now, do you agree?"

"Hell yeah."

"Now, raise your right hand and say, I Zaire..."

"Really, Mo?" He grinned.

"Yeah, nigga, I ain't playin'."

Boss shook his head and put his right hand in the air.

"I Zaire."

"Solemnly swear."

"Solemnly swear," he groaned.

"That I'm dead-ass about Monsieur," she said in a thick, New York accent.

"I gotta say it like that too?" Boss laughed, wholeheartedly.

"Yeah."

"A'ight...that I'm dead-ass about Monsieur!"

"There you go." She scooted close and planted her lips against his.

At first the kiss was small, gentle and very meaningful. But then, it grew bigger and more intense.

"Ahem." Dr. Bennet cleared her throat.

Mo, reluctantly, pulled away from her husband's embrace.

"Don't hurt me again," she whispered.

"I won't. Now, let's get back on our bullshit. Let's get back to us."

"Before I do, I have something else to tell you." She reached inside her purse. "I ain't gon' never get my waistline back. I'm so tired of yo' weak-ass pull out game. Congratulations, nigga, you gon' be a daddy, again." She handed him the positive pregnancy test.

Boss was speechless. All he could do was wrap Mo in his arms. She'd made him the happiest man on earth. At first, Mo was uncertain on telling him. Zaire wasn't even one yet and she had yet to tell him that she had postpartum depression, but the look on Boss face told her that everything would be ok. They'd just gotten through the biggest storm of their marriage. If they could get through this, they could get through anything. She had nothing to worry about. Boss was made just for her and she loved everything about him.

He had that brown skin Adonis thing going on that made her weak in the knees. Boss had the heart of a tiger and the soul of an angel. Everyone loved him. She could see it in the way people hung onto his every word. They wanted to be close to him, just like her. If he wanted to, he could have any woman he laid eyes on, but he just wanted her and the kids, and for that Mo was truly honored. Apparently, her love was enough. She was enough.

Over the years, they remained devoted to one other. Through sicknesses and family tragedies they supported one another. During rough times, neither strayed. Their journey wouldn't always be perfect. Loving her wouldn't be easy. They still had a lot of shit to work through. More battles were ahead. Sometimes, he'd hold the gun and she'd hand him the bullets, but Mo was in it for the long haul. For she'd experienced what it felt like to be loved by him and knew that there wasn't another man that would love her unconditionally and abundantly.

"All the signs been evident. This relationship is a sinking ship and we both 'bout to drown."– Lyrica Anderson, "Unhealthy"

Chapter 32

Gray

Gray stared down at the ten carat, oval-shaped, rose gold ring on her ring finger in awe. She was officially a married woman. After a 48-hour, required wait, she and Cam really went to the courthouse and tied the knot. It was crazy fast and totally out of her character, but she didn't regret her decision one bit. Cam had shown her more love in the past two months than Gunz had in ten years. They barely knew each other but Gray was confident they'd transition from friends, to lovers, to husband and wife without missing a beat.

The first order of business was telling Gunz. A week had gone by since she said 'I do'. Before she revealed her news, she had to put some things into place. That Wednesday afternoon, she sat on the windowsill, awaiting his arrival. She'd called him and said they needed to talk. The girls were in their room playing. Nervous energy raced through her veins. Gunz was sure to flip when she told him what she'd done. She didn't feel like arguing, but because of their kids, she owed him the right to know the status of her relationship.

Gray sat up straight and took a deep breath as the elevator door opened. He was home. There was no turning back now.

"Gray!"

"I'm in the living room."

"You going on a trip or something? What's up with the bags by the door?"

"That's what I wanted to talk to you about."

Gunz sat down on the couch and waited for her to continue.

"We're leaving," she said, matter-of-factly.

"Where y'all going? The kids got school tomor, don't they?"

Gray hung her head and scoffed. Gunz was a sorry piece of shit. He didn't even know if his girls had school or not.

"They have school tomor but we're not going on a trip. We're moving out."

"Moving where?" Gunz frowned, furiously.

"I got my own place."

Gunz stared into her bright blue eyes, flabbergasted. Silence gnawed at Gray's insides. Silence hung in the air like the suspended moment before a falling glass shattered on the ground. The silence was like a gaping void, needing to be filled with sounds, words, anything. The silence was venomous in its nothingness, cruelly highlighting how lifeless their relationship had become.

"You can leave but my kids ain't going nowhere."

"Gunz, the girls are going with me," Gray said, calmly.

"Where is this coming from?"

"Are you serious? Do you not remember gettin' a girl pregnant? This shit been coming."

"I know what I did, but that don't mean you get the right to take my kids away from me."

"You know I would never keep the girls away from you. You can see them whenever you want."

"I don't wanna be on no visitation shit. I want you and the girls here wit' me!"

"Well, I'm sorry to inform you but my life doesn't revolve around you anymore. I told you a long time ago I was done, and I mean it. You wouldn't give me the apartment, so I got my own. You will no longer hold this place over my head. I don't need it or you."

"I know this Tia shit got you upset, but you don't need to be making no rash decisions 'cause you're emotional." Gunz reasoned.

"Actually, I'm numb. The things you do no longer affect me. I have moved on with my life but you're too self-absorbed to notice that. This whole time we've been talkin' you haven't even noticed the ring on my finger."

Gunz glared at her hand. A diamond ring shined from her ring finger that wasn't the one he'd given her.

"Me and Cam got married last Wednesday."

This time, silence seeped into every pore of Gunz and Gray, like a poison slowly paralyzing them from either speech or movement. The silence stretched thinner and thinner, like a balloon blown big, until the temptation to pop it was too great to resist.

"Fuck you mean you married him? You belong to me!" He roared.

"Gunz, I haven't belonged to you in years. You and your dick is for everybody," she said, unfazed by his fury.

"You know I fuckin' love you!"

"Gunz, you don't love me. You don't even come home. I haven't seen you in days."

"You want me here, but you don't even fuck wit' me. You still angry over some shit I did last year!"

"Because… how do you say to me, Gray, I want to be with you and I want my family back and then you don't show up? You don't come home. You say one thing and then do another. I'm over it! I don't wanna do this no more!"

"The reason I don't come around is because you didn't wanna have anything to do with me."

"I DON'T WANNA FUCK WIT' YOU 'CAUSE YOU STAY FUCKIN' OTHER BITCHES!" Gray screamed at the top of her lungs.

"That don't mean you run off and marry that nigga!" Gunz got in her face. "I gave up my old life for you!"

"No, you gave up a life of crime, nigga! You did that for yourself! I motivated you to do it, so you wouldn't wind up dead or in jail! Yo' ass wanted to be a 60-year-old thug? You sound stupid as fuck right now!"

"If it wasn't for my drug-dealing past, you wouldn't have shit! I invested in that punk-ass magazine! I took you back after that nigga raped you! I helped you get your life back on track after you killed that nigga and had blood on your hands! I helped you sleep at night! I helped you get back on your feet! After all that, you got your li'l magazine and gave me your ass to kiss! And you wonder why I cheat!"

"Shut up! Shut the fuck up!" She forcefully pushed him in the chest. "You ain't gon' blame this shit on me!

You sit here and you tell me you want me back, and then you go runnin' to her! You must live with the bitch! Don't you? Y'all live together? 'Cause you ain't never here wit' me."

"Yeah, we live together, but she pay her own fuckin' bills." Gunz shrugged.

"So, you don't pay for the spot you rest yo' head at?"

"I mean… I bought the place, yeah."

"You mad 'cause I got married but you ran and bought your baby whore a place to live?"

"It was an investment."

"In what, y'all relationship? 'Cause if so, that's exactly where yo' ass need to be, instead of in my fuckin' face!"

"Fuck all that, Gray! You already know this is what I want! Me fuckin' other bitches is just for fun—"

"Oh my god, you are so fuckin' stupid! Do you really think you tellin' me you fuck other bitches for fun is gon' make me want you back?"

"You wanted the truth, so I'm giving it to you. I love you. I fuck other bitches 'cause you be holding out on that pussy. I wanna put all of this behind us. I want my family. You give me another chance, I'll leave that bitch where she's at. She only carrying my seed. This shit wit' her is business. Me and you is personal. What we got is a partnership. I would never put none of these hoes before you and you know that."

"Do I? I don't know shit 'cause at that basketball game yo' ass acted like you barely knew me. And you let that illiterate, ratchet, walking AIDS virus talk about my fuckin' daughter! You full of shit, Gunz! You keep sayin', Gray, I want you back! And, Gray, I love you! And, Gray, I wanna family, but I call your phone and you layin' up in the bed with another bitch! Who tells me y'all are in love and the only reason why you still deal with me is because we share a light bill together. I got my tubes tied because of you. Now, I can't have no more kids, but you get to go on with life and have as many kids as you want. ALL YOU DO IS FUCKIN' HURT ME! WHEN YOU WERE GETTIN' YOUR BUSINESSES OFF THE GROUND, I WAS THERE FOR YOU! WHEN YOUR FATHER DIED, I WAS THERE! WHEN UNCLE CYLDE DIED, I PUT MY FEELINGS ASIDE AND STOOD BY YOU, BUT YOU AIN'T NEVER DID SHIT BUT TURN YOUR BACK ON ME, DISAPPOINT ME AND LIE!"

"I love you, Gray. You are the person I love. You are the person I wanna be wit'."

"You don't love me," she repeated.

"As a man, I'm admitting my faults."

"You're not admitting faults 'cause you're blaming me."

"All you see is Gunz can provide. Gunz is that dude. Gunz got this. What about me? What about my heart, Gray? You don't provide that! And now you gettin' mad because I'm fuckin' with the next bitch? You walked away from me, Gray! You put that punk-ass magazine and your career ahead of me!"

Gray stepped back, as hot tears scorched her face.

"As much as I stood by you… ten years… and you couldn't even fuckin' marry me." Her heart broke with each word.

"But guess what, I's married now." She wiggled her fingers. "And I love him. He makes me feel stupid for even wasting ten years of my life on you. I ain't never in my life experienced a love like this. Just the thought of the taste of his dick in my mouth make me cum. He ain't nothin' like you. You will never measure up to the man he is. You ain't nothin' but a 42-year-old li'l boy. Me and my kids gon' be fine without you. I can't wait for them to meet Cam. I'm sure he'll be a better partner than you, a better provider than you, a better lover than you and I know for a fact he gon' be a better father than you!"

Gray knew she'd gone too far but didn't care. She meant every, single word. She loved Cam wholeheartedly and couldn't wait to start her new life with him. Protecting Gunz's feelings was no longer a priority for her. Finally, she was able to get everything she'd been harboring off her chest. It felt good to see him hurt. He deserved it and much more.

Heated that she had the nerve to speak to him that way, Gunz squeezed her shoulders, then slapped her with so much force she torpedoed into a glass vase. She and the vase fell onto the floor. Shattered pieces of glass pricked her skin, as he dragged her kicking and screaming across the marble floor. Gray couldn't believe what was happening. Gunz had yoked or up or pushed her, but he'd never actually hit her. She could hear the girls crying hysterically for him to let her go, but he wouldn't. Gunz was no longer there. There was no life in his eyes. He'd completely blacked out. Hovering over her, he reared his closed fist back and punched her in the face.

He'd told her if she ever tried to leave him, he'd kill her, and he meant it. Letting Gray go was too much for his brain to handle. He couldn't – no, wouldn't - lose her. She was his and a marriage certificate and a ring weren't going to change that. When and if he decided they no longer had to be together, it would be his decision, not hers.

Gray tried covering her face from his ruthless attack, but he removed her hand and punched her again. Her eye instantly swelled up. Gunz beat her so savagely that all she could do was burst into tears and beg him to stop.

"Get off my mama!" Aoki tugged on his arm.

Hearing the distress in his daughter's voice snapped him back to reality. Gunz stood back and eyed his handy work. Gray lay curled up in a ball on the floor, wailing, as if someone had died.

"You got me fucked up if you think you gon' have another nigga around my kids. You ain't gon' never see them again! C'mon, Aoki and Press! Y'all coming wit' me!"

"No, Daddy! I want my mommy!" Press cried.

"Don't make me tell you again," he warned.

Scared that he'd hit them too, Press and Aoki, reluctantly, followed their father.

"Gunz, please! Don't take my kids!" Gray tried to rise to her feet but was so weak she fell back down.

"Fuck you, bitch! You're dead to me!" Gunz slammed the door behind him.

After laying there for what seemed like hours, Gray pulled herself off the floor. In front of the mirror, she examined the damage that had been done. Gunz had given her a black eye and a busted lip. Shards of glass from the vase were stuck in her hair and clothes. Cuts and scrapes covered her back, arms and legs. Using a wet piece of toilet tissue, she wiped the dried-up blood from her lip and stared into her own empty eyes. She barely recognized herself. Gray gazed around the now deserted apartment. She was alone and hated it. Since Gunz couldn't break her sanity, he took the one thing that she loved the most - her kids. He knew it would break her and it had. Stifling a sob with the scuffed palm of her hand, she sunk to the floor and cried until she couldn't cry no more.

"I apologize.'Cause at your best, you are love and because I fall short of what I say I'm all about."– Jay-Z, "4:44"

Chapter 33

Chyna

The Isley Brothers' *For the Love of You* played softly, while Chyna sat in the middle of the floor surrounded by a slew of wedding gifts. She and Dame were back in New York after their whirlwind, three-week honeymoon. When they first resumed their romance, Chyna had revealed to him that she'd never left the country. Dame promised to rectify that, and he did. For their honeymoon, they visited Italy, Greece, Paris and the Almafi Coast. They sailed the blue seas on a yatch he'd charted, and stayed in the finest, five-star hotels each city had to offer.

Chyna had the time of her life. She and Dame got to focus on one another, sleep late, eat delicious food and make love night and day. Every morning when she awake, the side of his face and his large hand would be on her stomach. Dame would spend countless minutes talking to the baby. He wanted him or her to get acquainted with the sound of his voice. Chyna would just lay back with a huge grin on her face, smiling and laughing. This was the life she'd always dreamt of.

Her love for Dame grew each day. He'd given her everything she'd ever prayed for. He made all her dreams come true and loved her unconditionally along the way. Chyna and God had a love/hate relationship throughout the years, but she couldn't help but get down on her knees and thank Him. Her life was perfect. She finally had it all.

She was almost three and a half months pregnant. Her stomach had started to harden and pudge at the bottom. Now that the wedding was over, she couldn't wait to start showing. Chyna planned on being the flyest pregnant woman the world had ever seen. She'd already started cataloging her looks.

India was back in St. Louis, under the watchful eye of Delcious, until she was flown out to New York to be with them for the holidays. Thanksgiving was only a week and a half away. Chyna and Dame had gone 'round and 'round in circles about where she would reside now that they were husband and wife, but they still hadn't settled on St. Louis, New York or Chicago. Chyna honestly didn't care where she stayed, as long as she had her man and her daughter by her side.

Sitting Indian-style, she went through the mountain of gifts one by one. Their loved ones, family and friends had given them some of everything. They were given Keurig coffee makers, Versace plates, rose gold stemware, thousand-dollar flatware, a gold serving plate and a champagne bowl. Chyna didn't even know what a champagne bowl was, but she was gonna use it. Out of everything they'd been gifted, she loved the cash the most. At the wedding, they were showered with envelopes filled with money. After counting it all, the total came up to $70,000.

The only time she'd held that much money in her hand was when she won big in Vegas with Dame. There was so much shit she could buy with 70 g's, but Chyna wasn't going to touch any of it. She was going to put the money away for India and the baby. Easing her way off the hardwood floor, she walked over to Dame's wall safe that he had no idea she knew about. She'd stumbled upon it one day by accident. Dame had beautiful portraits of women and men from Sengal all over his home. One picture, in particular, caught Chyna's attention so much that she had to touch it. When she did, the portrait moved. Chyna thought it was about to fall but it didn't. It simply swung forward like a swinging door. To her surprise, behind it was a safe.

At the time, she didn't try to open it because she had no reason to, but there was no way in hell she was leaving 70 g's laying around. She trusted his staff but she didn't trust them that much. In front of the safe, she stood, contemplating the code and then remembered that Dame used her birthday for the passcode to his phone. Maybe the safe would be the same as well. Chyna punched 08-21-81 into the key pad and waited. Seconds later, the safe made a buzzing sound and then unlocked. Pleased with herself, she placed the money inside but didn't hesitate to peek around. Chyna was nosy as hell. She had to see what else was in there.

It wasn't much besides a couple stacks of cash, a gun and two, black, velvet jewelry bags. Curious as to what was inside, she grabbed the bags and pulled open the string. Chyna's brows dipped down when her eyes landed on L.A.'s chains, her Rolex watch and the pink diamond earrings that were stolen in the robbery. Every muscle in her body felt tight. Chyna was delirious. Panic began like a cluster of spark plugs in her abdomen. Tension grew in her forehead, limbs and mind, as she replayed the night of the attack. Her breathing became more erratic and shallow with each memory. In that moment, amongst her personal tornado, she understood how a drug addict and an alcoholic had the primal urge to flee.

"What you doing?" Dame said from behind, causing her to nearly jump out of her skin.

Eyes wide with fear, Chyna spun around. Her hands trembled at her sides.

"Where did you get these?" She held up the jewels.

With his hands inside his pants pocket, Dame clenched his jaw. He'd been doing so well at hiding the truth. Chyna couldn't find out like this. He loved her too much to hurt her. For the second time in his life, Dame wished he could rewind time and take back the irrational thing he'd done in the heat of the moment.

After Brooke left his hotel room, Dame allowed the darkness he felt to swallow him whole. Fires of rage and hatred simmered in his diamond-shaped eyes, as he weighed the pros and cons of the countless and creative ways he could exact revenge. Chyna had to pay. She had to suffer for toying and stepping on his heart, but he'd deal with her face to face. L.A., on the other hand, had to suffer now. He'd warned him to stay away from his belle. He'd told him not to tamper with what was his, but the nigga didn't listen. He'd disrespected him in the worst way. Disrespect wasn't tolerated in Dame's world at all.

"Mohamed!"

"Yes, nephew." He stood, stoically.

"We got a situation. I need for Lucas Abbott to be reprimanded."

"I'm on it."

Dame took a sip of whiskey and gazed absently at the plush, carpeted floor. When Chyna got back, she was in for a rude awakening. Not only was he going to break up with her, but he intended on making her suffer. Her suffering would be long and strenuous, just like his pain.

While his nephew stewed in his misery, Mohamed made a few calls to locate L.A.'s whereabouts. It didn't take him long to learn he was on a flight headed back to St. Louis. Since Dame didn't want him killed but spanked, Mohamed figured being robbed at gunpoint was punishment enough. It was terrifying enough to scare someone straight. Especially, when Dame sent word that it was him that did it. L.A. wouldn't dare disrespect him again. Hitting up their go-to jack boy, Berg, Mohamed set everything in motion and then notified his nephew on his plans. Dame gave the go-ahead and continued to drink his whiskey. A few hours later, Berg came to his hotel room to drop off the shit that was stole. He'd already been paid upfront.

"Is it handled?" Dame asked.

"Yeah, I ran into a li'l trouble but the problem was solved."

"What happened?"

"The nigga didn't wanna give up his shit so I had to pop his ass."

A slight chuckle escaped Dame's lips. L.A. was always a stupid, prideful nigga.

"Did you kill 'em?"

"When I left, the nigga was barely breathin'."

Dame hadn't wanted the nigga 6F, but if L.A. died, he wouldn't lose any sleep. He'd warned him not to cross him.

"And I thought you said your people out in Cali said the boy was alone?" Berg eyed Mohamed.

"He boarded the plane by himself."

"Well, he wasn't in the car by himself. We had to rough up his girl too."

Dame could give a fuck about L.A. and his bitch. He just wanted the nigga to hurt.

"The nigga didn't have much on him except this." Berg placed L.A.'s jewels and cash on the coffee table. "His bitch had a couple nice pieces on her too."

Just as he was about to pull out Chyna's jewels, Dame's phone rang. Dame knew by the ringtone who was calling. It was Chyna. The anger and resentment in him didn't want to answer, but the part of him that still loved her caused him to pick up the phone.

"What?"

"Dame!" She cried. "I'm in the hospital. I need you to get here now."

"You in the hospital?" He repeated, suspiciously.

Chyna tearfully gave him a quick rundown of what had transpired. Furious, Dame listened to every word. He wanted to remain mad but he knew Chyna like he knew the back of his hand. She wasn't feeding him some bullshit-ass story to cover her ass. She was telling the truth and he'd unknowingly fucked over the best thing that had ever happened to him.

"I'll be there in a second." He ended the call and focused his attention on Berg.

"As I was sayin', here go the bitch shit." Berg pulled out Chyna's Rolex and pink diamond earrings.

Dame's heart stopped when he saw her things splayed out before him. What the fuck have I done, he thought.

"What the fuck you mean y'all had to rough her up?" He picked up Chyna's jewels.

"My nigga had to smack her ass up 'cause she was takin' too long to run us her shit."

Before Berg could blink, Dame pounced on his ass. An anger like no other soared through his veins. The nigga had violated Chyna so he had to die. Dame didn't give a fuck. The beast in him had risen. Violently, he kicked Berg in the face, repeatedly. When he was done with him, he'd be leaving in a body bag. Blood poured from his nose and mouth with each kick. Usually, Mohamed tried not to interfere when Dame lost his shit; but this time, he had to. His nephew wasn't thinking straight.

"Nephew!" He pulled Dame off of him.

"Nah, Unc! Let me go!" Dame tried to attack Berg again.

"You can't kill 'em. He said we!" He shook Dame in order to get him to listen. "He said we. He had help."

Dame wiped the sweat from his brow and looked down at all the damage he'd done. Berg lay lifeless on the floor. His face was a dismantled mess. Dame hoped and prayed he could get the name of the other robber before Berg took his last breath but it was too late. He was already dead. Now, they would never know who the second robber was.

"FUCK!" He paced the room back and forth. "Chyna was in the car."

"What?" Mohamed panicked.

"That was Chyna on the phone. She was in the car. Brooke lied. She wasn't cheatin'. She was tryin' to get home to me."

Mohamed plopped down on the couch, in disbelief. They'd fucked up royally.

"Have you had these the whole time?" Chyna's lips quivered.

Fear set on Dame's face. The clock on the wall ticked like the timer on a grenade. He couldn't stop it, reverse it or slow it down. Each tick dragged him onward. He could no more avoid it than the beating of his own heart, as it pound with uselessness against it's cage of bone and cartilage. For months, the dread he harbored was an unseen demon sitting heavy on his shoulders. Only he could hear the sharpening of it's knives. Dame wanted to continue to lie, but the truth of what he'd done had been eating away at his insides. He'd cheated and nearly killed Chyna and their unborn child - all because he'd let his jealousy and insecruties get the best of him. He should've never listened to Brooke. He should've waited to react after he'd spoken to Chyna; but he didn't, and now here they were.

"Baby, listen. I can explain."

To Be Continued in Unapologetically Black.

Afterword

Oooooooh… no Dame didn't! Yes, Dame did! What a cliffhanger, right? Gunz and Dame both got some explaining to do. Gray's story will continue in her own book, which will be out next year, as well as the sixth book in the Chyna Black series titled: **Unapologetically Black**. I can't wait for you all to see where Chyna and Dame's relationship will go. There is also much more to Gray, Cam and Gunz's story. I hope you all enjoyed the first book in the First Wives Club series. I truly enjoyed every second of writing this book.

Special shout out and thank you to my bestie, Mo, who is the real-life Monsieur. She, of course, took her character very seriously and made sure that she was a true representation of herself. Also, thank you to my other bestie, Pancho. I got on his nerves calling him every five seconds to ask questions or to read him dialogue but he stuck with me. I love my friends and you all, my readers, to life. Muah!!!

Keisha xoxo

About The Author

Keisha Ervin is the critically-acclaimed, best-selling author of numerous novels, including: **The Untold Stories by Chyna Black, Cashmere Mafia, Material Girl 3: Secrets & Betrayals, Paper Heart, Pure Heroine, Emotionally Unavailable, Heartless, Radio Silence, Smells Like Teen Spirit Vol 1: Heiress, Mina's Joint 2: The Perfect Illusion, Cranes in the Sky, Postcards from the Edge** and **Such A Fuckin' Lady**.

For news on Keisha's upcoming work, keep in touch by following her on any of the social media accounts listed:

INSTAGRAM >> @keishaervin

SNAPCHAT >> kyrese99

TWITTER >> www.twitter.com/keishaervin

FACEBOOK >> www.facebook.com/keisha.ervin

Please, subscribe to my YouTube channel, to watch all my hilarious reviews on your favorite reality shows and drama series!!! YOUTUBE >> www.youtube.com/ColorMePynk

CPSIA information can be obtained
at www.ICGtesting.com
Printed in the USA
LVHW010845281018
595121LV00009B/385/P

9 781720 637868